————— ·⭑· —————

PRAISE FOR DONNA GRANT'S
BEST-SELLING ROMANCE NOVELS

————— ·⭑· —————

"Grant's ability to quickly convey complicated
backstory makes this jam-packed love story accessible
even to new or periodic readers."
–Publishers' Weekly

"Donna Grant has given the paranormal genre
a burst of fresh air…"
–San Francisco Book Review

"The premise is dramatic and heartbreaking;
the characters are colorful and engaging;
the romance is spirited and seductive."
–The Reading Cafe

"The central romance, fueled by a hostage drama, plays
out in glorious detail against a backdrop of multiple ongoing
issues in the "Dark Kings" books. This seemingly penultimate
installment creates a nice segue to a climactic end."
–Library Journal

"…intense romance amid the growing war between
the Dragons and the Dark Fae is scorching hot."
–Booklist

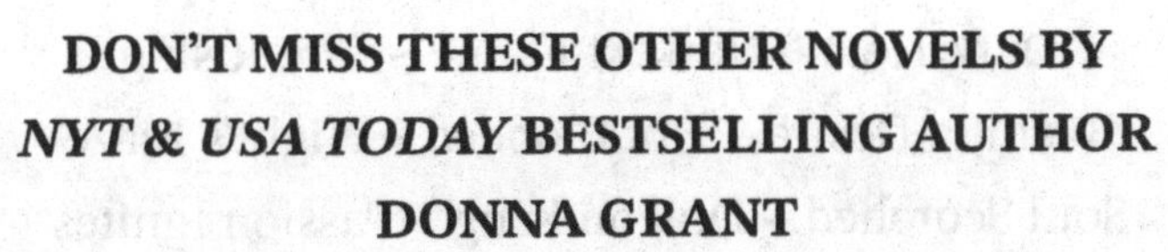

DON'T MISS THESE OTHER NOVELS BY *NYT* & *USA TODAY* BESTSELLING AUTHOR DONNA GRANT

☆ CONTEMPORARY PARANORMAL ☆

ELVEN KINGDOMS
Rising Sun ~ Dark Heart

DRAGON KINGS® SERIES
Dragon Revealed ~ Dragon Mine ~ Dragon Unbound
Dragon Eternal ~ Dragon Lover ~ Dragon Arisen
Dragon Frost ~ Dragon Kiss ~ Dragon Born

REAPER SERIES
Dark Alpha's Claim ~ Dark Alpha's Embrace
Dark Alpha's Demand ~ Dark Alpha's Lover
Dark Alpha's Night ~ Dark Alpha's Hunger
Dark Alpha's Awakening ~ Dark Alpha's Redemption
Dark Alpha's Temptation ~ Dark Alpha's Caress
Dark Alpha's Obsession ~ Dark Alpha's Need
Dark Alpha's Silent Night ~ Dark Alpha's Passion
Dark Alpha's Command ~ Dark Alpha's Fury

SKYE DRUIDS SERIES
Iron Ember ~ Shoulder the Skye ~ Heart of Glass
Endless Skye ~ Still of the Night

DARK KINGS SERIES

Dark Heat ~ Darkest Flame ~ Fire Rising
Burning Desire ~ Hot Blooded ~ Night's Blaze
Soul Scorched ~ Dragon King ~ Passion Ignites
Smoldering Hunger ~ Smoke and Fire
Dragon Fever ~ Firestorm ~ Blaze ~ Dragon Burn
Constantine: A History, Parts 1-3 ~ Heat ~ Torched
Dragon Night ~ Dragonfire ~ Dragon Claimed
Ignite ~ Fever ~ Dragon Lost ~ Flame ~ Inferno
A Dragon's Tale (Whisky and Wishes: *A Holiday Novella*,
Heart of Gold: *A Valentine's Novella*, & Of Fire and Flame)
My Fiery Valentine ~ The Dragon King Coloring Book
Dragon King Special Edition Character Coloring Book: Rhi

DARK WARRIORS SERIES

Midnight's Master ~ Midnight's Lover
Midnight's Seduction ~ Midnight's Warrior
Midnight's Kiss ~ Midnight's Captive
Midnight's Temptation ~ Midnight's Promise
Midnight's Surrender ~ A Warrior for Christmas

CHIASSON SERIES

Wild Fever ~ Wild Dream ~ Wild Need
Wild Flame ~ Wild Rapture

LARUE SERIES

Moon Kissed ~ Moon Thrall
Moon Struck ~ Moon Bound

WICKED TREASURES

Seized by Passion ~ Enticed by Ecstasy

Captured by Desire

Books 1-3: Wicked Treasures Box Set

⋆+˚｡⋆·˚ ⋆+ ☽ ◯ ☾ +⋆ ˚·⋆｡˚+⋆

☆ HISTORICAL PARANORMAL ☆

THE KINDRED SERIES

Everkin ~ Eversong ~ Everwylde

Everbound ~ Evernight ~ Everspell

KINDRED: THE FATED SERIES

Rage ~ Ruin ~ Reign

DARK SWORD SERIES

Dangerous Highlander ~ Forbidden Highlander

Wicked Highlander ~ Untamed Highlander

Shadow Highlander ~ Darkest Highlander

ROGUES OF SCOTLAND SERIES

The Craving ~ The Hunger

The Tempted ~ The Seduced

Books 1-4: Rogues of Scotland Box Set

THE SHIELDS SERIES

A Dark Guardian ~ A Kind of Magic

A Dark Seduction ~ A Forbidden Temptation

A Warrior's Heart

Mystic Trinity (a series connecting novel)

DRUIDS GLEN SERIES

Highland Mist ~ Highland Nights ~ Highland Dawn

Highland Fires ~ Highland Magic

Mystic Trinity (a series connecting novel)

SISTERS OF MAGIC TRILOGY

Shadow Magic ~ Echoes of Magic ~ Dangerous Magic

Books 1-3: Sisters of Magic Box Set

THE ROYAL CHRONICLES NOVELLA SERIES

Prince of Desire ~ Prince of Seduction

Prince of Love ~ Prince of Passion

Books 1-4: The Royal Chronicles Box Set

Mystic Trinity (a series connecting novel)

DARK BEGINNINGS: A FIRST IN SERIES BOXSET

Chiasson Series, Book 1: Wild Fever

LaRue Series, Book 1: Moon Kissed

The Royal Chronicles Series, Book 1: Prince of Desire

☆ COWBOY / CONTEMPORARY ☆

HEART OF TEXAS SERIES
The Christmas Cowboy Hero ~ Cowboy, Cross My Heart
My Favorite Cowboy ~ A Cowboy Like You
Looking for a Cowboy ~ A Cowboy Kind of Love

☆ MILITARY ROMANCE / ROMANTIC SUSPENSE ☆

SONS OF TEXAS SERIES
The Hero ~ The Protector ~ The Legend
The Defender ~ The Guardian

☆ STAND ALONE BOOKS ☆
That Cowboy of Mine ~ Home for a Cowboy Christmas
Mutual Desire ~ Forever Mine ~ Savage Moon

**Check out Donna Grant's Online Store at
www.DonnaGrant.com/shop
for autographed books, character
themed goodies, and more!**

RISING SUN

ELVEN KINGDOMS
BOOK ONE

NEW YORK TIMES & USA TODAY BESTSELLING AUTHOR
DONNA GRANT

RISING SUN
© **2024 by DL Grant, LLC**
Cover Design © 2024 by Hang Le
ISBN 13: 978-1-958353-31-8
Available in ebook, print, and audio.
All rights reserved.

Sneak Peek at DARK HEART
© **2024 by DL Grant, LLC**
Cover Design © 2024 by Hang Le

www.DonnaGrant.com
www.MotherofDragonsBooks.com

SHECRISH
Belanore
Flamefall
Rannora
Orgate
HUMAN LAND
DRAGON LAND
Stonemore
Iron Hall
Cairnkeep
ZORA

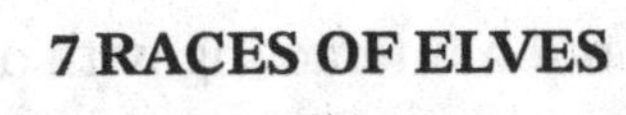

7 RACES OF ELVES

SUN ELVES (GOLD ELVES)
– recognized by their golden complexions.
Known for their levelheadedness, think things through.
Have long memories. Maintain a love of
freedom and personal expression.

Skin: golden brown
Eyes: amber, copper, gold
Hair: golden blond, tawny
Ability: Readers
Magic Color: yellow/golden

MOON ELVES (AKA SILVER ELVES)
– Isolated race who prefer only themselves.
Moon elf society values individual
accomplishment and rights.

Skin: very fair, silver tint
Eyes: various shades of blue (icy blue)
Hair: blue, silvery white
Magic Color: silver

STAR ELVES (AKA PEWTER ELVES)

– Nomadic, often interacting with other elves.
Have a knack for perceiving inner beauty.
Curious and adventurous. Can be focused and relentless.

Skin: fair skin
Eyes: violet/shades of purple
Hair: lavender, purple, silver
Homeland: nomadic
Ability: Healers
Magic Color: purple

SEA ELVES (AKA BLUE ELVES)

– Have webbed fingers and toes. Gills hidden behind
their ears. AKA as mermaids without the tails.
Among their own, delight in song, dance, and magic.
Toward others they are slow to bestow the gift of
their voice/artistry.

Skin: Blueish/greenish
Eyes: iridescent blue to silver white
Hair: bluish-black or greenish-black (oil slick)
Homeland: bodies of water
Ability: animals in the water
Magic Color: blue

WOOD ELVES (AKA COPPER ELVES)

– guardians of all things in the forest.
They live in complete harmony with the woods and
its inhabitants. Can be judgmental, but take time to
consider everything before passing judgment.
Once won, a Wood Elf's friendship is deep and lasting.
Some of the best fighters.

Skin: coppery skin
Eyes: Green or Hazel
Hair: Brown or Red
Homeland: forests/woods
Ability: good with animals; can sense truth/lies
Magic Color: green or copper

⋆+₀°⋆˙˙₊⟩ ○ ⟨₊˙⋆˙°₀+⋆

MOUNTAIN ELVES (AKA BRONZE ELVES)

– prefer the highest peaks. Rarest of the elves.
Cautious and aloof. Understand the importance of
community. Suspicious of strangers. Best weapon crafters.

Skin: white or brown
Eyes: Black
Hair: Black, Dark Brown
Homeland: mountains
Magic Color: bronze

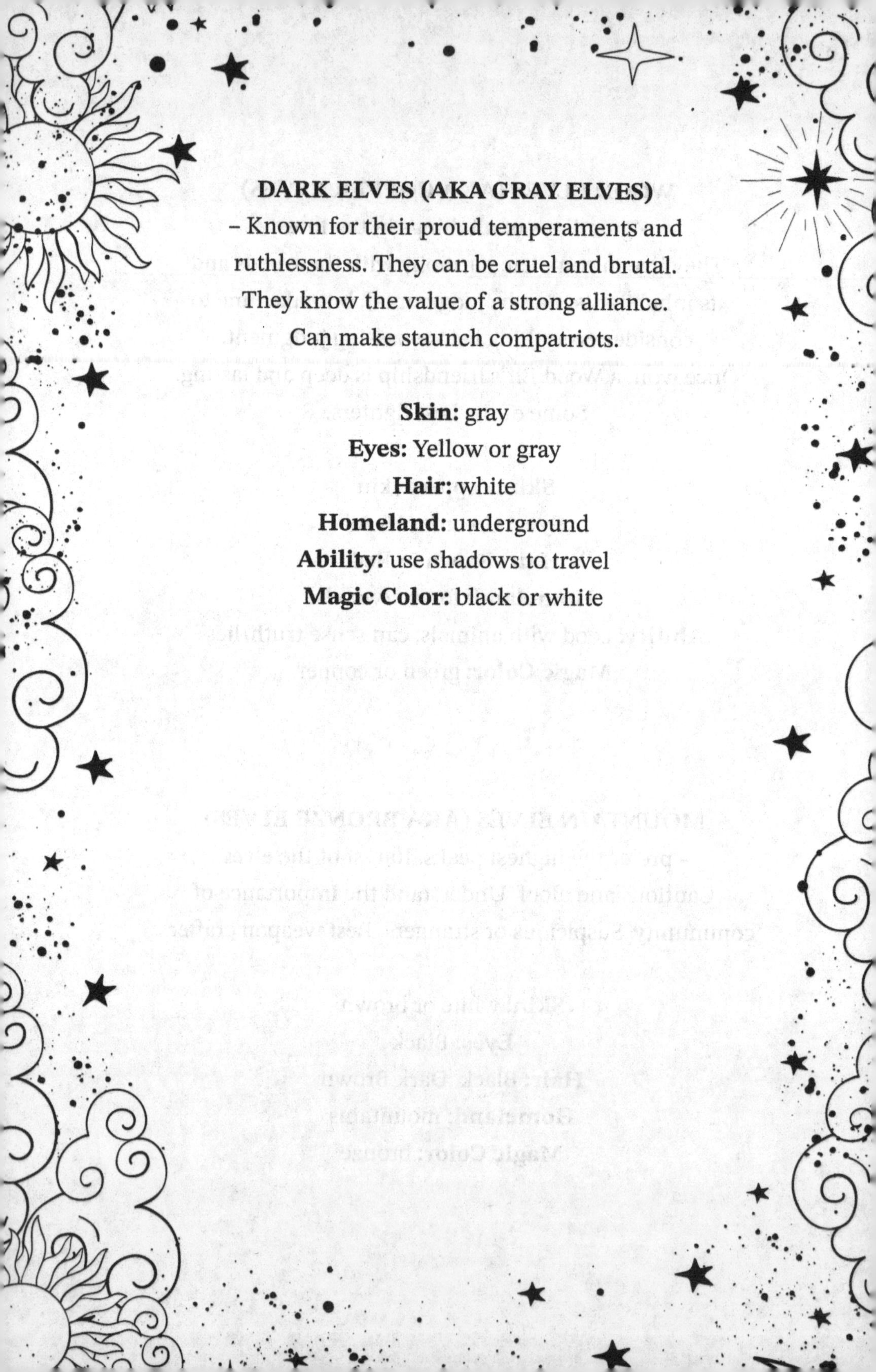

DARK ELVES (AKA GRAY ELVES)

– Known for their proud temperaments and ruthlessness. They can be cruel and brutal. They know the value of a strong alliance. Can make staunch compatriots.

Skin: gray
Eyes: Yellow or gray
Hair: white
Homeland: underground
Ability: use shadows to travel
Magic Color: black or white

RISING SUN

ELVEN KINGDOMS
BOOK ONE

1

Rannora
Fall

Ravi glanced at the sign above the tavern that read *Twilight*. It was an upscale establishment in the Geggin Square district of Rannora. He stepped inside and was promptly enveloped by a sexy ballad coming from a Star Elf swaying her hips seductively on the stage as she held everyone in thrall. Ravi took in the crowded business with one glance. His gaze swung to the left, and he nodded once to the stocky Wood Elf drying a glass behind the bar. The bartender returned the gesture. It was the only indication Ravi would get that all was well. And it was the only one he needed.

The elf's singing drowned out the sound of his bootheels striking the floor. He weaved through the tables toward a side door where another elf stood to make sure no one entered who wasn't supposed to. As Ravi approached, the guard let him through. The minute the door shut behind him, the sounds of the tavern dimmed and faded as Ravi continued down the narrow hallway. He didn't bother with any of the rooms on either side of him. His gaze was locked on the one at the end of the hall.

He surreptitiously adjusted the sleeves of his leather jacket as he reached his destination. Ravi paused for a moment to prepare himself before knocking once. The door swung open immediately. He briefly looked at the muscled elf in front of him before his gaze slid to the tall, slender occupant who waited within.

"About time," Durga stated, a brown brow raised, showing her impatience.

Ravi didn't bother to state that he was early. Durga had her way of doing things, and the people she allowed to stick around were the ones who learned to roll with her particular method.

He walked to her, noting the navy dress that showed off her coppery skin, signaling her as a Wood Elf. Intelligent, cunning hazel eyes studied him. Her brown locks were always pulled away from her face with nary a hair out of place. The only thing that changed was the placement of the bun. Tonight, it rested at her nape.

"I take my summons to mean you have an assignment for me." Ravi had just finished another mission but was never good at sitting idle. Durga knew that. It was in everyone's best interests to keep him busy. It didn't hurt that he had never failed Durga or the Defense Intelligence Agency in his many years of service.

She eyed him. "I do."

Ravi studied his mentor more carefully. Stress lines bracketed her mouth. She kept clenching and unclenching her hands at her sides. Wherever she was about to send him, it would be dangerous. "Tell me."

Durga cast a look at the other elf in the room. He quietly slipped out, leaving just the two of them. Only then did her shoulders sag, letting him see how anxious she was. "Do you remember when that dragon crossed our border?"

As if he could forget. It was all anyone had talked about for days. Some took it as a good sign, while others felt it meant their world was about to end. Ravi bowed his head. "Aye. Then it wasn't a rumor?"

"Rumor?" Durga snorted a laugh and shook her head. "It was no rumor. A dragon did cross into Shecrish, but it wasn't just any dragon. It was a Dragon King."

"The Dragon King?"

"Nay. *A* King. There are many of them."

Ravi walked to the right to lean a shoulder against the wall as he digested that bit of information. "What did this King want?"

"To track down the thing that's been killing others. The one we can't see."

"We can communicate with dragons?"

"A Dragon King can shift from his true form to that of a human."

Ravi blinked in surprise. "Shite." All the years of sharing a border with the dragons, and one decided to seek them out. "Did he track the thing down?"

"Sadly, nay. Kendrick—that's the King's name—did make a few allies, however."

Ravi crossed his arms over his chest. "That means he also made enemies."

"Unfortunately. Made worse by the fact that he fell in love with one of our most distinguished Asavori Rangers, and she returned with him to his land."

He stilled. "Tell me she went willingly."

"She did."

"And you believe whatever source told you?"

Durga cut him a sharp look. "Three different sources shared the information."

That did make it difficult to dismiss. "I take it you want me to bring her home."

"Nay." Durga shook her head as she walked a few paces from him and swung around, her deep blue skirts swirling around her ankles. "Kendrick came to us in peace. He worked with Esha to—"

"Esha?" Ravi repeated as he jerked from the wall, his arms falling to his sides. "Are you telling me it was Esha who left with him?"

"I am."

Ravi ran a hand over his face. Asavori Rangers were revered by both elves and humans in Shecrish. The Rangers were the first sent into any battle and usually the only ones needed. Esha was known by all. Ravi had met her a few times when his missions brought him near the Rangers' encampment in Flamefall.

"As I was saying," Durga continued, "Esha willingly worked with Kendrick. They tracked the thing slaying our people. In return, someone sent a nightwraith after them."

Ravi shook his head in surprise. Once the enormous creature had your scent, there was no escaping it. "They survived?"

"Kendrick is a Dragon King with magic that exceeds anything the elves have. He and Esha fought it in the forest. My people saw the entire battle."

Which meant Tarron, her cousin and the leader of the Wood Elves, had been one of those who'd passed on the information to Durga. That was one source. Ravi wondered who the others were.

"It seems Kendrick's arrival stirred things up in the Conclave," Durga continued. "There is reason to believe that someone on the Conclave sent the nightwraith after him."

For a long while, some had been calling for a reform in their governing Conclave, but it failed each time. Maybe now was the time to tackle that. "Tell me you know who is responsible. That crime needs to be dealt with immediately."

"It is being sorted out."

"By whom?" he demanded.

Her hazel eyes narrowed slightly. "I was going to give you that assignment, but another has taken precedence."

Ravi waited, knowing that no amount of pushing would get her to give up the information faster. Durga revealed things in her own time. For someone known for her impatience, she didn't have a problem making others wait. But he was already trying to imagine what could be more important than discovering who'd tried to kill a Dragon King.

Durga gathered her hands at her waist and drew in a deep breath. "I received intel earlier about a group intending to push us into war with the dragons by tossing an explosive device across the border. You need to stop that before it happens."

"Gladly. Where am I going?"

She hesitated. "That's the catch."

"You want me on this because you know I can get around anything. Nothing has stopped me before."

"I want you on this because you're the best agent we have, but there is a first time for everything."

"What aren't you telling me?"

"The location is deep within the Dangerous Peaks."

The only elves who dared to go anywhere near the snow-topped peaks to the east were the Mountain Elves who called them home. They were the finest weapons crafters, but they were suspicious of outsiders. Gaining their help would be difficult, though not impossible.

"You know how reclusive the Mountain Elves are. I'll need some time to find them and gain their trust," he began.

Durga shook her head. "I wish it were that easy. There is no time to get help from our mountain kin. You have to get to the Shaldorn stronghold immediately."

"I've never heard of it."

"That is by design. Few know of it."

He frowned as he took a step toward her. "But *you* know of this place?"

"We've had our sights on it, aye. Getting in is another matter."

"I can get in."

"You can't." She went on before he could argue. "Shaldorn is a place where the vilest in Shecrish go to do despicable things. From what I've learned, they have anything someone who walks in their circles could wish for."

Ravi shrugged. "I'll get in. There's always a way."

"There are two entrances, actually. Both are heavily guarded. It is a fortress, Ravi. The walls are too high to climb and watched from every angle. Only those with an invitation are allowed within."

"Then make sure I'm invited."

Her knuckles whitened as she gripped her hands tightly for a heartbeat. "We tried."

That meant someone had died. Ravi wanted to ask who but doubted Durga would impart that information. "So, how do I get in?"

"With the help of someone who has been inside. It has taken me all day, but I've found them."

"What makes you think they'll return to the fortress?"

"I'll make sure they do." She motioned for him to follow. "We don't have long to get this mission underway. We should get there in time to see the individual brought to us."

Ravi followed her out of the room. The moment she reached the hall, two guards moved in front of her and another two behind him. No one spoke as they entered a stairway that took them outside. The four guards split up to stay hidden while Ravi remained just behind Durga. Only a fool would attempt to attack her.

"Ah. There," Durga said and pointed.

Ravi followed her finger. He spotted three undercover operatives, then scanned the faces of those milling about the shops set up on the street. Finally, he saw the human. She was a waifish thing of average height with black hair in a thick braid that reached the middle of her back. She walked with the steps of one ready to bolt at a moment's notice, her gaze moving about as if she expected someone to shout that she didn't belong. She stood out amid all the finery in her worn black overcoat that had been mended so many times he couldn't believe it still held together, a black shirt with mismatched buttons, and pants with a hole in the knee. The strap across her chest connected to a bag. Her boots were old but well cared for.

The human sidled closer to a female Sun Elf deep in conversation with another. Before the human could pick the elf's pocket, Durga motioned with her hand. When she did, the operatives closed in around the woman. Ravi watched as she attempted to cradle her bag against her chest when the operatives grabbed her, but they yanked it away.

The moment she lost the pack, she lashed out with everything she had. Instead of quickly and quietly getting her off the street, there was a commotion as everyone turned to look at the trio of elves attempting to subdue the human. The female never screamed or spoke but fought as if her life was on the line. In a way, it was.

"This way," Durga murmured before turning and retracing her steps.

They didn't return to the room. Instead, Ravi followed her down a flight of stairs that led underground—fitting since everything the DIA did was in the shadows. It was a clandestine operation that few beyond the Conclave knew existed. The Rangers might be called in a fight, but the Conclave turned to the DIA before things escalated.

Ravi heard the scuffle before he saw it. The human female was so thin a breeze could blow her over, but she was quick. His fellow agents had her arms, but her legs and feet were free, and she used them efficiently. One of the men grabbed her hair and wrenched her head back. That didn't quell her. If anything, the human redoubled her efforts, managing to kick one of the men between his legs. That earned her a body slam against the wall just as yellow magic filled a Sun Elf's palm as he readied to unleash it on her.

Durga cleared her throat. All three men seemed to remember they had an audience. They suppressed their need to lash out, but their anger was palpable. Humans didn't have magic, so it made things worse for one to hurt an elf—worse, a female being detained. Their two cultures had always lived together, but the elves outnumbered humans twenty to one. Add in the fact that humans were magicless, and there was always simmering contention.

The trio took the female into a room and shoved her into a chair so hard that it tipped backward. She jerked forward, just barely managing to keep from falling over. The front legs of the chair banged against the floor as the human lifted her face and glared at the handlers.

Ravi and Durga stood outside in the hall, watching her through glass crafted with elven magic that appeared to be a picture within the room. It allowed Ravi to get a look at the woman. She sat up straight and settled as if she had come for a social visit.

He supposed she was pretty for a human—oval face with full lips and a stubborn chin. Midnight brows arched over eyes a deep blue that reminded him of the ocean. Her size belied her strength, but those eyes told him she had experienced things others could only guess at. She stared at the agents straight on, which told him she wouldn't cower easily.

It might be better if she did.

"Ready to meet your guide?" Durga asked.

Ravi's gaze jerked to her. "You're joking."

"You know me better than that."

He glanced back at the human. "She's...she's..."

"The only one who can get you inside."

"How can you be sure?"

Durga's gaze became icy. "If there was another way, I would've found it. The last thing I want is to bring an outsider—a human, at that—into this mission."

"She doesn't seem the type to be willing to help anyone."

"She doesn't have a choice."

Ravi blew out a breath. "Fuck."

2

The space was large enough to easily fit twenty, but it was still too small, especially with the lumbering elves scrutinizing her. But it was the shadow behind her that caught Yasmin's attention when they brought her into the room. It was no simple shadow but a Dark Elf. What was a Dark doing on the surface?

Yasmin tried not to cringe when one guard tossed her bag aside. She thought she heard a clink but knew she had wrapped the glass carefully. But what if she hadn't? What if she had to find more? It had nearly cost her everything to obtain it, but nothing would stop her from getting more if she had to. That was if she got out of here.

The door opened, and an elegant Wood Elf strode into the room. She had the haughty demeanor of someone who knew nothing but power and wealth. Her navy gown was made of the finest cloth, the stitching impeccable. Her hair was pulled severely back, showing off her pointed ears and the gold tips adorning them.

A man walked in behind her, moving to stand against the wall out of sight. His golden-brown skin marked him as a Sun Elf. Thick, golden-blond hair just brushed his shoulders. It was shoved away from his face as if he had run his hand through it. He stood indifferently, but there was nothing casual about him. He had an air of intensity, a hardness that warned he wouldn't hesitate to squash her like an insignificant bug. A penetrating copper gaze swung her way.

If she didn't have such disdain for elves, she would call him handsome. She had heard plenty of women talking about the hard planes of a face, the strong jaw, and a firm body. She knew the Sun Elf had it all in spades.

His burgundy jacket accentuated broad shoulders, while the decorative bands on the sleeves near his wrists put him firmly in the wealthy column. She could just make out the luxurious cream shirt beneath. Her gaze moved to black pants tucked into tall, leather boots that likely cost more than she had seen in her entire life. Which wasn't saying much. She wondered if he had ever been outside the Geggin Square district. He'd probably never known a day of work in his life.

"Hello, Yasmin."

Her gaze jerked to the woman. The Wood Elf spoke softly, but her gaze warned against defiance. Too bad Yasmin survived because of that rebelliousness. She knew nothing good would come of this meeting. The truth was, she didn't care what happened to her. Yasmin's concern was for getting the bag and its contents to the one who needed it.

"I'm sure you're wondering why we brought you in," the Wood Elf continued.

Yasmin decided it was best to keep her mouth closed for the time being. She fought not to look at the bag again. The woman walked toward her, hazel eyes boring into her. Yasmin didn't look away. Some would probably suggest it would be wiser if she did, but she had learned a long time ago that the only way to survive in Shecrish was to never show fear.

"You've been picked up by patrol for stealing before."

Yasmin thought about all the other times she had gotten away with it. Her gaze followed the Wood Elf as she leisurely walked back and forth in front of her.

"Your last stay was for three months."

Yasmin tried not to shudder at the memory. She wasn't sure she'd suppressed it completely. What they did to the humans they imprisoned was inhumane, but it wasn't as if anyone really cared.

"That was for your second offense. This is your third. That means a...lengthier stay."

Yasmin thought about the tiny, windowless cell they stuffed the humans into. Not tall enough to stand up in, nor long enough to stretch out your legs. One meal a day—if they remembered to bring food. Three months without sunlight or a breeze against your skin. Three months without feeling water or being able to stare at the moon. She had nearly lost her mind. She couldn't go back.

She *wouldn't*.

"Ah. I see your time there lingers in your memory." The Wood Elf stopped before her, making Yasmin tilt her head back to look at her. "Theft is a violation of the law."

The woman motioned to the bag. Yasmin clutched the side of the chair to keep from snatching it from them. The wood bit painfully into her skin. She felt one of her nails bend backward and her skin tear. She couldn't let them know how important it was to her. Yet she couldn't look away as one of the thugs brought the bag, and another carried a small table over to place between them. The Wood Elf took the bag and slowly opened it, removing the items inside one by one.

Yasmin bit her tongue as she saw the few meager food items laid out—provisions that were supposed to feed seven. It wasn't even enough for one person. Then, the elf drew out the bundle of cloth. She weighed it in one hand as she met Yasmin's gaze. The way she so carelessly unrolled it was almost too much to bear. The small bottle flew out. A shout of dismay locked in Yasmin's throat as the Wood Elf's hand snatched it out of the air and set it with the food.

"What is this?" she asked, her finger on the bottle.

Yasmin simply stared. It wouldn't do any good to tell them it was medicine or that she needed to get it to someone immediately. The elves didn't understand human sickness. They had healers for their afflictions. Healers would help humans, but only for an exorbitant price. And currency was never something Yasmin seemed to have enough of—for food or medical treatment.

Even if she somehow managed to convince her keepers to take the medicine to her home, they would discover the children there. Every child was accounted for in Shecrish, where no humanoid could bear offspring. Yet babies continued to arrive in unknown ways. They were quickly brought to the Domestic Ministry, where they determined which family the newborn would be placed with. No one was allowed to remove a child from their home or help one run away, regardless of the reasons. Everything went through the Ministry.

And that was the problem.

Starvation and abuse were reason enough for Yasmin to aid the children in her care. It had begun with sharing food with one and, somehow, had swelled to six. They counted on her. If she didn't return...

"It would behoove you to answer," the Wood Elf said, breaking into her thoughts.

Yasmin lifted her chin. "Why? You'll make up your own answer regardless of what I say."

"Do you want to go back into that cell?"

The words were clipped and angry, which was pretty much how Yasmin felt. So, she answered in kind. "Why don't you give it a try and tell me what you think of it?"

The Wood Elf leaned her hands on the table. "I can make these new charges against you go away."

"In exchange for what?"

The elf smiled confidently, making unease roll down Yasmin's spine.

"You have something we need."

Elves needed nothing any human had. Certainly not her. "I highly doubt that."

"Don't sell yourself short."

Yasmin saw the Sun Elf's gaze narrow as he looked past her—right where she had seen the shadow sitting in the corner behind her. She wanted to turn and look herself. She hated not being able to see it, but that would only alert them that she was aware of another presence. "I'm stating facts. You're elves. You have magic. There is nothing I have that you could want."

"Knowledge."

Yasmin bit back a grimace when the Wood Elf shifted, causing the flimsy table to sway and the bottle to wobble. "Knowledge of what?"

"A location."

A shiver of dread went through her. They couldn't be talking about... Nay. They probably didn't even know about it.

The woman was at her side so quickly Yasmin barely registered it. The elf's fingers barely touched her skin as she moved aside Yasmin's braid to expose the skin just below her hairline. Yasmin yanked her head away and got to her feet without considering retribution.

She glowered, her heart racing at having someone inspecting her hidden tattoo. "Don't. Touch. Me."

"Easy," the Wood Elf said. But it wasn't directed at her.

Yasmin glanced over her shoulder to find that the Sun Elf had come up behind her, his hands ready to grab her. She shifted to keep him in her line of sight.

"Apologies," the Wood Elf told her. "I wanted to see for myself. You bear the feather tattoo of Shaldorn."

Yasmin released a shaky breath. They *knew*. Her mind raced for a way to get out and run. Just as she was supposed to have done four years earlier. "I don't know what you mean."

"Don't play stupid. It doesn't suit," the female replied. "We need to reach Shaldorn. In exchange for your freedom, you'll take one of my operatives to the stronghold, get him inside, and bring him home."

"Nay."

"That isn't an option."

Yasmin squared her shoulders. "I've made it one."

"You're intelligent. You know how this will turn out. We can argue for days, but I don't have the time for it."

Yasmin needed to try another tactic. She kept tripping over the fact that they wanted to go to Shaldorn. She needed a few moments to collect herself. And she knew exactly how to get it. "I suppose the Dark Elf is that operative?"

The Wood Elf's smile was genuine. She swung her gaze to the corner. Yasmin followed and watched as the shadows parted to reveal the elf. He wore all black. His coat was long and cut into six thick stripes at the bottom. The shoulders had armor plating. He had long, white hair with silver metal around certain locks. Yellow eyes met hers and seemed to see right through her. The gray skin of his face was marred by several scars. One ran from the inside corner of his left eye and cut diagonally down the cheek to his jaw. Another dissected his mouth at an angle, right to left. A third ran from his left temple to his left brow, across his nose, and along the right cheek.

Behind her, she heard a soft curse. Yasmin held the Dark Elf's gaze, even when she wanted to look away. Dark Elves showed no mercy. Their brutality was legendary. Only a rare few showed themselves aboveground. The rest preferred their underground homes.

"I am not," the Dark stated.

Yasmin backed up until the wall was behind her. She wanted out of the room and to get as far away from the elves as she could. She'd had the chance once, and instead of getting away, she had shared her bread. Now, she was in a predicament she never thought to find herself in. Both would achieve the same result—her death.

"Perhaps an incentive is in order," the Dark said.

A muscle in the Sun Elf's jaw jumped. Yasmin looked at the table and the medicine. Such a small bottle, the glass so thin it amazed her the liquid stayed confined. Within the constraints of the glass was an elixir with the ability to heal.

The Wood Elf stepped back, allowing the Dark to speak. She caught the furious look on the Sun Elf's face and the Dark's answering smirk. There was something between the two. If Yasmin thought she could use it, she would do it in an instant.

The Dark walked to the table and looked at the food. He began returning each item to the bag. Until he came to the medicine. He palmed it, pretending to put it with everything else. Yasmin's heart skipped a beat. He was up to something, and whatever it was, it couldn't be good. She watched him carefully, waiting until his eyes met hers. She hadn't dealt with a Dark Elf before, but their reputation preceded them.

"You're in a unique position," the Dark said as he set her bag aside. "You have information we require."

"Then I'll draw you a map."

He grinned. "It isn't that easy, and you know it. We can get to the stronghold. It's getting *in* that is proving problematic."

"If you know Shaldorn as you say you do, then you know you ask the impossible," she retorted.

He released a slow breath and came around the table. "Will it be difficult? Dangerous, even? Without a doubt. Impossible? Nay."

Yasmin glanced at the Wood Elf. Her gaze then moved over the three bullies who had dragged her into the room, stopping at the Sun Elf. He had backed up, but he hadn't returned to his position in the corner. He stood with his arms crossed and feet wide as if waiting for her to do something reckless.

He wasn't wrong.

"You don't understand," she said, sliding her gaze back to the Dark. "None of you do."

The female shrugged. "You're right. We don't. And it doesn't matter. The fact is, we have to get inside. You have a choice. The cells, or a trip to Shaldorn."

A place she swore never to return to. She knew what went on behind those high walls. The misery, the pain, the horror. She had lived it, breathed it. She had barely gotten out last time. There was no way she could return. She would take the cell. She could do it. Prison was better than Shaldorn.

The Dark moved his arm. As he did, he flashed the bottle in his hand. "What would you do for a life?"

She met his gaze, her hatred for elves growing to new heights.

The Dark raised a brow, waiting. He knew the vial contained medicine. His threat was clear. Help them, and he would get the treatment where it needed to go. Refuse, and she would be locked away, the bottle destroyed.

Yasmin wanted to scream at the gods for putting her into such a predicament, but it wouldn't do any good. The only one who could save her was herself. That was how it had always been, and it was how it would always be.

She had stolen and saved to scrape up enough coin to buy the medicine. Little Jaya was counting on her. All the children were. She had promised to always be there for them. She couldn't turn her back on them now. Even if it meant going back to Shaldorn.

If she survived this...nay, *when*...she would get as far from Shecrish and the elves as she could. It didn't matter what she might run into somewhere else on Zora. Anything was better than elves.

Yasmin turned her head to the Wood Elf. "Take the bag where I need it to go, and I'll do what you ask."

"Give us the location," she replied.

The moment Yasmin stated the locale, the Dark grabbed her bag and walked out the door. The Wood Elf was next, followed by the surly Sun Elf, and then the trio until she was alone. But she wasn't really. They were watching.

The elves were always watching.

3

"Dain? Really?" Ravi asked Durga once they were in the hall and alone.

She turned to face him, her hazel eyes hardening. "Are you questioning my decisions?"

"I'm questioning him."

"So, you *are* questioning my decisions."

Ravi blew out a breath. It took him a moment to gather the calm he was known for. "This is about him."

"It's about me since I brought him into this. He's here because he was with Esha and Kendrick."

Ravi should've known there was more to the story Durga had shared. There was *always* more where she was concerned. "What haven't you told me?"

"Plenty," she retorted saucily.

Ravi tried again. "About Dain."

"He sought out the Dragon King," Durga said with a little smile.

Somehow, Ravi wasn't surprised. "I can only guess for what purpose."

"Perhaps you should ask him."

Ravi clenched his teeth as Durga walked away. He had handled that poorly. Durga never responded well to being questioned. Ravi wanted to know more about Kendrick. It would mean seeking out Dain, and it wasn't as if the Dark would bother telling him anything resembling the truth. Ravi's objective was something much more dangerous at the moment.

He turned to look through the glass once more. The human sat on the floor, her back against a wall, hugging her legs to her chest. There were no tears, no banging on the door. What was she thinking about? No doubt coming up with a way to double-cross him. She might have agreed to Durga's request, but it was under duress—not exactly a way to head off into a remote area where one of theirs had already been killed.

He could argue there was another way in, but Durga always explored every option. If she said there wasn't, then there wasn't. Ravi trusted her. It wasn't something he could say about too many. His world was one of fabrications and deceptions, which meant he always expected others to lie to him. It was safer that way.

His gaze narrowed on the woman as he realized she had given in quicker than expected. She hadn't begged for her freedom or wailed at the unfairness. She had been calm and collected through nearly all of it. The only time he'd seen any cracks in her armor was at the mention of the cell and when Durga touched her.

The way the human had launched out of the chair surprised everyone but him. He'd seen her body tense, and her muscles tighten, right before fear flashed in her gaze. Nay. Not fear. Panic.

It had only been for a moment, though, and he would've missed it had he not been looking for it.

Not only was his guide a human who couldn't be trusted and was being forced to help, but she was also hiding something. He blew out a breath. Everyone hid things. He didn't care what it was, as long as it didn't hinder their operation. And that was the rub. Because he couldn't be sure. It was why he preferred to work alone.

His thoughts turned to her bag. She had been most interested in it, especially the small vial that had been so carefully bundled. What was it? A drug, perhaps? Maybe that's what she was trying to hide. Ravi spotted one of the guards holding the bag. He strode to him and took the satchel. A look inside showed there was nothing but the meager items of food.

"Fuck," he muttered.

Ravi went looking for Dain before realizing exactly where the Dark had gone.

"Where are you going?" Durga asked as she poked her head out of a room he passed.

"I'll be back."

"We have details to discuss."

Ravi halted and turned to look back at her. "We're going to need Dain. I'm fetching him."

"Ravi," she began.

"I'll be back," he repeated.

He made his way to the East Haffeb district. It was the opposite of the glittering, beautiful Geggin Square. The structures used for homes looked as if they would fall down at any second. Dozens of people lived in a single building, their clothes nothing more than rags hanging on their bodies. The emptiness in people's gazes was difficult to miss, but the children's sunken cheeks and listless bodies made Ravi question the Shecrish Conclave's decision to grant children to those who couldn't feed or care for themselves, let alone others. It had always been the Conclave's opinion that everyone should have a child if they wished it, regardless of their standing. He had to wonder when anyone from the Conclave had last been to East Haffeb.

He found the location the human had given. Ravi half-expected it to be a trap. Instead, what he found was a mercantile store, which surprised him. He headed toward the shop when he spotted Dain standing off to the side, watching him. The Dark tilted his head and raised a brow. Ravi sighed and diverted toward him.

"I wondered how long it would take you," Dain said.

Ravi eyed him. "You're attracting attention."

"I'm not the only one."

"Why are you here?"

"Why are you?"

Ravi should've known he wouldn't get anything from the Dark. He started to turn away.

"It's medicine," Dain said, stopping him.

Ravi slowly turned around. "What?"

"The bottle Yasmin had. It's medicine."

"How do you know?"

"I make it my business to know things about humans. Perhaps you should do the same."

Ravi crossed his arms over his chest. "She didn't look ill."

"I don't believe it's for her. Neither was the food."

Ravi frowned. "You really think she gave us the correct location?"

"I believe she wants the medicine to get where it needs to go. My guess is the shop owner will know exactly who the medicine is for."

It was a plausible theory. Ravi nodded once. "You think we'll find something more to keep her in line?"

Dain mumbled something as he rolled his eyes and walked into the store. He returned soon after, shaking his head. He'd gotten nothing, but that wasn't a surprise. Few knew how to deal with a Dark since they preferred to stay beneath the surface. There were some elves in East Haffeb, but it was more where humans congregated.

"There was a young lad inside," Dain said. "His head snapped up when I mentioned Yasmin. He knows her."

"That doesn't mean he'll know where she lives."

Dain just shot him a flat look. "I thought you were good at this?"

"Now isn't the time to st—"

"There," the Dark interrupted.

Ravi swallowed the rest of the sentence and followed Dain's gaze. He spotted the lanky form of a lad teetering on the verge of manhood, slipping from the store's side entrance and hurrying away. He had an eye patch over one eye. Dain followed him. Ravi trailed after both of them. They didn't go far. The lad entered a building with part of the roof gone and the door leaning against the wall, off its hinges.

"What are you doing?" Dain whispered frantically as Ravi walked around him.

Ravi snorted. "Going inside."

He strode to the building, eyeing how unsafe it appeared. He didn't know or care what Dain was doing. "Hello?" Ravi called out as he paused at the door.

When no one answered, he carefully lifted the leaning slab of wood and peered inside. The outside might look questionable, but the inside was clean and orderly. Ravi turned his shoulders to the side and ducked through the doorway. He settled the door back into place and turned around. Out of the corner of his eye, he spotted a flash of blond hair dashing away. Above him, he heard the patter of tiny footsteps. Children.

"Hello?" he called again, moving slowly. "I'm not going to hurt you."

Something sharp poked him in the middle of his back. An adolescent voice, just beginning to deepen, said, "That's what they all say."

Ravi raised his hands and turned his head to the side. He saw the lad from the shop. "Easy, now."

"You're the one who entered our home without invitation."

"You're right. I apologize for that. How about you lower the weapon, and we can discuss why I'm here?"

The boy grunted. "Right. You're here for a conversation. How about you tell me what you've done with Yasmin since you're holding her bag?"

Damn. Dain had been right.

When Ravi didn't answer fast enough, the tip of the blade pressed through the material of his jacket and shirt, pricking his skin.

"Tell me!" the lad bellowed, his voice cracking at the end.

"She's fine," Ravi said carefully.

"She's not here, and you are. She's far from fine."

The rage in the lad's voice was startling. Was this her brother or another family member? Ravi's mind sorted through the options. "I'm not here to harm anyone. I'll leave now."

"So you can come back with more of your kind?" the lad said, his voice heavy with distrust. "Because you elves always speak the truth."

Ravi closed his eyes in exasperation. Now he knew what the female was hiding. She was a dissenter. One of the humans who hated elves and everything they stood for. The dissenters believed that anything that befell the humans was always the elves' fault. Never mind that humans and elves had lived together for countless centuries.

The soft cry of a child in pain came from above and caught Ravi's attention. He thought of the vial Dain had said was medicine. "Someone is sick."

"It's none of your concern," the lad snapped, his voice cracking again.

"Why didn't you take them to a healer?"

"Look around. Does it look as if we can afford that?"

Ravi frowned. Healers did charge more for human treatment, which he had never agreed with, but surely one would have seen the child. "Then let me take them."

"We know what accepting help from an elf gets us. No, thanks."

"So, you'll let the child die?"

"Yasmin has medicine. She'll bring it."

Ravi opened his mouth to answer when Dain appeared at the top of the steps.

"Enough," the Dark stated, his yellow gaze locking on Ravi.

His attention slid past him to the lad. "Yasmin did get medicine—or what she thought was medicine."

The blade lowered, and Ravi took the opportunity to turn sideways to look at the boy. Shock slackened the youth's face. Dark hair was trimmed short, and the first hint of facial hair was just beginning to show.

"That took all our coin," the lad mumbled.

Dain turned and disappeared into a room. The lad hurried after him, Ravi forgotten. After a moment, Ravi followed, climbing the steps two at a time. He reached the top and went into the room Dain had entered. A little girl of no more than five or six lay on a blanket, sweating and pale. Dain gently laid a hand on her forehead, his face clouded with anger.

"She's gotten worse," the lad said. "We've tried everything."

Dain looked up at the lad. "I have a friend coming to help. Will you bring her up here?"

The lad hesitated before motioning to someone. Ravi turned to look behind him and found a girl a year or two younger than the lad rushing away. Ravi took a closer look around the room and found three other children of various ages. There was much Ravi wanted to know, but he found his attention on Dain and his gentleness with the child as he bathed her head with a cool, wet rag. The little girl whimpered, in obvious pain.

They didn't have to wait long for Dain's friend, a Star Elf, to arrive. The healer said nothing as she quickly got to work on the child. Dain remained next to the girl until the healer nodded. Only then did he stand and look around the room at the rest of the children.

"She's going to be fine now," Dain announced. "She'll still need some rest, though."

The oldest lad lifted his chin. "We'll look after her."

"I have no doubt." Dain bowed his head to the lad and motioned for Ravi to follow him downstairs.

Ravi lowered the bag and backed away. The children rushed to it and pulled out the food. They didn't devour it as he'd expected. Instead, they divided it up so everyone got the same amount. He took one last look at them before meeting Dain downstairs.

"Do you know what this place is?" Dain asked.

Ravi shrugged. "I can guess. She's stealing kids."

"Stealing?" an adolescent voice dripping with bitterness asked.

At the snort, Ravi lifted his head to see five children at the railing, looking down at them.

The lad shook his head and continued. "Yasmin saved each of us. I got this," he said, pointing to the patch over his left eye, "from the people raising me. We've been starved and abused in ways you couldn't begin to consider. Yasmin protects us. She gave us the only home we've ever known."

Ravi eyed each of their thin frames, their hunger and misery obvious. If the human had really wanted to help, she would've taken them to the Ministry to let them deal with things with the families, but he knew it was pointless to say anything. The children saw her as their savior. They had no idea that what she did was against the law and doing them more harm than good.

Ravi walked out, Dain on his heels. He didn't get far before the Dark stood in front of him, fury rolling off him.

"Is everything black and white to you?" Dain demanded.

"I can see they're suffering. That doesn't give her the right to step in."

"And who would? The Conclave? The city? Because that's worked so well in the past."

Ravi shook his head, his anger growing. "She's a dissenter. She's keeping children not granted to her. She could be locked away for life for such crimes."

"Feeding, caring for, and sheltering children in need is a crime?" Dain's lip lifted in a sneer. "And you wonder why the Dark Elves prefer to stay underground."

4

The hours stretched endlessly. Yasmin waited for what was to come next. She didn't want to remain in the room but also didn't want to return to Shaldorn. A look around the space had shown her there was no getting out except through the door guarded by the three goons who had taken her in the market.

Food was brought, but there were no more interrogations or additional threats. Perhaps the elves thought they had done all they needed. Sadly, they had.

She ate because she needed her strength for the trip and because it had been a day since she had last eaten. While alone, she used the time to think about what she was being coerced into doing. The female Wood Elf had been careful about how much she gave away, but Yasmin wasn't stupid. These people weren't just elves on some adventure. They were the real thing. Defense Intelligence agents.

Who was the elf she would take into the mountains? Was it the

Dark? At least he had been willing to help her. Not that she believed he had. But she couldn't think about Jaya and the medicine, or she would lose it. Nay. Yasmin had to stay focused on what she *could* do something about at the moment.

She shook her head slightly to clear it. Somewhere out there, the elf she would take to Shaldorn would attempt to double-cross her somehow. She had to be mentally and physically ready when it happened. They would likely wait until she got them inside the stronghold. It might have been four years since she had last been inside those icy walls, but a person never forgot certain things. She remembered every corridor, every nook and cranny. She knew which of the maze of stairways led to which parts of the fortress, which led to nowhere...

And which led to the dungeons.

Life had dealt her a difficult hand, but Yasmin had managed to stay alive. It wasn't always pretty or even just, but she was still walking around. That had to mean something. And the kids needed her. She would return for them. Somehow, someway.

She had dreamed of leaving Shecrish. Of finding another life somewhere without the elves. If she didn't play this treacherous game accurately, she would never get the chance. But that was something to think about later once she'd held up her end of the bargain. After—because there *would be* an after—she would return to Rannora, grab the kids, and they would leave. It would be incredibly risky to take all of them, but she couldn't—and wouldn't—leave a single one behind. They deserved a better life. Everyone had let them down. She wouldn't be one of those people.

Yasmin felt eyes on her. She couldn't tell where it was coming from, but she knew she was being watched. She leaned against the wall and closed her eyes. Let them think she slept. She dozed, snatching rest while she could. She had always been a light sleeper, but now she had to be on guard more than usual.

She wondered if the elves had taken her bag to the shop. The Dark had made it seem as if she could trust him, like he would get the medicine to Jaya. Her eyes burned at the thought of sweet, tiny Jaya. The child was timid and shy but had the sweetest disposition despite the physical abuse she had endured.

Her illness had begun with nausea and vomiting and escalated at an alarming rate. Yasmin had tried all the herbs she knew about and then sought others' advice. Nothing seemed to work. She had gone to one of the Star Elves for healing, but he had taken one look at her and shooed her out of the store before she could talk. Jaya became sicker with every hour. Yasmin only had one other choice. She managed to convince a human physician to take a look at the child. Thankfully, she had agreed to help.

The door opened. Yasmin lifted her lids and turned her head to see the trio of guards. They motioned for her to stand. The one she had kicked in the nuts looked as if he hoped she would refuse. She didn't know why they hadn't used magic on her, though she was thankful.

Yasmin climbed to her feet and made her way to the door. One of them turned and began walking. She fell into step behind him while the other two took up positions at her back. They led her down various hallways before going up a short flight of stairs, and then through another door to the outside. The sky was dark, the stars glittering like jewels above her. She didn't spot the Wood Elf or the Dark.

Nor the Sun Elf.

They led her to a carriage and ushered her inside. One of the guards sat inside with her while the other two rode outside. The moment the door closed, the horses were in motion. They drove through alleys behind the building to the fringes of Geggin Square and then continued through Rannora until they reached the city border. To her surprise, they approached a quaint house, and the carriage came to a halt. A moment later, the door opened. Yasmin disembarked and looked around to find a guard motioning for her to go inside.

She walked up the curving path with its overflowing beds of bright flowers and stopped at the stoop, staring at the orange door. Yasmin hesitated for only a moment before rapping her knuckles twice on the wood. The door opened to reveal the Wood Elf from earlier. Yasmin nodded to her.

"Come in, please," the elf said.

Yasmin stepped inside. Her gaze moved past the entrance to land on the Sun Elf, who stood in the main area with a surly expression. He took one look at her before turning on his heel and leaving.

The Wood Elf motioned for her to follow. Yasmin realized that she had changed from her navy gown into one that made her coppery skin glow even more. Another set of elaborate gold tips decorated her ears. Yasmin's gaze swept the areas of the house she could see, but there was no sign of anyone else.

"No one is hiding to jump out at you," the woman stated. She smiled and beckoned Yasmin inside. "Come."

Yasmin softly shut the door and walked to her. "What is this place?"

"A safe haven."

"And you? Who are you?"

The elf smiled and sank onto a chair before indicating that

Yasmin should take the one across from her. "I wondered when you would get around to asking."

"Does that mean you won't tell me?"

She laughed, the sound soft and melodic. "You may call me Durga."

Yasmin watched as Durga poured them some tea from a setting Yasmin hadn't noticed until then. She loved tea, but it was a luxury she hadn't been able to afford in years. "Thank you," Yasmin said after Durga handed her a cup.

Durga sat back with her own cup and regarded her. "I'm able to find out things about people, but it has been difficult to learn anything about you before Shaldorn."

"Good."

"Do you have something to hide?"

Yasmin lifted one shoulder. "Doesn't everyone?"

"That they do."

"I'd like to know how you discovered my time at Shaldorn." Because if the DIA could find her, then so could the Trinity. Which put everyone around her in incredible danger.

"That is information I'm unable to provide you. Suffice it to say I deal in the dark places."

"You are DIA."

Durga grinned behind her cup. It didn't last long, however. "There has been a slight change in plans."

"Meaning?"

"Our timetable has been moved up."

Yasmin drank her tea, letting it fill her mouth before savoring the sweet, floral flavor. "To when?"

"If I had my way, you would leave now." Durga glanced to the side, her lips compressing slightly. "A complication prevents it. It's being worked out. Regardless, you depart at dawn. You'll spend the next few hours here."

Yasmin wondered what could be holding up the mission and then wondered why it had been brought about so rapidly. She had a small reprieve, but it would be over soon. Then, she would be heading back to the nightmare.

"Do you have questions?" Durga asked.

Yasmin cradled her cup in both hands on her lap. "You put a lot of confidence in me to get your agent to Shaldorn and back."

"He has a map. I wouldn't suggest attempting to divert him. That wasn't a question."

"Wasn't it?" Yasmin sipped her tea. "How much do you know about Shaldorn?"

Durga released a long breath. "I know what it is."

"I'm not sure you do. Otherwise, you wouldn't force me to return."

"If I had another choice, I would take it."

"Everyone has a choice."

Durga's lips curved slightly. "I like your spirit, Yasmin. The fact is, all of Shecrish is in danger. If it means saving everyone, I'm willing to send my agent, as well as coerce, force, or bribe you to take him, knowing that both of you may die."

"At least you're honest about that. Why tell me?"

"You should know. It isn't something I can tell the public, but they aren't the ones risking their lives." Durga leaned forward and set her empty cup on the tray. "I know about the children you're looking after. They'll be watched."

"In case I return sooner than expected."

Durga folded her hands in her lap. "You don't trust me, and

you have every right to feel that way. Trust is earned, and it goes both ways."

"Aye. It does." Yasmin held Durga's gaze, not backing down.

The Wood Elf smiled. "Few things in this world are truly ours. Things can be taken away. Food, clothes. A home. But we have our word. A promise given, a vow made and kept, can mean more than riches. And if broken, it can mean that no one believes us after. Would you not agree?"

"I would."

"Then let me begin. I give you my word that no charges will be brought against you if you take Ravi to Shaldorn, get him inside, and then return him to Rannora."

Yasmin considered that. "He could find his way home."

"This is about completing a mission."

"I'm not one of your agents."

"You are for this."

So much for Yasmin running back without this Ravi, whoever he was. She couldn't ignore those charges. Yasmin couldn't talk to the children and get them prepared to meet her somewhere either.

"Do you accept?" Durga pressed.

What choice did she have? Spending forever in a cell if Durga informed the Conclave about the children would break her mentally and emotionally. Or she could face her past and certain death. At least there was a chance at freedom by taking Ravi to Shaldorn. "I accept."

"I want your word, Yasmin."

She drew in a deep breath and then slowly released it. Yasmin never gave her word without meaning it. As Durga had said, it was the only thing no one could take away from her but herself. The only thing she truly had. "And if your agent leaves me behind?"

"He won't."

"Neither of you understand Shaldorn and its dangers."

"It doesn't matter. You know why I'm sending you. There is always a chance of things going awry during a mission. You two will need to learn to rely on each other. I fully expect both of you to watch each other's backs and help each other out. He won't leave you, and you won't leave him. Do I have your word?"

Yasmin nodded. "You have my word."

"Good. Now that that's settled, is there anything else?"

"My bag...was it delivered?"

The woman's hazel eyes were direct as she nodded. "It was."

Yasmin held her breath as she waited to hear news about the children, but the woman said nothing. Still, she had to know. "Was the medicine administered?"

"The child is on the mend."

Tears burned Yasmin's eyes. She wished she was there to hold Jaya, but she would when she returned. The children were what she had to keep thinking about. They were the ones who would get her home.

"There is food in the kitchen, a bath ready for you in the chamber down the hall, and some new clothes for the mountains. If you need anything, don't hesitate to ask."

"You should send more than one agent."

The Wood Elf's gaze slid past her toward the hallway. "Get some rest while you can."

Yasmin watched her rise and walk to the hall. A moment later, she heard the sound of a door closing. Then, she was alone. Well, as alone as someone with two other people in the house could be. She went to the kitchen and found so much food she could only stare in wonder. It would feed her and the kids for a week. If only she could get some to them. She loaded her plate and then headed to the hallway. There were three doors. Two were shut. She went to the open middle door and looked in.

A tub filled with water still hot enough that ribbons of steam rose from it was inside. There was a braided oval rug in bright colors between it and the large bed. An actual bed. It had been some time since she had slept on anything but a blanket.

She walked over, shutting the door softly and setting the plate of food on a table. Then she fingered the clothes on the bed. They were similar in color and style to what she already had, but without the holes and mended areas. There were even boots and thick socks to keep her feet warm.

Yasmin stripped and sank into the water. She sighed, enjoying it more than she should. She stayed until the water began to cool. The soap was unused, and beneath it was a drying cloth. She brought the bar to her nose and inhaled the warm, earthy, woodsy scent of sandalwood. She lathered it over her body twice and her hair three times.

She stood and began to dry with a cloth softer than anything she had felt in a long time. Yasmin wrapped it around herself and expected to finger-comb her hair as usual, but she saw a brush on the bedside table. She grabbed it and sat on the rug to detangle her locks as she nibbled on the food.

There were more items to be found. A new bag sat on a chair. Beneath it were new underthings and strips of leather to tie back her hair. Inside the bag was a coat, gloves, a scarf, a cap, a rolled blanket, food, and a water flask—everything she would need for a trip to the mountains.

Yasmin packed it all back into the bag and crawled into the bed. She lay within its plush covers and attempted to sleep.

Durga found Ravi standing outside. It was still several hours before dawn, but she never slept before a mission. She might not be going on this one, but that didn't matter when so much rested on its success. "Spit it out," she said.

He stood with his arms crossed over his chest as he stared in the direction of the mountains. At just the right angle, the very tips of the peaks could be seen through the tops of the trees. "What?"

"You know what."

"She's a fucking civilian, Durga. And a dissenter. And is being forced. It won't end well."

"You'll make it work."

He blew out a breath and turned his head to her. "I can't trust her."

"We have one chance to get the explosive, Ravi. One. It's being sold at Shaldorn during its once-a-month gathering next week. Would you rather try to track it through the mountains or the jungles of Shecrish before it reaches the border?"

A muscle ticked in his jaw. "Nay."

"Then what's your real problem? Is it Yasmin? Or is it the fact that Dain brought this information to me?"

"It's both," he muttered.

"Get over it."

Ravi glanced at her. "The human isn't an agent."

"You've worked with other humans."

"They were trained. A few of them actually do well in our line of work. She isn't one of them."

Durga had mentored Ravi for years, but there were times she could cheerfully knock his head off. "*She* has a name. Use it." Durga sighed loudly. "Dain risked his life bringing this intel to me. His superiors have no idea what he did or that he's been working with us. Our two agencies have never gotten along, and you know it. Dain is walking a tightrope. I don't blame him for getting called back before he could take you and Yasmin to the mountains."

"Now, we get to trek through the peaks."

"You've never turned away from a mission before, no matter how risky or treacherous."

Ravi's copper eyes met hers. "I'm not now."

"Is this where you tell me again that I should be questioning her?"

"You know the more information we have, the better the mission."

Durga shrugged. "If the original plan still stood, I would be interrogating her right now. But it doesn't. She's angry and defensive because I've put her in an impossible situation. You have days with her to get all the information you need. Get over your anger and do your job."

"She's a dissenter."

"Maybe. Maybe not. It doesn't matter. We all have a job to do to save lives. That's what matters at the end of the day."

"Aye," he said and turned his head away.

"Then I suggest you get yourself ready. Everything rests on your shoulders, just the way you like it."

He smiled for the first time since she'd seen him at the tavern. "Aye, I do."

Yasmin hadn't realized she'd dozed off until sounds from within the house woke her. She glanced outside to see the sky lightening from black to gray. Dawn approached. And with it, her past.

She rose and dressed with care. She took her time combing her hair before braiding it. Habit had her checking the bag and its contents. Yasmin tucked the small knife she always carried with her into her boot, then downed the last of the food from the night before.

That's when she found herself staring out the window. She wished she knew what she had done to the gods that they would put her in this predicament. She tried to live a good life. She only stole when she had to—which seemed to be all the time. Why hadn't she left Shecrish? She'd had four years to leave, yet she remained.

There was no getting out of what she had to do. She had given her word. Yasmin slung the strap of the bag over her shoulder and walked from the room. She followed the sound of voices to the kitchen and found Durga with the Sun Elf. More food was set out.

"Ah, there you are," Durga said. "The clothes fit well. That's good. Grab some food while you can."

Yasmin set down her bag and got a napkin to put several items in. She wrapped it up and carefully placed it in her pack, all while the Sun Elf stared at her. She noted his boots were the same as hers. She really hoped he wasn't Ravi.

5

"**A**re you ready?" Durga asked as she handed over a cup of tea.

Yasmin bowed her head in thanks and accepted it. "Not really."

"I like your honesty." She laughed.

Yasmin drank the tea as her mind wandered. She wanted to ask Durga to tell the children that she would return. She and Sameer had come up with a plan. If anything were to happen to her, he knew what to do. She hated that she couldn't send word to them, but she didn't trust any of the elves around her. Durga might be nice, but she had known *nice* before, and it hid a soul as black as pitch.

She was so wrapped up in her thoughts that it took her a moment to realize she had missed some of the discussion. Yasmin smoothed a hand over her hair to tuck a flyaway strand behind her ear.

"...isn't going to be an easy journey. Shaldorn is located on one of the highest mountains within the Dangerous Peaks," Durga said. Her gaze briefly met Yasmin's before moving to the Sun Elf. "Because of the inclement mountain weather, it will be better to cut across the plateau before heading into the mountains."

That was at least two days of hard travel across some of the thickest rainwoods of Shecrish. But she was right. It was better to limit their time in the mountains. There was more than just weather to worry about once they began climbing the peaks.

Yasmin looked at the Sun Elf. So, this *was* Ravi. He had changed out of his lavish attire from the night before and now wore a short-sleeve tan shirt with no collar and buttons down the front. The garment lay softly against him, showcasing thick neck sinew and even bigger arm muscles. Deep brown breeches were tucked into well-worn boots. The top portion of his golden hair was tied behind his head, and he kept his eyes on the woman speaking, never once looking Yasmin's way.

"Yasmin?"

She started, her gaze jerking to Durga. "Aye?"

"I asked if you had everything you needed for the excursion."

"The items will make the trip bearable."

"We've packed as much food as possible," Durga continued. "I didn't want to weigh down your pack. The coat we supplied took up a lot of room."

Nothing would keep them warm once they reached the Dangerous Peaks, but Yasmin kept that to herself.

The Wood Elf sighed and flattened her lips. "Yasmin, as you may have guessed, this is Ravi. Ravi, Yasmin. It's nearly dawn. You should be off. Good luck to you both. Remember, you both gave me your word."

Yasmin didn't budge. Ravi still wouldn't look at her. It was bad enough that she was being forced on this *excursion*. Now, she learned it was with someone who hadn't even bothered to speak to her before now. She stared at him, daring him to look her way. Finally, those copper eyes met hers. The disdain reflected there was palpable.

"You both gave your word," Durga repeated.

Yasmin adjusted the strap of her pack on her shoulder. "I gave my word to you, just as Ravi did."

She had known she would be taking an elf and had been prepared to hide her hatred and get the job done. But for some reason, Ravi rubbed her the wrong way. Perhaps it was his unconcealed contempt.

Durga cleared her throat. "You two are to watch each other's backs. That's the only way this will work."

"I'll do my part," Ravi said after a stern look from the woman.

That hard gaze swung to Yasmin. She thought about the knife in her boot. She would be prepared for any double-cross. "I'll do my part."

"Great," Durga said with a too-bright smile.

Yasmin looked from the woman to Ravi before turning on her heel and walking into the rainwood. The thick vegetation and soaring trees soon enveloped her. She didn't wait for Ravi as she pointed herself northeast and began walking fast. They had a lot of ground to cover, and there was no use dawdling.

She heard a rustle behind her. Unable to help herself, she glanced over her shoulder and spotted the Sun Elf five steps behind her. He didn't look her way. At least he wouldn't bombard her with conversation. Silence was her preferred way to deal with elves. It wasn't as if they needed to talk. Neither wanted the other on this journey, and it was best to just get their *excursion* over with as quickly as possible.

Yasmin kept to the path as much as she could. Her stride was steady, and since her legs were shorter, she would set the pace. She was leading, after all. That made her grin. Was that what galled the Sun Elf? He didn't seem the type who played a supporting role to anyone.

They had been traveling for about an hour when the rain began. She didn't slow. She was surprised to find that her jacket and pants were waterproof, keeping her relatively dry. She'd find out about the pack later, but if the clothes were treated, she surmised the bag was, too. However, that didn't stop the water from dripping from her head, down her neck, and then rolling between her shirt and skin. It helped to cool her from the oppressive humidity, though.

Yasmin didn't stop until the sun was directly above her. At least the rain had halted. She looked at the small pool of water and dropped her pack near one of the catalpa trees. Some of its tall, narrow roots protruded from the soil. She sat on one and rolled her head from side to side to stretch her neck. She spotted Ravi near a tree, far enough away that she'd have to shout to talk to him. Yasmin sent up a silent prayer of thanks and dug into her pack for food.

The bag had done a good job of keeping the water out. She rubbed the material between her fingers. She couldn't imagine how much it had cost. If she returned, would she get to keep it? She'd demand it because then she could sell it and have enough coin to feed them for days. Maybe even a week.

One of these days, she would figure out a way for the children to have as much food as they wanted. She recalled what it was like to have hunger gnawing at her belly. It still happened, but it had been worse as a child. Or maybe she was just used to it now.

She dug out the food she had wrapped in the napkin and devoured everything within. She was still hungry, so she sniffed a piece of dried meat before taking a bite. It was delicious. She tried to hide her surprise. She'd had plenty of dried meat before, but this was unlike anything she had ever tasted. Yasmin closed her eyes and savored the perfectly mixed spice-to-meat ratio. Maybe she could ration how much she ate so she could bring some back to the kids. They should be able to know what great food tasted like. It would be a treat to make up for her having to go away.

Yasmin went through her piece quickly. Too quickly, actually. She had to fight against grabbing another. At this rate, she wouldn't have any for the children. Her gaze covertly slid to Ravi. Unless she took some of his. It would be easy once he slept. He'd probably never miss it. It wasn't as if she'd let him starve. If it came down to him needing it, she'd hand it over.

She drank deeply from the water flask. There were plenty of sources of water on the plateau. Between the many lakes and rivers, they would never be without. She rose and walked to the pool. The water was clear, allowing her to see the various fish swimming beneath the surface. They didn't pay her any mind as she knelt near the edge and lowered her flask to refill it. She saw the shadow of a krelite rising toward her and quickly stepped back. It wasn't a predator exactly. Mainly because it wouldn't eat her. It just wanted to play, but in doing so, it could hold her underwater until she drowned. The krelite couldn't distinguish between a Sea Elf and anyone else. It just saw a playmate.

As she stood, she looked up and found Ravi watching her. His eyes lowered to the water as the krelite returned to the bottom. Only then did he refill his flask.

She said nothing as she readied herself. Once the straps to her pack were looped around her arms and it rested against her back, she glanced at Ravi to find him waiting. They set off again. A grin formed when she heard the ruckus of some cooroda. She looked up to find them swinging from tree to tree, howling and chattering excitedly. They were harmless. Well, unless someone had catalpa fruit. They were a particular favorite of the cooroda.

It was only then that Yasmin heard the sounds of the rain-wood: the sway of leaves from the breeze. Water dripping after the rain. The loud and various bird calls. The cries of the cooroda mixed with other animals. The rainwood was a beautiful place, but there were lethal threats, as well.

Like the elf behind her.

6

It had been some time since Ravi had someone on a mission with him. While he didn't like his guide's political views, she had proven a bit of a surprise already by remaining quiet. Thankfully, she kept a steady bearing and a quick pace, which meant he didn't have to hurry her. And she rarely looked back to see if he was still there. If he lagged, it would be his problem—not that he would fall behind.

He thought back to when Durga had detained the human. If anyone else had given him the information, Ravi would've believed them liars. But Durga had never led him astray. That wasn't to say she never would, but she wouldn't do it on purpose. Precious few could be trusted in their line of work, and they both knew how imperative it was to maintain that trust.

Durga had given him his first mission. He'd thought himself so important at the time. It had been a menial job, but she must have seen something in him because she brought him back to the academy with her, where he began his training.

So, when she sent him somewhere, he went. Always. It didn't matter how risky or problematic. Because he came through for her each time. That wasn't what bothered him about this assignment, though. Nay, that lay solely with his *guide.*

He'd spent the rest of the day before and well into the evening poring over everything Durga had collected about the Shaldorn stronghold. It was pitiful how little intel they'd gathered. They didn't even have a clear indication of who ran it. Most of the information in the file was thirdhand knowledge overheard by agents. No one who had been inside had ever been interviewed. He locked his gaze on the back of the female's head as she walked ahead of him. The fact that so much rested on the human getting him inside and back out left Ravi uneasy.

She could—and probably *would*—double-cross him. She hadn't wanted to return to Shaldorn. Her reaction had been visceral, her fear tangible. Someone with that strong of a response being compelled to do something they didn't want to do was a recipe for disaster. Sure, Durga's threat of a year in the cells was enough to make anyone hesitate.

Ravi had seen the prisons the humans were thrown into. They weren't places he would even put his enemies. The female had endured a month in one already. Anyone who knew what awaited them would do *anything* to avoid finding themselves in one again.

Perhaps the human had capitulated quicker than anticipated because she realized she had no choice. More than likely, she had concluded there was only one way to potential freedom, and that was to agree to the situation. If he were in her shoes, he'd wait until they reached the mountains before leaving him behind. They would be far enough away from Rannora for her to make her escape.

Durga had said the human wouldn't go back on her word. But Ravi knew she would. She was a cornered animal with only one thought: survival. Whether that included the children she looked after or not remained to be seen.

Ravi's thoughts turned to the other thorn in his side. Dain. He would give the Dark his due. Dain was good at his job, but that didn't mean Ravi wanted him around. And he certainly didn't want to work with him. Dain was…Dain. Like most Dark, they had ideologies that rarely, if ever, lined up with the rest of the elven communities. Dain was no exception.

However, Dain had somehow gotten into Durga's good graces, which meant Ravi never knew when Dain would show up. The fact that the Dark knew Kendrick and had spent considerable time with the Dragon King made Dain an asset to their current mission —even if it rankled Ravi. Of all the elves, why had Dain approached the Dragon King? What had Dain sought? Because the Dark Elves didn't do anything without reason. Ravi would eventually uncover whatever it was.

He watched as the female kept her attention on the cooroda above her instead of where she was going. She was light on her feet, though, deftly skirting anything in her way. Humans had always been a part of Shecrish, but the elves outnumbered them forty to one. It put them in the awkward position of being minor citizens. They didn't have magic, which meant they were at the mercy of the elves.

Humans were a part of life. Ravi didn't have strong feelings about them one way or the other—at least the ones who abided by the laws. He drew the line when it came to dissenters. He didn't care if anyone objected to the laws and wanted to change them. He opposed the systematic dismantling of society to throw it into chaos on the chance that humans could take over. The fact was that humans couldn't defeat the elves. Not without magic.

And that's what kept things stirred up.

For as long as he could remember, Ravi knew there were malcontents. It started with protests. Humans demanded to be represented in the Conclave. No one stopped that. Humans ran for positions all the time, but they lacked the votes. When they couldn't get onto the Conclave or even the smaller city councils, the protests became larger, louder. There was rioting. Elves and humans got hurt. A child had even been killed.

Yet that wasn't enough. Next came the bombs. There were five explosions over a three-month period that killed dozens of both humans and elves. Since the humans had started it, the Conclave that ruled Shecrish stepped in and put an end to things. But it didn't quash the insurgents, not completely. They were still there, working in the shadows. He worried about what they might try next. The elven communities had gotten complacent. Even the humans who weren't a part of the rebels thought they were gone.

Ravi and the DIA, as well as the Conclave, knew differently.

A rumble of thunder sounded before the skies opened, and more rain came. Ravi shook droplets from his face as the precipitation turned from light rain to a downpour. The female never stopped. She strolled through the rainwood as if it were nothing. The sounds of the city were long behind them, and only the jungle surrounded him. Hot. Humid. Wet. Lethal. He had been born in the city but had spent enough time in the forests to know the perils.

There was also the fact that they weren't alone. Wood Elves were everywhere, though you only saw them when they wanted to be seen. Durga had contacted her cousin, Tarron. He knew about

Ravi and the human's path through the rainwood. Whether they intersected was anyone's guess. Ravi would prefer it if the Wood Elves stayed away. He didn't want the human to say something they would both regret. She had spoken to Durga with some semblance of respect, but she had given him none.

He hadn't given her any either.

That was fine if it was just the two of them. He didn't want that with any other elves besides Durga. Ravi trudged through the rain and turned his thoughts to Shaldorn. The female was meant to get him to the fortress, inside, and back home. But he might need her to complete his mission.

Durga was right. It would be up to him to learn everything he could about Shaldorn from the human. The more he knew, the easier it would be to coerce her into doing what he needed to complete the assignment. It wouldn't be the first time he'd had to set aside his feelings about someone to achieve a successful mission, and it wouldn't be the last.

Ravi blinked the rain from his lashes and checked their heading. The female had deviated a little but not enough for him to be concerned. He had a map of the stronghold's location. There was a road to Shaldorn, but they were going another, longer way. He'd know if she took them off course.

As much as Ravi didn't like working with Dain, things would've been infinitely easier and quicker had the Dark been able to take them straight to the mountains using the shadows. Dain could only get them so close, though, since Shaldorn had special lanterns that broke through the Dark's shadows.

Durga had believed it safer if they traveled on foot, especially after she lost an operative. She took the loss of one of her people hard. So, here he was, walking through the rainwood with an enemy he'd rather be taking to prison than toward a place that, if he wasn't careful, could end his life.

It became difficult to see in the forest with the sun sinking. The thick canopy of trees gobbled up most of the light, allowing only meager strands to filter through. He lengthened his strides to bring himself closer to the human. If she noticed, she didn't give any indication.

The rain began slowly tapering off and then finally stopped altogether. Water dripped from the leaves overhead, making it seem like it was still sprinkling. The entire Corrial Plateau that made up Shecrish was one large rainwood. All except the mountains. When he was younger, he'd once claimed he would live in the mountains. It had been a foolish child's dream. The reclusive Mountain Elves were the only ones who dared to call the Dangerous Peaks home.

The female's steps slowed as she looked around. Ravi watched her survey the area, then walk a little more before slowing to take a closer look. She did it thrice more before sliding the pack from her back. That was the only indication he got that they were stopping for the evening.

The huge leaves from the twisted cycad tree arching overhead were the perfect protection against any rain during the evening. After she had found her spot, Ravi chose his. Again, far enough away from her that there wouldn't be any talking, but close enough that he could keep an eye on her.

He settled beneath a grouping of twisted cycad leaves, thankful that the ground was dry. He didn't like sleeping on wet soil. He didn't bother stretching out. Instead, Ravi used his pack to prop himself up as he ate dinner. A sound above drew his attention. He saw a teba, with its green and black scales, slowly stalking its prey. A monguar released a cry in the distance. The large, feline predator didn't usually bother elves, but he couldn't be so sure about the human.

Ravi glanced at her location to find her gone. He jumped up and started toward her when he saw her pack on the ground. He came to a halt as she emerged from behind a tree.

"Surely, you don't need to follow me as I relieve myself," she stated with a glance his way.

He told himself to return to his spot, but the longer he stared at her, the angrier he became. "You think this mission is a jest? A prank we're playing because we're bored?"

Her dark head slowly lifted to him, blue eyes locking on him. "Hardly. Especially when we're talking about *my* life."

"And mine."

"You have no idea what you're getting yourself into. You think you can just waltz up to Shaldorn and find a side door. Maybe you think you can scale the walls and enter through a tower. There won't be any of that."

He needed intel, but he couldn't set aside his anger. Not yet, at least. "Why didn't you say that before?"

"We both know none of you would have listened. All of you had a single purpose, and you don't care what has to happen or whose lives you destroy to achieve it."

Ravi took a step toward her. "If you knew what was at stake, you might not be so careless with your words and things you know nothing about."

"Durga told me about the explosive."

"And you still would rather not help?" he demanded, his fury escalating.

Her throat bobbed as she swallowed. "You obviously know very little about Shaldorn if you would ask me that."

"You're right. I don't know anything about it. Why don't you tell me?"

"It won't matter what I say. Durga wouldn't change her mind, and neither will you."

He shook his head. "Because I'm attempting to divert a potential war."

"And I want to stay alive."

"You expect those at Shaldorn to come after you?"

Her shoulders lifted as she drew in a breath. "I know they will. The moment they learn I'm alive, they won't stop until they have me."

Ravi wasn't sure whether to believe her or not. Something about her words made him pause, though. "Why?"

"Because I did what no one else has been able to do. I escaped."

7

Yasmin's dreams were filled with Shaldorn and the evil within. She woke bleary-eyed, and her mood was foul as she greeted the gray morning. Her first months after fleeing Shaldorn had been plagued with never-ending nightmares. She had seen the Trinity waiting to grab her everywhere she looked. It had taken over a year before the trio of elves had stopped appearing in her dreams. Though the fear of them finding her never faded.

She could've told Durga every harrowing, ghastly moment of her time at Shaldorn, but Yasmin had recognized that the elf wouldn't relent, no matter what she said. A possible war with the dragons was terrifying, but Yasmin would rather face a horde of dragons than those at Shaldorn.

Yasmin rose and stretched the kinks from her neck, careful not to make any noise. She wanted a few moments to herself before she had to engage with the Sun Elf. A glance in his direction, however, showed he was already awake.

"Great," she murmured beneath her breath, rolling up her bed sack.

"Something wrong?"

She closed her eyes and bit back a tart reply. Yasmin returned everything to her pack after grabbing a piece of dried meat. "Not a thing." She rose and faced him.

He smirked, and she felt the desire to shove him into a pile of blood loxa. Watching them swarm him would be as entertaining as the red welts dotting his body from their bites. They wouldn't kill him—well, enough of them could, but he'd mostly just be very, very uncomfortable.

The picture of him writhing in pain brought a smile to her face. She bit into her piece of dried meat. "We need to pick up the pace today. We're going to encounter at least one storm in the mountains. Depending on the severity, we could lose hours or even days. It's better if we get there ahead of schedule. Otherwise, you co—"

"I could miss the deadline," he said over her. "Good point."

She raised her brows. Had he really agreed with her? Yasmin didn't point that out lest he take it back. Instead, they took a few moments separately to eat and ready themselves for the day. It wasn't long before they headed out.

It was a repeat of the previous day. More jungle, a few stops, and no talking. At times, she almost forgot the elf was with her. Then she'd catch sight of him or hear him and be reminded why she was out here to begin with.

The fear she had lived with for years returned tenfold. She thought about different ways to run away and slip back to Rannora to get the children—that was if Durga didn't have anyone watching them, and Jaya was well enough to travel. But Yasmin had no coin, and taking the kids on the run with her wouldn't be right.

She could leave them behind. Some might even say that was the best option, but she couldn't do that either. They were her family. They depended on her, but she needed them just as much. Nay, she would never abandon them.

That left her with the third option of carrying through with her promise. She hadn't been able to figure a way out then, and she still couldn't. With every step she took farther away from Rannora, she realized she might have to do the unthinkable and face the Trinity.

It wasn't in her nature to be cruel. But she could be. She had been. Still, she never liked it. She had learned to release animosity and bitterness. It only harmed her, not the ones who had hurt her. It wasn't easy to let things go, however. She had worked hard at it, but those who had injured her didn't give her a second thought. Why should she give them any of her time?

Life was what a person made of it. She had discovered that through an unimaginable amount of agony and tears. She did what she had to do until she could do what she wanted. Even if every fiber of her being screamed for her to run far, far away. Whatever was at Shaldorn didn't concern her. Ravi barely tolerated her. If it came down to saving her life or completing his mission, she knew without a doubt which he would choose.

As she walked the rainwood, she thought about the stronghold, pulling up a mental picture after years of trying to erase it. She made herself return to a time she'd attempted to scrub from her memories. Mentally, she walked the corridors and recalled the faces and names. Forced herself to remember the smells and sounds.

And the voices.

Her toe caught a root. She pitched forward. Yasmin tried to adjust so she didn't fall, but the pack's weight threw her off balance. She managed to get a foot under her, but it only threw her off balance more, causing her shoulder to glance off a tree. The pack was roughly yanked backward. It twisted one of her arms as she continued to fall. Before she knew it, she tumbled to the side and rolled into one of the lakes.

Yasmin broke the surface and took a deep breath, seeing Ravi rushing toward her. It was on the tip of her tongue to tell him she was fine when something yanked her beneath the water.

Ravi shouldn't have been so far behind her. He'd seen the female trip and attempt to right herself, only for her pack to get caught on a branch and be wrenched off before she tumbled into the water. He'd run to help and saw the tentacle gently unfurling from the depths to wrap around her and yank her under.

He dropped his bag and dove into the lake after them. The krelite were sweet, but she'd drown if he didn't get to her soon. He spotted the animal attempting to play with the human, who valiantly fought to untangle herself from its grip. The krelite was taking the female into the bottomless depths, most likely toward one of the many underwater tunnels connecting the plateau's lakes and rivers.

Kicking his feet as hard as he could, Ravi swam toward them. The krelite noticed him and thought he had come to join the play. It paused, allowing him to reach them. He didn't fight when the krelite wrapped a tentacle around him, just tried to get the human's attention. Unfortunately, panic had seized her.

Ravi kept the krelite's attention on him. He stroked a tentacle softly, lulling the animal into a near sleep state. It was difficult with the female thrashing about. Humans couldn't hold their breath as long as elves could, and her lungs likely demanded air. But the krelite wouldn't release them until he made it sleep.

The female began to gasp, bubbles coming from her mouth as she ran out of time. He kept his gaze on her, willing her to look at him, but her eyes were elsewhere. At least with her no longer fighting, the krelite began to drift off. The minute the tentacles loosened, he moved toward the female and freed her. He wound an arm around her and swam to the surface as fast as he could.

Ravi got to the edge and hauled them both out, dragging her away from the water before another krelite wanted to play. He rolled the human onto her back, but she was too still. Her eyes were closed, and her chest wasn't rising or falling.

"Shite," he said as he got on his knees and began pressing on her chest.

He pumped several times before her eyes fluttered. Water dribbled from her mouth. The minute she coughed, he had her on her side to help her vomit up the water she had inhaled. When she finished, he became aware of his arm around her and the weight of her breast against the back of his hand.

She turned her head to look at him, and her eyes flared in surprise.

Ravi removed his arm and got to his feet. He wiped the water from his face and looked around. "Good enough spot to stop for the noon meal, don't you think?"

Yasmin's throat was on fire from the mix of coughing and throwing up. Her lungs ached, but her chest was what really hurt. She gently touched her ribs. The act of breathing was so painful that she wanted to stop.

Ravi walked to his pack as if he hadn't just pulled her from the water and gotten her breathing again. She carefully sat up and looked into the lake. It would be an eternity before she forgot the absolute terror that had gripped her as tightly as the krelite when she realized she was about to drown. She had fought to hold her breath for as long as she could. The krelite had no plans to release her. How had Ravi gotten her loose?

Her gaze swung toward him just as he got her pack untangled from a broken limb. He set it near a tree and walked away to his own spot. Yasmin didn't want to eat. She wasn't sure her throat could handle it at the moment. She took her time getting to her feet while doing her best not to wince from the pain in her ribs. It was a small price to pay for being alive. She should thank Ravi.

Yasmin walked to the tree and opted to stay on her feet. It was too painful to move too much. She thought the words. *Thank you.* It was simple and direct. Easy. Yet she couldn't form them on her lips. She drew out her water flask and took a hesitant sip. Something warm would soothe her throat better, but the water would do for now.

She tucked the flask into an outside pocket of her pack and drew in a deep breath. As she released it, she looked at Ravi and tried to say those two simple words. Yet they still wouldn't come. It was petty of her to withhold them merely because she didn't like the elf.

While she had known the cruelty of elves, a few had been kind. It wouldn't be right to classify all elves as malicious, but from her experiences, most were exactly that. Ravi clearly didn't like her and likely had only saved her because of his mission. But he had helped her.

"Thank you."

He didn't look up from whatever he was studying. "Couldn't let you drown when I still need you."

"Of course, not." That's what she got for trying to do the right thing.

After a long moment of silence, Ravi lifted his head. She saw him looking at her out of the corner of her eye. She tried to ignore him, but he wouldn't look away. Finally, she turned her gaze to him.

"Next time a krelite gets you, stroke their tentacles gently. It soothes them to sleep. That's when you can slip away." He paused. "You're welcome."

She nodded. The information on the krelite was useful. Trying to remember that while fighting for air might be difficult, though.

It started raining before they resumed their hike. Her boots squished with each step, and she couldn't wait to get them off to dry overnight. She didn't enjoy the thought of not having protection on her feet, but she hated wet boots even more. She didn't exactly relish soggy clothes either, but she could endure those.

The rain didn't let up for the rest of the day. Despite the weather and her pain, they still made good time. Finding a dry location that evening was impossible. She was about to accept that they would have an uncomfortable night when Ravi pulled something out of his bag. A moment later, after he began setting it up, she realized it was a tent.

Yasmin eyed it enviously. She tried to sit, but the pain was too intense. She finally gave up and leaned against a tree that shielded most of the rain from her. She closed her eyes. Her throat felt better, but her ribs would bother her for some time to come. That would make the trek in the mountains more treacherous than it already would be, but it wouldn't be the first time she'd had to cross those peaks injured.

Something touched her arm. Yasmin's eyes flew open, and she readied to reach for the blade in her boot when she saw Ravi beside her. He had her pack in his hand.

"The tent is for both of us," he said, then walked away.

He might have saved her life, but she didn't relish being that close to him. She looked at her boots, moving her toes against the squishy socks. But she really wanted a moment to get dry. Yasmin swallowed her pride and followed Ravi to the shelter. It was nice, too. The dark green shell camouflaged well in the forest.

She stifled a yelp when she had to bend over to get inside. Every move was excruciating as she crawled in and turned to sit. She closed her eyes and sent up gratitude for the tent. And maybe a tiny bit of thanks to Ravi for sharing it.

8

The sight of the female attempting to get comfortable was a reminder that he had brought her back to life earlier. And in the process, had probably injured her ribs. He hadn't been thinking about that while pumping her chest, though. She hadn't complained once. Nor had it stopped her from keeping up their pace. Begrudgingly, he had to give her credit.

"How bad are the ribs?" he asked.

She shot him a quick glance as if surprised he had spoken. He was just as astonished.

"Fine, as long as I don't take deep breaths. Or move."

He imagined the pain was a lot worse than she was letting on. "There are some herbs in your bag that should help."

"I'll be fine."

Irritation flared. "Is it elves in general you have a problem with, or just me?"

"You don't want me to answer that."

"So, elves in general." He shook his head. "You're only hurting yourself by not taking the herbs. If you wish to walk around hurt, that's your business, but I won't let you slow us down."

She snorted as she yanked her pack in front of her, a flare of pain crossing her face. "I didn't know they were in there. And as for you not *letting* me slow you down, have fun getting into Shaldorn on your own."

He gritted his teeth because she had him there. And she knew it. He looked out the tent entrance, regretting his brief lapse of judgment in offering to share it. He bent his legs, propping his feet on the ground and wrapping his arms around his knees to link his hands. Ravi didn't know how long they sat in silence before, out of the corner of his eye, he saw her studying the small bag of herbs. They weren't just any herbs. The master healers, the Star Elves, had mixed magic into them. Some elven factions could manage minimal healing, but most turned to their star kin in times of need.

They're the ones who mixed the bags for the female and him. Hers was different, being human and all. He saw her open the bag and lean down to smell it before worrying her lip.

"If you don't know how to mix it..." he began.

"I know how."

He rolled his eyes. So much for trying to help.

More time passed without her doing anything but sitting there with the bag. Ravi missed the previous night when there had been some distance between them. She was too close now. He could hear her breathing, taking in the small hitches every once in a while, alerting him to her discomfort.

The trek across Shecrish through the rainwood was relatively easy. There were some undulations across the plateau, but they weren't getting near anything difficult. Nay, the toughest portion was yet to come, and she wouldn't be able to hike the mountains in her current condition. The more he thought about it, the more irritated he became. She hadn't wanted to be here. She would use her injury as a way to get out of bringing him to Shaldorn. He would if he were in her position.

It wasn't as if the krelite had taken her based on something she had done purposefully. Her tripping and falling had all been an accident. Just as her drowning had. He understood all of that. His problem came now when there was a remedy for her bruised—and possibly broken—ribs. In her eyes, she had found a way to get out of this without breaking her word.

"If I have to carry you up that fucking mountain as you point the way to the stronghold, I will. You're not getting out of this," he stated.

There was a long stretch of silence before she said, "I can't take these herbs."

"Oh, this should be good," he said, turning his head to her. "And why not?"

"It has lake root in it. I have an adverse reaction to it."

Ravi swallowed the rest of his words and took the bag from her. He brought it to his nose and inhaled. Sure enough, he smelled the distinctive grassy, minty, almost sweet aroma. Lake root was a known herb used by healers for humans, though some Star Elves favored it over others. He closed the bag. None of them had thought to ask if there was anything the human needed to avoid.

He set the sachet aside and dug into his pack for his bag. After a sniff, he knew there was no lake root included. Ravi held it out to her. "This was made for me, but you can try it. It won't heal you completely since it wasn't made for a human, but it'll speed the process."

To his surprise, she added a pinch of the proffered herbs to her water flask. After shaking it well, she brought it to her lips and drank.

"Thank you," she murmured.

He nodded and tucked the bag away. Now that he had spoken to her, he was very aware of the silence that stretched between them, broken only by the sound of the rain. It wasn't awkward, at least not at first, but he found himself listening to her breathing, waiting to hear if the pain receded. It was too soon. He knew that, but he couldn't help himself. She would have to drink the entire flask and give the magical herbs an hour or two to take effect.

As the silence stretched, it became uncomfortable. At least for him.

"How bad of a reaction?" he asked.

Her brow furrowed as she looked at him.

"The allergy. How bad?"

She drew in a deep breath. "It can kill me."

He ran a hand down his face and shifted positions so he sat cross-legged. "You're lucky lake root has a unique smell."

A grunt was her response. Then, "The pain is lessening."

"Already? That's good."

He cast her a quick look to find her unbraiding her hair. She ran her fingers through the long midnight strands, her eyes closed. He hurriedly looked away. It felt too much like invading her privacy. He kept his gaze directed anywhere but at her after that.

At least he did until he heard a small grunt. Ravi looked her way before he could stop himself. She was attempting to lean forward to remove her boots. He knew she would refuse if he offered to help. Instead, he simply rolled to his knees and effortlessly removed both sodden boots and socks from her. Something fell out of her boot to the blanket she sat on. He looked from the knife to her. She held his gaze without saying a word. Ravi handed her the blade and then set her boots and socks aside before resuming his seat and taking off his own.

"Rain and humidity here," she said. "Ice and dryness in the mountains. Not sure which is more miserable."

"The cold," he answered.

Her lips quirked in a brief smile as she carefully lay down and curled up on her side, away from him. "I agree. By the way, the coats won't be enough. No number of layers will keep out the kind of cold that's up there."

He didn't bother to look away from her now. She couldn't see him anyway. Her breathing seemed easier. He wanted to ask how she'd learned of the allergy, but the answer was simple. She had been injured and sought a healer. Why hadn't the Star Elf used magic instead of herbs? Maybe she hadn't been able to afford it and took the magical herbs instead.

"Why are you going to Shaldorn?" the human asked.

He blinked and looked out to watch the rainfall. "Because someone has to."

"And that someone is you?"

"Usually."

She rolled partway onto her back to look at him. "Do you enjoy being the one they send in during a crisis?"

He looked into her dark blue depths. They were eyes that had seen and experienced much. They should belong to someone much older. He cleared his throat, wondering why his thoughts had taken him down that road. "I do."

"You seem the type who works alone."

He dipped his chin. "I am."

Her gaze lowered as she nodded. "It's easier, isn't it? Not having to worry about anyone else."

"I suppose." He wondered about her suddenly talkative mood. Then he saw her dazed, glassy eyes. The herbs were affecting her. She might have only used a little, but they had been crafted specifically for him, which meant a higher dose of magic. "Do you have any other reactions to herbs or magic?"

She blinked slowly. "Haven't had any in…a long time. Not after…"

"After what?" he pressed when she didn't continue.

"Can't talk about it."

He frowned.

"I won't slow you down." She swallowed loudly before licking her lips. "I can push through the pain."

Ravi reached over her for the water flask in her pack and removed the top. He brought it to her lips and helped hold her head up. "Drink."

She quickly sucked down the rest. Then he gave her some of his water. She kept her eyes closed the entire time. He gently laid her head down and turned to put his flask away. When he looked at her again, her eyes were locked on him.

"We're not coming back from this. You know that, right?" she asked.

He watched a lock of her black hair tangle in her lashes as she blinked. "I've come back from every mission."

"We're going to a place devoid of morality."

"You were there. You lived."

She rolled away from him and curled into a tight ball. "I don't think I did."

The words were said so softly he thought he might have imagined them. Soon, her breathing evened into sleep. Ravi made himself as comfortable as he could with her sharing the space. He thought it'd keep him awake for most of the night but he quickly sank into sleep.

When he opened his eyes, the rain had stopped. He looked at the human, but she still slept soundly. He used the time to put on his boots and go for a walk to stretch his legs and empty his bladder. It was still an hour or so until dawn. He refilled their water flasks in the lake.

All the while, her words kept reverberating in his head. *We're not coming back from this.*

He wanted to ask her for specifics. Would she tell him? Would she even remember their conversation? He knew it was the herbs and magic that had loosened her tongue. He didn't know her plans, but his was to get the explosive device from the enemy and return to Rannora with it so he could hand it over to Durga. Ravi didn't expect to escape Shaldorn without leaving some bodies in his wake.

Those who were building the weapon to attack the dragons wouldn't just stop because Ravi took it. They would build another. Which meant they had to be stopped. He didn't exactly enjoy taking lives, but he justified it by telling himself that he was saving innocents and removing evil from the world.

Sometimes, that was enough.

Other times, it wasn't.

He crawled back into the tent and sat next to the female. He'd read her file. There was little to it other than her previous theft of food and confinement. She had refused to give them more. Not even Durga had gotten anything else. Whoever the human was, she didn't want anyone peering into her past. If he didn't know better, he'd say she was a spy.

9

"It's almost dawn."

The softly spoken words jerked Yasmin from sleep. Her eyes flew open. It took her a moment to remember where she was and who the deep voice belonged to. She stared at the side of the tent for a moment. Then she used her arm to push herself into a seated position. The moment she was upright, her head swam and her stomach lurched. Yasmin dropped onto her elbow.

She could hear Ravi moving about outside the tent. She needed to get moving. But first, she had to lay back down. Yasmin lowered herself onto the blanket and took slow, measured breaths.

Ravi poked his head inside. Their gazes met, and a frown formed between his brows. "What's wrong?"

"I need a moment."

"Is it your ribs?"

She swallowed and shook her head. "It's the magic. I'd forgotten just how much it affects me."

He squatted down, balancing on the balls of his feet with his arms resting on his knees. His gaze was unnerving. Her stomach settled enough that she braved sitting up again. She didn't look at him as she reached for her socks, thankful to find them dry. A vague memory of Ravi removing her socks and boots filled her head. She hurriedly got her footwear on and then moved off her blanket to roll it. The world swam again, warning her that she had moved too fast.

"Easy," he said.

They didn't have time for such bothersome setbacks. "It will pass."

"What will?"

She tried to continue to roll her blanket, but he snatched it from her. He caught her gaze and lifted a brow, waiting for an answer. Yasmin blew out a breath. "I'm already feeling better."

Ravi stared at her for another few moments before handing her the blanket and standing. She waited until he'd walked away before putting the blanket into her bag and reaching for the water flask. Yasmin only wanted to wet her mouth, but the minute the liquid touched her tongue, she realized she was parched. She wanted to gulp it down, but she regulated herself so as not to upset her stomach again. She didn't bother with food. It would only come back up.

Yasmin exited the tent and only then realized that her hair was loose. She didn't remember taking it down last night. What else didn't she remember? She'd known there was a chance that some of her memories would be foggy or gone altogether, but it was a chance she was willing to take to diminish the pain. The thought of Ravi carrying her up the mountain told her that nothing short of death would stop him from getting to Shaldorn. She'd made the decision then to only take a little of the magical herbs. But even that smidgin had knocked her sideways.

She looped her arms through the bag and settled it against her back. There was only a slight pull on her ribs—a vast improvement from the previous day when it had taken everything she had to stay on her feet. She felt Ravi's eyes on her and missed when he pretended that she wasn't there. His focused gaze made her think that something had happened during the night, something she couldn't recall. But she wouldn't ask. It was better if she acted as if nothing was amiss.

Yasmin braided her hair as he tore down the tent and stuffed it back into his pack. Then they set off. This time, he remained only a few steps behind her. The more she moved around, the more the effects of the herbs wore off. No longer did she feel as if she would topple over if she didn't plant her feet firmly. How she hated that feeling—and the memories it provoked.

Memories that were better left shut away, never to be revisited.

Or acknowledged.

That time in her life was over. She'd made sure of it. When she walked away, that had been the end. Death would've been preferrable to continuing on as she had been. And there were times she had begged the gods for death.

About an hour later, her stomach growled. She didn't pause to take out one of the precious pieces of bread from her pack. She ate in small bites, ever aware of Ravi's eyes boring a hole into the back of her head. She almost turned around and demanded to know why he was acting differently. But did she really want to know? What if she'd let something from her past slip? Or about the children? Then again, maybe she'd told him how deep her aversion to elves went.

She quickened her steps. They had one final river to cross. She might not have been this way in years, but it was ingrained in her memory—though she had been walking in the opposite direction. She had raced out of the mountains, uncaring where she ended up. Then, she had seen the rainwood and had run headlong into the tangled forest, grateful to be alive. Now, she was headed back into the snow and ice where death had danced around her daily.

Yasmin mentally shook away the past and focused on the present. She felt more like herself, and they were still ahead of schedule. If she pushed hard, they could make the foothills by early afternoon. The Dangerous Peaks were icy and continually topped with snow. Only the lowest parts of the mountains were free of those conditions. That didn't make them any less threatening, however.

By lunchtime, her stomach was growling loudly. She devoured two pieces of dried meat and the last portion of bread while trying to ignore Ravi's gaze. If he wanted to talk, he could. She wouldn't cave and demand to know why he kept gawking.

The spot she had chosen was stunning. The trees swayed with a light wind, the leaves caressing each other, bringing a lulling melody. Brightly feathered birds darted from branch to branch, calling loudly, looking for their mates. She saw delicate clilrillas with their four bright blue-and-white-patterned wings clumped together on the side of a tree.

When Ravi rose and walked toward her, she stood and slipped her pack on. "We're making good time," she said and started walking again.

"What happened this morning?"

She shrugged. "Nothing."

"It looked very much like something."

If she didn't tell him, he'd keep pestering her. "I have a slight reaction to magic."

"You knew that and still took the herbs?"

Yasmin rolled her eyes. Was he really that dense? "I did."

"You could've warned me."

"Because you care that much?" she asked as she glanced at him over her shoulder.

A frown seemed permanently etched into his forehead. "Because without you, I can't get into Shaldorn and keep the peace between us and the dragons."

"That's right. For a moment, I forgot why I was out here."

"Is everything a joke to you?"

"Far from it. I liked it better when we didn't talk."

He grunted behind her. She took it as agreement and walked faster to put more distance between them. She soon forgot about their conversation and his frown when she spotted the mountains through a break in the trees. The rainwood was dense enough that it cloaked the outside, almost as if sheltering those within its borders from prying eyes.

All she got was a glimpse of one snow-capped peak, wind tangling the snow and pulling it into the air. One glance. But there was no getting rid of the growing dread within her. Yasmin looked away. She had been hurrying toward the mountains, trying not to think about them or what lay in their icy slopes. It had been stupid to compartmentalize things so firmly. She'd done it because she hadn't wanted to face the peaks or what they meant. And yet, there they were, looming in the distance like a seething beast waiting to reclaim one of its own. Even when the foliage closed in around her again, she sensed the anticipation of the mountains.

She was trapped in a situation with no good outcome. And she *had* given her word. She wished she were one of those who could promise something and ignore it later. But she wasn't. She didn't have coin or standing, and few friends. The only things she had were her wits, her drive, and her word. They bound her more firmly than any threat could.

Yasmin heard the sound of the river long before she saw it. Every instinct she had told her not to keep going, yet that's exactly what she did. She spotted the water through the trees. Before she knew it, she was at the edge. Ravi moved up beside her. She watched the river flowing southwest where it eventually dumped into one of the larger lakes, which would empty into the largest of the plateau's waterways, the Ever Reaching River.

"This way," Ravi said and turned to the west.

She followed as he walked alongside the swiftly moving water. The river was deep and had rapids in many places thanks to the runoff from the mountain. It wasn't anything she wanted to chance. She could keep her head above water, but she wasn't strong enough to swim against such a current or the rapids.

Ravi's strides ate up the ground to where she almost had to jog to keep up with him. It wasn't until he came to a sudden stop that she saw what he had brought them to. The rope crossing was just that. Three strands of rope hung in a *V* over the river, with smaller strips keeping them all connected. He didn't hesitate to start across it.

Yasmin watched the way the *bridge* swung with each step. Before she knew it, he was on the other side. The look he shot her told her that he didn't want to tarry. She almost told him to keep going, but she knew he wouldn't.

She drew in a deep breath and slowly released it as she reached for the rope with shaking hands. The cable was so thick her fingers couldn't wrap around it. With a hand on each side, she slid her foot along the bottom rope. The cord creaked loudly, protesting her weight. She cautiously moved a step forward. The bridge swayed, and the rope groaned again. The drop to the water would be short, but the bridge also hung over the wildest part of the river because it was the narrowest.

"Just keep walking," she told herself.

But she had to force her feet to take the next step, and then the next. It was slow going, but she eventually progressed to the other side. When she stepped onto firm ground again, she hoped to never see another crossing like that in her life. She'd swim or find another way around. Or maybe never cross it.

Yasmin expected a rude comment from Ravi, but surprisingly, there was none. She took the lead again and headed straight toward the mountains rising before her. She couldn't stand to look at them, so she diverted into the forest once more.

The ground became increasingly more difficult to trek over the next few hours. There were sharp rises and deep trenches as they crossed the foothills. Each time she put her hand on one of the boulders, she heard its soft song.

She let her fingers linger there, soaking in the words. It had been so long since she had heard them so loudly. The city noise drowned out the song, but she had also closed herself off to it. But she needed it again.

And the mountains answered.

When she saw the valley littered with boulders and flat rocks lying across them as if someone had placed them there, she knew it was where they'd camp for the night.

Ravi spent a long time looking at the mountains soaring next to them. Yasmin found a place among the rocks and watched a group of cooroda in the nearby trees making a commotion as the beautiful melody of the stones surrounded her. She observed the young animals clinging to their mothers and noted the swollen bellies of other females about to give birth. There were older males who guarded everyone, protecting the group from predators. Younger males mimicked them, learning for the day they would take their places.

"What is it about the cooroda that you like so much?" Ravi asked.

She shook her head. "It isn't the cooroda, exactly. It's all animals. See the females expecting? See the mothers and fathers with their young? True families. Each child knows who their parents are. Each parent knows their child."

"A family isn't always blood."

Yasmin thought about the children she looked after. "That's true. But haven't you ever wondered about your parents? The mother who birthed you? Did they not want us? Were we taken or given away?"

"It doesn't do any good to ask those questions because there aren't any answers."

"Maybe because we're not looking for them. Don't you want to know why animals can have offspring and we can't?"

Ravi stared at the human's profile as she watched the cooroda. "There have been those who sought the answers you want. They never found anything."

"Maybe they weren't looking in the right places. For all anyone knows, we could have people on another part of the realm where they take children away to bring here because we can't bear them ourselves."

It was a good theory, and one he had heard before. But also something that had never been looked into or investigated. At least, as far as he knew.

"I'm going to leave Shecrish," the female stated. "I'm going to travel and see if I can find those answers."

"You might find more questions."

"Maybe. But anywhere is better than here."

His brows snapped together. "Has life been so bad? You were found in Shecrish and given to a family. You weren't allowed to starve, nor were you forgotten."

"It might have been better if I had been."

That brought him up short. "Were your parents so bad?"

She slowly turned her head to him. "They weren't my parents."

"They were the ones who raised you. They might not have birthed you, but they were still your parents."

"They weren't my parents," she stated again, her voice dropping an octave as her blue eyes turned icy.

Ravi shrugged. "Suit yourself." But his curiosity had been stirred. Had she been given to a human or elven family? All elven children were placed with elves. But human babies could be given to either.

She looked away, her shoulders tense. "You fit in Shecrish. I don't. No human does. There are others like me out there somewhere. I'm sure of it. I'm going to find them."

"Do you plan on taking the children with you?"

Her head snapped back to him as her gaze searched his face. "Did you hurt them?"

"I would never harm a child. Though the oldest one is a bit rough around the edges."

Her nostrils flared as anger tightened her face. "You know nothing about them or the hardships they have endured."

"You should've allowed Rannora's council to deal with that."

"Right," she said with a bark of laughter. "Because that always works out so well."

Ravi ran a hand over his jaw, feeling the whiskers scraping against his palm. She hated elves, and he didn't exactly care for her. The only thing that softened his opinion was her obvious concern and affection for the children in her care. "It wasn't medicine you purchased."

"It was. She promised. I gave her every last coin I had." The human looked at him again, her chest rising and falling rapidly. "Is Jaya...? Durga said she was better."

"Dain knew it wasn't medicine. He didn't bother telling me until after he brought a healer in. Jaya was in bad shape, but the Star Elf healed her."

The female squeezed her eyes closed before turning her head away. She sat in silence for a long moment. Finally, she cleared her throat and asked, "And the other children? Did Durga take them away?"

"As far as I know, they were left where we found them. You can thank Dain for that."

"If I ever see him again, I will. And, nay. I won't abandon them. Ever."

Ravi stared at the back of her head. He saw her reach up to her face and wondered if she brushed away a tear. He couldn't imagine much could make the female cry. She was too thorny and hostile for such an emotion.

"We made good time today," she said into the silence.

"Things would've been a lot easier had Dain been able to bring us as planned."

She ducked her head and picked at a broken nail. "Why don't you two like each other?"

"He's a Dark Elf."

Finally, her deep blue gaze slid to him. "Maybe, but he was willing to help you. Would you do the same for him?"

"Doubtful," Ravi answered honestly.

She gave a light snort. "That's what I thought."

"What is that supposed to mean?" he demanded.

"That he's willing, but you wouldn't return the favor. He put aside personal preference to do something he thought was important."

"You don't know either of us."

She shrugged. "I saw enough of your exchange to come to the right conclusion. You just don't want to admit it because it makes you look bad."

It was on the tip of his tongue to argue the point, but he decided against it. She wanted to rile him as he had done with her earlier. "Apparently, your contempt doesn't include all elves."

"I have met a few who were kind."

"A few," he repeated with a snort.

She shifted to look at him. "Let's get something straight. You don't like me any more than I like you. We're stuck together. You need me, even if it galls you to admit it. Trust me, I'd rather be *anywhere* but here with you."

"I don't have a problem with humans as you seem to have with elves. My issue is that you harbor children that should be with their families. And you're a dissident."

One slim, arched brow lifted. "You take a look at a person or scene and think there is only one story. I live with those children. Therefore, I must have taken them."

"Taken them or pressured them into leaving their families."

She laughed, but there was no mirth in the sound. "And this is my problem with your kind. Elves think they know better than humans. That there is only one way, and it must be the elven way."

"I'm not naïve enough to think there aren't elves out there who harm others. The eldest lad told me about his eye."

If it was possible, the female's gaze hardened even more. "That didn't sway you, did it?"

"If there's an issue, he should've gone to the city council."

"A human child's word against two elves? Aye, that always works out so well."

Ravi shifted to face her. "Why didn't you do something, then?"

"Me?" she asked with a blink. "You're right. They would absolutely listen to me."

"They might." But even as he said the words, he knew they were a lie.

She rolled her eyes. "No one bothers anymore because nothing gets done. Sameer would've been returned to the *parents* who hurt him and would likely have died within months. They hated him because they weren't given an elven baby. It wasn't his fault the Domestic Ministry chose them as his parents, but they took it out on him. When we return, maybe I'll show you the scars they left on his body throughout the years. He crawled out of the house the night they took his eye. He was bleeding and dying when I found him lying in the street as elves walked over him as if he were garbage. Literally walked over him. He had been starved until he was nothing but skin and bones. I should've had trouble picking up a boy of thirteen summers."

Ravi inwardly cringed at the picture she painted. He couldn't imagine anyone walking over someone injured, be they elf or human. He certainly wouldn't have.

"Shall I tell you about the other five? Shall I go into their stories of horror and abuse, detailing each until you can't decide whether to be disgusted or irate? Each of those children came from an elven home. And their *parents* never bothered to search for them or even tell the authorities they were missing. I know because I checked every week. Those children are alive because I was there when no one else was." She glared at him as if the very sight of him sickened her. "Elven kind hides behind magic and sanctimonious arrogance, but they aren't any better than humans. You just want to make us think you are."

Before Ravi could reply, she rose and walked away. He watched as she skillfully climbed over the rocks. She was right. He had taken one look at her and passed judgment. His aversion had deepened when he learned about the children. His job was to look past what a person showed the world to who they really were. His life depended on it. Yet he'd let his contempt color his views of the human.

He inwardly winced. He hadn't even bothered to call her by her name. Not aloud and not in his thoughts. Maybe she hadn't noticed. It wasn't as if she had called him by *his* name. He couldn't say if she would be as petty as he had been by calling her *the human* or *the female*.

Dain had realized what had happened to the children. A Dark Elf had seen what Ravi hadn't because he'd been angry that Dain was there. He shook his head. He was glad Dain had made him leave the children as they were. Though Ravi wished he would've sent them food and clothing. Why hadn't he thought of that?

The fem—Yasmin had put herself at risk in taking care of the kids. She had certainly cut him down to size with her words. Her rage had been palpable, and she had every right to it. It sickened him that anyone out there would take their anger or resentment out on an innocent child. When he returned to Rannora, he would find the parents of each of those children and report them to the Rannoran Council as well as the Shecrish Conclave.

How many more children were out there suffering? It was probably more than he wanted to think about. Not just in Rannora but also in Belanore and all the small villages across the plateau. Someone needed to stand up for them. He couldn't bring attention to himself with the work he did, but he would find someone who could.

Ravi's gaze swung to Yasmin. Her back was to him as she settled on the flattest ground she could find between two boulders. She dug into her pack, carefully pulling out some food. He stood and walked in her direction, jumping to the ground behind her. She turned her head slightly.

"Save that. I'm going to get us some fresh meat," he said before walking away.

11

The stones had warned Yasmin that Ravi was approaching. She had expected him to reprimand her for the way she had spoken to him. She hadn't guessed he would go hunting. Her shoulders dropped, and she let out a sigh. When it came to the children, she couldn't control her temper or her words. They were all alone in a world that was all too ready to beat them down. They needed someone to show them compassion and love, which is why she had taken them in.

Leaving Shecrish was the answer. There would be hardships aplenty, but they would have each other. All she had to do was make it back from Shaldorn. She had done it once. She would do it again.

For them.

They were her family.

By the time Ravi returned, the last bit of pale blue clung to the sky as the sun set to a magnificent yellow and orange. He had a chickupine in hand. She took it from him and began plucking the feathers as he built a fire. Before long, the bird was roasting, and her mouth watered at the delicious smell.

Ravi stared at the flames, seemingly lost in thought. Yasmin raised her gaze as the woonsada, with their leathery wings, large ears, and fur-covered torsos, flew erratically around them, catching insects drawn to the fire. Her stomach growled, and she hoped Ravi couldn't hear it from his position across the blaze.

Ravi drew in a breath and then slowly released it. "You know the legend of the dragons, aye?"

"I do. Their land borders ours. No one is allowed to cross into Idrias for fear of what the dragons will do."

"That's right, but no one has seen a dragon for hundreds of years. There were rumors they were gone, that they'd left Zora. Some elves wanted to enter Idrias and find out if the dragons were still there."

"That is unwise."

A ghost of a smile played on his lips. "In that, we agree. Just because you don't see a dragon doesn't mean they aren't there. That became true when one visited us recently."

"A dragon crossed into Shecrish?" she asked in disbelief. "I didn't think they were supposed to."

"They aren't. But it wasn't just any dragon, it was a Dragon King. Apparently, some can shift from their true form to that of a human."

Yasmin sat up straighter, suddenly impatient to hear more. If dragons could look human, then that confirmed there were others like her on Zora.

"Kendrick, the King, crossed the border when he was battling a foe we share. It's invisible and strikes when we least expect it. He teamed up with the Asavori Rangers to hunt it."

"Wow," she murmured. How she would've loved to meet Kendrick. If anyone would know if there were other humans like her, it would be a Dragon King. He might even be able to take her to them. The stones sang louder when she thought about the King.

Ravi turned the chickupine over. "Dain worked with them, as well. During all of this, Kendrick and Esha, a Ranger, fell in love."

An elf and a dragon? Now that surprised her.

"Then someone sent a nightwraith after them."

Yasmin shuddered at the thought. She had never seen one of the giant predators firsthand, and she hoped she never did. "Did it kill the dragon?"

"Kendrick killed it." Ravi scratched at his neck. "There is speculation that someone from the Conclave sent it."

"But why? Kendrick came to help."

Ravi nodded and blew out a breath. "Exactly. I was to be assigned to that before I was told to go to Shaldorn to stop the sale of the explosive. The Dark Elves have an undercover operative in Shaldorn. They're the ones who got word to Dain about the device."

"I don't understand the reasoning for angering the dragons. They've left us alone all this time."

"Aye. We don't know which group crafted the bomb or who plans to use it. My objective is to steal the device before they hand it over in three days' time."

Yasmin licked her lips. "How can you be sure you'll get to it?"

"Because that's my job. But first, I have to get into the stronghold."

Which fell on her. "I can't understand why anyone would want to bring down the wrath of the dragons."

"For change."

Her eyes widened as understanding dawned. "You think it's humans."

"A dissenter group has been very vocal about bringing about change. They've used explosives before."

She bit her lip and shook her head. "Select humans are invited to Shaldorn, but most are elves. Those of my kind who walk around freely are few. They're also extremely rich and powerful, even among the elves."

"That can't be very many."

"It isn't." She eyed him. He was being particularly agreeable that evening. Was it because of her words earlier? No doubt he'd return to his grumpy self in the morning.

"You said freely," he said, his gaze locked on her. "What do you mean?"

Yasmin tried to look away from his copper eyes but was unsuccessful. "The workers at Shaldorn are all human."

"What do they do?"

She pulled her gaze away as a woonsada flew near her, gobbling up a morsel. "Cook, clean, entertain. Everything."

"And which were you?"

Yasmin picked at her fingers. "It's been some years since I was there. Things rarely change, but we need to expect that some have. Before, we were marked."

"Your tattoo," he interjected as he glanced at her neck.

She fought not to reach up and touch the spot. "Aye."

"That could be easily hidden."

"Guests couldn't see them, but it wasn't for them. It was for us. To remind us who we belonged to."

"*Belonged* to?" Ravi spoke the words in a tone that suggested he might not have heard right.

Yasmin shrugged. "Did you think we could come and go as we pleased?"

"Are you telling me you were prisoners?"

"That's one word for it."

His nostrils flared. "If you escaped, then there's a way out for us."

She glanced toward the mountain, apprehension growing the closer she got to the stronghold. Ravi cut meat from the bird and handed it to her. She took it, her fingers burning. Yasmin moved the meat from one hand to the other until she could hold it without scalding her skin. Then she took a bite and closed her eyes at that taste of fresh meat. It felt wrong to enjoy such a meal when the children were merely scraping by. But they were strong. They would hold out until she returned.

Yasmin swallowed and wiped her mouth on her sleeve. "Getting into Shaldorn is hard. Getting out is impossible."

"You did it."

"With help."

He shrugged as if that didn't matter. "There's always a way out."

Would she be able to speak to the stones without Ravi discovering her secret? If they were to get out alive, she would have to. "You need to understand something about Shaldorn. They're meticulous about who they allow inside. Everyone there has something they want kept secret. Whatever their peculiarities. You're going to see all kinds."

"I've seen everything. Nothing will shock me."

She snorted. "Something will. Though it might not be those in attendance. It could be the things they have for sale." She took a small bite and chewed while studying the contours of his face in the firelight. Once she swallowed, she said, "Weapons and magic will be front and center. It's what everyone assumes goes on there."

A golden brow rose on his forehead. "I assume there's gambling and rooms where discussions take place in secret."

"Most of Shaldorn is private rooms. The exchange you want to stop will happen in one of them."

His lips flattened for a moment. "Locating those involved could be a problem since we won't know which room they choose."

Yasmin had an idea, but she kept it to herself for the moment. A lot could have changed in the time since she had been at Shaldorn. She needed to be prepared for that. The stones might be able to help her sort it out.

"What else happens there? What are you afraid of telling me?"

Her attention returned to Ravi. "For all intents and purposes, it is a market. You say you've been around all kinds. I doubt you've been around these types of people. They're the worst sort. The kind who wears a pretty mask to show one side of themselves, but in Shaldorn, that mask is removed to show their true selves. Nothing they ask for is too heinous or revolting. If they want to hunt a human child and have enough coin, it'll happen."

"When you say hunt..."

"Aye," Yasmin nodded. "I mean hunt. Like you did our meal."

A muscle in his jaw tensed. "Shite."

"Weapons and magic are bartered and sold. So are animals, humans, and even some elves. There are five groups within Shaldorn. Those on the very top run things. They're called the Trinity. One, Two, and Three are who everyone answers to. They're always around. Then you have the elite. Those are the guests who come to enjoy the predilections offered at the fortress.

Mostly elves, but you will see some humans. The guards are next. Huge brutes who seem to enjoy the violence. They watch everyone. Lastly, there are the marked. There were many names for us. Recruits, workers, staff. There were more of us than any other. They are the ones who keep Shaldorn running behind the scenes and walk among the elite."

"You interacted with these people?"

She looked away as she thought of her last evening at Shaldorn when she knew she had to leave or die there. Freezing to death was a better alternative to what had awaited her that night. "I did. Not all the staff do. Only certain ones."

"Pretty ones, you mean," he guessed in a soft voice.

Yasmin lifted her gaze to him. "Those of us the Trinity believed would get the elite's attention."

"What did you have to do?"

"Then you have the last group," she said without answering him. "Those are the ones the elite bring to trade or sell. There are those the owners have decided won't do as staff. They're of all ages and social standings. I know one of the elite had a feud with someone and had their daughter kidnapped."

Ravi poked the fire before adding another piece of wood. "What happened to her?"

"They stripped and tied her to one of the columns in the main area. The elite were told to have fun. They beat her with whips, chains, and even their hands. She never begged for mercy, never cried out. Not even when they took her into one of the rooms where they had their way with her. The men rotated in and out of that room for days." Yasmin squeezed her eyes shut in an attempt to block out the memory. "There wasn't much left of her by the time they finished. I think she died without them knowing."

"Why didn't you tell anyone when you escaped?"

Yasmin stared into the fire and unbound her hair. She dug into the pack to find the brush and slowly began pulling it through the length as a way to soothe herself. "Staff members try to run away nightly. Sometimes, groups of them go in hopes that at least one of them will get free. No one does. Those who make the attempt are brutally killed and displayed as a warning to others."

"Yet they keep trying."

"Freedom is worth the risk of death," she murmured. "I looked for a way out from nearly the moment I arrived. Years passed before I got up the nerve to try. I was almost caught once. It scared me so bad that I didn't try again for months. After that, I was more determined than ever. But I wanted to do it right. Yet I still didn't manage it on my own."

"Did the one who helped you get away, too?"

Yasmin's throat tightened as she shook her head. "Neela covered for me and gave me a head start. The guards came after me. That night, I chose death over being brought back. I had nothing but the clothes I wore. My shoes weren't made for the snow, but I didn't care. I ran headlong toward death with open arms."

"Yet here you are."

She shifted to brush another section of hair. "Here I am. And all the while, they've continued to look for me. I see guards walking the streets of Rannora. I've seen them stop any human who looks even vaguely like me."

"What would they do if they caught you?"

Yasmin met his gaze. "Kill me."

"I won't let that happen."

"You won't be able to stop it."

"I just might surprise you."

She sighed and dropped her hands to her lap. "You may be all you say you are, but you are just one elf. There will be dozens of guards. The instant they think anything is off, they'll surround us."

"Then you'd better be a great performer, because it's going to take both of us to pull this off and get out alive."

"They'll take one look at me and know who I am. It'll be over before it begins. You'll have to go in alone."

12

Ravi held Yasmin's gaze as he watched the flames reflected in her dark blue irises. She hadn't hidden her fear about Shaldorn, but he was now beginning to understand the depth of it as well as who she was. "You'll be with me, but they'll never know it's you."

"You want me to wear a disguise?"

Her uncertainty was understandable, and Ravi didn't take it personally. "I'm not talking about a change of clothes."

"Good. Because that wouldn't work." She paused then as if just hearing his words. "Then what, exactly?"

He shrugged. "I'm an elf. What do you think?"

"Magic."

"The DIA has perfected a dose. We use it all the time."

"You saw how I reacted to the herbs."

He'd been thinking the same thing. "Hopefully, you won't have a reaction."

"Magic is magic. It doesn't matter how it's used."

"If it doesn't work, then you stay behind."

Her lips parted in shock, and her brow furrowed. "Truly?"

"I must stay unnoticed. I can't have attention placed on me. If that means leaving you outside to wait, then I will."

"Interesting. Especially after Durga's warning to me."

Ravi blew out a breath. "I've completed my previous missions because I learned to pivot when needed. This would be one of those times. Durga was right about one thing, though. We need to trust each other. Or this will be over before it begins."

"Trust."

"I'm not suggesting we be friends. Just…friendly."

She lifted her eyes to the sky, as she had several times that evening, the brush in her lap.

The longer she went without speaking, the more Ravi realized he had made a mistake by letting the acrimony between them grow. Durga was more worried than he had ever seen her about a mission. That, coupled with what little Yasmin had shared about Shaldorn meant he couldn't go into this assignment as he had others. He needed to put aside his personal issues and think about what was at stake.

"Shaldorn is the last place you want to be," he said. "I assumed you'd be happy not to step within its walls again."

She pulled her hair over one shoulder, her fingers raking through the waves. "I'm already too close to that place." She blew out a breath as she lowered her gaze to him. "You know nothing about it. Or those who preside over it. They consider it their kingdom. It's a maze of floors and stairways that took me months to learn. If you go alone, you'll die."

"Then prepare me for Shaldorn and everything and everyone connected to it. You and I are all that stand between those bent on conflict and those set on peace. There can only be one outcome."

Yasmin gave a slight shake of her head. "If we're caught, they'll kill us. There won't be time to ask questions or escape. No time to get word to the undercover agent to ask for help. It will be instant. Going to Shaldorn is suicide. It would be better to reach out to Kendrick and warn him about what is happening."

"That is happening through Esha's sister, Savita. She's a Re—"

"A rune Reader," Yasmin said over him. "I've heard of her."

Ravi leaned back on one hand, unable to tear his gaze away from Yasmin as she braided her hair until it lay in one thick plait over her shoulder. "If the device is allowed to detonate, the dragons will have to respond. The best thing for everyone is to steal the explosive before that happens."

"You've done something like this before?"

"Nothing this important. What about you? How good are you at stealing?"

Her lips quirked into a grin. "Better than most."

"I imagine you are," he replied, hiding his smile. He took the chickupine from the fire and pulled off another piece of meat for himself before handing her the rest. "Eat up. It might be a few days before we get fresh game again."

"This will be the last meal like this until we return. Unless you can hunt in the snow."

Ravi leaned back against a boulder as he ate. "I've never been past the foothills."

"It won't be easy getting to Shaldorn."

"Nothing in my job ever is."

She regarded him over the flames. "Why a spy?"

"I've a knack for it."

"But is it what you want to do?"

He shrugged. "I've never stopped to think about whether I want to do it. It's important work, and I'm good at it. What about you? What are you good at?"

"You mean besides stealing?" Yasmin shrugged and continued eating. "I don't know."

"How often do you nick things?"

"As often as needed. Believe it or not, I do try to earn coin. It isn't easy to find work. The children need to eat. They need clothes, shoes, and medicine. I do what I have to. I've only ever been caught twice."

He threw a bone into the fire and licked his fingers. "Durga was looking for you, so I wouldn't consider this last capture as being caught." Ravi wondered how Yasmin would fair joining the DIA. She had the qualifications. And Durga certainly seemed to like her. "What if you had a steady job?"

"You mean spying?" she asked, her brows raised. She shook her head. "I don't think so."

"Why not? You don't hesitate to do what's needed. You know when to fight and when to stop. You have quick fingers. I suspect you'd be great undercover. And nothing seems to scare you."

She finished the last bite and wiped her hands on her pants. "Everything terrifies me. The things I've done, that I did to survive. Fleeing Shaldorn, stealing food and clothes, and staying hidden from everyone was all done for freedom."

"We need a human on the team. Think about it. It would give you steady pay where you could find a better home, which means more for the kids."

"I plan to leave Shecrish, remember?"

He lifted one shoulder. "There's an opportunity if you change your mind."

She settled against the rock, and he realized it was curved, almost as if cradling her. He had to admit that she had chosen a nice area to camp for the night. Especially where they were sleeping. It was the smoothest out of all the places he had considered.

Ravi lay back to sleep. He closed his eyes, but they didn't stay shut for long. He found himself staring at the mountains rising around him. Tomorrow would take them into the Dangerous Peaks. The chill already came down from the mountains to tease him with what was to come. Or maybe it was his imagination. What he did know was that it would be the most treacherous mission he'd ever been sent on. So many lives rested on his shoulders. He couldn't fail.

He had told Yasmin that he was good at pivoting when needed. That was because no plan ever went exactly as it should. Things always happened, and an agent was only as good as their ability to get out of tricky situations. No one would be coming to their aid. Everything rested with him and Yasmin.

They were an unlikely pair, to be sure. It was anyone's guess if she would get him to Shaldorn. He had a map, but it wasn't detailed. Not to mention, he knew nothing about the mountains. Climbing the plateau's sheer cliffs didn't make him a mountain climber. Then there was the weather. He shivered thinking about it.

Many obstacles stood in his way. Some might even say Yasmin was one of them. He would continue to press her for information about Shaldorn. Even if only half of what she said about the fortress was true. He had to be prepared.

As much as he hated to admit it, he wished Dain were there to get them close to Shaldorn so he didn't have to traipse across the unforgiving peaks. But the Dark wasn't there. Ravi preferred to work alone. It was easier to only worry about himself. Yet a team came in handy at times—like now.

Even if Savita got a message to Esha, and she was able to convince Kendrick and the other dragons that it was a rogue group in Shecrish that wished them harm, it didn't mean all the dragons would stand down. That was why Durga was sending him and Yasmin to Shaldorn.

Ravi rolled his head to the side and looked through the fire at his companion. There were layers to her he hadn't anticipated. He wanted to ask her more about what she had seen at Shaldorn, but he wouldn't. Not unless he had to. The truth of her past and what she had done was hers alone. Talking about Shaldorn clearly took her to a dark place. He suspected facing the stronghold would do a lot worse. He would need to remind her that she had escaped when so many others hadn't.

They had a way out as a last resort. Ravi didn't want to blow the Dark Elf's cover, but he would if it meant getting the device safely away. That was the only reason. Nothing else mattered.

Not his life.

Not Yasmin's.

When Ravi opened his eyes, Yasmin was awake. She stood next to a boulder with her hand on it as she stared up at the mountain. He yawned and stretched before getting to his feet.

"There's a storm coming," she said. "We need to reach the ridge before it does."

Ravi looked to where she pointed. "Give me five minutes."

He walked to the river and splashed his face with cold water to help wake him. He ran his fingers through his hair before pulling the strands together at the back of his head and fastening a strip of leather to secure it out of his face. Then he checked the area to make sure no one had followed them. He searched the trees for Wood Elves, to no avail. He hadn't seen any, which meant they didn't want to interact. But they would report back to Durga.

Ravi returned to camp. The fire had long since gone out. Yasmin now wore a black coat and a deep gray scarf. She had also tugged on a thick black cap to cover her head and ears. Ravi hadn't thought they would need that gear until later, but he didn't know the Dangerous Peaks like she did. He put on his coat, hat, and scarf with his gloves stuffed into his pockets. Then he rolled up his blanket and secured it in his pack.

He walked to Yasmin and tore his last piece of bread in half to share with her. She took it with a nod of thanks before returning her gaze to the mountain. "Something troubles you."

"We'll have to move fast. It's been a warmer-than-usual summer that has pushed into autumn."

"There's still a lot of snow on the peaks."

She cut him a look. "Melting snow."

"We'll make it."

Yasmin adjusted her pack and finished the bread. "We don't have a choice."

She set out then, moving quickly between the boulders, jumping effortlessly. Ravi followed, placing his feet where hers had been. The way she moved over the rocks, it was as if she had been born to them. A hand on one, a foot on another. Not once did they hamper her movements. He almost fell twice but managed to catch himself and keep up with her.

"Keep up," she said over her shoulder.

He shot her a glare, but she didn't see it. She was too busy wending her way through an undulating field of boulders. Then they were ascending the mountain. The slope started easy but quickly grew more difficult. They moved in quick bursts of speed between the precipitous inclines. She kept to the wooded areas, but they wouldn't always have that to shelter them. Her gaze constantly rose before scanning around her. Ravi followed her example, glancing behind him on occasion, too.

When Yasmin paused and squatted next to a tree take out her water for a drink, Ravi was grateful. Nothing could prepare anyone for the steep slopes if they hadn't been on one before. He drank deeply and surveyed their next section while trying to ease his labored breathing.

"The next segment is easier, but we'll be out in the open," Yasmin said.

Ravi slowed his breathing. The cold had descended upon them sometime in the forest. He hadn't been aware of it until now because he had been exerting himself. He fastened his coat. "You think someone is watching."

"I always assume someone is watching."

"Smart."

She chuckled under her breath. "We'll rest again when we reach the next ridge. We still have two more before we get to the top."

"I take it the sections after that aren't easy?"

She looked at him and shook her head. "I hope you can climb. We have a vertical bluff to scale."

"I can handle it." He hoped he could in the cold. He'd only ever done it in the heat and humidity.

She put her water flask back into her pack. "Ready?"

They set out after his nod. The gradient from the woods to the summit of the next ridgeline was gradual, though the rocks slid beneath his feet if he wasn't careful. It didn't take them long to get to the top. He paused there and took in the sight of the never-ending sea of peaks before him, varying in height and size, some with tips so pointed they looked like they could slice the sky. Others were more rounded. But snow enveloped them all. He could see the wind whipping around the summits, causing a dusting of snow to become airborne. The higher they went, the colder it would be. His lungs already ached from breathing in the icy air.

Ravi bent over, bracing his hands on his knees. His gaze was drawn to Yasmin as she studied their next section to climb. She was bent over, her hand on a rock before she finally stood.

"I have the way," she informed him.

He straightened and walked to her as he pulled the water flask from his bag. Ravi was shocked to discover that he emptied it in two swallows.

"There's water ahead where we can refill the flasks."

He eyed their next climb to find some clumps of snow on the ground the sun had never reached. "Are you sure?"

"It's the best route."

A heartbeat later, he was trailing behind her again. They wound around the snow, never once touching it. Their feet landed on firm rock each time, almost as if steppingstones had been placed there for them.

13

Gray clouds snuffed out the sunlight and any speck of the blue sky, but Yasmin could do nothing about the impending storm. She glanced over her shoulder to find Ravi behind her. Her lungs burned from the cold air, and her legs wobbled, threatening to buckle with every step. Still, somehow, she kept going.

It was either that or get caught in the storm.

Yasmin flattened her hand on a stone as she passed. There was no warning sound from it, so she continued on her course. She waited for Ravi to ask how she knew which direction to go. He was too caught up in staying on his feet at the moment to think of it, but he would eventually.

What should she say?

What *could* she say?

The truth would be the easiest, but he wouldn't believe her. She had never told a single soul. For many years when she was young, she had thought it was all in her mind. She had realized the truth during her time at Shaldorn. The rocks were the main reason she'd escaped and made it off the mountains. They told her where to go. Just as they did now.

It felt like an eternity before they reached their destination. Each ridge took them higher on the mountain. But this was just one of several they had to climb and descend before reaching Shaldorn.

Yasmin stood at the ridgeline and turned to look behind her. All she could see of the rainwood was the canopy of trees. Rannora was somewhere to her left, and Belanore to her right on the opposite end of the plateau. Straight ahead past the border was Idrias—dragon land. If only she could fly. She would take to the skies and travel around the realm until she found the perfect place to settle. It would be far, far from Shecrish and Shaldorn.

Something touched her arm. She looked over to find Ravi holding out his refilled water flask for her. She took it and drank, letting the frigid water fill her stomach. He dug out her canteen and went to replenish it from the water that trickled between the rocks to fall far below. Yasmin watched him. Sweat beaded his brow while the white cap covered his golden-brown hair and pointed ears.

"How do you feel?" she asked.

He tapped his temple. "Head aches a bit."

"It's the altitude. I'm feeling it, too. Keep hydrated. It'll help."

His breath billowed around him as he stood beside her to gaze over Shecrish. "I've never seen it like this before."

"Have you ever been outside of Shecrish?"

"Never had a need."

"You're about to."

"The Dangerous Peaks are still part of our land."

Yasmin took another drink before putting the water away. "You're not going to think so for long."

One more section to go. It was the toughest of them all. She placed her hand on a boulder to check the direction one last time.

Yasmin could see the course plotted in her mind. She didn't understand how it worked, but she didn't question it. There was a slight incline to walk before they reached the cliff. She would've steered clear of this area if the rocks hadn't told her which way to go. Climbing with cold, stiff fingers was a recipe for disaster. The other ways she could've gone were even more hazardous. So, they ascended.

"Follow where I'm going," Yasmin told Ravi. "Move quickly but carefully."

She hadn't needed to say anything. He did it instinctively. At least he didn't have an issue with a human taking charge. Perhaps it wasn't as obvious now. Or maybe he hid it better. Yasmin cleared her thoughts as she got her first toehold and reached above her for a handhold.

"To the left."

The stones continued to guide her, directing her where each foot and hand should go. The rocks were freezing, and the wind was bitter as it whipped around her. She shot quick looks down at Ravi when she could.

"There's a good hold right here," she called when she moved past it.

A moment later, he said, "Got it."

Minutes stretched endlessly as they inched their way upward. The temperature began to plummet, signaling that the storm was almost upon them. Yasmin didn't hurry herself or Ravi. This kind of climb took complete concentration.

She reached the top as the first snow flurries started to drift around her. She threw her leg over the edge and pulled herself up to roll onto her stomach. Then she scrambled back to the ledge and looked over. She watched Ravi as he held himself with both feet and one hand while flexing his other.

"You're almost there," she called.

If he replied, the wind took it. He had pulled his scarf up to cover his mouth and nose so only his eyes were visible. She pushed to her feet and saw the rock overhang behind her. That, along with the tent, would have to do for shelter. At least they would be out of the falling snow. A grunt sounded behind her. Yasmin spun to find Ravi pulling himself to the top.

"Fuck," he murmured.

She started toward the overhang. "We can rest inside once the tent is up."

Yasmin rubbed her cold, aching hands together as Ravi slipped his pack off and tugged out the tent. They put it up together, working as swiftly as they could with stiff fingers. Finally, it was up, and they slipped inside.

"I know you don't like to be touched, but all we have is body heat," he said.

She nodded and slipped out of her pack. It felt so good to be sitting down to rest her legs. "Too bad we can't have a fire."

Ravi poked his head outside. "The snow is falling rapidly already. We just made it."

He fastened the flap entrance and sat beside her. They both scooted closer to the other. He was right. All they had was body heat, and she knew better than to snub that. Especially in this weather.

· · ·

"How are you doing?" she asked.

Ravi grunted and took out his water flask. They sat shoulder to shoulder, staring at nothing while the wind howled outside. Every once in a while, the sides of the tent bowed inward from a gust.

"Is the sun always hidden?"

Yasmin startled at his deep voice. She blinked, shocked to find that she had begun to drift off to sleep. She was so exhausted. "It does come out, but it's rare. The clouds keep it hidden for the most part. You're thinking about your magic, aren't you?"

"A Sun Elf needs the sun," he said with a half-hearted shrug.

Each elf species could do certain kinds of magic, but all elves could do what they called simple magic, which consisted of fire and light. A Sun Elf, who took their power from the sun, crafted fire more easily than a Dark Elf. Ravi drew his magic from the sun, and being without it could mean trouble. Unless he'd been smart enough to bring an amulet filled with sunlight.

"I brought an amulet, just in case," he said as if reading her mind. "I've never had to use one before since I've never been without sunlight for long."

Yasmin brought her legs up to her chest, attempting to get warmer. "How long can you go without the sun and still use your magic?"

"I've never had to find out."

"You will soon."

He took out his blanket and spread it over their legs. "That I will. How long did you live here?"

Yasmin stretched out her legs before getting her blanket and using it to cover their torsos. She held it up to her chin. "Eleven summers."

"That's a long time."

"Any time is too long in that place."

Ravi was silent for a moment. "Tell me more about Shaldorn. I need to know the layout."

"There's a road in and out of the mountains. That's the easiest way to travel, but it also has its perils. If you come down the lane, guards will spot you well before you reach the stronghold. Then there's a gate so they can check everyone. If you get through it, you'll proceed to the next area. There's another, larger gate there, but to get to it, you have to disembark from the carriage and walk through a two-story house. There are guards everywhere. Each person is checked against a list of who has been invited and who hasn't. Guests are allowed to bring someone, but they have to be on the list."

"Then they get into Shaldorn?"

Yasmin shook her head. "After the second gate, there is a path that leads to Shaldorn, but with the intermittent weather, they are brought to an underground tunnel. The trek is long enough that guests climb into carriages driven by guards supplied by Shaldorn. The tunnel comes out the side of the mountain, where the carriage then delivers the guests to the front door. From there, they are welcomed inside for food, drink, and entertainment."

"No wonder our agent was killed," Ravi muttered.

Yasmin pulled out some food and bit into a piece of dried meat from her bag. "The stronghold is built atop a mountain surrounded by towering peaks on either side. The structure itself has four floors, though one is hidden belowground. That's where the staff is kept."

"Let me guess. There are no exits there."

"No windows or doors to the outside. Four doors besides those to the bedrooms. Those connect to stairwells with guards at each entrance."

He turned his head to her. "How in the world did you escape?"

"I jumped from a window on the second floor."

Ravi's brows furrowed. "You jumped?"

"A possibility of death versus certain death. Which would you choose?"

"The possibility. Still, that took courage."

She scoffed. "I wouldn't go that far. I was scared of dying in Shaldorn. I knew what was coming for me, and that terrified me more than freezing to death."

"What was coming for you?"

"I caught the attention of someone. He...he isn't a nice person. No one he chooses lives through the night."

Ravi looked toward the fire. "Do you know his name?"

"Aye."

"Tell me."

"Why?"

"Because I'm going to make sure he doesn't hurt anyone else."

Yasmin didn't know how to feel about that statement. No one had ever stood up for her like that before. "He isn't your mission."

"I can take care of two things at once."

"If I see him, I'm going to kill him."

Ravi jerked his chin to her feet. "You're going to need more than that little dagger in your boot."

"It'll get the job done."

Yasmin licked her lips and turned her thoughts back to Shaldorn. "The first floor is where people mingle. There will be hallways with benches set into alcoves. There is food everywhere —set on tables and carried around on trays by staff. The drinks are only handed out by the staff. The first floor has some rooms. Most of them are kept open so people can come and go to participate as they wish."

"And what is in these rooms?"

"At least two of the rooms are for gambling. Sometimes, it's one of the staff naked on a table covered in food. The elite eat off them before they pass them around for sex. The first floor is for fun. The second is the market. Buyers peruse the booths to see if anything catches their eye. The rooms on that side are private. Guards will be at every door. Once one is occupied, no one is allowed in unless granted by someone within."

Ravi rubbed his hands together. "That's likely to be where the exchange happens."

"I think it'll be on the third floor. The security there is triple what it is anywhere else in Shaldorn."

"Can you get us up there?"

Yasmin looked at Ravi, their gazes meeting. "It's going to be tricky."

"We can do it."

14

The cold had settled into Ravi's bones, and he wasn't sure he would ever shake it off. They hadn't even gotten very far into the mountains yet. Yasmin had warned him, but he hadn't listened. They generated some heat sitting together beneath the blankets, but a fire would have been better.

His body was weary from pushing so hard to reach the summit before the storm. They were lucky she had noticed the snowstorm headed their way. The thought of being stuck out in it made him wince. It was uncomfortable in the tent. He couldn't imagine being huddled for any bit of warmth in the midst of the snowstorm. And yet, that was likely to happen. When he got back to Rannora, he planned to get better gear for anyone venturing into the Dangerous Peaks. For now, this was all they had.

Ravi attempted to sleep. Yasmin had drifted off almost as soon as she lay back. He managed to doze in short bursts, but he kept waking when the wind buffeted the tent. Whether it was the cold or the stories about Shaldorn, his mind wouldn't shut off long enough for him to rest. He was used to little or no sleep on missions, so he could push through, but nothing—not any kind of training or reading—could prepare anyone for the mountains.

Very few who called the plateau home ventured into the peaks. The cold and rough weather kept most everyone away. He was at a disadvantage, and that didn't sit well. As soon as he got back, he would push Durga to begin training exercises on the slopes immediately.

He closed his eyes and listened to the soft whoosh of the wind while ignoring the pain of the headache that wouldn't relent. Beside him, Yasmin rolled onto her side and scooted back against him. He shifted closer to her, seeking any warmth he could find.

When he next lifted his lids, he found his head listed to the side. He felt something against his shoulder and looked to see Yasmin's cheek pressed against him. He was warm. Not completely, but more than he had been since first stepping foot onto the mountains.

Yasmin stirred and moved her head away. Almost immediately, she rolled onto her back. She turned her face away and yawned, then slid out from the blankets. He instantly missed her warmth. His eyes tracked her as she stretched before peeking out the opening.

"Well?" he asked.

Yasmin quickly shut the flap and crossed her arms over her chest to retain her warmth. "The snow stopped. Dawn is about an hour away."

"How much time did we lose yesterday?"

"None."

"Should we get an early start then?"

Her lips compressed briefly before she slipped beneath the

covers again. "The snow reflects light and would help to illumi-nate the way, but it will be dangerous to venture out before sunrise."

"What are the chances we'll run into another storm?"

"Extremely likely."

Ravi nodded at that. There was still a dull ache in his head, and he wanted to use whatever time he could to cover the distance. "Then we should take whatever opportunity we have."

"Agreed."

They rose and saw to their morning routines, made quicker by the fact that they shared the tent again. Ravi stretched his back and neck, working out the kinks. They ate while taking down the tent. When he finished getting it into his pack, he looked for Yasmin. She stood near the overhang with her hand on the stone and her eyes closed. Ravi quietly watched her. He was good at detecting when someone lied. He wasn't as proficient at it as the Wood Elves were since that was their inherent magic, but anyone who studied others for a living learned to pick up on things.

Despite Yasmin's issues about where they were headed, he hadn't sensed any treachery or duplicity. That didn't mean there wasn't any, though. She had been pleasant since he had suggested they get along, but that didn't mean she wasn't planning something. He would keep an eye on her as he would anyone. He always hoped he wouldn't be betrayed, but he expected it. After all, lies and betrayal were fundamental elements of his profession. He had spoken his fair share of fabrications to get away alive and complete missions.

Yasmin had escaped a terrifying life at Shaldorn. Nothing could make him return to such a place. Yasmin likely felt the same. She was only here because of Durga's threat. The first agent sent had died, and no one would think twice if a second met the same fate. It's what he would do for his freedom.

And then he'd get as far from Shecrish as he could. Yasmin had already spoken of doing exactly that.

Her hand dropped from the wall, and she opened her eyes. Taking a deep breath and turning to him, she jerked when she found him staring. "There are three routes we can take."

"And they are?"

"The first will take roughly half a day longer, but it's easier. And there are one or two places we could find shelter if we have need of it."

Ravi widened his stance and crossed his arms over his chest as he listened. "And the other two?"

"The second involves a good deal of climbing. It is a shorter course, but we could get stuck without anywhere to go for shelter against another storm." She paused. "The third is the quickest route. We could cover a lot of ground and make up even more time."

He could argue that she was getting them to Shaldorn quicker so they could return sooner, but the problem was that she didn't *want* to get to Shaldorn. No matter the reason. "What's the catch?"

She blew out a breath, a white cloud puffing from her lips. "First, there is a bit of climbing. I pushed us hard yesterday, and neither of us might be up for it. After the climb, we would head slightly west to bypass the second route. It would bring us to a frozen lake. With our hotter-than-usual summer, the ice could be thin."

"We'd be crossing the lake?"

"We would. It's a large body of water. If we can get across it without mishap, we'd gain almost half a day."

Ravi considered that. "I gather most go around?"

"Most stick to the road," she replied.

Did he trust her enough to take them to a frozen lake where he could slip through the broken ice and freeze to death? Durga didn't think Yasmin would turn against him after giving her word, but Ravi knew she would the instant she saw a way out. And he didn't blame her.

But this was about more than what either of them wanted. It was about the future of Shecrish.

"I like the idea of reaching Shaldorn early to scout around before we sneak inside."

Yasmin tugged on her gloves. "Then the lake is the course to take."

"You think it's safe?" he asked to hear her response.

She made a sound in the back of her throat. "I cannot and will not guarantee safety for any part of this journey. Every path has its perils and drawbacks."

"Say we take the third route. What happens after the lake?"

"We climb. It won't be as grueling as yesterday, but it will have to be done regardless of which course we take. If we cross the lake, the section we climb will be a tad easier than elsewhere on that peak. After that, we'll descend into a shallow valley."

Ravi watched her carefully. "Before we ascend again."

"That's right. We have this mountain and one more before we reach Shaldorn."

"Then we should get moving."

The moment he stepped out from the overhang, he was met with a world of white so bright he had to blink to adjust his eyes. The snow reflected the fading light of the two moons, making it bright enough that it momentarily blinded him. Yasmin made a path in the ankle-deep snow—not deep enough to slow them, but enough to be an irritation. She didn't seem to care. Maybe because this was nothing compared to what she had tolerated during her escape.

He had so many questions. Had she stashed food away? Was someone waiting for her with supplies? Did she have a direction planned, or did she just head out into the wild? She'd said she hadn't been allowed to leave Shaldorn on her own, but that didn't mean she hadn't been taken from the stronghold. Perhaps she had set her own course. Yasmin had admitted that she'd planned for a long time.

She'd spent eleven summers in that place. Given the things he had learned about Shaldorn, he was astonished she had survived that long. But perhaps he shouldn't be. Yasmin was nothing if not a survivor. She took whatever was thrown at her and turned it to her advantage however she could.

Snow crunched beneath their feet, breaking the silence of the morning. Their breaths puffed around them. Yasmin trudged onward as if on her own. There was no conversation. She didn't pepper him with questions or try to get him to promise anything. In fact, she had asked very little.

The fact was, he was more curious about her than she was of him. Who were the people who'd raised her? How had she ended up in Shaldorn? What had she been forced to do at the stronghold?

He may not want to know the latter. Wickedness was a part of the realm. Corruption, fraud, and immorality were things he dealt with on each assignment. Some people courted such vices willingly, while others were drawn to them by a dark side they attempted to hide. Still more found themselves involved without realizing it until it was too late.

And then there were those, like him, who fought against such crimes.

Everyone knew the truly wicked were out there. He'd run across a few himself. But now he would come face to face with many of them. Ravi wished he had more agents waiting to take them down. He might not be there to do that this time, but he would remember faces and names. And he would go after them.

"Who runs Shaldorn?" he asked.

Silence stretched between them. He was about to repeat the question when Yasmin stopped before a cliff. She gazed up at the wall of stone and sighed. "I never spoke to or met the person in charge. That's who the Trinity answers to. I only ever dealt with the trio of male elves. One, Two, or Three oversaw everything. They're the ones we're brought before if there's an issue." Yasmin's dark blue gaze turned to him. "And we didn't want there to ever be an issue."

"They were strict, then?"

"There are many rules. And there was no bending them. If we stepped out of line even a little, we were punished."

Ravi told himself it didn't matter, that he didn't need to know. Yet he heard himself ask, "How?"

"They had various ways. Each of them had a favorite. Two's was withholding food. Three loved beatings. He had special whips made."

"And One?"

"Confining us."

"Why are they called One, Two, and Three?"

She shrugged. "That isn't a question anyone dared to ask."

Ravi didn't get a chance to say more as she began her climb.

The rocks were jagged and rough, but at least it wasn't a sheer cliff like before. Yet somehow, the climb was just as difficult.

"After everything I've told you about Shaldorn, you still think you can complete your mission?" Yasmin asked from above him.

He lifted his gaze to find a handhold before glancing at her. She was a faster climber and already near the top. "Lives are at stake. I have a job to do, and I'm going to do it."

"You could've brought others with you to help."

"The more of us there are, the more likely it is we'll be seen."

"I hope you have a way to contact your people in case you need it."

He frowned at her choice of words. "Don't you mean in case *we* need it?"

"That's what I meant."

But he knew it for the lie it was.

Yasmin shook out her arms after she reached the top. She was sweating from the exertion but couldn't remove her jacket to cool off and risk losing the body heat she had acquired. There was a brief moment when she looked out over the vista and could believe she was the only person on the realm. Sometimes, she wished that were true.

The sound of small rocks tumbling made her turn around. She spotted Ravi as he crested the top and straightened to his full height.

He came toward her, stopping inches away so she had to crane her head to look at him. "I wouldn't suggest double-crossing me."

"No one likes being threatened, and that's exactly what you and your people have done to me from the beginning."

His copper eyes hardened. "Lives are at stake."

"So you've said. Repeatedly."

"Don't you understand the importance of what we're doing?"

She wanted to step back to put some distance between them,

but she wouldn't give him the satisfaction of knowing how his nearness unsettled her. "Does it surprise you that, indeed, I do? I think perhaps better than most. I know the kinds of guests who visit Shaldorn. I know their depravity and debauchery. I know exactly how they would get off on the chaos of a dragon invasion, all while staying safely tucked away somewhere a battle wouldn't touch them."

"You gave your word. That means something to you."

Yasmin looked at the sky to see the first glimmers of sunlight peaking over the horizon. "I've spent the last four years doing my best to forget my time at that place. I tucked those memories away and fought each time they tried to rise. I've moved on."

"And we pulled you back in," he said softly.

Her gaze swung back to him. Anger churned, but she kept it leashed. "I'll get you there. I'll make sure you're inside. I'll detail every floor and room. I'll even wait for you to bring you back. But I *will not* go in," she said, shaking her head. "No disguise will prevent them from discovering me. And when they do..." She shivered, unable to finish the sentence.

The tension eased from Ravi's shoulders. "I can protect you."

"Don't make such promises. No one can protect me from those elves. Besides, your focus is on finding the device." Yasmin cleared her throat and tried to shift the subject. "Shouldn't you have a partner or something?"

His copper gaze slid away. "I did. Once."

If he could pry into her past, she could do the same with him. "What happened?"

"I learned that I work better alone."

"Exactly," she said, seizing his words. "I'll guide you there and back, but I'll be a hindrance inside. As you said, you don't want to bring attention to yourself. You even said that I could wait for you."

He cut her a dry look. "I take it that's the lake."

Yasmin faced the valley and looked down at the frozen water. It was thick enough and the same white as the snow, so it could be mistaken for ground instead of ice. She wouldn't have known had the stones not told her. "That's it."

"It's difficult to tell how big it is."

She pointed to the right. "Do you see where the rocks rise up at the base of the mountain?"

"Aye."

She then pointed to the left. "Do you see the trees that look like they're in a line?"

"I do."

"That is how wide the lake is."

He mumbled something beneath his breath that sounded like a curse, then looked down, leaning over a boulder that sat hip-high. "I take it the lake comes all the way to us?"

"Aye." She eyed him. "There's no skirting it. I might have left that out earlier. There is still time for us to backtrack and take another path."

"We're here. We'll take this one." He swiveled his head to her. "How are we getting across?"

She shrugged one shoulder. "The safest bet is to stick close to the edges where the ice will be the thickest. We'd save a little time going straight across, but I don't know if the possible danger is worth it."

"It isn't. Let's stick to the edges," he said as he eyed the lake.

She noted that he was squinting. "Is your head still bothering you?"

"A little."

That made her frown. Hers had stopped hurting. His should have by now, as well. "Do you need to rest? Take some of the herbs?"

"I'm fine for now," he told her.

Yasmin nodded and began carefully picking her way down. It was a short descent. The real problem was the lake. She paused before stepping onto the ice. She slowly put her foot down, then shifted her weight. On her second step, she slipped. She wind-milled her arms to regain her balance before she fell.

Her heart was thudding against her ribs when she finally righted herself. She looked up to find Ravi watching her, a deep frown furrowing his brow. "I'm fine," she told him. "I just had to find my footing."

"I'll keep some distance between us," he replied.

She began inching over the ice and then raised a hand to let him know she had heard. Her ears strained to listen for any sounds of breaking ice, but so far, she only heard her breath and her boots shuffling across the lake. A glance ahead showed she had a long way to go before she reached the other side. If she didn't have to walk so cautiously, she could be across the ice quickly. Her real issue was not being close to the rocks. She might be able to distantly hear their song, but she had to touch them to really hear what they said. And without them, she'd have no warning of danger.

Yasmin looked over her shoulder. Ravi was about fifteen paces behind her. He kept his attention on the ice and took slow, measured steps. He had seemed sincere about his promise to protect her, but no one could do that. Only she could. It had always fallen to her. Things had gone very wrong the times she had put her trust in someone else.

It was Ravi who had first broached the subject of her waiting outside Shaldorn for him. And she would take him up on the offer. He had said it, and he couldn't go back on it now. There was nothing he could say or do, no threats or promises he could make, that would make her step foot in that place again. Death awaited her there. She was already testing fate by returning to the mountains. Even getting as close to Shaldorn as she needed would be challenging.

There were too many memories there, and none of them good. Those who sought pleasure inside took it from others with a smile as if they were entitled to it simply because of who they were. Shecrish would be better off if all those individuals were wiped from existence. But she knew that wouldn't stop the cycle. More would step in, and it would begin all over again.

"We're each born for a purpose, Yasmin. Yours is to bend to the will of elves in whatever way we decide."

The voice of Laboni, the elf who had called herself *Mother*, filled Yasmin's head. She jerked, causing her foot to slip. She overcompensated and went down hard on her arse. The sound of ice cracking was deafening.

"Yasmin?"

Her heart thudded against her ribs. What was Laboni's voice doing in her head?

"Yasmin?!"

She closed her eyes and tried to get ahold of herself. She couldn't let herself unravel. Not now. Not after so many years.

"Yaz!" Ravi's voice was getting closer.

"I'm fine."

There was a long pause. "Is the ice cracking below you?"

Yasmin moved aside some snow on either side of her and shook her head. "I don't see anything."

"Crawl slowly away from that area before you get to your feet."

She gingerly moved to her hands and knees and crawled to the side. She felt a slight pain in her back that would likely cause more discomfort as the day wore on. When she was safely away, she got to her feet and turned to Ravi. "See? I'm fine."

The doubt on his face said he didn't believe her.

"We're halfway there," she announced and then turned to continue walking.

Yasmin kept her mind focused on getting across the lake so no more intrusive memories from a long-buried past could show up. Walking over the ice was grueling, taking more mental capacity than she had at the moment. At least she didn't hear any other cracks, which meant the ice just might hold.

Still, it came as a surprise when she reached the edge of the lake. Yasmin happily moved off the ice to stand amid the stones. The first thing she did was remove her glove and put her hand on one. No warning waited for her, just a calming song. She sighed in relief. If she were alone, she would collapse to the ground, but she wasn't. It wouldn't do for Ravi to see any weakness from her. As a human, she already had far more than he. There was no need to add to it.

"Are you hurt?"

She turned at the sound of his voice. He stood near enough to reach out and touch her, but he didn't. She couldn't ever remember a time when she hadn't had to stand on her own. Sometimes, like now, the weight was crushing, and she wished she could share it. But that wasn't her lot. She had accepted things long ago. He wanted to know if she was hurt? She had scars aplenty, but most couldn't be seen.

But she knew he wasn't asking about those. He wanted to know about her fall.

"I'll be sore by tonight, but it won't slow me down," she said, putting her glove back on.

He looked away. "We've made good time. Let's rest after this climb."

Yasmin almost told him she'd be good to press onward, but she realized she wanted a few moments. "All right."

"You're pale."

She sniffed and grabbed a rock to start climbing. "You're still squinting, which means your head still hurts."

"I'm fine."

"So am I," she retorted.

Nothing more was said as they made the quick ascent to the summit. Yasmin carefully sat on a rock and removed her pack while Ravi turned in a circle to look around.

"I can't see the rainwood anymore. It's like we're on another realm," he said.

She looked at the clouds above them that looked close enough she could reach out and touch them. "In a way, we are."

His gaze latched onto her. "The fall hurt more than you want to admit."

"It startled me."

"I don't have to be your enemy, Yaz."

The only other person who had ever called her that was Neela. It made her think of her friend and how she hadn't been able to escape with Yasmin. She braced her hands on her knees and dropped her chin to her chest. "I'll be okay. I hurt some, but nothing that warrants herbs."

"You'll let me know if that changes?"

She lifted her head to look at him. She saw real concern on his face, and she didn't know what to do with that. "Worried about me?" she quipped, needing them to get back to their proper places.

One side of his lips quirked into an almost smile. "I wouldn't dream of it."

"Good."

He moved away to find a seat and took in the view while digging out food. There were only a handful of clouds, letting the sun's rays find them. She lifted her face and let the warmth sink into her. When a cloud blocked the sun, Yasmin fished out a piece of dried meat. She was still getting used to having something in her stomach for each meal, even if it was the same thing each time. Food was food. Anyone who had gone without was grateful for whatever they could get.

That made her think about the children. She hoped they were all right. Sameer would make sure they were. He was a natural leader. Others gravitated to him. He had an innate charisma that was impossible to ignore. Each of the kids had something special about them, and Yasmin made sure to always point it out. Life had beaten them down, and she undertook the job of building them back up. She wanted them to have a chance at a future. A real one.

The kind she'd never had.

Her thoughts shifted to Ravi's job offer. He wouldn't have the final decision. That would likely fall to Durga or even someone above her. The idea of a steady job where she wouldn't have to worry about coin to purchase food or clothing was thrilling to Yasmin. However, that would mean remaining in Shecrish. She would be working alongside elves, requiring her to trust them. And what if they sent her away for days or weeks at a time? The children had been deserted by others before. She wouldn't do that to them. For any reason. She would find another way. Somehow.

Yasmin missed the children terribly. It was an ache in her chest. She couldn't wait to hug each of them and learn everything they had done while she was gone. She hated that she hadn't gotten to see them before she left, but she would make it up to them.

First, she had to survive Shaldorn.

16

It was obvious that Yasmin was sore, but she wouldn't admit it. Not that Ravi was much better about his head. At least the descent into the valley below would be an easy one. Though he wouldn't actually call it much of a *valley*. The walls were short and curved, leading to a shallow bowl-shaped gorge—perfect to hold melting snow to form the lake.

A partially frozen waterfall toppled from a mountain to his left. It dropped down to meet rock thrice more before plunging into a small pool that fed a stream. The view of the waterfall from his vantage point was breathtaking with its icy blue and white colors.

Ravi drew in a deep breath. The high elevation meant thinner air. It also meant he tired quicker than usual. Each time he thought his headache was lessening, it came roaring back. He hoped the effects of the altitude would wear off before they reached Shaldorn. He had to be in top form both mentally and physically.

He bit into the dried meat and chewed as his thoughts

returned to Yasmin. When he first mentioned her not entering the fortress with him, he hadn't realized the sheer size of the place. Now that she had explained more of it to him, he knew he would need her.

Unfortunately, he had only made that task more difficult by opening his mouth before. If Durga were here, she'd tell him he had been without a partner for too long and was used to doing things alone. She was right. He had been and was. It was why he had first told Yaz she didn't have to enter the stronghold.

He had until they reached the Shaldorn to change her mind.

The problem with that was that he understood why she was so against it. It had been a place of agony, suffering, and torment for her. He could force her hand by making threats against the children or her—those tactics weren't new to him. He'd always used whatever was required to get those he needed to cooperate. He knew the right words and inflections to use in his tone. It always worked.

And yet, he wasn't sure he could do any of that with Yaz.

By the time he finished eating, Ravi was no closer to figuring things out. He looked at the descent, wondering which way they would travel. He had depleted his water again, but there was more in the valley. He slid his gaze to Yasmin. She was on her feet, standing a little way from him with her hand on a rock, and her face turned to the sunlight.

She wasn't the only one taking advantage of the sun. The Dangerous Peaks with their near-constant cloud cover played havoc with his magic. He would need to save what he had for when he reached Shaldorn—he would need every bit of magic then.

While he basked in the sun's rays, his gaze lingered on Yasmin. There was something to how she always had a hand on a rock with her eyes closed before she told him which direction they should take. If he didn't know better, he would think she had magic. Mountain Elves took their power from the rocks. But Yasmin's curved ears confirmed her status as a magicless human.

He stared at her profile. High cheekbones, slim nose, perfect pouty lips. Strands of black hair had fallen from the confines of her cap to tease her sharp jawline. She had a graceful beauty about her, one that would catch others' eyes. Once more, he wondered what had happened during her time in Shaldorn. How many males had lusted after her? How many had forced themselves on her?

A flare of anger, sharp and fiery, cut through him when he imagined a male choosing her for his companion. Had she gone willingly? Yaz was a fighter, but more than that, she was a survivor. He could see her enduring whatever she had to in order to flee Shaldorn. But whatever had been done to her, and whatever she'd willingly done at the stronghold, it hadn't broken her. It had strengthened her spirit and toughened her before spitting her back out into a world where she still fought and scraped by.

Her eyes opened, and her gaze met his. For a heartbeat, they stared. Even from the distance, he could see the blue of her irises. But when he had towered over her earlier, he had gotten an up-close look. They were a dark, vivid blue like the vast sea. Strands of pale silver mixed with the cobalt like whitecaps on a windy day, while a band of navy encircled the iris. Her eyes were like her. Intense. Astute.

Mysterious.

She was the first to look away. "We should attempt to make it through the valley before the sun sets."

Ravi forced his gaze from her and stood to look down at the river and the trees so heavily covered in snow their limbs sagged. Night came quicker in the mountains once the sun set behind them. Shorter days meant less time to travel. He took another look at the sky. Clouds were beginning to close in. "What do you suggest?"

"We could make it to the other side, but I doubt we'd make the climb before night fell."

"That was my thought, as well. Let's see how far we can get."

She bent to get her pack and slung it onto her back. "Watch your footing on the way down. There are some loose rocks hidden by the snow."

"Understood," he said, readying himself.

The descent looked easy, but it took longer because of the loose stones. Both he and Yasmin hit a couple of areas but were able to right themselves before falling. If they hadn't been taking their time, they would've been caught up in the rock and snow and would have possibly taken a tumble down the slope, which could have resulted in broken bones. He had the herbs, but after seeing how Yaz had reacted to just a pinch of them, he didn't want to give her more.

The basin was spectacular. The gently curved area was thick with evergreen milkbark trees known for their thick, rough bark and cones that encased their seeds. Snow and ice glistened in the fading sunlight, giving the area a mystical feel.

The snow was deeper in the valley, coming up to his calves as they plodded through it toward the stream. It wasn't until he entered the forest that he heard the familiar sounds of animals. He wondered if he could catch something for dinner.

As if reading his mind, Yasmin looked at him with a smile. "Don't bother. The animals will hide the moment they hear us."

Almost on cue, the sounds stopped. Ravi did pick up a few bird calls, but he couldn't pinpoint where they were. They wove through the woods where the snow wasn't quite as high. He found himself touching the trees. He hadn't realized how much he had missed them until he was with them once more. There were few places he could go around Shecrish that wasn't covered in trees. Even the cities and villages were created around them instead of removing them.

Ravi grinned when he realized his headache was abating slightly. It no longer throbbed and was only a dull ache now. He didn't even care that the clouds were quickly covering the sun. He felt better than he had since they'd begun their climb into the mountains. Even Yasmin seemed more relaxed.

They had climbed the cliff face and crossed the frozen lake without incident. By his calculations, they were more than halfway to Shaldorn. If they kept up their pace, they would reach it with time for him to scout the area—and convince Yaz to accompany him within the walls. He would succeed, and then she'd be back in Rannora with the children.

He suddenly frowned, a thought taking root. Did she have a lover? Were they scouring the city for her? Had the children gone to them for help? "We never asked if someone would be missing you."

"The children. But you knew that."

"There's…no one else?" he pressed.

She glanced at him over her shoulder. "Would it have made a difference?"

"Probably not."

"Then you don't need to worry about it."

Now that he'd asked the question, he wanted to know the answer. He parted his lips to ask again when her voice reached him.

"Tell me something about yourself," she said. "You know a lot about me."

"I know very little about you."

She chuckled without turning around. "You know more than most."

"Why are you so private?"

"I asked about you," she said, turning her head to the side.

Ravi flattened his lips in annoyance. He didn't talk about himself. Those who knew him already knew most of his history. He spent his time going from one assignment to another. There weren't opportunities to meet others, and when he did, he didn't form attachments. Not when he would soon leave for another mission.

"Ravi?"

Her voice jerked him from his musings. It was the first time she had called him by his name. And he liked it. "There isn't much to tell."

"Tell me how you became a spy."

He adjusted the straps of his pack and closed the distance between them so less than two steps separated them. "I had an affinity for picking pockets. I found it amusing how easy it was. I never kept what I stole. I returned it to the owners and advised them how to keep their items more secure."

"Of course, you did," she said with a shake of her head.

He heard the smile in her voice. "I was bored, and that occupied my time. I attempted to pick Durga's pocket one day. She was an operative at the time. Instead of turning me in or reprimanding me, she offered me coin if I'd go into a building and eavesdrop."

"I assume you took her offer."

Ravi grinned as he remembered. "I did. I got the information she needed, which helped to close her mission. A few days later, she found me again and offered me another opportunity."

"How old were you?"

"Thirteen autumns."

"She was training you."

He laughed. "I enjoyed every moment of it, and I've been working for her ever since. The better I became, the more assignments I got."

"You don't regret any of it?"

"None."

Yasmin glanced at him. "And your parents? They didn't mind?"

"They were pleased I had something to do."

The sound of water reached them. Ravi looked around Yasmin and spotted the river. The edges of it were frozen, the ice trying to connect in the middle, but it flowed too quickly in places and wouldn't freeze entirely.

"There's a story there," Yasmin said as she halted beside the river and looked at him.

Ravi faced her. "Tell me about your family, and I'll share it."

"I didn't say I wanted to hear it," she replied, turning her attention to the river. "I merely said there was one."

He grinned, exchanging a look with her. They both knew she

wanted the story. He also wanted to know about the couple who'd raised her. How had she ended up at Shaldorn? Had they taken her there? Had she been kidnapped? If so, were they searching for her still? There were so many questions, and he doubted he would get anything out of Yaz.

She dropped her pack and dug out the water flask. Ravi's mouth was dry and he realized how thirsty he was. He removed his bag and found his own canteen. He tested the ground near the river's edge to make sure the ice would hold, then removed his gloves and leaned over, dipping the flask into the water to fill it.

He hissed as the frigid liquid splashed his hands and fingers. They were practically frozen by the time the container was full. He took a long drink to soothe his parched mouth and throat, then refilled what he had taken and looked over at Yasmin, who was filling her own flask. Her eyes met his right before he heard the crack of ice.

"Yaz!" he bellowed.

Ravi was on his feet and diving for her in an instant. She moved but wasn't fast enough. Magic filled his hands as he shot it toward her, grabbing her and tossing her aside. She landed on his side where she had been moments before.

Just as the ice broke, and he plunged into the river.

17

Yasmin landed hard, her gaze locked on Ravi as the rushing water swallowed him. She scrambled to the edge in time to see him pop to the surface, gasping for air. He attempted to pull himself out, but the quick-moving river was too much for his shivering body.

"Ravi!" she hollered, shock thrumming through her.

Yasmin jumped to her feet and ran down the side of the river, looking for a place to grab him. She rushed ahead, dropped flat onto her stomach, and extended her arm.

"Ravi! Grab my hand!"

His head bobbed beneath the surface, but he still managed to reach out. She strained her arm toward him, dread curdling her stomach. Her focus was on his hand, still lifted above the water even as he was dragged under again and again. She swallowed, her heart in her throat. She couldn't miss him. If she did... She couldn't finish the thought.

He was getting closer. The water roared in her ears, or maybe it was her blood. She scooted out as far as she dared, her other hand tightly gripping the bank. Ravi's head broke the surface, and their eyes locked.

"Come on," she whispered.

Then he was there. Their fingers brushed, and she cried out when she thought she had lost him, but then he reached for her again. She latched onto his hand with everything she had. But even that proved difficult. The current refused to let him go. But she wouldn't allow him to be taken.

Yasmin dug her toes into the snow and clutched Ravi's arm with both hands. She got his head above water, but his eyes were closed. Worse, his fingers barely gripped her. She pulled him close until, finally, he was at the riverbank. His teeth chattered loudly, and his lips had a blue tinge.

"Ravi? Can you hear me? You're almost out, but I need your help, okay? I can't do this alone," she pleaded. "Ravi?"

There was no answer. Her fear grew, consuming her until it was all she could think or feel. Yasmin squeezed her eyes closed and shut out the inner voice telling her she would fail. She didn't have time for that. She had to get Ravi out of the water and dry.

She glanced around, looking for something to help her, but she was utterly alone and saw nothing. The current tried to take Ravi, and her with him. Yasmin used one of her hands to steady herself. It went through the snow and landed on something solid. She heard the singing then. Every stone around her joined in on the song, the sound deafening. But it did the trick to calm her.

Without releasing Ravi, she shifted into a sitting position so she could wrap her arms around his chest and dig her heels into the ground for leverage, all the while praying they didn't fall into the river. She gritted her teeth, stretched out her legs, and pulled.

At first, no amount of effort seemed to move him. He shook so violently she could barely keep hold of him. Yasmin tried again, only getting him an inch or so free of the river.

"Come on!" she bellowed to the gods.

The rocks sang louder. She loved having a connection to them, but right then, she wished she had another kind of magic that could help. Instead, she wiggled backward and tugged Ravi again. Her leg muscles strained to the point where they shook from the effort. Again and again, she repeated the movement until she freed him from the water.

"Shite. Shiteshiteshiteshiteshite," she muttered as she carefully laid him down and jumped to her feet.

Ravi curled in on himself, instinctively seeking warmth. She didn't know if he was conscious or not.

"Hang on. I'll be right back," she told him.

She ran to get their packs and then raced back to him. No matter how hard she tried to pump her legs, they wouldn't go any faster. Yasmin got her foot tangled in her pack strap as she tried to toss it aside. She landed hard on her knee but didn't feel anything. Her fingers were stiff with cold and wouldn't move as they should. She got her foot free and yanked off her jacket to drape it over Ravi before shifting her attention to his bag.

Yasmin yanked it open. She was in such a hurry that she dropped it twice while trying to get the tent out. She had only helped once with it, but it had proven easy to set up. Thankfully.

She kneeled beside him. "Ravi? I have the tent up, but I can't lift you. Help me get you inside so you can warm up."

There was no response.

Panic seized her. "Ravi? Ravi!"

His eyes fluttered open.

The surge of relief she felt made her head swim. "I need to get you inside the tent. Do you understand?"

She thought he nodded as she removed her coat that lay over him. When she put her arm under him, he tried to sit up. Getting him to his feet took twice as long as putting the tent together. For every moment he stayed in his wet clothing, the more time it would take for him to warm up.

Yasmin had his arm around her shoulders and hers at his back. He leaned heavily on her, and it was all she could do to remain standing while supporting his weight. The tent was only a few steps away, but it felt like a hundred miles.

Then she felt him start to lean forward and attempted to steady him. "Ravi."

He made a sound. She thought it might have been a word, but she couldn't make it out with the way his teeth chattered.

"Just a few steps. Come on. We can do this," she coaxed. "Shuffle your foot forward. I'll do the rest. That's it," she said with a smile when he did as she'd requested. "I got you. Now, the other one. Good. Good. You're doing good. Do that for me again."

They just might make it. Yasmin glanced at the tent. Why hadn't she pulled it closer to him? She hadn't been thinking of that. She'd been too worried about not getting it up to think about the placement once it was. If the situations were reversed, he would have considered that. He would've known exactly what to do. She knew nothing. If he died, it would be her fault.

Suddenly, she was face-first in the snow. Yasmin pulled her arms from Ravi as he mumbled something. She tucked his arm against him and rolled him onto his back. Then she wiped the snow from his face to make sure he was unhurt. There was no way she could get him on his feet again. She would have to drag him inside.

"It's all right," she said, the words for both of them. "I've got you."

Yasmin got to her feet again. She got the blankets from her pack and his, spread one on the bottom of the tent, and set the other nearby. Then she grabbed his jacket in her stiff fingers and pulled. Just like when she got him out of the river, she heaved him inch by inch. She was breathing hard and covered in sweat, her stomach knotted with dread and worry.

Finally, she had most of Ravi inside the tent. There was no time to rest, though. She got their packs and her jacket and brought it inside before her attention returned to Ravi. His body still shook, but he was unconscious now. Yasmin moved as quickly as she could to unfasten his coat. Then she struggled to get him into a sitting position. Keeping him there proved difficult as he kept falling backward. She had to prop a knee up at his back to keep him sitting while having both of her arms free to wrestle with his soaked clothing.

The scarf and cap came away easily. It took more effort to free his arms from the coat. But even that was easier than his shirt and undershirt clinging to him, making a sucking noise as she pulled them from his body. They joined the rest of his clothing near the opening.

Yasmin carefully laid him down and set about maneuvering him deeper into the tent. Sweat trickled down her face as she struggled to get all of him inside. She had to turn him onto his side and bend his legs to do it. Her knee gave out just as she tugged one final time. She pushed aside the need to rest and crawled around him to close the tent flaps. Next, she hastily removed his boots and socks. Then his pants. She was efficient and quick in stripping him, not allowing herself time to look at his body. Once he was free of the clothes, she covered him with the other blanket.

Getting out of her clothes was much easier. She shivered at the cool air against her bare skin before sliding between the blankets and scooting her body against Ravi's. It would be better if they had another blanket. And a fire. But all they had was each other. He felt like a block of ice. Regardless, she pressed herself against his front, her arm reaching around him to hold him against her, willing her body heat to extend to him.

She closed her eyes and felt her heart rate begin to slow, as did her breathing. Adrenaline had kept her going, but she was rapidly succumbing to exhaustion now. As she lay there, she began to think of what she should do next. He had the magical herbs, but she didn't know how much to give him or even how to get it down his throat if he wasn't conscious. Would they even work to warm him since it wasn't technically healing? She needed to dry his clothes, but that would require a fire they didn't have. Yasmin tucked the blanket tighter around them.

She should've paid closer attention to the ice at the riverbank. It was the first thing she should've done. Instead, her thoughts had been on Shaldorn. Ravi had used his magic to save her, and in return, was now suffering the consequences of her carelessness.

Ravi brushed his cheek against her hair. She held him tighter and squeezed her eyes closed when they burned with unshed tears. A moment later, his arm went around her. She rubbed her hands up and down his back as he continued to shiver. She tried not to notice the hard lines of his body, the firm muscle everywhere they touched.

There had been moments after she fled Shaldorn when she had

been just as cold. A few times, she thought she might die. Yet the gods had thought differently. She wondered who Ravi would've brought with him if she *had* died all those years ago. Would he have attempted to get inside Shaldorn on his own? He seemed the type who would try. Was that because he enjoyed being the hero? Or did he do it because he loved the profession? Maybe it was a little of both.

Yasmin inwardly snorted. Since when did her thoughts turn to such contemplations about an elf? Ravi wasn't her friend. But what did you call someone who had saved your life—twice? The only reason he had was because he needed her. But would it be so bad to have an elf for a friend?

She pushed such thoughts aside. They were musings brought on by trepidation and nothing more. Each time the gods had tried to crush her, she found a way through. These...thoughts about Ravi were there because she had been thoughtless and put him in this situation. She was nothing more than a means to an end for him, and she would do well not to forget that. He was an elf. She was human. And much more than her lack of pointed ears and magic separated them.

Slowly, her body began to relax. Sleep crept over her, and she gave in to it. She tumbled into dreams where she was the one who fell into the river, and Ravi laughed as she begged him to help her. Then she was in Rannora, clinging to all six children as Ravi led an army of armed elves into their home to return the kids to their families. No matter how hard she tried to hold on to them, they slipped from her grasp. The next thing she knew, she stood in the middle of a kitchen with bright yellow cupboards she knew well. She heard voices and turned to find Ravi standing next to Laboni, both of them pointing and laughing at her.

"You're back where you belong."

Yasmin came awake with a start in the semi-darkness. She lay still as her heart thudded in her chest. She heard a heartbeat in her ear and realized it was someone else's. She lay sprawled across Ravi's chest, her leg thrown over his. He had one of his arms wrapped around her while the other lay over her arm draped across his stomach.

By the steady beat of his heart and his even breathing, he was on the mend. She extracted herself from him and covered him with the blanket. She dressed quickly, shivering as the now-cold material settled against her skin. She opened the tent flap and stepped out into the twilight with his wet clothes, shutting the entrance behind her to keep the warmth inside.

Yasmin wrung out his clothes before looking for a place to put them. She had no choice but to spread them across some low-lying branches. She was shivering by the time she returned to Ravi, eager to climb beneath the cover and find warmth again.

When she removed her clothes again, she put them under the blanket to keep them warm, then slipped between the blankets and sidled up next to Ravi until their shoulders and legs touched. She closed her eyes and tried not to recall the hard ridges and firm muscle of his body. His heat enveloped her, and she briefly wondered if she should wake him. She decided to let him rest.

Yasmin woke on her side with Ravi curled around her back. She used his arm as a pillow, while his other hand lay possessively on her hip. It was like being cocooned in warmth and safety, and oddly, she enjoyed it. Soon, she was drifting back into slumber while contemplating her enjoyment of his touch.

Heat pulled her from sleep. She pulled her arms from beneath the blanket and opened her eyes to find herself on Ravi's chest again. He made a very comfortable pillow. She didn't even mind that he held her securely against him. There was something comforting—reassuring, even—about listening to his heartbeat.

But it was the feel of his cock growing thicker against her thigh that made her stomach flutter. Her traitorous body instinctively wanted to rock against his. She forced herself to remain still even as her sex throbbed with a deep, carnal hunger. The reaction was shocking...and thrilling. Desire pooled low in her belly as she felt herself grow damp.

Her hips undulated, the contact with him sending pleasure shooting through her. She stilled, horrified at what she had just done. Yasmin squeezed her eyes shut and begged for sleep while attempting to ignore her body's cravings.

She tried to roll away from him to keep her dignity and cool off, but his arms tightened, refusing to let her go. Of all the people she could have responded to, why did it have to be him?

18

Yasmin woke freezing. She was curled in a ball on her side alone. She rubbed the sleep from her eyes and looked around the dark tent. The blanket was gone. She found it puddled at their feet. With a curse, she yanked it back over them and glared at Ravi in the darkness. He was on his back, his head turned away. She could just make out his silhouette. He didn't make a sound. Yasmin touched his shoulder and snatched her hand away when she connected with his burning skin.

"Shite," she murmured, tucking the blanket more securely around him after she got out.

She dressed in the dark with hands shaking in fear. Her gaze darted to Ravi often. She needed to find his herbs and mix some for him. How long had the fever raged? Why hadn't she checked sooner? What if he died?

Yasmin halted her thoughts there. She searched for his pack but couldn't tell which was which in the darkness. She cursed the fact that they didn't have any light. Durga had given them everything. Why not a light? The answer was simple. Ravi *was* their light. Unfortunately, he couldn't help with that now.

She sat back on her haunches and felt the same crushing fear she had when he went into the river. She couldn't tell how late in the night it was or even if dawn was close, but she couldn't see anything in the tent. Her best bet was to go outside. She grabbed both bags, crawled to the closed flap, and silently opened it to look outside. The snow seized the meager light and held tightly so the ground seemed to almost glow.

It was still night, which meant she needed to be careful about predators. She drew in a deep breath and left the tent, shutting the flap behind her. The moons were hidden behind the clouds, making it even harder to see, but there was enough illumination for her to find what she needed in the bags.

Yet she knew without a doubt that something was out there. Her gaze slowly scanned the area, moving from tree to tree, then to the river and beyond to more trees. She looked at the limb where Ravi's clothes were. Only, they were gone. She bent and retrieved the blade from her boot, setting the packs down before slowly turning in a circle and searching for whatever was out there.

Her gaze kept returning to the left and the tree nearest the river, but she couldn't see anything. She glanced down at her blade. It was small and would do the trick in a tight spot, but it wouldn't do much against a predator. And there were plenty of those in the mountains.

Yasmin didn't have time for this. She needed to get the herbs to Ravi soon. A shadow moved near the tree she stared at. It took a moment for her gaze to pick out the person leaning a shoulder against the trunk. He wore thick furs, a hood pulled up to cover his head and pointed ears.

"Took you long enough to spot me," he said.

Yasmin's knees went weak at the sound of Manu's voice. She hadn't realized how anxious she had been until then. She had wondered if she would see him, but Mountain Elves were distrustful of outsiders and kept their distance.

"It's good to see you," she said, walking to him. "I could've used you earlier."

"You did fine on your own."

She stiffened as his words registered. "You saw it?"

"Aye. I was on my way to you, but you had it under control."

"Under control," she said softly, fury roaring through her. "I was struggling, or couldn't you see that?"

"I saw."

She felt his black eyes on her. "You saw?" she repeated in disbelief. "You saw and did nothing?"

Manu straightened from the tree. "You forget, I know your strength. You continue to believe you're broken and defeated, but you were far from that when I found you four years ago, and you've only grown stronger."

"He could've frozen to death," she stated, ignoring his words.

Manu grunted. "You got him out of the water."

"Barely."

"Are you angry because I didn't rush to your aid, or that you once again managed on your own?"

Yasmin fisted her hands at her sides. "I don't have time for this."

"Is he feverish?"

She blinked at the quick change of topic. "Aye."

"I saw him rubbing his head." Manu took something from a pocket and held it out to her. "Get this in him quickly. He has to swallow it."

Yasmin looked at the bottle. "He has his own herbs."

"Those aren't from the mountains. They won't help. These will. They've been crushed to powder. Something in the mountain water causes some elves to become ill. It's simple if treated early, but the fever can kill."

She closed her fingers around the bottle. "How much do I give him?"

"All of it."

"In water?"

"Straight into his mouth," Manu said. His other arm held out Ravi's clothes. "I've dried them. Take them into the tent or they'll freeze again."

"Thank you."

"You shouldn't have returned," he said when she started to turn away.

"I didn't have a choice."

"You could've let the river have him and freed yourself from whatever he has over you."

She studied Manu for a moment. She couldn't help but remember the first time she had seen him as he walked through the blizzard as if it were nothing before gathering her in his arms and carrying her to safety. It hadn't taken her long to learn that he had been tracking her. "How long have you been following us?"

"Long enough."

Which could've meant a few hours or days. Manu wasn't exactly the talkative type. He was the reason she was alive now, though, and she would forever be in his debt. Manu had said the gods sent him to her, but she didn't believe that. She wondered why he hadn't asked who Ravi was. Could it be that he knew? She knew better than to dismiss anything when it came to Manu. "Are you here to guide us to Shaldorn?"

"You seem to be doing that well enough on your own. Who told you to take this path?"

Yasmin shrugged. Manu might have saved her life, but that didn't mean she would share her secrets. "A guess."

"You haven't been in the mountains in four years, yet you somehow know the back way to Shaldorn."

She needed to get him off this subject, so she shifted to another that might make a difference and gain his assistance. "A device is being sold at Shaldorn. The buyer intends to toss it across the Idrias border."

"Because a Dragon King paid us a visit?"

Her brows rose. How did the Mountain Elves seem to know things when they never left the peaks? "Aye. How did you know that?"

"We live in the mountains, Yasmin, not another country. Get those herbs in him. Quickly." He turned and walked away.

"Where are you going?"

There was no answer. Soon, the night swallowed him, just like when she'd awakened in another cave all those years ago and found Manu gone. He appeared out of nowhere and left just as swiftly.

Yasmin slipped back into the tent with everything and had to give her eyes a moment to adjust. Then she spread Ravi's clothes beneath her side before returning their bags to the corner. She could just make out his silhouette. She wished there was more light to see him. He hadn't moved since she'd come in.

After removing her shoes and sitting beside Ravi, she placed a hand on his forehead. The fever still burned. She had never heard of such a sickness and was surprised that it hadn't ever affected her. It must have something to do with the differences between humans and elves.

Her fingers slid into his hair, pushing it away from his face. The locks were thick and cool against her palms. He looked so peaceful. She wouldn't even know anything was wrong if she didn't know about the fever.

"Ravi?" she called. "Can you hear me? You're ill. I need to get these powdered herbs into you, okay? They will end the fever."

He made a sound. She didn't know if it was an agreement, but Yasmin held out the small bottle Manu had given her and dumped some of the herbs into her palm anyway. Then she set the bottle aside and parted Ravi's lips. He turned his head away. He was unconscious and not intentionally fighting her. Or maybe he was. It sounded like something he'd do.

"Ravi, please," she begged. Then she changed tack. "Your mission is at stake. You've never failed. If you don't take these herbs, we'll never get to Shaldorn."

She watched his face, trying to see in the darkness. Her fingers ran up his jaw, covered with a thickening beard since they'd left Rannora, and moved to his mouth. His lips were soft and pliant beneath her fingers. He didn't fight her as she parted them. She brushed the pad of a finger against his lips before tugging his chin down to open his mouth wider. He grunted but didn't turn away. Yasmin carefully pinched a small amount of the herbs and placed them into his mouth.

Manu had said no water, but she didn't know how she was supposed to get them down Ravi's throat. She didn't want to dump them all into the back of his mouth and have him choke. So, she gently ran her thumb and forefinger along his throat in hopes he might swallow. It took some time, but she finally felt his throat bob.

Yasmin smiled and repeated the steps until all the herbs were gone. There was no reason for her to continue to caress his face and throat, but she couldn't seem to stop. She told herself it soothed him, but in reality, she was the one who wanted the contact. She stayed in that position until her hip ached, and one side of her arse had gone to sleep.

She thought about earlier when she had felt his arousal. Her sex throbbed at the memory. Desire slid sensuously through her, making her legs clench, and her nipples tighten. She looked down, her fingers lingering on his lips for a heartbeat longer. Then, she slowly moved away before she did something foolish.

Yasmin tugged out both of their water flasks and set them nearby. He would want them once the fever broke. She yawned and decided to try to sleep some more. It didn't take long for her to remove her clothes and put them on top of his beneath the blanket. As she slipped under the cover, she put her hand on his forehead and felt the sweat beading.

"At least the herbs work quickly," she muttered.

She tried to turn on her side, but Ravi pulled her down beside him. As soon as she rested her head on his chest, she felt his body relax. Yasmin didn't read too much into that. He was ill and sought comfort. She had been the one to warm him. His body recognized that. If he were awake, she would be the last person he'd want next to him. She didn't take offense to that. She felt the same about him.

Or she had before.

She didn't know what she felt now. Her emotions were too jumbled after the river incident. She would sort it all out in the light of day when he was healed, and she had time to think. Fear and the darkness had created this mess. And Ravi's hard, naked body.

Yasmin squeezed her legs together and felt a throb of longing, a craving that wouldn't relent. She swallowed and closed her eyes. Ravi's steady heartbeat lulled her. He murmured something and settled back into slumber.

Despite her exhaustion, sleep evaded her. Her mind ran rampant with lustful thoughts of all the ways she wanted him. His chest was close enough she could press her lips to it or run her tongue along his skin. Her palms itched to move over his hard body. Her fingers flexed, coming into contact with the thick sinew of his arm. She felt the power of his legs beneath hers, slung across them.

She cautioned herself about such thoughts, but her body rebuked the warning. She didn't want to feel these things but couldn't turn them off. It wasn't Ravi. He might be handsome and had rescued her twice, but she had never felt such things for Manu. It had to be because they were naked.

Once she left Shaldorn and her body was hers to do with as she pleased once more, she hadn't let anyone touch her. Why did she crave it now? Why Ravi?

She tried to turn away, but he tightened his hold again, refusing to let her go. Yasmin waited for the flare of fear at being detained, but it didn't come. Nor did she really want to put distance between them. Not when he felt so good against her. She settled back down and closed her eyes. His large hand splayed across her back, and she felt every inch of his palm. She wanted to hate it, to despise his touch. What would that hand feel like cupping her breast? Teasing her nipple? Or sliding between her legs? Inside her.

What would he feel like inside her?

Yasmin bit back a moan. There was no stopping her thoughts as she pictured him over her, thrusting inside her, his hard length sliding in and out and touching her exactly where she needed. Or maybe his hands gripping her hips as he drove into her from behind.

She rocked against him as her fantasies played out in her mind.

A groan rumbled in his chest. Her eyes snapped open, and she stilled. What was wrong with her? Ravi was ill and unconscious. She had no business acting in such a way without his consent. Yasmin had never been more embarrassed and ashamed of herself than in that moment. She cleared her thoughts, forcing all the images into a box she locked away. She removed her leg from his and then evened her breathing and endeavored to sleep.

When she finally tumbled into slumber, her dreams were filled with Ravi's very willing body doing sinful, wonderful things to her.

19

The instant he woke, Ravi became aware of three things: He was warm, his cock was rock-hard, and a soft, naked body lay half on top of him. He didn't need to look down to know it was Yaz. His fingers flexed against her supple skin. Her warm breath fanned his chest. She had one bent leg over his, near his arousal. His balls tightened greedily.

And with that came a soul-deep longing to slide his palms down to her arse and grind against her before rolling her onto her back and kissing her.

His breathing quickened. Need scorched his veins. He could feel her breasts against him. His hand rested on the curve of her back. A slight downward shift, and he could cup her bottom. He swallowed, the sound loud in the silence.

Yaz shifted her cheek against his chest. Strands of inky hair had come loose from her braid and lay across his shoulder as if beckoning him to touch them. She shifted her leg, and it brushed his rod. He barely bit back his moan.

She stiffened the instant she woke. Ravi calmed his breathing. He didn't want her to know that he was awake. If she knew, she would likely be off him the next second. She fit perfectly against him, and he liked her there.

Gradually, the tension eased from her muscles. Ravi didn't know if he was more surprised by his decision to remain or hers. His thoughts were muddy after the river. Ravi recalled going into the icy water but didn't remember exiting the river. Still, he did have a memory of Yasmin getting him to his feet. She must have done it because they were inside, and he was warm.

He wondered how much time they had lost. It was hard to tell whether it was day or night, but since Yasmin hadn't risen, he remained where he was. It was peaceful, and he wasn't sure if that would continue when they faced each other. He never would have imagined that the prickly human could put away her barbs to lay languidly against him. But he liked it—perhaps too much.

Ravi bit back a groan as his cock grew harder. Desire thrummed through him, hot and thick, consuming his thoughts. It was all he could do to keep it in check. If he didn't put some distance between them, he would do something they both regretted. The only reason her naked body lay against his was because he had needed to get warm. He would've done the same for her. It didn't mean she wanted him.

But what if she did? Ravi's heart beat faster just thinking about it.

Suddenly, she deftly moved her leg away from him. Next, her arm disappeared from across his abdomen. He snapped his eyes shut as she rose onto her elbow and tenderly rested her palm on his brow. Then, she was gone. Away from him and out from under the blanket. A whoosh of cool air slammed into his side before the cover dropped again. He immediately wanted to call her back to him.

Ravi slightly opened his eyes. He saw her dark silhouette standing with her back to him as she quietly dressed. She made a soft sound when she realized her hair had come loose. Instead of braiding it again, she stuffed the long tail of the plait and the stray strands under the cap she slipped onto her head. She paused long enough to put on her boots and then exited the tent so skillfully that he only saw a brief glimpse of the outside before she refastened the flap.

He released a breath he hadn't realized he'd been holding, then palmed his aching arousal, wishing he had time to see to himself. Ravi sat up, bending his knees to plant his feet on the ground as he rubbed his eyes. He looked around for his clothes but couldn't find them. Surely, she hadn't tossed them away. Maybe she had gone outside to get them.

A moment later, the entrance opened wide enough for her to poke her head inside. She stilled when she saw him, then entered the tent. He could make out the subtleties of her face now. She had her gaze directed at his chest, and he glanced down to find the blanket pooled around his waist.

"Thank you." He wanted to say more but wasn't sure what words to use or how to phrase them. So, he kept with a simple gratitude.

"It was nothing," she replied with a shrug, looking away.

"It was something."

She jerked her eyes back to his. "Did you think I would leave you?"

"I wouldn't blame you if you had. I know what we're asking of you is more than anyone has a right to do."

She shrugged again.

"You saved me."

Yasmin briefly met his gaze. "You saved me twice. I didn't check the ice by the river. I should've—"

"Things happen."

She was silent for a moment, her thoughts seemingly distant. "It was careless. You could've...well, it was bad." She cleared her throat and handed him a water flask. "You should drink. The fever was intense."

Ravi accepted the water and frowned. "Fever? From what?"

"I thought you would know. There is something in the water that affects some elves. Your headache was an indicator."

He shook his head. "I had no knowledge of any such thing. Why didn't you say something?"

"I wasn't sure."

"Are you not at risk?" He was suddenly concerned about her welfare.

"It only affects elves."

Ravi nodded once and drank deeply, realizing he was parched. He had a weird taste in his mouth. "The fever broke on its own?"

She didn't look up when she said, "I used some herbs."

He finished the water and reached over for his pack to see how much of the herb mixture was left. To his surprise, it didn't appear as if any more were gone. Ravi looked at Yaz. "You should've warned me about the fever."

"I should have."

Something in her voice made him think she was keeping something from him. It could be because they had slept skin to skin, but since she had believed he was asleep when she left, he didn't think that was it. "Why didn't you?" he pressed.

She blew out a breath and swung her gaze to him. "You know why."

Of course. She was angry, and it was her way of getting back at him. "How did you know how much of the herbs to use?"

"I guessed."

"How much did you use?"

"The right amount." She lifted the blanket where she had lain and tugged out his clothes. "They're warm and dry. It's nearly dawn. You slept through yesterday afternoon and the evening."

Something wasn't right. He couldn't put his finger on what it was, but he would. One way or another. "We lost the time we had made."

"But you're alive." She handed him her flask and took his empty one.

Because of her. She got food from her bag. He heard her stomach grumble in hunger and wondered what had happened during the night. Before he had time to ask, she took her pack and left.

Ravi wondered what she would've done had he thrown aside the blanket. She could hardly meet his gaze. Had he said something? Done something? All he remembered was being so cold that he didn't think he would ever get warm.

He finished her water and dressed. Only then did he exit the tent. Snow flurries danced in the air, teasing his face and tangling in his eyelashes. His gaze immediately sought Yasmin. She stood beside the river, looking across it in the direction they were headed. Her hair was once more braided and hanging down her back. His boots crunched on the snow as he walked to her.

"What happened last night?" he asked.

She shook her head. "Besides the fever and getting your body temperature up? Nothing."

"Did I say something out of line?"

"Nay."

"Did I do anything?"

Her deep blue eyes met his in the pre-dawn light. "You slept."

Ravi thought about his erection this morning. Perhaps that's what made her nervous. Surely, she knew a man didn't have control of such things. Maybe he should tell her it had nothing to do with her. He couldn't say for sure or not if it was a lie. The more he thought about it, the more he wondered if she wasn't the cause.

Even now, standing in the cold and knowing something was wrong, he wanted her. Desperately. The urge to pull her against him, have her cheek pressed against his chest, and her arms around him, was overwhelming. He wanted to touch her face, her lips. He needed her against him. He couldn't explain it.

How he wished he knew what'd happened during the night. Maybe he was reading too much into things, searching for something that wasn't there. He nodded once, deciding to let things be as they were. He retraced his steps and returned to the tent to grab his bag and find food. The thought of sustenance made him realize he hadn't eaten since noon the previous day. He devoured some dried meat before dismantling the tent and packing it away. When he finished, Yasmin was still at the river. Something was on her mind. Since she faced the direction of Shaldorn, it was obvious what it was.

The sky was lightening to a soft gray by the time they wordlessly set out. He didn't ask her which way they were going, and she didn't offer. He was still trying to sort out his body's reaction to her. He tried to tell himself that it was just the confines of the space and the accident. He'd had a human lover before, but he preferred elves. While he didn't have relationships per se, he did have those he shared his bed with on occasion. They were liaisons that benefited both parties since he had no intention of settling down—not with the work he did.

They walked along the riverbank until they came to where a tree had fallen across the water. Yasmin was the first across it. He almost asked her why she was fine walking over a tree, but the rope bridge had made her hesitate.

Once across, she led them through more forest. Ravi saw something out of the corner of his eye, but when he looked, there was nothing there. He could've sworn he saw movement. Mountain Elves lived among the Dangerous Peaks, but few saw them. They were the rarest of all the elves. So much so that he had never seen one. As far as he knew, they never left the mountains.

Sea Elves came into the cities sometimes. Even Dark Elves came up from underground. But never their mountain kin. Ravi wondered if they had gone extinct like the Desert Elves. Would anyone know if they had since they kept to themselves?

After he crossed the river, Ravi halted before running into Yasmin's back. He looked over her head to see why she had stopped. A huge, white animal stood before them. It nuzzled the snow as if looking for food. Yasmin pushed against him, tapping his leg. He got the hint. Ravi walked backward, glancing behind him to make sure nothing was there. He wrapped an arm around Yasmin when he reached a tree and tugged her behind it with him. They both leaned out to keep an eye on the creature.

He bent low until his mouth was by her ear and whispered, "What is that?"

"An ostoose. Let's hope it doesn't pick up our scent."

"We could run."

She shook her head. "It's too fast."

Ravi looked up at the tree branches. "We could climb."

"It can, too. We have to wait."

He realized he still had a hold of Yasmin. He didn't care that layers of clothing separated them. He knew what her flesh felt like. She didn't push him away, so he remained. They stood in silence, barely breathing as they watched the ostoose search for food. The animal began walking away, but Yasmin didn't relax until it was far out of sight.

"We need to get out of the valley," she said.

He loosened his arm when she stepped away from him and it fell to his side. The instinct to pull her back against him returned. He fisted his hands and lengthened his strides to catch up with her.

"There's much you need to know about Shaldorn," she said into the silence.

To his surprise, she began talking about the fortress. She described hallways, tunnels, and stairways. She spoke of stairs that led nowhere and passages that someone could become trapped in. He learned about the rooms the staff knew as the dungeons. It was where they were taken and punished. He didn't need to ask if Yaz had been there. He heard it in her words as she described the rooms in detail.

She paused when they came to the end of the woods. Anyone looking would be able to see them when they crossed the last part of the valley. He got a look at the ascent up the slope. It was rockier, and the angle was steeper.

He barely had time to glimpse it before Yaz started walking again. She picked up where she had left off in continuing his education of Shaldorn. When they got back, he needed to get all of this in writing. If she would cooperate. It would also give him a reason to see her again.

Before he knew it, they had reached the edge of the valley. Yaz was the first to start the trek up. The incline was so steep they had to lean over and use their hands. She talked all the while. He now knew there was a back entrance to Shaldorn, but there were also secret doorways few were privy too. She gave him those locations, and he filed it all away for later.

Halfway up the slope, Yaz began asking him questions about Shaldorn to see how much he had retained. He was able to answer over half of them correctly, but it wasn't enough. So, she repeated the information. And the next time she tested him, he passed.

She held out a hand once they reached the top of the mountain and helped him over the edge. Their gazes met. She was the first to look away. Ravi turned and looked back at the valley. It had almost been his last resting place. But that was why he wanted to remember it. For him, it was where something had shifted with Yaz.

Every mission held danger, but this one was even more treacherous. And they hadn't even reached Shaldorn. He turned back to find Yaz with her hand on another rock, her gaze distant. He followed her line of sight to the next peak. There, nearly on the top, he could just make out the roof of a building. Shaldorn. The stronghold rose out of the rock and snow to dominate even the peaks.

He slid his gaze to Yasmin and studied her profile. He didn't need to ask what she was thinking. It was written all over her face. Dread. Anger. Trepidation. Ravi started to grab her hand and give it a squeeze before he remembered that she didn't like to be touched. He thought about how easily she had slept against him, but would she welcome his touch now? He didn't have any words of comfort. What did someone say to another who had to return to such a place? There was nothing he could say that would make it better.

"I'm sorry you have to be here," he said.

She drew in a deep breath and slowly released it. "We all have to do things we don't want to do. It's just a place."

It was more than that. It had been her prison, and inside it, her tormentors. No matter what she did or didn't do, what had been done to her or hadn't been done, Shaldorn had left its mark, fashioning her into the person she was now. She had an inner strength he had never seen before.

Yasmin swung her head to him. "It will be tricky from here on out. Stay close."

20

The wind became their tormentor, an adversary persistently swirling around them, intent on their deaths. And it nearly succeeded on more than one occasion. The stones had warned Yasmin that this section of the mountain was precarious, but they'd failed to tell her just how hostile the conditions were.

Everything was against her and Ravi. The weather alternated between snow and sleet, pummeling them relentlessly. The jagged rocks gave the illusion of security but sliced her palm and Ravi's forearm almost as soon as they began their descent. Then there was the ice in the crevasses and on any flat surface hidden beneath layers of snow, waiting to make them slip and fall.

It was such a grueling descent that they had to stop frequently to rest both their bodies and their minds. Worse, they were running out of water. By noon, they had only reached the midway point on the mountainside. The valley descended far below, a labyrinth of boulders and layers of thick snow between them and it. More water awaited them there.

If they could make it.

Yasmin rubbed her chest where it ached from the cold that seemed to seep into her very bones. Snow had replaced the sleet, and it fell fast enough that it caused issues seeing into the distance. She had halted her instruction on Shaldorn because it became too difficult to talk and descend, but there was so much more to tell Ravi. Her gaze moved from the valley to scan the area around them. Was Manu around? Did he still watch them? Should she have told Ravi about him? She probably should have. But Ravi would've wanted to look for the Mountain Elf, and she knew Manu wouldn't make himself visible. She closed her eyes and huddled in her coat, her thoughts turning to that morning when she had been toasty inside the tent. She longed for that heat now. And Ravi's body alongside hers.

"How is your hand?"

His words jerked her out of her thoughts. Her eyes snapped open as she glanced to where he sat beside her. She had opted not to wear gloves to better grip the rocks, but it had come at a price. "It hurts, but I can't tell if it's from the injury or the cold."

"Both, probably." He moved closer to her, sitting on the same rock. He tugged down his scarf to expose his face. Then he held out his hand. "May I?"

Yasmin gave him her left hand. He cradled it carefully while gently unwinding the strip of his shirt that he had torn off to use as a bandage to stop the bleeding. He brought her palm closer to his face. A shiver went through her when she felt his warm breath skimming over her skin. She couldn't look away from his face. His beard had gotten thicker. It seemed to add to his masculinity, accentuating his incredible jawline and mouth.

Her gaze dipped to his lips. She remembered parting his lips the night before. They were close to her hand, and she wondered what his mouth would feel like against her skin. She knew the sensation of the rippling muscles of his body against her, but she wanted more. Yasmin had been held by him and against him. And damn if she didn't want to be cradled in his arms once more.

"The injury looks good. It's nearly closed," he said.

His finger was soft, tender as he tested the herbs he had put into the cut. She had wanted to refuse the herbal magic, but there was no way she could continue without the use of her hands. So, she relented—and worried she might become out of it like when she'd drunk them. But there had been no ill effects so far. That would be just as dangerous as descending with an injury.

She inhaled slowly as bumps rose across her flesh each time his skin contacted her palm. She didn't feel the cold or the sting of the cut. All she felt was *him*.

Ravi's gaze lifted to hers. She became lost in his copper eyes, noting the darker shades that tended toward brown, and the lighter that glinted like his golden skin. His cap was pulled low over his brow, but strands of his hair had fallen loose, the golden strands like a beacon against a world drenched in white.

"Yaz?"

By the gods, his voice. It was deep and soft. Sensual. Hypnotic. Had there really been a time when she had hated hearing him talk? Now, she could listen to him say her name for eternity. "Aye?" she asked when she found her voice.

He stared at her for a long time, his hand still cupping hers. Suddenly, he looked away and shook his head as he began covering the injury with the bandage once more. "The cut should be fully healed within a few hours."

She wanted to ask what he had been about to say, but maybe it was better if she didn't. The moment he returned her hand to her lap, she felt the absence of his warmth and something else she couldn't quite name. She wasn't ready to end whatever was happening between them. Not yet, at least. "And the wound on your arm? Would you like me to look at it?"

"I already did. It's healed."

Yasmin hadn't realized how much she wanted to touch him until then. "That's good." Her voice caught, and she quickly looked away.

Out of the corner of her eye, she saw him put his scarf back into place to protect his face. She tugged on her gloves since her fingers were becoming stiff. She could always remove them again if the climbing became too difficult.

She stood. "We should get moving. We need to make it to the valley before dark."

Yasmin found it difficult to concentrate. She was aware of Ravi. Of where he put his feet, where he placed his hands. And each time his gaze slid to her. It was maddening. She didn't want to think about him. But she did. Constantly.

The next hour went by without incident. They even covered more ground than she had expected. They paused for a rest before continuing, both taking note of the deepening gray of the sky. It wasn't long before the snow became sleet once more. She shivered and longed to be in the valley so they could get inside the tent.

Yasmin tested each place before she put the full weight of her foot onto it, yet still she slipped. She caught herself but became aware of a hand on her arm. She looked back at Ravi, their gazes meeting before he slowly released her. She nodded her thanks and continued on, but the skin beneath her clothes where he had touched heated from the contact.

They progressed as quickly as they dared. The sun never returned, making it difficult to keep track of the time as the sky turned darker and darker. The sleet halted hours later, but they were already soaked to the bone. She could see the valley. It was near enough to touch but still so far away.

The last part of the slope became so steep they had to walk down sideways. The huge boulders were hidden beneath piles of snow. One fall, and they would find out just how deep. She put one foot in front of the other, her gaze locked in front of her until they reached the valley.

She and Ravi didn't speak. Unlike their previous location, this vale was barren of anything except ice and snow. Wind lashed across it, whipping up snow and swirling it about with a howl that made her want to plug her ears. There was no shelter from the gusts. It blew from seemingly every direction. Yasmin blinked, suddenly realizing how dark it was. She looked around for water.

"Here!" Ravi shouted over the wind.

She followed him as he headed to the right, skimming along the outer rim of the valley. Yasmin stumbled, but he thankfully didn't see her. She wrapped her arms around herself, shaking so badly she wasn't sure she could stay on her feet. She was about to tell him she couldn't go on when he stopped.

Yasmin tried to help him when he pulled out the tent, but he waved her away. It was probably better. She couldn't feel her hands anymore. She probably would have been more of a hindrance than anything. As soon as the tent was up, he motioned her inside. She made an effort not to dive in, but she wasn't sure she managed it.

Ravi poked his head in and motioned with his fingers. "Give me your flask. I'm going to fill them."

"I can help."

"You're frozen. Warm up. The water is close," he told her.

It took her far too long to take off her bag and hand him the flask. He left and shut the entrance. Being out of the wind helped tremendously. Yasmin took off her shoes and kept them near the flap. She then removed her coat and got the blankets from the bags. For a moment, she almost spread them out like the previous night but wrapped one around herself and huddled with her legs close to her chest as she waited for Ravi's return.

The moment he opened the flap, the howl of the wind became deafening. He was inside in a flash with the flap shut behind him. He handed her both flasks before taking off his shoes. He was in a squat when he turned to her.

"What?" she asked at his stare.

"Your clothes are wet."

She swallowed hard. "So are yours."

"Come," he said as he unfastened his coat. "We have to get warm and out of these damp clothes."

Yasmin watched him for a heartbeat, ridiculously excited to have exactly what she wanted. But this would be different. He'd be conscious. That meant it would likely be awkward. Then again, she was too cold to care.

She threw off her blanket and got to her feet to undress with her back to him. Meanwhile, he laid a blanket down as their base. She peeked over her shoulder when she discarded the last of her clothes, but Ravi was messing with something in his bag, sitting with a part of the blanket over his lap. She used that time to slide between the covers and curl onto her side.

It wasn't long before he settled beside her. She felt his warmth and scooted closer.

"Shite, Yaz," he grumbled as he turned to face her. His arm snaked out and dragged her against his chest. "You're like ice."

"It's how you felt last night," she said between chattering teeth.

Almost immediately, it became impossible for her eyelids to remain open. She hadn't gotten a lot of sleep the night before. He rubbed a hand up and down her arm, and she tugged the blanket tighter. Slowly, she began to thaw.

"You should've told me."

She was almost asleep when he whispered the words. Yasmin shrugged. "Nothing you could do."

"It doesn't always have to be you against the world."

"It's how it's always been."

"Not while I'm around."

She smiled. Perhaps, but he wouldn't always be around. That was just the way of things.

His arm was heavy as it settled along her hip and down her leg. It felt nice.

He felt nice.

21

Ravi lay awake long after Yaz had drifted off. He listened to the wind and thought about the following day. If everything went to plan, they would reach Shaldorn. They were right on schedule. There hadn't been much time for conversation with their demanding descent, but he had been thinking about her.

There had been a moment when she'd let her guard down as he inspected her injury. He'd been ensnared by her blue eyes and wanted to know what she was thinking, even as images of their tangled bodies filled his mind.

Ravi had told her she didn't need to face the world alone, but he did the same thing. Though he suspected their reasons were different. Trust didn't come easily in his line of work. He found it simpler to keep everyone at arm's length. But Yaz had somehow wormed her way past his defenses.

He closed his eyes and settled his arm in the indent of her waist with his hand resting over her stomach. He'd tried to find a way to get her in exactly this position all day. Perhaps he should thank the gods for giving him what he wanted. If only things weren't so complicated.

His thoughts returned to Shaldorn and everything Yaz had shared. He knew exactly what he could say to force her to join him. But she would hate him for it. Well, she would loathe him even more than she already did. But this was about Shecrish. Thousands of lives meant more than one person. Yaz would have no choice but to come with him inside Shaldorn's walls.

But he didn't want to take her. He didn't want her anywhere near that place. The gods, however, had other ideas.

It was more than pleasantries between him and Yaz. He thought it was more than them saving each other. Being friendly had turned to friendship. He never saw that coming. However, that would change in an instant on the morrow. Still, she was a human of her word. She would help him achieve his mission. No doubt she would make their return trip exponentially more difficult, but he would accept whatever she threw at him. He'd deserve it and more.

It would likely crush everything they had built over the last few days. If there was another way for him to succeed, he would do it.

He wondered if she would consider working for the DIA. She would make an excellent agent, and the job would give her stability for the children. Even if she did join the agency, she would likely ensure their paths never crossed again. Which was too bad. He liked her.

The irony wasn't lost on him.

His arms tightened around her, knowing this could be the last time he held her. He would never know her secrets, never fully gain her trust. He wouldn't get to see one of her rare smiles and know what it was to run his fingers through her hair. He would never know the taste of her kiss or the feel of her body clenching around him as she climaxed.

For the first time in his career, Ravi didn't want to be the person running the operation. He wanted someone else to force Yaz so he could keep what they had developed. He wanted to be the one she turned to and sought out when her burdens became too heavy.

But that wasn't in the runes for them. Their paths had been laid out long ago, destined to cross and briefly mingle, only to deviate. But she would leave a lasting impression.

This small, human female had taken on the world, accepting each battle as it came. She never went looking for them, and she never cowered, never hid. She faced whatever it was head-on, daring the gods and fate to bring her down. She might have stumbled a few times, but she had gotten right back up, stronger than before. He didn't need to know the details of her past to come to that conclusion, but he saw it in her each day.

And for this brief moment, it was just the two of them.

Ravi came awake slowly, surprised he had fallen asleep. He reached for Yaz, but she wasn't there. He lifted his lids when he heard a noise. She leaned away from him, digging in her pack. Her hair was loose, the damp midnight strands drying as they cascaded down her back.

Without thinking, he reached for a lock of her hair and wound it around his finger. She glanced over her shoulder. It was dark inside the tent. He couldn't see her face and cursed the fact that he hadn't turned on the light. He wanted to see her and put every inch of her to memory.

"Did I wake you?" she asked. "Sorry. I was hungry."

Ravi rolled onto his back, careful not to tug the blanket she had clutched to her chest. "Aye. We should eat."

He sat up and used a small portion of his magic to ignite a light no bigger than his palm. He set it near him, where it shed enough of a glow to see. It was difficult to keep his eyes off Yaz, especially with them sitting naked beside each other.

As they ate in silence, he wondered what she would think of him when all this was over. He'd shared little of himself—practically nothing, really. And she had asked. Initially, he hadn't told her to be spiteful. After all, what was the point of giving her any information? At least, those had been his thoughts once. Now, he *wanted* her to know who he was. She had shared. He wanted to do the same. Maybe it would make her think better of him later. It probably wouldn't, but it seemed important right now.

"I had a partner once," he said.

She shot him a startled look, her brows furrowed. There was a beat of silence before she asked, "Oh?"

"Well, we worked on some assignments together. We weren't always paired up. I prefer to work alone."

"You don't say?" There was a ghost of a smile on her lips.

Ravi chuckled, shrugging his shoulders. "I can be difficult."

Her lips did curve into a grin then. "So can I." She looked away. "Is that why they aren't here now?"

He chewed and swallowed before saying, "We are no longer

partnered because their loyalties came into question. It occurred while we were on a mission."

"They betrayed you."

He nodded, glancing at her.

"It was a female, wasn't it?"

He swiveled his head to her. "What makes you say that?"

"The way you talk about it. If it had been a male, you'd be angrier."

"You don't think I'm furious about it? It nearly cost me my life."

Yaz pulled her hair over her far shoulder and watched him, waiting for him to continue.

"It was a female," he said with a sigh. "Took me too damn long to figure out what she was about."

"Because you were too close to her. That's what happens to lovers."

Ravi leaned back on one elbow and shook his head. "How did you piece that together?"

"The way you talk about it. You're angry, aye, but more at yourself for not knowing what she was up to. You also hold a lot of resentment toward her for betraying you and the agency. You stopped her, didn't you?"

"I did."

"Then you triumphed."

"I'm not so sure about that." He ran a hand down his face, scraping his beard. "She used me. She used everyone. I thought what we did mattered to her. She had goals other than keeping Shecrish safe. Coin and power was what she was after. She stole confidential information and sold it to the people we were in the process of taking down. She told them my plan. They were waiting."

"What tipped you off about her?"

He shrugged. "It was a gut feeling that something wasn't right. I thought she was in danger. I told her and attempted to stop her from going, but she ignored my words. That's when I knew she was involved."

Yaz handed him a flask and drank from her own. "That changed you. Every decision, every choice, alters us. That's just the way it is. I spent a lot of time being bitter and hating everyone, but my decisions put me in Shaldorn."

"How so?"

She licked her lips and looked down at her hands in her lap. She was silent for so long he didn't think she would continue. Then she took a deep breath and slowly released it before saying, "I ran away from the people raising me."

"Your parents."

Yaz snorted and rolled her eyes. "They're not my parents. They didn't give birth to me."

"That doesn't mean we shouldn't consider the people who raised us our parents. What if the children with you began calling you mum? Would you stop them?"

She slowly shook her head. "Never. But you need to understand that not every couple the Ministry grants children to are meant to have them. They may want them, but they shouldn't be allowed."

Ravi thought about his parents and nodded, waiting for Yaz to continue.

"They were affluent, and they loved to show off. They had been granted an elven boy three years before the Ministry gave them me, but he died a year before I came. They gave me the newest and prettiest things, and we constantly went out, like they were showing me off. They were very strict, though they never physically harmed me."

Ravi's gut clenched at the words because he feared what was coming.

She played with the ends of her hair as she got a faraway look in her eyes. "I got sick. I was too young to remember the details of how it began, but I remember being unable to move. Laboni, my mother, took me to a healer, who helped. A couple of weeks later, I was sick again. It was the same thing. And back to the healer we went."

"They couldn't figure out what ailed you?" he asked.

Yaz made a sound in the back of her throat. "They just said I was a sickly child. Laboni and her husband got a lot of attention for that. Everyone felt sorry for them since they had already lost one child. Many of their friends commented on how great they were to undertake having such an ailing human. There would be times when I felt good, and they quickly brought me out of the house on display. But I was sick more often than not. Laboni got some herbs from the healer since we were there so often. She added them to my meals, which was why my food had to be prepared separately. It's true something was put into my food, but it wasn't the herbs from the healer. It was lake root."

Ravi slowly sat up. He couldn't believe what he was hearing. "Are you telling me your parents were poisoning you?"

"I know for sure Laboni was. I saw the bottle. I dumped my food out that night and didn't eat. I went to the kitchen while everyone slept and searched for the bottle. I knew as soon as I smelled it that it was the source of the weird scent in my food."

"How old were you?"

"Twelve."

He ran a hand over his face. "You were a bloody child."

"A *human* child."

"It shouldn't matter," he bit out.

Her gaze met his. "But it does."

"What did you do?"

"I dug around for the herbs from the healer, which I took to help myself get better. I also hid food in my room. For the next few days, I ate only the food I had and took the herbs. I healed and got stronger. And I began to plot my escape. Because I knew it would continue. I couldn't trust them and knew no one would believe me. I snuck out in the dead of night, taking only the clothes on my back and a few coins I'd found."

Ravi stared in amazement at her. "Did they look for you?"

"Not that I know of. I went far from the neighborhood so they couldn't find me. I lived on the streets, wandering during the day and finding any place I could at night where I'd be safe. When I dared, I bought food until the coin ran out. After that, I learned to steal. I was good at it, and it kept me fed. I did pretty well until I picked the wrong pocket one day."

He quirked a brow, impatiently waiting for the rest of the story.

"I'll never forget her. She was a beautiful Moon Elf with stunning blue hair and ice-blue eyes. She was out of place among the human community, dripping with wealth. I didn't think she'd miss one of her many bracelets. But she caught me. It wasn't anger when she turned to me, though. She smiled. There was kindness in her eyes. I was filthy, my clothes in tatters, and my hair in knots. I can't imagine how I must have looked since I only ate once a day. She didn't toss me away, though. She asked if I wanted a better life.

One far away from Rannora, where I would have new clothes, a bed, and three meals a day."

Ravi realized his hands were clenched into tight fists in the blanket. He forced himself to relax.

"I hesitated because it sounded too good to be true. She assured me I could leave if I didn't like what I saw. I took her at her word and followed her into the carriage. We went straight to Shaldorn. It was the first time I had been out of Rannora, and I was so excited. The gods had finally answered my prayers. The first time I saw Shaldorn, I was awed by its size and beauty. She ushered me inside, and I was bathed, dressed, and fed in short order. When I didn't eat straight away, she asked why. I told her what Laboni had done. She explained that it was the lake root that had made me ill. I smelled my food, but there was none of the scent I was used to in it. So, I ate. I ate until I was nearly sick. For two days, I did nothing but eat and wander the front of Shaldorn. I didn't see the Moon Elf again after that first night. I asked for her. I even inquired about her name, but no one would tell me. Finally, a staff member asked if I wished to remain. I couldn't imagine leaving. It was heaven. I was safe for the first time."

Ravi followed her hand as it tucked her hair behind her ear and adjusted the blanket under her armpits.

"I was taken to my new rooms after I declared I would remain, and that's when I discovered the truth about Shaldorn. It's a place where the wealthy play, but it's a prison for the rest of us."

Rage, unlike anything Ravi had ever experienced, rushed through him. They had taken a child from the streets, one starving and homeless, and offered her a dream. Anyone would've taken it.

And he could imagine many, many had.

22

Yasmin opened her eyes, disturbed by the silence that greeted her. The wind must have stopped sometime while they slept. She stared at the side of the tent, trying to determine if Ravi was still asleep. She slowly rolled onto her back and found his side empty. Disappointment filled her.

It hadn't been her intention to tell him about her past. Maybe it was because he'd opened up about his. She wished she hadn't spilled so much, but what was done was done. There was no taking it back. Even after telling him, she couldn't look at him. She merely lay down and turned her back to him. It wasn't long after that he extinguished the light, but he didn't reach for her, which hurt.

Her sleep had been riddled with dreams of him—or rather his body and all the things she wanted to do to it, mixed with the horrors of Shaldorn. It made for a restless night. But she was a light sleeper. How had she not heard him rise?

Yasmin rubbed the sleep from her eyes and sat up. She sighed and reached for her undergarments first. Once they were in place, she shoved off the blanket and tugged on her socks. Her under-shirt came next, followed by her shirt. She stood and had just put her foot into one pant leg when Ravi returned. She froze as their gazes met. He quickly looked away and closed the flap behind him as she got her trousers on and buckled.

"The sky is clear," he said. "It looks to be a beautiful day."

That was too bad. She had been hoping for a massive storm that would keep them right where they were. Though she couldn't decide if it was to stay away from Shaldorn or to be with Ravi. Naked and sharing covers.

He tugged off his gloves before rolling the blankets. "The climb will be intense. It's nearly straight up."

"It's going to be tough."

"Can we make the climb to Shaldorn today?"

"If the weather holds, maybe." She took a moment to braid her hair again.

Ravi sat back on his haunches. His gaze landed on her, watching her. "About what you told me last night—"

"I don't want your pity," she said before he could continue. "I didn't tell you my story so you'd feel sorry for me. I ended up at Shaldorn because of my decisions."

"You were a child," he stated in a clipped voice. "One, I might add, who had been homeless, starving, and alone. Anyone would've accepted the kindness shown to you."

She shrugged and tugged on her boots. "It was too good to be true. I should've realized that."

"You need to forgive yourself for being lured. There's no embarrassment in that. They would've gotten you to Shaldorn one way or another."

He was probably right, but that didn't diminish the shame she had carried since. And now she was about to face that evil once more. At least she didn't have to go inside. It was enough to face the stronghold, knowing what was happening within its high, thick walls.

She ate quickly. They took down the tent and packed it away in short order. And then she gazed across the valley to the wall they had to scale. She looked around for a rock so she could ask it which way was the easiest, but all she found was ice and more ice.

"What's our direction?" Ravi asked as he came up beside her, settling his pack on his back.

Yasmin shook her head. It looked as if the snow was hanging onto the side of the mountain by sheer force of will alone. One wrong move could have it tumbling down, and them along with it. She needed to get her bearings before she killed them both.

"Yaz?"

She walked away from him, searching for a rock, any rock. She dropped to her knees and began clawing at the snow, hoping she could locate one. When she found nothing, she jumped up and walked to the side where the mountain rose. There was too much snow for her to find anything.

"Yaz."

She spun around and started back at the mountain they had descended yesterday. There were rocks there. A hand wrapped around her arm, halting her. She jerked her head to the side, her eyes clashing with copper ones.

"What is it?" Ravi wore a deep frown, his concern clear.

Yasmin swallowed and searched his gaze. Could she tell him? Did she dare? It wasn't as if they were friends. They were barely friendly. Though she could argue that sleeping naked with someone could bridge the two. She didn't know what he would do if he learned her secret.

"What's wrong?" he urged.

Ravi might be a good man. He might even keep her secret and never use it against her. But she couldn't take that chance. She looked away and said, "I need a better view to determine which way we need to go."

"Are you sure it isn't a rock you need?"

Her head whipped to him as her heart skipped a beat. Did he know? That was impossible. He couldn't. Or...did he? "What?"

"I see you touching them at every opportunity."

"Do I?"

He gave her a flat look, all concern gone as irritation took its place. His fingers loosened, and he dropped his hand. "Do whatever you need to do, but hurry."

"I'm trying to get you to Shaldorn as you want. If we go the wrong way, the snow might not hold us. I'd think you would rather I not hurry."

His nostrils flared, but he didn't reply. He turned his head away instead.

She dropped her pack and ran the short distance to the other mountain. Her breath came out in big puffs of white before her face. She kicked and scratched at the snow at its base, hoping and praying she'd find a stone so she didn't have to waste time going back up. Why hadn't she thought to ask yesterday? Why hadn't she taken precautions on one of the many times they had rested?

Yasmin slapped at a mound of snow, releasing her fury.

Ravi watched Yaz in the soft gray light of the approaching dawn. She was distraught, and he didn't think it had anything to do with their conversation about Shaldorn. The distress had tightened her face once he'd asked about their route. But it wasn't until he'd brought up the stones that he had seen the flash of panic in her eyes.

What was she hiding?

He wanted to go to her and help her look for the rocks, but he didn't think she would appreciate him nearby. The fact that she wouldn't admit what she was doing was enough to make him keep his distance. Yet there was no denying she had a secret. But how did stones fit into it? Now, if she had magic, he could understand.

His thoughts skidded to a halt. Ravi looked at Yaz in a new light. As far as he knew, no humans had magic. If one did, surely they would've come forward. The implications would ripple out, not just with humans but also elves. No one would keep that to themselves. Especially no human.

Unless that human was Yaz.

She frantically searched the snow for a rock. Then, suddenly, she stilled. Her hands were covered with snow, but he knew she had found a stone. Her chin dipped to her chest. She stayed there for several moments before her shoulders moved in a deep breath.

Ravi wanted to continue watching her but forced himself to turn his back on her. He had to be wrong about the magic. It would irrevocably alter Yaz's life. Her status would likely be elevated, and she would have no trouble finding a job, which would put a proper roof over her head for the children. Not to mention regular meals. If she had magic, she would've used it against those at Shaldorn. Or even to get away from Durga. And him.

That still didn't answer the question of why she needed to touch the rocks. Maybe he was putting too much thought into it. She had spent years at Shaldorn. Perhaps it was something she'd been forced to do there and just couldn't shake. Maybe it embarrassed her, which is why she tried to keep it a secret.

Aye. That made much more sense than it being magic.

The soft crunch of snow alerted him that she approached. She scooped up her pack as she reached him and kept walking. "This way."

Ravi shook his head and fell into step with her. She glanced up the side of the mountain on their right. He studied it himself. It was the first place he'd looked when he emerged from the tent that morning. He'd been sure someone was there, but no matter how hard he looked, he couldn't locate anyone.

"We need to be on the lookout for guards," Yaz said.

He nodded, but when he realized she wasn't looking at him, he said, "Understood."

"They didn't use to spend a lot of time on this side of Shaldorn. There are easier ways to reach the compound." Yasmin wasn't sure why she'd blurted that. Ravi hadn't said anything else about the stones.

"How far is the fortress once we reach the ridge?"

"Too close."

Yasmin kept her chin up and her strides long as they hurried across the valley. They were more exposed here than anywhere else. She caught Ravi looking around, his unease evident. Even when they reached the edge of the valley, and Yasmin tested a section to begin the climb, he kept scanning the area. She looked at the mountains, again wondering if Manu was out there.

She glanced over to see Ravi still searching. "Ravi," she called. When he looked at her, she said, "Once we start, there's no stopping."

"I'm ready," he stated with a brief nod and pulled up his scarf.

23

Ravi knew he should be concentrating on the climb, but he couldn't stop thinking about Yaz. How many people had forced her into circumstances beyond her control? How many had ignored her?

How many had hurt her?

He could argue that Durga and the society had put the lives of every person before Yasmin's when she coerced Yaz into taking him to Shaldorn. Durga could probably be excused for her part. But him? What he planned to do once they reached the top? That would be unforgivable. He would be worthy of Yaz's vitriol then.

But did he have a choice? She was there specifically because she not only knew how to get into Shaldorn but also because she had knowledge of the compound few others did. That expertise would allow him to find the parties where the device would be handed off. And it was Yaz who would find them a way out of Shaldorn.

If they had more time, if Ravi had days to spend inside

Shaldorn to learn the layout and the movements of those in charge, as well as the guards and guests, he wouldn't consider bringing Yaz. But time wasn't on his side. If he hadn't fallen into the river, if the storm hadn't hit yesterday, they might have reached Shaldorn sooner.

If. He had never liked that word. It was too indecisive. He was a doer, an elf of action. He didn't sit around and dither. He saw a problem and got things done. *If* never factored into things. Yet, for this assignment, that seemed to be in all of his sentences.

From the valley, the wall had looked completely vertical. It wasn't, and that was a good thing since most of it was snow and ice with rock protrusions. Still, it was steep enough that it felt like a vertical climb. He paused and shook out his hand, trying to get warmth into his fingers. Ravi had climbed the sheer walls of Shecrish's plateau multiple times. It was one of his favorite hobbies. But scaling the Dangerous Peaks was another matter entirely. He was ready to wish the snow or ice a farewell forever.

Ravi glanced up at Yaz. She grunted as she kicked her foot into the snow for a firmer hold. Like everything she did, she kept a steady pace and made good progress. Whenever Yaz was near the stones, she set her hand on one for a heartbeat.

His gaze lingered on her for a second, his thoughts shifting to her elf parents and what they had done. He had called her a survivor before he knew about her past. Ravi tried to imagine her jumping from the compound and rushing into the mountains without a coat or supplies. A brisk breeze blew past him as he climbed, so frigid it stole his breath. How had she not frozen to death? Or gotten lost?

The sun rose into the sky, its rays shining so brightly off the snow that it nearly blinded Ravi. No amount of squinting helped, but he wouldn't complain. He needed the sun. He soaked it up while he could, praying it would be enough when the time came to call on his magic. When his arms tired, he paused. When his legs cramped, he shifted his weight from one to the other to ease the muscles.

Ravi drank sparsely. He wanted to ensure he had enough water to get to the top. He noted that Yaz did the same. They paused long enough to dig out some dried meat when their hunger became too great. There wasn't anywhere to sit, so they ate quickly to get back to climbing.

It would've been the perfect opportunity for Yaz to prolong their ascent, but he was learning that wasn't who she was. She was doing everything she could to get him to Shaldorn in time for the buy. Despite her past. Despite her trepidation.

Despite everything.

Ravi gritted his teeth when his fingers took too long to grip a rock. He cupped his gloved hands around his mouth and blew. He didn't know how Yaz was climbing without gloves. His fingers were frozen. Hers couldn't be much better.

The sun inched past its zenith. It seemed to signal change everywhere as clouds drifted in. Not the big, fluffy kind, but the blue-gray ones that promised snow as the temperature plummeted. It wasn't long before the clouds covered the sky in every direction, sealing out the sun. Ravi felt the loss both physically and magically.

Descending amid the storm the day before had been miserable. Going through that again on their current climb would be agonizing. Ravi noticed there was more distance between him and Yaz, so he pushed himself to move faster.

Yaz scanned above her before looking at him. Her scarf was tightened firmly around her lower face. "I see it," she called, her voice muffled.

He didn't need to ask what she saw. "How close are we?"

"Not close enough."

That seemed to spur them both. Find a handhold, find a foothold, and pull up. Repeat, again and again. Sometimes, the snow gave under him. Ravi stiffened, waiting to fall, but as long as he followed Yaz's path, he never did.

He had kept his eyes forward and up, but he chanced a glance down. The valley was so far below it seemed like another world. If either of them fell, they wouldn't survive. Not in the time it would take the other to get to the bottom and administer the herbs.

Ravi drew in a deep breath of icy air and coughed as it stung the inside of his lungs. Sweat dripped down his forehead and into his eyes. The combination of freezing weather and sweating from the exertion was a horrible combination. Gods, he couldn't wait to return to Rannora and the humidity that didn't try to steal his every breath. The wind picked up, and the threatening clouds continued their trek across the sky, spilling neither snow nor rain.

The climb seemed endless. It would've been a good time to contemplate different means of obtaining the device, but he couldn't. The ascent was too taxing, both mentally and physically. Ravi lost track of the sun behind the dense clouds. He thought it might be close to dusk, but he couldn't be sure. He was lost without the sun amid all the ice and snow.

Ravi blinked against the fading light. They had to be near the ridge. He looked up, expecting to see Yaz, but there was nothing but unending white. Suddenly, her head peered over the ridgeline. She flashed him a tired smile and motioned him onward.

It gave him the extra push he needed to climb the last bit. Ravi nearly shouted with joy when he crested the ridge. He threw a leg up as Yaz grabbed his arm and helped him over before they huddled behind a grouping of boulders. He rolled onto his back, uncaring that his pack was still in place. He stared up at the darkening sky, wishing he could linger and rest. Ravi sighed and then got to his feet, his body protesting. He found Yaz sitting on the ground. He held out his hand, she accepted, and he pulled her up. They locked gazes, their bodies close, and their hands linked.

"Let's never do that again," he joked.

He couldn't see her lips behind the scarf, but her eyes crinkled at the corners. "That might be difficult."

"We're going back the same way, aren't we?"

Yaz shrugged and released his hand. "Not if we're followed. They'd be able to pick us off easily."

"You have another route?" He fisted the hand that had held hers so he wouldn't reach for her.

"I will."

Ravi wasn't a man who trusted easily, but he believed her. She hadn't led him wrong yet, and there had been plenty of opportunities. It was the first time in a long while that he had a partner he could trust.

He looked beyond her to the fortress that towered above them, fighting with the mountain peaks to reach the clouds. Shaldorn. It was still a short distance away. Trees dotted the way, but they would mostly be out in the open, making them easy to spot if anyone was looking.

Yaz slowly turned and faced the compound. He moved a half

step closer when he saw her shiver, a movement that had nothing to do with the temperature. Ever since Durga had told him about the stronghold, Ravi hadn't been able to get to Shaldorn quickly enough to complete his mission. However, now that he saw the structure through Yaz's eyes, there was so much more at stake than just obtaining the device.

His gaze shifted to her. He wondered what was going through her mind. Was she frightened? Angry?

Worried?

It was difficult to tell with her face hidden as it was. She stood with her back straight, unbowed. Yaz could likely take on the entire realm alone, yet he wanted to be there to protect her and ensure that no one ever hurt her again. It was a new emotion, this need to safeguard another in such a way. It had no business filling his mind before such a daring operation. Ravi wished someone else were with him, someone who hadn't suffered at the hands of those at Shaldorn. Someone who didn't stir...things within him. Besides, Yaz had been through enough. She shouldn't have to suffer further horrors.

Yet it was out of his hands now.

Or was it?

Yaz drew in a deep breath and glanced his way. "There are guards inside Shaldorn whose main purpose is to watch for anyone outside."

"How are we going to get close without being seen?"

She pointed to the sky. "Both moons are at their lowest right now. We should be able to make it using the trees as cover and avoid being seen. Unless the guards are patrolling outside."

"How often do they patrol?"

"Depends. I've been away for four years. I don't know their routines now."

He pointed to the thick snow. "What about the tracks we'll leave?"

"Let's hope they think ours are from other guards."

"I'll walk in your tracks, so we only leave one set."

She nodded. "Good idea."

He reached into his pack and pulled out the last of his food. He gave her some and took the rest for himself. He would worry about provisions for their return later. It had been a long day and wasn't ending anytime soon. They needed to keep up their strength for what was ahead.

Yaz didn't linger, preferring to eat as they walked. She charted a course to the first tree, moving quickly through the thick snow. He devoured the dried meat and finished off his water within moments. Ravi looked behind him and thought he saw movement. He paused and studied the area but couldn't find anything. The mountains were causing him to imagine things. He shook his head and turned forward, putting his foot in Yaz's tracks to the next tree.

He didn't like being out in the open. He saw a dozen places he would put sentinels that could've spotted them the moment they crested the ridge. No alarms were sounded, and he didn't hear any shouts to halt. That didn't mean someone hadn't seen them, though.

Ravi scanned the side of the compound with its many windows. Only a few were darkened. There were torches along the high outside wall. To unsuspecting visitors, it might seem inviting, welcoming even. The striking façade hid the ugly truth.

He wondered how Shaldorn had been kept a secret for so long.

But he knew the answer. The wealth and power of individuals who wanted their playground kept away from prying eyes. The Dark Elves had known of it long before anyone at the DIA. Ravi probably still wouldn't know about the fortress if it weren't for the potential conflict with the dragons.

Yaz reached the next tree and stopped behind it. She turned to him. He thought she looked paler than before. He wanted to tug down her scarf and tell her that everything would be fine. But he didn't dare. Something had shifted within her. It was like a wall had come down between them. He understood why, but that didn't mean he liked it.

Ravi opened his mouth to speak, but she turned and made a beeline for the next evergreen. The looming structure grew closer. He heard the distant cords of music from within. Yaz didn't pause at the next tree. Instead, she kept walking as if she couldn't stop. He suspected that if she halted she might not move again. Ravi half-expected her to turn and bolt.

And he wouldn't have blamed her if she did.

He glanced between the low branches of one of the evergreens heavy with snow and spotted a guard with his back to them. They needed to hide before they were spotted. He lunged for Yaz, but she had spotted the guard, too. They diverted to a tree to the left and plastered themselves behind it. They were so rough that the limbs moved, causing snow to fall from the branches.

They looked at each other, listening for movement. When none came, Ravi leaned around the branches and surveyed the building. He found the guard in the same location and realized he was pissing. The guard then righted himself and turned to look around. Ravi jerked back out of sight. When he looked again, the guard was gone.

He nodded at Yaz. She carefully checked her side before once again heading to the tree they had been on course for. They moved quickly in case another guard appeared. Ravi continued to look behind him, but there was no movement anywhere.

At the tree, Yaz blew out a breath. He noticed that she kept her back to Shaldorn. The flickering torch flames along the outer wall stretched their long fingers as if trying to reach them. Ravi remained behind the wide branches of the evergreen while getting a better look at Shaldorn. Someone had taken their time crafting the compound. The architecture was intimidating and flamboyant, its presence impenetrable and ominous.

Or maybe that was because he knew what went on within its stone walls.

"How do we get in?" he whispered, eyeing the building. When Yaz didn't answer, he slid his gaze to her. She was breathing rapidly, her eyes wide with fear as she glanced around like a cornered animal ready to bolt.

"I can't. It's... There's..."

He'd realized some time ago that he wouldn't force her to enter Shaldorn. Even if he hadn't, he wouldn't now. She was in no state. Being this close to the place she had barely escaped was too much. Besides, it wouldn't be the first time he'd entered somewhere and had to sort things out himself. He'd complete the mission. Like he always did.

Ravi tugged down his scarf and gently touched Yaz's shoulder. Her wild eyes jerked to his. She was so good at hiding her trauma. If she hadn't shared it with him, he never would've known. But she couldn't hide it now. It stood between them.

When they left Rannora, he hadn't cared about why she'd left Shaldorn. He had told himself everyone had something in their past, but it had been a lie so he wouldn't feel anything. It was always better that way. Emotions got in the way.

Like now.

But he couldn't change that. He wouldn't.

He fought the impulse to pull Yaz into his arms and shield her from the world. He didn't because he feared she would reject his embrace. She had proven that she didn't need anyone. Especially him. Odd how that disappointed him so. He was the same. Life was easier alone.

It had been his mantra for years. Somehow, after a trek through the mountains, that no longer applied.

He glanced down and noticed that she gripped his arm tightly. He didn't know if she held on to steady herself or to shove him away. It was enough that she touched him in any capacity.

"It's okay," Ravi said, keeping his voice soft to calm her. "Tell me how to get inside, then make your way back to the boulders and wait for my return. If I'm not back by dawn, leave."

She blinked twice. Her gaze was directed toward him, but he didn't think she saw him. She was lost in her memories. Bringing her to Shaldorn had allowed the past to rear its head. He should've expected this. He should've prepared. He'd heard the terror in her voice when she spoke of Shaldorn, and he had done nothing.

He stepped closer, bringing his face near hers. "Yaz? Did you hear me? You aren't going inside. I just need the way in."

24

Yasmin saw Ravi's lips moving, but the roar in her ears obscured his words. Her chest was tight, making breathing difficult. She had been drowning in the unbidden memories since the moment she allowed herself to look at the building. In an instant, she was back within Shaldorn's walls, living a nightmare she would never wake from.

It was Ravi who steadied her. She gazed into his copper eyes and struggled to determine reality from illusion. Her body warmed where his hands rested on her shoulders. Slowly, the nightmare crumbled to reveal trees, an inky sky filled with stars, and Ravi. His gaze was filled with concern. Her fingers began aching from the way she clung to him. She wanted to be closer to him. She needed to know he was real.

His lips moved again. She tried to focus on his voice, which she had come to love hearing. Deep and smooth. She strained to listen to him, willing the roar to die away. Gradually, his words reached her. The unforgiving band around her chest loosened as what he said penetrated her mind. She didn't have to go inside, wouldn't have to face the past and see all those she had left behind. Yasmin drew in a shaky breath at the reprieve she hadn't known she needed. She feared he would find a way to force her inside. That was the deal she had made. Her vow.

Ravi watched her intently. "Yaz?"

A portion of his face was lit by the flickering torches. She dared another glance at Shaldorn. Her eyes burned with unshed tears of regret. She was ashamed that she had given in to her anxiety when so many lives were in jeopardy. She had marched her way across the mountains while ignoring the doubts and worries that cropped up, shoving them aside as she always had. But she had to face not just her fears but also the friends she had left to suffer. Ravi's face swam in her vision as tears gathered.

"It's all right," he said, giving her a soft smile. "Stay hidden. I'll find you."

He lowered his arms and turned to leave. A tear dropped onto her cheek. Yasmin refused to release him. Ravi's head swung to her, a small frown furrowing his brow. There was no way she could let him go into Shaldorn alone. It didn't matter how good he was. He wouldn't get far without being caught. The mission would fail, and the device would be sent to Idrias. Whether she liked it or not, she was his only chance.

Yasmin tugged down her scarf, hating that her hand shook. "I'm coming."

"You're in no condition to do that," he said as he moved closer.

She briefly closed her eyes at his nearness. It would be so easy to rest her head on his chest. Just for a moment. That's all she needed. But she was too scared to do it. "I'm aware that I…" She paused and tried again. "I know that being here has drudged up things I wasn't prepared for. I should have known. It's just...it's easier not to face the past."

"It is." His hands lifted to cup her elbows.

Yasmin swallowed and inched closer. "The exchange happens tonight. There isn't time to meander around, trying to find your way. It wouldn't matter how well I explained each level, you would get lost or, worse, found. But I know the way."

"It would be better to have you with me, but I can't ask you to come."

"You aren't. I gave my word."

He glanced to the side. "I don't care about that."

"I can do this. We both know you need me."

"Yaz," he began.

She put a hand on his chest. "I know what I said before, but being here, seeing this...place?" she said as she glanced at Shaldorn, "I can't run anymore. I won't. I have a chance to stop a catastrophe."

"And if your fear takes you again?"

Yasmin pressed her lips together, knowing what she had to do. "You won't be caught with me. I'm not just saying that to convince you. It's a fact."

His copper eyes searched hers. "How?"

"I have a secret no one else knows. Something I've kept my entire life." She jerked her chin to Shaldorn. "The stones tell me where to go and if there's danger."

Ravi didn't scoff or laugh at her. He released a long, slow breath. "The stones. That's how you got us here. That's why you are always touching them."

"It is," she said, lifting her chin and waiting to hear what he would say.

"They talk to you?"

"In a way. If you want to steal the device, then I need to be with you."

Ravi lifted his gaze and stared at the imposing structure. After a moment, he slid his gaze back to her. "Are you sure you can handle it?"

"I can. I'll have to stay out of sight, though. They will recognize me."

He disregarded her words. "First things first. Let's get inside so we can warm up."

She looked forward to getting out of the cold. Even if it was within Shaldorn. Ravi looked down. She followed his gaze to find her hand on his chest and her other on his arm. Yasmin lowered her arms to her sides. She chanced a look at him, and for a moment, thought he might say something. But the moment passed.

Yasmin turned and put her scarf back in place. Her emotions were under control. For so long, she had snubbed and disregarded the past, believing it was better for her to forget it existed. She could push it as far down as she wanted, but it would never leave her. She didn't know if facing the past would help, but it certainly couldn't hurt. No matter what, she couldn't fall apart once they were inside.

"Ready?" she asked without looking at Ravi.

"Aye."

She sent up a silent prayer to the gods and checked for guards before hurrying across the space from the tree to the structure. As soon as she reached it, she placed her hand on the stones. Even through the gloves, Yasmin heard them. They immediately showed her where the guards were without her asking, as if they knew what she needed.

Yasmin grabbed Ravi and tugged him after her into an alcove before the guard above looked out the window. He didn't question her as they flattened their backs against the building. They heard a male's voice before someone dumped liquid from a window into the snow where they had been.

Ravi shot her a look. She grinned, shrugging. The stones then showed her there was a clear path to the hidden door at the back. She motioned for Ravi to follow as they kept close to the wall and hurried down the long stretch to the next alcove. Once there, the rock she needed to push to open the door was glowing. At least, to her. Ravi didn't seem to notice it.

Yasmin met his gaze as she pushed on the rock. A soft scraping noise was the only sound that broke the silence as the door unlatched. She pushed it open wide enough for them to slip through, and Ravi shut it behind him. They crept quickly down the narrow, dimly lit hall. Yasmin tugged off her gloves and ran her fingers along the stones. She heard their warning and quickly rounded the corner and moved out of sight as the guard appeared.

"That was close," Ravi whispered.

She felt his warm breath and realized he had lowered his scarf. Yasmin did the same before stuffing her gloves into her pockets. It was warmer inside, but not enough to thaw her just yet. She planted her hands on the stones and closed her eyes as their song surrounded her. She let her question fill her mind.

They showed her the path that would bring them to an empty staff chamber where they could decide their next move. When she opened her eyes, she saw Ravi watching her. His expression gave nothing away, and she found she wanted to know what he thought of her ability. But perhaps it was better if she didn't.

"This way," she told him.

He stayed one step behind her as she followed the stones' directions. It had been years since she'd walked these corridors, but little had changed. If she became confused, all she had to do was touch the stones for them to remind her of the way.

Yasmin's lips split into a grin when she saw the door to the room on the left. Her steps lengthened to reach it. She went to grab the handle to open it, but Ravi beat her to it. He gave her a silent look, letting her know that he would go in first. She stepped aside as he quietly opened it and peered inside. Then he pushed it wide and waited for her to enter before he closed and locked it behind them.

"The room was empty," she said.

He shrugged as he looked around the small, barren chamber. "I wanted to be certain. Why are we here?"

"To plan." She dropped her pack and unfastened her coat, then removed her cap and scarf and stuffed them into her bag. "It's still early. We have an hour, maybe two before the exchange happens."

Ravi turned to look at her. "How can you know that?"

"I don't. I'm going on how things were done in the past. There isn't much happening right now."

"I hear music. Conversation."

"There are those who jump at the chance to spend a night at Shaldorn when the opportunity arises. They're the ones you'll find downstairs right now. They arrived yesterday and will likely stay tonight before they have to depart in the morning. Others will begin arriving soon, and the conversation will grow even louder. Of the Trinity, One is always around. Two will appear once the majority of the guests arrive. Three will emerge shortly after that. Once all three are seen, that's when you know things are beginning."

Ravi tugged at his scarf so it hung around his shoulders. "Meaning?"

"The staff is already making the rounds with food and drink. The guests won't say the night has begun until the market is open, and the other staff is brought out."

He considered that for a moment before nodding. "All right."

"I have a friend here who will assist us. Neela helped me escape. We can trust her. First, we need to change out of these clothes and into something that won't make us stand out. There are a few places where we can watch the happenings."

Ravi ran a hand down his mouth. "We could stay hidden, but it would be better if we mingled with the guests."

"I can't. Remember?"

"I have a solution for that."

"What?"

"I'll explain as you take us to your friend."

25

Ravi glanced behind him as he followed Yaz down yet another hallway. They were a maze. She touched the stones a few times as they walked, her frown growing.

"What is it?" he asked.

She shrugged. "The stones can't locate Neela."

"Maybe she found a way out."

"Maybe."

But he heard the doubt in her words. Yaz kept walking. He watched her fingers trailing along the stones and wanted to ask if it was because she needed to confirm directions or if she simply needed to feel them. He was still coming to terms with the fact that she had such an ability. He had considered it before but quickly disregarded it. And why wouldn't he? Humans didn't have magic.

Until now.

Were there more humans with magic? Perhaps it was called something else. That could be why elves didn't know of it. But if humans had such abilities, they would alert the elves. Yaz hadn't wanted to impart her secret because she feared what might happen. But she had trusted him.

Ravi alternated between scanning the area around him and watching her. Whatever had happened to Yaz outside seemed to have passed, but he knew it could rear up again at any time. The past did that. Especially when it was as harrowing and atrocious as hers. He didn't know what Yaz had experienced during her time at Shaldorn, but he could guess.

She stopped before a door and knocked quietly. When there was no answer, she tried the handle. It turned beneath her hand. Ravi gently pushed her inside to get them out of the hallway, immediately checking the room to see if anyone was there.

"This is Neela's room," Yaz said.

Ravi had an uneasy feeling. "We can't stay here."

Instead of replying, Yasmin picked up a discarded shoe near the bed. She examined it closely, her brow furrowing. She let the shoe drop and walked to the wardrobe, flinging open the doors. Her hands yanked the clothes apart before she dropped her arms to her sides.

"What is it?" he asked.

"These aren't Neela's clothes. She was my height but very voluptuous. Her feet were as small as a child's." Yaz pointed to the shoe she'd dropped. "That is much bigger. And these clothes are for someone much taller."

Ravi strode to the door. "We need to go. Now."

Yasmin shut the wardrobe doors and hurried to him. She placed a hand on the stones for a heartbeat before looking at him and nodding. They exited the room quickly and headed in the opposite direction. There was no time to ask where they were going as Yasmin quickened her steps until she was nearly running. She skimmed her fingers along the stones before taking a sudden right.

He heard steps coming toward them and looked over his shoulder. A guard walked along the corridor behind them, focused on the food in his hand. They turned a corner, safely out of sight. They walked down another section before Yaz turned left down another hallway and then another. Finally, she walked through a door.

Ravi entered the dark room. A moment later, Yaz found the lights. Ravi was surprised at the various wardrobes and trunks filled with clothes. An open door was on the far wall.

"Take your pick," Yaz said.

He eyed the assortment. "What will you wear?"

"I'm still not sold on accompanying you."

He dug inside his pack until he found the small vial with the clear liquid and then held it out to her. "I've used this before. All the agents have. It works on elves and humans without any negative effects."

Yasmin looked at it silently.

"Durga suggested I bring it in case we needed to pass you off as an elf."

Blue eyes slid to him. "I know what it is. I've seen it sold in the market upstairs."

"That's impossible. No one has this other than the DIA."

"I've seen one of the guests take it and change from a Wood Elf to a Sea Elf. The spell only lasted a few hours, however."

Ravi glanced at the container between his fingers. "Our scientists worked on this for years to perfect the formula. It gave us an edge. If it's out there, then someone within our ranks betrayed us."

He shook his head to dispel those thoughts. Now wasn't the time for that. "Ours is a better formula. It lasts for an entire day."

"That does make me feel better. I'd hate to revert back to human in the middle of things."

"Durga had this mixed for you. I don't know if you'll keep your coloring or if it'll change your entire appearance. The point is, no one should recognize you once you take it."

"Are you sure?"

"I've used it many times."

She bit her lip.

Ravi was reminded of how much she detested elves. Changing into one might be as difficult for her as entering Shaldorn. "It's been years. I doubt anyone will recognize you as you are, but I understand your dislike of my kind. If—"

"What do I need to do?" she asked over him.

"Drink it. You'll feel the effects quickly."

Yaz blew out a breath. "Then I guess I need to find some clothes."

She walked to a wardrobe and began sorting through it. Ravi chose the first thing he found that looked like it would fit. Yaz took a little longer. He dropped his pack, ready to change.

"Not here," she said, heading through a second door he hadn't seen.

He picked up his pack and followed her into the next room. It held shelves of shoes and chests of jewelry. He found a pair of boots while Yaz rummaged for a while and set out her clothes. Finally, she beckoned him to follow her to yet another side door and into a chamber with two chairs, a toilet, a sink, and a mirror. He spotted a doorway and looked inside to find a square tub.

"We have to get the smell of the mountains off us," Yaz said as she took his clothes and laid them out on one of the chairs. "Everything we need is here. We should be left alone. Do you wish to bathe first?"

"You go," he told her.

He dropped his pack near the chair as she went into the next room and turned on the spout to fill the tub. He put his gloves, hat, and scarf into his bag, then removed and folded his coat. He sniffed it and wrinkled his nose before putting it away. Yaz was right. They did need to get the stink off.

Ravi made his way to the arched mirror and rested his hands on the edges of the square bowl atop the wooden table, while a spigot protruded from the tiled wall below the mirror before curving elegantly downward toward the sink. A tall, slim cabinet sat to the side. He opened the doors and looked at the different soaps, as well as some shaving cream and a razor.

Ravi glanced at himself in the mirror. He scratched at his beard before he grabbed what he needed and turned on the water. When he looked into the mirror again, he noticed that the door to the bathing chamber wasn't shut completely. He could see the tub through the gap. He stared, wondering, hoping to get a glimpse of Yaz. He had held her naked body, but he hadn't seen her.

He inwardly shook himself at his yearning and dragged his gaze away to begin the tedious process of removing his beard. It took longer than he remembered. Or perhaps he lingered on the chance he got to see Yaz.

After he'd rinsed his face, he patted it dry with a cloth as movement in the mirror caught his attention. His breath locked in his lungs when he caught sight of Yaz's leg extending from the tub. His blood heated, rushing straight to his cock as he ran his gaze upward from her foot to her calf and toned thigh, only to halt at her hip because of the drying cloth she held against her.

His balls tightened as need thrummed like fire in his veins. Ravi lowered his gaze to the sink and braced his hands on either side. A hunger unlike anything he'd ever known pumped through him. Images of her bare flesh pressed against him only amplified the longing. He recalled how his hand had rested on her lower back, his fingers gracing the curve at the base of her spine. He remembered her sigh and the way her lashes brushed his chest. He felt the phantom press of her breasts.

He squeezed his eyes closed as blood pounded in his ears. His cock was hard and aching. The sound of a door closing snapped his eyes open. He lifted his head and searched the room through the mirror. He was alone. His gaze darted to the doorway of the bathing chamber. The door was open, and there was no sign of Yaz.

Ravi straightened and turned on his heel. He stopped at the threshold and looked at the tub and its draining water. Then he glanced over his shoulder at the closed door on the opposite wall. Yaz must have gone there to change so he could bathe. He blew out a breath before walking to the tub. It was larger than he'd first thought. Big enough for two people. What would she have done if he'd suggested they share it?

"Fuck," he murmured and ran a hand down his face.

His palm met skin, jarring him from his musings. Ravi took a good look around the room. Nothing seemed out of place. Yaz must have put everything back as it had been without him having to tell her.

Ravi waited until the water was gone before he turned on the spout. As the tub filled again, he found soap and a drying cloth and stripped. He couldn't wait to get the past few days off him. He didn't wait for the tub to fill before climbing inside and quickly scrubbing himself. He would've enjoyed emptying out the dirty water and refilling it once more to lounge for a bit, but that would have to wait for another time.

He started the water draining as he dried himself. Afterward, he used the cloth to wipe down any water that had splashed. Then he replaced the soap. Only then did he grab his old clothes, fold them, and put them away in his bag. Once that was done, he dressed in the borrowed clothes, his gaze going to the closed door where Yaz had gone. He wondered who his clothes had belonged to. Or did those at Shaldorn have them lying about for anyone who might have need of them?

Ravi shifted his shoulders in the jacket. The elf he saw in the mirror seemed changed somehow. Nothing on the surface looked different, but he felt it. He grabbed a comb and raked it through his hair. He was debating whether to pull it back as usual when the door opened. His gaze locked on Yaz as she poked her head around the corner. Her eyes widened when she spotted him.

"Too much?" he asked, glancing down at his clothes.

He wondered what she thought as her gaze lingered on the long, dark green dress jacket with gold buttons and a high collar. The long-sleeved shirt beneath was the same shade of green, as were the trousers tucked into tall black boots.

"You look very handsome," she said as she approached.

Ravi's mind went blank when he caught sight of Yaz. She had chosen a gown in a soft purple. Not so light it could be called lavender, but too pale to be called purple. The *choli*, or blouse, stopped just beneath her breasts to expose her midriff. The sleeves covered her arms to below her elbows. The entire garment was covered in embroidered silver thread. The long, circular, flared skirt, or *lehenga*, had more of the silver embroidery starting at the waist and woven all the way to the hem. Draped across one shoulder was the sheer *dupatta* in the same soft purple, edged with embroidery.

Ravi's eyes lingered on the exposed portion of Yaz's stomach that highlighted the indent of her waist. He spotted the silver *jhumkas*, or large, bell-shaped earrings amid the long strands of her black hair. That's when he realized her hair was free of the braid and parted down the middle. A silver *maang tikka* ran along her part, with a crystal dangling against her forehead.

He fought the urge to reach out and stroke her hair. He hadn't even realized he had closed the distance between them. It took him a moment to find his voice. "You're a vision."

A quick grin flitted over her lips as she looked away.

Ravi couldn't stop staring. He cleared his throat and searched for the vial before handing it to her.

Her face gave nothing away as to what she was thinking. "What will this do to my... ability?"

"It doesn't interfere with elven magic. You should be fine."

"I hope so, because we're going to need the stones." She bit her lip before holding out her hand.

He set the bottle in her palm, letting his fingers linger on her skin for a heartbeat. When she hesitated, he repeated, "No one will recognize you."

"I hope you're right."

"Even if they do, I wouldn't let any harm come to you."

Their gazes met. "You wouldn't be able to stop them. No one can."

"I would." And he meant it.

She drew in a deep breath and slowly released it. Then she removed the stopper and tilted her head back, draining the vessel. Her face scrunched up as she swallowed then gagged. "Shite. That was horrible."

Ravi frowned. "I've never tasted anything."

She swayed. He instinctively reached for her, pulling her against him to steady her.

"You should sit," he said as he maneuvered her to the chair.

He spotted her bejeweled sandals after he lowered her and squatted beside her as she put her head in her hands.

"I don't feel so good," she mumbled.

26

The room was stifling. Anytime Yasmin opened her eyes, it swam around her, making her stomach revolt. A flash of heat rolled through her body.

"I've got you," Ravi said, winding his arms around her again. "Just breathe."

She was attempting that very thing, but every second, another place on her body screamed in agony. The song of the stones became so loud that it felt like her eardrums were about to explode. Yasmin covered her ears, but touching them became impossible. They burned and sizzled as if a hot poker were being held against them.

Yasmin had no idea how long she endured the torture before it finally began to ebb. When she opened her eyes, she was on the floor, leaning back against a strong, familiar chest while Ravi held her. She tipped her head to his shoulder and released a shuddering breath.

"Yaz?" His voice was laced with worry.

She looked down to find her hands holding his. It took effort to relax her fingers so they weren't digging into him, but she couldn't force herself to release him. "Aye."

"Fuck. You scared me."

"How long was I out?"

"Moments. I've never seen anyone have that kind of reaction."

"Do you have humans who take it?"

There was a beat of silence before he said, "I know they have, but I've never seen it."

"I see." She sat up and reluctantly let go of his hands.

"I was told there might be some pain but that it would be minimal."

"They lied." There was no heat in her words. It wasn't Ravi's fault.

He leaned to the side as he peered closely. "How do you feel?"

"Worse than I did after you revived me from drowning."

Relief crossed his face. He stood and held out his hands. "Are you ready to stand?"

She accepted his help and was soon on her feet. "How different do I look?" she asked when she couldn't stand his staring any longer.

"See for yourself," he said and turned her to the mirror.

Yasmin kept her gaze down as she walked to the sink. Her heart thumped wildly in her chest. When she was little, she had dreamed of being an elf. Would she be a Wood Elf? Maybe a Sun Elf. Or even a Sea Elf? After all these years, she would finally get to find out.

Slowly, she lifted her gaze until she stared back at a reflection that was her but different.

Her hair was no longer black but a deep blue. Her eyes were

such a light shade of blue they were nearly white. Her skin was paler and now had a silver tint. Those weren't the only differences, though. Pointed ears stuck out of her hair.

She reached up and touched one of them. Sensations coursed through her body at the simple stroke. She ran her fingers over her cheek, mesmerized by the silver sheen of her skin. It brought out the embroidery in her attire. It was like she glowed from within.

Her gaze shifted to meet Ravi's in the mirror as she dropped her arm. "When I was a child, I used to imagine what I might look like as one of you."

"You look good as a Moon Elf. How do you feel about it?"

"I don't know." And that was the truth.

She used to believe that if she had been born an elf, she wouldn't have had the problems she did, but as an adult, she knew that everyone had something to bear. Would things have been different had she been an elf? Maybe. There were never any certainties about anything.

"May I?" Ravi held out his hand, showing the silver tips.

Yasmin nodded. She gripped the sink when he gently slid first one and then the other onto the points of her ears. She needed to see all of herself. She walked to the dressing room and studied herself in the full-length mirror leaning against the wall. The purple hue blended nicely with the silver and blue of her coloring. She didn't recognize herself. Surely, no one else would. She could stand there all night and stare in wonder, but they had work to do. When she turned to look for Ravi, he stood leaning a shoulder against the doorframe, watching her.

"Can I pass for an elf?" she asked.

He pushed away from the door and closed the distance between them. "I think you could do anything you want. But, aye, you more than pass as an elf." A small frown marred his features when she touched her ears. "Are they bothering you?"

"The stones became louder than I've ever heard them during the process."

"And now? Can you hear them?"

Panic clutched Yasmin's chest. She had been so focused on her appearance that she hadn't thought about her ability. With determined steps, she made her way to the wall and put her hand on the stones. She immediately heard their hum. She silently asked them if it was clear to leave. Their answer was instantaneous.

"I can," she told him with a smile. "It's clear. We should make our way upstairs."

"You said there are guards at every stairway. How will we get past them?"

She grinned. "Some staff are meant to be seen, but many are not. There are hidden passages throughout Shaldorn so they can move about."

"And they don't have guards watching them?"

"Everything is guarded."

He gave her a pointed look. "How will we get past them?"

"I'll get us past." She walked out, leaving Ravi to catch up to her.

"Yaz," he said in a low, warning tone.

"The voices are already getting louder above. We don't have time to waste."

"You don't have a plan, do you?"

Not yet, but hopefully she would by the time they reached the main floor. The stones once more led her through the corridors to one of the hidden passageways. The top of Ravi's head brushed the ceiling and he had to bend slightly, but they weren't in it for long.

They exited into another hall. Yasmin held them back as staff hurried past without noticing them. Then she led them to the left and up a flight of stairs before halting.

"What is it?" Ravi whispered in her ear.

She shivered at the feel of his breath against her cheek. "On the other side of that door is where we need to be."

"I'm guessing there's a guard there."

"There is."

"Will he leave?"

She shook her head. Her hair felt odd against her new, pointed ears.

"Some guests came a day or so early, aye?"

His hand was near hers on the railing. She looked at his long fingers, recalling how they had held her. "Aye."

"Have any of them ever ventured into the staff area?"

"On occasion." She turned to look at him over her shoulder as she realized his plan. "Brilliant."

He grinned, and she was conscious of just how close they were.

Yasmin cleared her throat and turned around. "We'll play innocent."

"I had another idea."

"Oh?"

He walked around her on the stairs. "Do you trust me?"

Funny how a few days before, the answer would have been a firm *nay*. "I do."

Ravi held out his arm. She didn't hesitate to put her hand against his large palm. He held her as they walked up the last few steps. He leaned back against the wall and tugged her closer. Yasmin's heart beat double time as she found herself standing between his legs. He placed her hand on his chest before he loosely set his on her waist, his fingertips touching bare skin. Shivers raced over her flesh at the contact.

"We could do as you suggested and say we got lost," he said softly. "Or…"

"Or?" she prompted when he didn't elaborate.

His gaze dropped to her mouth. "Or…we could get caught."

It took a moment for his words to register and decipher what he meant. He wanted them to get caught kissing. The thought sent a thrill through her. She would finally know what it was to kiss Ravi.

"I'll act surprised when this door isn't one to a bedroom," Ravi continued. "We just need to look flushed with desire."

That certainly wouldn't be a problem since that's exactly what she was. She nodded in agreement as she looked at his mouth.

"Just play along," Ravi urged.

She had no time to respond as he laughed loudly and banged his elbow against the door. "We're almost there, love. Then you're all mine."

Ravi went to turn the handle when the door flew open. A guard stood above them, his frown intense as he eyed Ravi and then her. Yasmin quickly looked away for fear the guard would recognize her.

"Apologies," Ravi said as he tugged her against his side. "We snuck away to find some alone time. I think we took a wrong turn."

"You're in the staff area," the guard stated.

Ravi swung his head to her and ran a finger along the side of her face. "We've been thwarted, but not for long." He turned his attention to the guard. "Can you show us the right direction to the main area?"

Yasmin remained silent as the guard directed them. Ravi kept his fingers intertwined with hers as they walked away. Once they turned the corner, she expected him to release her, but he didn't. She breathed a sigh of relief.

"He didn't know me," she whispered.

Ravi grinned. "Told you." He scanned the area. There were only a handful of people. "Where to now?"

Yasmin didn't need to ask the stones which way. She and Ravi were mixed in with the other guests. Eyes darted their way. She knew she looked different, but she couldn't stop wondering if someone would still recognize her.

"Keep walking," she said.

Ravi took her hand and looped it into the crook of his arm. They continued down the corridor toward the sound of conversation and music. The closer they got, the harder it was for Yasmin to continue walking.

Ravi's hand covered hers on his arm. "You can do this."

She squared her shoulders. She had promised him that she would be fine. She shot him a smile as they entered Shaldorn's main greeting area. There was a dazzling display of clothes and jewels from males and females alike. Food and drink flowed freely as guests mingled about the room.

Alongside them were staff members. Those moving through the throng wearing all white and holding the highly polished trays with beverages and fare were unseen by the guests. Yasmin's gaze latched onto a human boy about Sameer's age who had to hurriedly step out of the way as one of the guests backed into him and nearly caused him to drop the tray.

Then there were the other staff members. Those in the same attire as her and the other guests in attendance. The only difference was that they were human and marked as Shaldorn's property. Yasmin stopped herself from touching the tattoo on her neck when Ravi turned to face her.

"Don't," he whispered, bringing her hand to his lips and kissing her knuckles.

How had he known what she was about? Was it etched on her face?

He steered her toward one of the giant pillars and turned her back to it. He searched her gaze. "Forget the mark. You aren't that person tonight."

27

Ravi never should've put his mouth to Yaz's skin. Now, all he wanted to do was lower his head and place his lips against hers. He'd nearly done it in the stairwell when she looked at him with a flicker of surprise and a flash of longing that sent blood straight to his cock. The temptation had been heady, his desire thick.

Then he remembered that she was acting a part. They were both supposed to be performing. And that was the problem.

Ravi wasn't.

He had to get ahold of himself. He knew better than to let his emotions in while on assignment. Obtaining the device was his goal. Nothing—and no one—could get in the way of that. Not even Yaz.

"You're playing a part," Ravi said, as much to her as him. "The person you were outside these walls doesn't exist tonight."

Her lips softened into a smile for the benefit of a couple passing them. "I understand."

He leaned closer so his mouth was next to her ear. Anyone watching them would think they shared an intimate moment. He inhaled the scent of sandalwood that lingered on her skin from the bath and briefly closed his eyes as it spread through his body. This ache for her was growing out of control.

"You watched these people for years," he whispered. "You know their actions, their movements. Become whoever you want to be."

Her head turned slightly toward him, her mouth brushing his cheek. "Is this what you do? You become different people?"

"When it calls for it." He leaned back to meet her gaze. He missed the deep blue color of her eyes.

"How do you not forget who you are after being so many others?"

Ravi glimpsed a tray bearing drinks coming close. He stopped the woman and grabbed two glasses, handing one to Yaz. "I've never thought about that."

She quirked a brow, her look suggesting she didn't believe him. Yaz took a sip and said, "You've played a part since we left the city?"

"Nay," he said, sharper than intended. "There was no need."

He watched the glass touch her lips as she took another drink. Ravi tore his gaze from her and scanned the room. The floor was quartz cut in diamond shapes with smaller diamond-shaped onyx situated between them. Six enormous obsidian columns towered over them, supporting the elaborately painted ceiling above.

The grand salon was large and brightly lit from every angle to show off the beauty of the room and its occupants. Sconces lined the walls, and a colossal chandelier hung from the ceiling. Standing candelabras edged the room.

He took a closer look at the walls, noting the many doorways. He spotted stairs leading upward. He lifted his gaze to the second and third floors above, each with a balcony that ran the circumference of the main area. Yaz had said people watched from above. He saw many of them leaning on the iron railings, drinks in hand. He couldn't see faces. Once out of the room, the lights became dim. The main salon was the place to be seen. Everywhere else was where things happened. Deals, trades, and other transactions. All of it turned his stomach.

Ravi swept his gaze around the people near him and saw a male ogling Yaz, displaying flagrant interest. The Sea Elf grinned at Ravi and motioned to the Wood Elf on his arm. In answer, Ravi turned his back to them and led Yaz away.

"We should make a round," she said behind her drink.

He rolled his shoulders to take out the tension. They kept smiles on their faces, nodding to others as they walked. Ravi knew any of those in attendance could be the ones who had constructed the device or the ones purchasing it. Dain's undercover operative had only given them a name. A single name. Kumar. They didn't know if he was the buyer or the seller.

"That is a lovely color on you," said a voice.

Ravi was pulled from his thoughts as they paused so Yaz could speak to the female. As the two of them exchanged compliments, Ravi found himself nodding to the Sun Elf opposite him. "Brutal weather outside. We're glad to be out of it."

"Us, too," the male said. "I'm Manish."

"Nice to meet you. I'm Navin, and this is Abha," Ravi said. "This is our first time in attendance."

That caught the female's attention. She shot them a wide smile.

"Is it? There's so much to experience. I recommend the orange room."

Yaz stiffened slightly beside him. He put a hand over hers on his arm. "I've heard of that. Is it really what I think it is?"

"If you mean a roomful of naked bodies waiting to please you, then aye," the female said. She looked Yasmin up and down. "I think the two of us could have fun together." Then she looked at Ravi and her companion. "As well as all four of us."

Ravi nodded, keeping a smile in place. "That sounds enticing."

"We did say we would try anything," Yaz said as she met his gaze.

"Perfect," the female said. "We have to make the rounds. Manish must speak to his friends before we have any fun."

Manish gave her a crooked smile. "The meeting won't take long. Look, Kumar is already here."

At the mention of the name, Ravi looked in the direction Manish pointed. Ravi couldn't make out who Kumar was.

"We'll find you shortly," the female stated as they walked away.

"Did you see Kumar?" Ravi asked in a soft voice.

Yaz shook her head. "Who is that?"

"That's the name of the person I'm looking for. Shite. I've lost the couple amid all the people."

"Let's keep walking," she suggested. "Maybe we'll find them again."

Ravi guided her through the room. It wasn't long before it began to thin as others made their way upstairs into the different rooms. But there was still a large crowd in the salon. They hadn't spotted Manish and his companion again, which meant Ravi hadn't gotten eyes on Kumar. They could be anywhere. He looked up.

"They won't go up yet," Yaz stated.

He glanced her way. "How can you be sure?"

"I know this place. Now, wipe that frown away and smile. You're supposed to be having a good time."

He finished his drink and waved to a passing staff member. The human girl paused long enough for him to set his empty glass on the tray. Yaz placed hers on it, as well.

"Hello," Yaz said to the girl. "Where is Neela? I heard she was someone I needed to see."

The girl's dark brown eyes jerked to Ravi before she answered. "Neela is gone."

"Gone? Gone where?" Yaz pressed.

Ravi looked at Yaz because he knew what was coming. He had deduced as much when they'd visited Neela's old room.

The girl swallowed. "She's dead. She died four years ago."

Yaz said nothing more, and the girl walked on. Ravi maneuvered them to a semi-secluded spot. He sensed Yasmin's shock and regretted not saying something sooner about her friend. He'd forgotten about it until Yaz mentioned her. "Do you need another drink?"

"Neela's dead. Because of me."

"You don't know that."

Yaz snapped her light blue eyes up at him. "I do."

"Then get your revenge."

"Oh, I plan to."

She tugged him to continue walking. Once out among the crowd, she put away her anger. They sampled some delicious food. His stomach rumbled for more after having only dried meat for so long. He looked around. Each Dark he spotted made him wonder if it was the undercover elf. Or had they disguised themselves as

Yaz had? Ravi didn't want to blow their cover, but he might need to do it to secure the device.

He and Yaz talked to other people as they moved about the room. It wasn't until he heard a loud *dong* reverberating that Yasmin faltered. He looked at her to find her gaze locked on something. Ravi followed her line of sight and saw a woman being led out by two guards, with two more behind her. Her hair was pulled back to show her rounded ears, just like all the other staff.

The four guards brought the woman to a stop in the middle of the salon. Everyone gathered around, voices rising in excitement. A disembodied male voice from somewhere above began the bidding process. The offers came quickly as they vied for the woman.

"There's no reason to stay. We should head up to the second floor," Yaz suggested.

Ravi led her to one of the two sets of stairs on either side of the salon. Everything in Shaldorn was done on a massive scale, and the stairs were no exception. They were white quartz with a solid black runner down the middle.

"Not much has changed," she said as they walked up to the second level.

He glanced below at the woman being sold as the bidding came to an end. "What will become of her?"

"It wasn't announced beforehand, meaning whoever wins will get to decide what they wish to do."

Ravi glanced at Yaz. Her voice gave nothing away, and neither did her face. But her tight grip on his arm was another story. "Once we get the device, we'll return and end all of this."

"That is a nice thought," she said with a smile.

"Someone needs to do something."

She briefly met his gaze and nodded. "I agree. But you can't end evil like this. It might be snuffed out for a short while, but it always returns. One way or another."

In all the years he had been fighting to stop crimes in Shecrish, he knew how true her words were. That didn't mean he would let it continue.

They carried on along the perimeter of the second-story balcony. Soft music continued to play, and more conversation milled around him. A person had been sold below, and no one cared.

"The market is to the right," Yaz said.

They walked so closely together that their bodies brushed again and again, making him yearn for more. He turned her to the right and proceeded down a wide hallway that opened into another larger corridor. The market was just as she had said. Booths were set up along the walls from one end to the other.

As they passed, he saw many things being offered for sale. Ancient swords probably stolen from wealthier households. Modern blades crafted specifically for the Asavori Rangers, impossible to come by unless someone was at Shaldorn's market. His steps slowed when he reached a booth with dozens of the same containers he had given Yaz earlier.

"Careful," she whispered.

He flashed her a grin to let her know he was in control. The booth's owner was all too happy to explain what the vials were and how they worked.

Ravi raised a brow. "Are you telling me that yellow one would make me look human?"

"I am," the Wood Elf behind the table declared with a wide smile. He leaned forward and lowered his voice. "I have no idea why anyone would want to be human, but some elves like to indulge in such things. If they want it, I supply it," he replied with a shrug.

Ravi studied the table and the colored liquid in each tiny container. "You craft these potions?"

The Wood Elf laughed, flashing white teeth. "I have my hand in some things, but I'm not the scientist behind it. There are others for that."

Ravi grunted.

"Most of these will be gone by the end of the night. Get it now or wait until the next gathering. If I have any then. I never know what I'll bring with me."

Yasmin lifted her face to his. "I may wish to try one, too."

The Wood Elf's smile widened as he looked between them, his excitement for a transaction evident. "I have a special price for couples. Second vial is half off."

"We'll think about it." Ravi turned away and put the elf's face to memory.

They hadn't gone far when Yasmin nudged him and said his name. Ravi followed her gaze and spotted Manish and his companion from earlier. Next to them stood a Sun Elf surrounded by bodyguards.

"I think we found our target," Yaz whispered.

Ravi zeroed in on the Sun Elf. "Let's find out."

28

Yasmin had walked Shaldorn's rooms many times. She had witnessed grand entrances that turned heads, but no one dominated a room like Ravi. He was striking in his dark green attire, which highlighted his golden skin and hair.

And others noticed.

Both male and female gazes followed him, raking over him from head to toe with lustful appreciation. She had done the same herself earlier. Ravi wasn't dressed any better than others in attendance. He simply wore the clothes better. As if he had been born to the world of wealth and privilege.

She glanced at him, noting the ease in which he walked among the splendor and depravity. How others moved out of his way without him uttering a word. He might be used to moving in criminal circles with his job, but fitting in among the rich was something else altogether.

His long fingers lifted her hand from his arm before he sidled closer and rested his palm on the bare skin of her back. Heat spread through her, his touch like a brand. He held out a hand across them to halt a female who had been about to back into Yasmin. The elf hurriedly apologized before looking at Ravi. Her lips softened, and desire flared in her eyes. Yasmin looked at Ravi to see if he'd noted her reaction, but his gaze was elsewhere. And the satisfaction that gave Yasmin should've caused her alarm.

Ravi deftly moved them down the corridor. Yasmin was all too aware of his hard body continually brushing against her while her skirts tangled around his legs. She knew what it was like to lay naked against him, to have him curled around her body. All of it was branded in her mind.

And on her soul.

Her dreams were filled with him. Running her palms over his firm body. Wrapping her hands around his arousal to feel his heat and hardness. Taking him into her mouth and bringing him to orgasm as he called out her name. Him thrusting into her as he claimed her mouth.

But that was all it would ever be. Fantasies. Fiction. A dream.

Their steps slowed, and Yasmin put away such thoughts to focus on those around her. Ravi moved them behind the couple they'd met downstairs. They were close enough to hear the conversation but situated so that neither Manish nor his companion could see her or Ravi. To the left of the couple was Ravi's potential target, Kumar. Yasmin noticed the elves steps away from Kumar, eyeing everyone as a threat.

Ravi didn't linger. He guided her away as they continued to pretend as if they were perusing the various vendors. A muscle jumped in his jaw when he saw the merchant who had human children for sale. No matter how many times Yasmin witnessed the kids' empty expressions, it always cut her to the bone.

They didn't stop. Not even when the merchant tried to wave them over after noticing their attention. Ravi reached the end of the hall, and they turned to wander up the other side. They had both gone quiet. She could imagine what he was thinking about Shaldorn. No matter how far she had gotten from the stronghold, no matter how often she scrubbed herself raw, the stench of Shaldorn still clung to her.

"Was it Kumar?" she whispered.

Ravi turned his head toward her and dipped his chin. "I didn't hear a name. He had men with him."

"I noted the bodyguards. Four, right?"

"Six. There were two others farther away. One of them near Kumar eyed me suspiciously. We couldn't linger."

"Let me get close. I won't bring nearly the attention you do."

"Every eye in here is on you."

She snorted as they came to a halt. "They're looking at you."

Their gazes met, and a half smile curved one side of his lips. "I know for a fact they aren't."

"I don't know who you're looking at, but I can point to at least ten people looking at you."

He dipped his head toward her as he briefly looked around. "I see them looking at you."

"We were supposed to blend in. I think we missed that mark."

His copper eyes sparked as he chuckled. "I blend in."

"Are you saying I don't?" she teased, needing a moment to push away the darkness that threatened to envelop her.

"I'm saying that you're beautiful." His voice dropped to barely a whisper as he added, "Elf or human."

Her heart missed a beat.

He wound his finger around a strand of her hair that had fallen over her shoulder. Their gazes held as tension grew.

If she didn't think of something to say, she would pull his head down for a kiss. How was it that he had the ability to make her forget where she was? For just a moment, it had only been the two of them. And it had been wonderful. She didn't want it to end, but it had to. At least for now.

"I've watched a lot of people in my life. Those who have been raised with wealth move about that community easily. Like you," she pointed out.

He shot her a lopsided grin as he released her hair. He briefly looked over her head in Kumar's direction. "My father inherited a tidy sum. We moved about those circles, but both of my parents were scientists and would rather spend time in academia than with anything else."

"You mean you."

"Aye," he replied with a half-hearted shrug. "I got in the way, and they liked to throw money at me to get me to occupy myself. I was doing just that when Durga found me."

Yasmin liked how he moved a fraction closer, so their lower bodies touched. "I'm sorry."

"I'm not." He smiled, his expression genuine. "Things worked out as they were supposed to."

She glanced down at his chest to the gold button with the mandala design.

"They're moving," he murmured.

"Let me get close. I can do this," she assured him.

Ravi guided her forward so they could make their way back to Kumar, who now stood at the railing looking down at the salon below.

"You need this," she pushed when he didn't answer. "Don't you trust me?"

Ravi blew out a breath and kept his voice low. "It isn't about trust."

"Then you don't think I can get close."

"It's about putting you so close to danger, and me not being able to get to you in time."

Her stomach fluttered in delight at his words. "I'm not without skills."

"I need you to get us out."

That speedily extinguished the elation. She kept her smile in place, but it felt hard, brittle. Thank the gods he wasn't looking at her. She didn't want him to see how his words could cut so deeply.

"Don't worry. I'll get you out." They reached the group then.

Without another word to Ravi, she sidestepped out of his grip and slipped away, moving through the crowd like a shadow. She swallowed, his words reverberating in her head. It would behoove her to remember that everything he did and said was for his *character*. He was only after one thing, and it wasn't her. She might look like an elf tonight, but it would wear off soon enough. Then she would be human again, and it would be like none of this had ever happened.

All of it confirmed that she needed to get away from Shecrish. She needed her own people. She needed to *belong*.

To someone.

Or somewhere.

Yasmin felt a hand touch her arm as she passed a female. She nodded at the elf but didn't tarry. Yasmin continued to weave her way through the gathering. It wasn't long before a male attempted to stop her. She kept walking. She heard talk about her after she passed, but she didn't care. The elf she was pursuing was too important.

In her past life at Shaldorn, she would've had to stop and speak to all who sought her attention. She would've had to smile, laugh, and act interested. She would've had to flirt and permit them to touch her wherever and however they wished. This time around, her body was hers. So were her thoughts and actions. Everyone here sickened her.

She fisted her hands and wished she had her dagger. Though it was better that she didn't lest she pull it out and start cutting throats. Would anyone even miss this wretched, immoral mob? She doubted it.

The closer she got to her target, the more clustered the crowd. It was as if everyone was drawn to him. Yasmin got as close as she could to the railing before the mass of bodies stopped her. She tried to push through, but no one would let her past. Finally, she blew out a breath and tapped a male on the shoulder. The Dark Elf turned around.

She flashed him a bright smile. "Excuse me. May I get around you?"

His yellow eyes looked her over before he nodded. As she passed, he trailed his fingers along her back where Ravi's hand had previously been. It was all Yasmin could do to keep moving forward and not knock his hand away. Little by little, she got through the crowd until she was at the balustrade.

She glanced to the left and then the right, shocked to see that she was next to a bodyguard with Kumar on the other side of him. The Sun Elf saw her looking and smiled before bowing his head of short blond hair. She demurely lowered her eyes before returning her gaze to him. His attention was drawn to his other side with conversation, but his gaze returned to her.

Yasmin would definitely gloat when she brought Ravi information.

A lot.

Her smile froze when her gaze dropped to the main floor. A buzz of excitement ran through the crowd as guards wheeled out a tall, narrow, clear box. Her blood pounded in her ears as they sat the case upright.

Yasmin couldn't look away, even though that's what she wanted to do. She was trapped, caught. Stuck. She knew what was coming, and there was nothing she could do about it. No way to stop it.

The room swam. Her palms were damp, and her knees threatened to buckle. She tried to back up and leave but bodies prevented her from going anywhere. Then guards roughly hauled out a woman dressed in all white.

And she didn't go quietly.

She fought with everything she had, kicking and biting while cursing everyone.

It became difficult for Yasmin to draw breath into her lungs as she watched everything play out as if a nightmare had come to life. A guard unlocked a door in the box. They brought the woman toward it. One of the guards backhanded her, and she went lax instantly.

Yasmin nearly touched her cheek. She knew the feel of such a blow, how it reverberated through the cheekbone and then down the jaw and across the entire head. With the woman dazed, the guards stripped her and threw her into the container. Her arms were at odd angles, and her light brown hair hung in her face. Then they closed and locked the door.

There was nowhere for the woman to move now, no way for her lungs to expand to take a full breath. No way for her to move her hair or scratch an itch. She would be stuck like that for however long the Trinity deemed it. A few hours, maybe. Or longer. There were small holes drilled at the top for air, but they had covered it before to let spectators watch someone slowly suffocate.

Yasmin knew the humiliation of being in the box, the pain.

The abject terror.

She wanted to look away. She tried, but she couldn't. She had returned to a place of wickedness, and now she was one of the onlookers. And she was doing nothing to stop it. Didn't that make her as bad as them?

"Breathe," said a familiar voice in her ear.

Ravi's arms wrapped around her as he stood at her back like a barricade.

"Breathe," he whispered again.

But she couldn't. Because she was the one in the box now, seeing others laughing and pointing at her. Delighting in her misfortune and discomfort.

She became aware of Ravi pulling at her fingers that gripped the balustrade. Then all she saw was his chest. One moment, they were at the guardrail, and the next, they were in a dark corner with his hands cupping her face. She reached for him, needing to have something solid to hold on to.

"Yaz. I need you to look at me," he bade.

It took a moment to focus on him, then locked on to his copper eyes.

"Good. Breathe with me. You're hyperventilating. Slow breath in."

She followed his example.

"Now release it gradually." He nodded as they breathed out together. "Good. Again."

Yasmin did as he instructed until the panicky feeling began to loosen its hold. He kept his hands on either side of her head. She didn't know what she enjoyed more, his fingers in her hair or their warmth.

She tried to look away as embarrassment filled her, but he refused to allow it. "You don't have to say it."

His thumb gently caressed near her mouth. "They put you in that box, didn't they?"

Her eyes burned with tears. The words lodged in her throat, leaving her no choice but to nod.

"I'm sorry," he whispered.

"It's in the past."

His gaze moved softly over her face. "I brought you to the past."

"You had to." To her surprise, she realized she had fisted her hands in his jacket. She glanced down, wishing there were no clothes between them.

It was nice to stand with him, alone and separate from the horrors a few steps away. She studied his mouth. He dropped one of his hands to her waist. With the other, he skimmed the pads of his fingers along her jaw, leaving a trail of heat in their wake.

Ravi's head lowered. Her lips parted eagerly. She needed to feel alive, and there was only one person she wanted to touch her. Time stood still as they drew together. Her lids fell shut as she waited for his lips to meet hers.

The moment was shattered by a loud cheer that filled Shaldorn. Ravi jerked upright, trying to figure out what was happening. But she knew.

"They covered her air holes," she told him.

He looked down at her as anger gradually filled his gaze. "This place needs to be destroyed."

She wanted nothing more. But at the moment, she feared she might never get free. If Ravi hadn't found her, she…she wasn't sure what would've happened, and she didn't want to find out. "I was close to the target, but I didn't hear his name."

Ravi's lips thinned. "It's him. I heard his name when I was looking for you."

29

The color was gradually returning to Yaz's face. She had been so pale, her breathing so labored that he feared she would faint. He hadn't panicked when she slipped from his grasp. That didn't occur until he realized what was happening below. He had suspected it might affect Yaz, but he hadn't comprehended to what extent until he saw the horror on her face.

He'd shoved everyone out of his way to get to her, uncaring about the attention put on him or the commotion he caused. All that mattered was getting to Yaz. And when he finally reached her, she had been so lost in her head that she hadn't known it was him. She had such a death grip on the railing, he'd had to pry her fingers loose, one by one.

He should've felt better once he reached her, but that wasn't the case. The only thing he could do was take her away from the scene below. When he turned around, the mob of people instantly moved out of his way. He'd done his best to shield Yaz from them, talking loudly about her consumption of alcohol so no one would think she was upset about the woman below. The way Yaz stumbled in a daze helped, but he couldn't be sure if anyone believed him.

Thankfully, most were more interested in witnessing the female's humiliation and didn't pay much attention to him. Ravi was able to find them a quiet place, but Yaz was lost to him. Nothing he said got her attention. Not until he held her face between his hands. It wasn't until her eyes finally focused on him that he felt any relief. Then he began to pull her back from the brink.

Breath by breath, he watched the darkness fade from her.

The stark fear that had taken him had been all too real. He hated how it ran through him like sludge, eating at him from the inside out. It had been seconds, but it felt like an eternity. He shouldn't have held her face like a lover. It came too close to the things he dreamed of doing to her. It didn't matter that her fingers latched onto him as if he were all that kept her from drowning. Or that she gazed up at him as if he were her hero. He had no right to touch her. Even if he longed for it to be otherwise.

Ravi was compromised. He knew it, but nothing could be done about it. He'd let his emotions rule him before, and it had nearly cost him his life. He'd sworn never to be in that position again. Yet inexplicably, it had happened somehow. Without his knowledge or consent.

He cared for Yaz.

More than he should.

More than she would likely allow.

But how did he stop the feelings that careened out of control?

Did he even want to? He asked himself that over and over as they gazed at each other. Then she leaned in to him, her lips parting. He wanted to kiss her, longed for it more than he could remember yearning for anything. He couldn't stop himself even if he wanted. And he didn't want to.

Joyful shouting broke through his haze. Ravi straightened and looked out at the crowd. Everyone was interested in an innocent's death. A human woman at the mercy of elves, stripped of her clothing and dignity and thrown into a box so slender the guards had to shove her into it. It would be a long, horrible death.

Many questions filled his mind, but he couldn't find the words to ask Yaz any of them. Besides, he wasn't sure he wanted the answers. Yaz knew what the female was about to endure. It made Ravi want to unleash his vengeance on everyone taking part in such a barbaric event.

And he wanted to take Yaz far from Shaldorn and erase its existence from her mind.

It was a silly thought. Nothing could remove memories. He should know. He had tried.

"Ravi?"

He briefly closed his eyes and swiveled his head to Yaz. The frightened, vulnerable woman was gone. The strong, unshakable one stood before him once more. How had he not seen beneath her veneer of irritable indifference for what it was? How had he not realized she had been doing her best to shield herself from more harm?

There had been plenty of opportunities for her to ruin the mission and get away. No one ever would've found out. Instead, she had kept her word. He had laughed when she first told him her oath meant something to her. He hadn't believed it. But she had proven him wrong with every step that brought her to the one place in all the realm she didn't want to be. Ravi wasn't sure if he could've done the same in her shoes.

Yaz had more internal fortitude than a hundred elves. She deserved more. So very much more than what she had gotten so far.

"What is it?" Yaz pressed when he remained silent.

It wasn't as if he could tell her. He had to shove aside his emotions and bury them beneath the mountains they had crossed. For both their sake's. Otherwise, he could get them killed. Maybe he would be able to embrace his emotions once more someday. But that wasn't now.

"I'm thinking," he said as he scanned those around them. "Are you still sure about the location?"

"I can only go by what I knew when I was here."

He held out his arm to her. Their eyes briefly met before she tucked her hand into the crook of his elbow once more. "Let's go."

Ravi kept his attention on the guards and anyone else who looked like a threat. The problem was everyone at Shaldorn was a threat, be they guard or guest. If they ran into trouble, no one would help. He wasn't even sure the undercover elf would show themselves with the likes of those in attendance.

"There is only one set of stairs leading up to the third floor—at least one that's visible. There's a second, but it's hidden from prying eyes," Yaz said in a low voice as they walked.

"Perfect for a clandestine meeting."

"The stairway will be guarded. We can't take it." She motioned to the set of steps that led to the third floor. "We'll have to take those."

He shifted them as they walked around a group still ogling the woman in the box. He studied Yaz and caught her glancing down into the salon. He knew what she was thinking. It was the same thing he was. The human had a little time before her air ran out. Yaz wanted to save her. He did, too. The odds of that happening, however, were unlikely.

And he didn't have the heart to tell Yaz that.

They reached the stairs, where guards stood on either side, watching everyone pass. Yaz ignored them, but Ravi gave each a surreptitious glance. There were no visible weapons, but that didn't mean the guards didn't have any.

He waited until they were halfway up before asking, "Do you know how many will be in the room?"

"I've never been in one when such a deal was taking place, but there are usually guards inside." Her fingers tightened on his arm. "Things might have changed."

"Don't second-guess yourself. You know this place. Which room?"

She shot him a glare. "It has been four years."

"How many things changed when you were here?"

"Few."

"Then I doubt they would now. Which room, Yaz?"

She blew out a breath and moved closer. "It won't be easy to get to. We certainly won't be able to merely walk up to the door."

He eyed her. She would make an excellent operative. "I gather you have an idea?"

"Maybe." She motioned to a wall and led him to it.

They pressed the left side of their bodies against it and looked cautiously around. They stood together intimately, her hands on his chest, his at her waist. Their faces breaths apart as they looked into each other's eyes.

"Tell me," he urged.

She glanced at his mouth, making his blood heat.

"Directly across from us is a hallway where our target should walk past after coming up the hidden stairs. We'll briefly see them before they head into the secure room. It could give us an idea of how many Kumar has with him."

Ravi located the place she referred to. "Got it."

"You've seen how huge this place is. You've seen the number of guards," she continued.

"The ones in uniform. There are others I suspect are disguised. I know my target has those."

"Exactly. My point is, getting out of here will be nearly impossible."

He flexed his fingers on her hip before dragging his hand upward to touch her bare flesh above the waist of her skirt. He returned his gaze to her. Her hands spread up his chest. "Nothing is impossible. The stones will help you lead us out."

"If we aren't caught."

"We won't get caught."

She dropped her gaze to his chest for a moment, smoothing the material she had clutched earlier. "We'll be going into a room full of elves. The moment they see us, they'll not hesitate to draw weapons and use magic."

It was a reminder that he hadn't seen the sun in hours, which meant his magic wouldn't come as easily. It was always there, but the sun made it easier to command. "I'm not unprepared."

"Neither am I," Yaz said and held up a cylinder.

Ravi frowned as he looked at the gray liquid within. He remembered seeing one of the weapons vendors selling it. "Where did you get that?"

"Sticky fingers, remember?" she replied with a grin. "I thought we might need some additional help. This will create smoke for us to disappear. At least, that's what I heard the vendor telling someone."

He dug into his pocket to withdraw a tiny urn that fit into the palm of his hand. "You aren't the only one with skills."

Her eyes crinkled at the corners as her smile widened. "I didn't see that one. What does it do?"

"If the vendor can be believed, it creates a storm."

"What kind of storm?"

He shrugged. "That, I don't know."

"Will it be enough?"

"It'll have to be. We don't have time to steal anything else."

"True." She looked into his eyes. "We only have one shot at this. We'd better get it right."

He wondered when it had gone from *him* securing the device to *them*. Not that he minded. He wasn't sure Yaz was even aware of what she had said. "First, we need to have a place to meet up if we get separated."

"It's highly doubtful we'll be able to steal the device without it alerting others. Shaldorn will shut down. Literally. The doors and windows will be locked, and no one will get out."

"There's always a way out."

Yaz gave him a shrewd smile. "There is. I saw it once. It was long ago, but I think I can get us there again. We'll have to get to the staff level first. And that will be the challenge. The instant the alarms sound, it's going to be chaos."

"Exactly. Everyone will be running around. That'll help us blend when we're making our getaway."

"There's a door directly below us on the main floor. It leads to the staff level. We'll meet there."

"If we get split up."

She bit her lip. "About that. I have an idea."

Ravi listened as she laid out her plan. There were times he walked into a building knowing little more than where the exits were located and where he needed to be. He was good at improvising, but this wasn't that sort of assignment. This was the kind that needed a plan, and Yaz had a good one.

"Are you sure about this?" he asked.

She gave him a firm nod. "My part isn't much. You're doing the majority."

That wasn't exactly true. Yaz intended to put herself front and center, the place he should be.

"Do you have another plan?"

He shook his head. "Not a good enough one."

"There isn't time to think of another. Look," she urged.

He glanced over to see their target followed by bodyguards passing across the hall, just as she had predicted. Whatever arguments Ravi had dissolved. It was time to put her plan into motion. Then, before he thought better of it, he briefly pressed his lips to hers. He didn't allow himself to linger, or he might never stop kissing her. "Stay safe," he whispered.

"I will. Be careful," she replied softly.

And though it went against everything he wanted, he walked away. As his feet carried him to the next hallway, all he could think about was how good it had felt to finally put his lips to hers. He wanted to look back before he turned the corner, but he didn't. Ravi shoved his feelings aside, locking them tightly away until he could take them out again later. He counted the doors to the thirteenth one on the left and tested the handle. It turned beneath his hand. Inside was the closet Yaz had described.

He shut the door behind him and flicked the switch that turned on the light. The shelves inside the closet had an array of clothes, weapons, drying towels, and other supplies. But he wasn't there for any of that. He looked at the grate overhead and grinned.

30

Yasmin's body buzzed with surprise and pleasure. She pressed her lips together, still feeling his mouth against hers. The kiss had been all too brief. He had leaned away before she even realized what was happening. She should have pulled him back for another deeper kiss.

She became aware of the stones singing loudly, a reminder that she couldn't sink into her thoughts about Ravi in such a dangerous place. Yasmin listened to the stones over the loud voices around her. With Ravi gone, she missed his presence. Now, all she had were the stones. She kept her hand flattened against them while wishing she didn't have to do what she was about to do. But it was the only way. The stones had shown her the way as she and Ravi leaned against the wall.

She drew in a deep breath and slowly released it. It did nothing to calm the rising storm of emotions swirling in her belly. What a fool she had been to tell Ravi she would be fine helping him inside Shaldorn. Her trauma went too deep for her to be able to walk these halls without the past threatening to yank her back to when she'd been imprisoned within its gilded walls.

She couldn't let Ravi down. For the next little while, the mission's success rested on her shoulders. The lives of everyone in Shecrish was a cumbersome burden. She didn't know how Ravi did it day after day with no thought for his safety. Instead of making things easier for him, she had been sullen and snappy. If only she had known then what she did now.

Yasmin slowly let her hand drop from the stones. She squared her shoulders and started toward the hallway. She walked as if she owned the place. All the while, her insides were mush, her legs jelly. It took extreme effort to keep herself upright. Sweat broke out over her body. Her palms were damp, and her heart careened wildly.

A gap in the bodies at the balustrade showed the woman in the box. Rage coalesced with her fear, giving Yaz the last push she needed. She made her way to the door with two burly guards protecting it. They glared at her. She recognized the Dark Elf on the left. He was a cruel bastard who had slapped the staff around anytime he got the chance. The scar near the outside of his right eye was courtesy of her during her first week at Shaldorn when he'd cornered her for the sheer fun of it.

Yasmin had lashed out with hands and feet that day. Her nail had caught his face, inflicting the wound that left the scar. The commotion had drawn others, including the Trinity. From then on, he'd had it out for her. The times she was punished, he always managed to be there to help dole it out.

She looked him square in his gray eyes without worry that he would recognize her. If she believed it, then so would anyone else. "Step aside."

"This is a private gathering." Both he and the Wood Elf next to him stood straighter and moved closer together.

If she had elven magic, Yasmin wondered if she would've used it then. How many times had the Dark grinned at her pain? How many others who hadn't fought back as she had had he hurt? How many had he cowed simply because he could?

She lifted her chin and gave him a glare. "Kumar is awaiting my arrival. The meeting can't commence until I'm there."

The guards exchanged a look.

Yasmin held her arms at her waist, her hands linked as she raised a brow and tapped a toe impatiently. "Would I know there's a meeting here if I wasn't invited?"

It was the Wood Elf who relented and opened the door. A muscle in the Dark's jaw moved beneath his gray skin. Yasmin slid past him and into the room. The door clicked softly shut behind her. She had a moment to get her bearings. She had only been in this room once before, but she would never forget the octagonal shape, the blood-red rugs, or the ceiling painted to look like the night sky.

She had gotten past the guards. Now came the difficult part.

Yasmin swallowed. Five men were gathered in a circle, conversing with drinks in their hands. She noted the two guards on the far wall, standing so still they nearly blended in. A quick look to either side showed two more guards near her. One looked at her curiously.

She wished she could touch the stones. Or Ravi. Was he in place? Was he ready? It was too late. She had already begun.

Ravi pulled himself into the shaft and carefully replaced the heavy iron grate. He shoved his hair out of his face and wished he had tied it back to keep it out of the way. He crawled a short way until he found the grate in the secret hallway where Kumar's protection stood. Given what he could see, he gauged the distance between the three. The middle bodyguard was closest to him.

He hadn't brought any weapons. Luckily, his quarry had. Ravi slowly and quietly lifted the grate and set it aside. He dropped down onto the elf below him and snapped his neck before they hit the ground. Ravi unsheathed the sword at the dead bodyguard's waist and turned to the guard on his right. He heard the other approaching quickly behind him.

Ravi dove, rolled past the lifeless body, and came up to stand behind his enemy, putting both of his adversaries together. The passage was narrow and difficult to move in, forcing them to come at him one at a time.

"You might as well give up now," the Wood Elf said. "You're not getting out of this alive."

The Sun Elf behind him grunted in agreement.

Ravi grinned and motioned for the Wood Elf to come. "Let's see, shall we?"

The body of their friend lay between them as their swords clashed. Ravi didn't want the noise to draw attention from those within the room. He needed to end this quickly. When the Wood Elf lunged, Ravi grabbed his extended wrist and pushed him against the wall, pinning him there. Ravi then thrust his sword into the elf's heart before yanking his blade free just as his opponent kneed him. Ravi shoved the elf down and pierced his spine.

Ravi looked one way down the hall and then the other, waiting to see if the noise had drawn others. When no one came, he walked to the left, his strides eating up the distance. He found the entrance and rested his hand on the handle, then pressed his ear against the door to see if he could hear what was going on within. Only silence greeted him.

He looked at the stones and wished he could hear them. He curled his fingers around the handle.

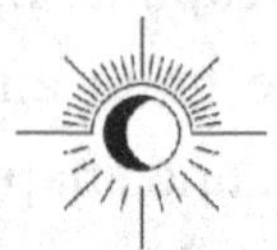

Yasmin walked deeper into the room. She was nearly upon the group before anyone noticed her. Her heart thumped so loudly she was sure everyone could hear it. The first to see her was a Moon Elf. Yasmin gave him a smile that he returned.

She searched for One, Two, and Three, but thankfully they weren't in attendance. The others noticed her one by one, parting to reveal another occupant. The female was gowned in sparkling silver, but that's not what caught Yasmin's gaze. It was the elf's face. It was the very same one who had smiled and offered Yasmin a home at Shaldorn. Yasmin's steps faltered, and she couldn't decide whether to attack or run.

The Moon Elf was as beautiful as Yasmin remembered. Her blue hair was swept up in elaborate twists and braids, and white and sapphire tips rested on her pointed ears, matching the extravagant necklace around her neck. There was a clink of bracelets as the elf's arms dropped to her sides.

"And you are?" she asked.

It was the same voice from when Yasmin had been a child. Curious and fascinated. Yasmin had known she would face her past, but she hadn't expected her. She wanted to run, but she was rooted to the spot, as if threads from the rug had wrapped around her ankles to lock her in place.

Yasmin recalled how nice the Moon Elf had been. How she had sat with Yasmin those first few nights at dinner. How she had held Yasmin's hand and dressed her in finery. She had duped Yasmin. Now, it was Yasmin's turn to return the favor.

"What a curious question when you're the one who invited me," Yasmin replied.

Kumar walked to her and took her hand. He brought it to his lips and kissed her knuckles as his golden eyes studied her. "I didn't get the pleasure earlier. What is your name?"

The first name that came to mind was the woman who had raised her. "Laboni."

Kumar's fingers tightened on her hand as he turned his head to the female. "What is the meaning of this, Gita?"

"I don't know," Gita insisted.

Yasmin took the opening and said, "If I'm not meant to be here, then how did I get past the guards?"

"A very good question," Kumar stated. "Gita, I had your assurance that all would go as planned."

The other men in the room looked between Kumar and Gita.

"It will," Yasmin assured him. She laid her other hand atop the one squeezing hers. "I'm here to ensure that."

His gold eyes searched her face before he turned to Gita. "I don't have time for games."

Yasmin didn't hide her grin as she saw the brief flare of anger in Gita's eyes. Yasmin couldn't have planned this better herself. Had the stones known that Gita would be here? They must have. They had known what Yasmin needed.

She moved closer to Kumar and looked at Gita as she whispered, "She requested that I be the intermediary between the two of you to keep things...calm. I know nothing other than there will be an exchange. I'm to facilitate that."

"That isn't what we agreed," Kumar said to Gita.

Yasmin twisted her lips. "Past experience has made her more careful."

Gita's nostrils flared, but she said nothing. She was waiting to see how this played out.

Kumar released Yasmin's hand. She moved between him and Gita, looking from one to the other. "Shall we begin?"

"Aye. I want this finished," Kumar replied.

Gita stood calmly. She slid her gaze to the side and nodded to one of the men, who lifted a gold chest from behind a table. He brought it to Gita, and she opened the lid to reveal silver and gold coins and loose jewels of all sizes.

Yasmin looked at Kumar and surreptitiously dug the cylinder from her skirt pocket. "Your turn."

Kumar's man brought out a domed wooden box engraved with protection runes of the gods. One of them held it out for Kumar to open the lid. Inside was an orb, nestled among the white silk.

At first, Yasmin thought it was a solid piece of obsidian. Then she saw the flashes of something that appeared to be lightning within it. She didn't know what the device would do, but it didn't matter. The fact that it had been built to do harm was enough to make her want to get rid of it.

The room was as quiet as death, everyone looking at everyone else. It was the only reason she heard the soft click of the door latch. She didn't wait around to see if it was Ravi. The instant everyone's attention shifted to the doorway, she threw the cylinder. It shattered on impact, the room filling with thick smoke.

Ravi only got a glimpse of Yaz's purple skirt before the smoke enveloped her. Others coughed. One of the bodyguards—a Dark—tried to use his shadows to move the smoke, but it didn't work. There were shouts of dismay and a crash to the left. The smoke spread quickly, reaching from wall to wall and hanging there.

Ravi rushed to where he had spotted Yaz, but he couldn't see his hand in front of his face. He bumped into someone. Ravi checked to make sure it wasn't his target or a guard before knocking the elf out. Ravi then checked to make sure he didn't have the device on him before standing.

He heard a scuffle and soft grunts that sounded like a woman, but he couldn't be sure where they were coming from. And he couldn't call out for Yaz. Ravi forced himself to set aside his need to find her and searched for his target and the device instead. He stilled, closed his eyes, and used his hearing. That's when he heard someone moving on his left. There were footsteps and labored breathing, followed by a cough.

Ravi reached out, his fingers brushing someone through the smoke. He coughed against the irritation in his throat and tightened his fingers on clothing. He carefully stepped over the prone elf on the floor at his feet and yanked his find to him.

It was another male he didn't recognize. The elf flailed in his arms, gasping for breath, his cheeks puffing like a fish. Ravi easily subdued him, dropping him unconscious next to the first, but came up empty for the device after a quick search.

He stood and backed away from the two on the floor to follow the sounds of others coughing and gagging as they called for help.

Ravi coughed into his jacket. His lungs burned, and his eyes watered. He wanted to shout for Yaz but didn't want to give away his position. He had to trust that she could handle herself. The stones would show her the way. He wasn't going anywhere until he had the device.

Ravi heard a male cry for help, the words garbled between coughs. A flare of green on the far right showed a Wood Elf attempting to use magic to disperse the smoke. If only Ravi had been inside before Yaz had broken the container. He might know who had the device—and what it looked like.

Coughing mixed with shouts of help mingled with calls for the exit. He heard them fumbling as they ran into each other and bounced off the walls. Someone fell over the bodies on the floor. Ravi took the opportunity and lunged forward to grab whoever it was.

He hauled them to him. The instant he saw it was his target, he slammed Kumar against the wall. Ravi put his face near his. "Where is the device?"

Kumar shook his head before turning it to the side, seized with a coughing fit.

Ravi shook him. He kept his voice down so as not to draw notice from the remaining bodyguards. "Where is it?"

"I...I don't know," Kumar answered breathlessly before coughing again. "I had it before the smoke. She...b-b-betrayed... me."

Ravi gripped him tighter. "Who?"

Kumar doubled over in a coughing fit. Ravi would get nothing else out of him. He drew back his fist and punched his target in the face to knock him out. Ravi checked him for the device before leaving him slumped against the wall.

31

The smoke billowed faster than Yasmin had anticipated. She briefly lost sight of Gita in the ensuing pandemonium. Yasmin grabbed her skirt and raced after the Moon Elf. The smoke got into her nose and mouth, choking her and causing Yasmin to cough, her eyes burning and watering. She caught sight of Gita's silver skirt and lunged.

Somehow, Yasmin managed to get her fingers on the thin material of the *dupatta*. It ripped loudly as she yanked it from Gita. The elf yelled for someone. Yasmin couldn't make out the name, but it didn't matter, not when she saw Gita moving through the smoke.

Yasmin dove forward and wrapped her arms around full skirts. The instant she held Gita, Yasmin twisted to land on her side. Gita lost her balance and tumbled to the ground, but the elf didn't stay down.

An elbow landed hard in Yasmin's abdomen, robbing her of breath. She knew if she lost her hold on Gita, the elf would get away. Yasmin couldn't let that happen. Not when she had such an opportunity. She scrambled to her feet, clawing her way up the heavily adorned skirts as Gita hit and dragged her across the rug.

Yasmin got her arms around Gita's midsection before planting her feet to halt them. The elf leaned forward to get away. When that didn't work, she responded with a round of elbow punches and kicks. A blow connected with Yasmin's nose and left her dazed. A moment later, something warm and wet ran down her face. She refused to let go, though. She wrapped her legs around Gita and used her body weight to slow them. The elf flipped Yasmin onto her back and landed another hit on her jaw.

Yasmin's vision was edged with dots. Her fingers tightened as the two rolled on the floor, each trying to gain an advantage. Which was why it took Yasmin so long to realize that if Gita could use both hands to strike her, then she didn't have the box. Yasmin couldn't decide whether to let Gita go and look for the box or release all her years of hatred and anger onto the elf.

A flash of green magic caught Yasmin's attention. It made her think of Ravi's clothes. He was in the room with all the madness. Was he looking for her? Had he found Kumar and the device? She couldn't see anything. There was no way to find Ravi or the weapon, but she had Gita.

Yasmin brought her fists up and slammed them into the elf's jaw. It dazed Gita enough that Yasmin was able to climb on top. She reared back her hand to punch Gita when the elf shoved both hands into Yasmin's stomach and released a round of magic.

The force of it pitched Yasmin backward. She crashed into a table before dropping to the floor. The pain was blinding. Everything hurt. It was like someone had shredded her lungs, and each time Yasmin attempted to breathe, smoke filled her body until she became wracked by coughs—which only doubled her agony.

Tears ran down her face as the smoke burned her eyes. All she wanted to do was lay there alone, but she would likely die if she did. The only way to survive was to get to her feet. That proved harder than expected.

Just getting to her hands and knees took every effort, all between coughing and holding her stomach where the elf had hit her. Yasmin wiped the back of her hand across her mouth. It came away streaked with blood and soot. She blinked several times and scanned the area for Gita, but the elf was long gone.

Yasmin shook her head, refusing to admit defeat. Gita could still be in the room. Yasmin crawled a short distance to the wall and used it to pull herself to her feet. She bit back a cry of pain when something pulled in her stomach. She dragged in a deep breath and tasted fresh air. Swinging her head to the side, she watched the smoke waft through an open door. She heard a scuffle and saw Ravi fighting one of the bodyguards on the other side of the room. He drew the cube he had stolen from his pocket.

She scanned the room for Gita or Kumar when she spotted the wooden box. She forgot about her pain as she raced to it, sliding on her knees to wrap her arms around it just as a guard reached for it. He yanked at it. She lifted her gaze and met Ravi's right before he threw the cube.

There was a deafening *whoosh*, a heartbeat before a monsoon filled the room. Yasmin was drenched immediately. As the guard's attention shifted, Ravi seized the opportunity and kicked him in the face. He toppled backward with a howl as he released the box.

The rain dispersed the last of the smoke. Those still in the room beat a hasty retreat. Yasmin gathered the box tightly against her and raced to the door closest to her. She paused and looked back to see Ravi rushing through a door on the opposite side.

Yasmin slipped out of the room and plastered her back against the wall. She clawed at the hair stuck to her face and breathed in fresh air, even as water continued to soak her. Panic gripped Shaldorn. The occupants' screams and shouts were drowned out by the roar of the storm that continued to gain momentum.

Yasmin scanned the faces of those who rushed past her as they shoved others aside to get down to the main floor and the entrance. Some rammed into her painfully. She got caught up in a group, and it pushed her farther down the wall. Yasmin protected the box with her body and planted her feet. Eventually, the crowd moved around her. She knew few would make it out before Gita sealed the fortress. The guests, however, didn't know that.

She waited until the area thinned out. The storm made it difficult to see, just as the smoke had. But at least she could breathe easier now. Yasmin reached to open the box's lid with a shaking hand. She sighed with relief when she saw the device inside. Now, she needed to get to Ravi so he could complete his mission.

Yasmin looked first one way and then the other. The device was likely safer in its confines, but the box was bulky and heavy. Not to mention, people would be looking for it. It would be a lot easier to take the device out. She could put it into her pocket and make her way down to Ravi.

The only problem was that she knew nothing about the device or how it could be detonated. She had found the box on the floor, which likely meant it fell. No one would've put it down if they'd had a choice. If the device hadn't detonated then, perhaps it would be safe for her to carry it.

She blinked water from her eyes and frowned at her thoughts.

There was a very real chance the bomb could go off. But there were two good things about that. The first was that she wouldn't need to worry about getting caught at Shaldorn, and the second was that there would no longer be a potential conflict with the dragons.

But if it went off as she held it, she would never kiss Ravi again.

Yasmin scooped the orb into the palm of her hand. She was surprised by how cool it was against her skin. Before she could change her mind, she dropped it into her pocket. The weight of it pulled the right side of her skirts down, but she ignored the awkward balance. She inched toward the door, then leaned around the corner to glance inside the room before tossing the box inside. Yasmin gathered her skirts in her hand and ran to a staff door. She threw it open as she rushed through.

A startled cry brought her to a halt as she spotted a group of staff huddled together in the stairway. Water dripped from her and billowed through the door she held open. Someone came up behind her and shoved a hand into her back. Yasmin tumbled down the stairs, only to be caught by a couple of staff members.

"Get me out!" a male voice bellowed behind her.

Yasmin got to her feet and turned to face the elf. She knew his kind. He didn't care about anyone but himself. There was a way out from this stairway, but she wouldn't tell him that.

She looked up at him in fear, her voice shaking as she said, "This isn't an exit. We need to go back."

The male didn't hesitate to leave them behind.

After he was gone, Yasmin turned to the staff. "Stay here until the storm is contained," she warned before racing down the stairs.

No one stopped her, no one questioned her—because that

wasn't what the staff was supposed to do. From the first day, they were taught that guests could do whatever they wanted. She almost told them to follow her, but she would likely put them in more danger if she did. They were better off where they were for the time being.

Yasmin trailed her fingers along the stones and heard their answering song. They showed her the empty passages where she was to meet Ravi. She ran as if her feet had wings. Down corridors, around corners, zigzagging through hallways and down steps.

She didn't stop. Not even when her side began to ache. She felt the thud of the device knocking against her leg as she ran. Every once in a while, she reached for the stones. All the attention was upstairs, leaving doors unmanned. All Ravi had to do was get to the lower level.

It was no surprise when she reached their meeting place first. She sucked in breaths of air and wished to be out of the wet gown and into her clothing once more. Her chest heaved as she fought to even her breathing. Then she put a hand on the stones and asked about Ravi. They showed her that he was drawing close, but she couldn't determine where he was.

Yasmin paced, antsy to get going. She touched the device through the material of her skirts. She considered going to get their clothes and packs. She could've been there and returned by now—and able to change.

The warning scream of the stones punched through her thoughts. She went to reach for them to find out what was going on when she heard something behind her. She spun around to see Gita striding down the corridor, her face twisted in a murderous rage. Her hair had come loose and hung in wet tangles, her clothes were ripped and soaked, and one of her ear tips was missing.

Yasmin had done that to her. If the elf wanted another fight, she'd give it to her.

"There's nowhere you can go," Gita said as she walked closer. "The doors won't open again until I tell them to. Enjoy these last minutes. They'll be your final ones."

Yasmin grinned. "You do love making threats."

Gita stopped, her wet skirts swishing around her legs. "It's a fact, not a threat."

For the first time, Yasmin looked past Gita and saw One, Two, and Three bearing down on them. She didn't stand a chance against the Trinity. There was nowhere for Yasmin to go.

"I rule Shaldorn," Gita continued. "Your mistake was imagining you could outsmart me."

The Trinity stopped two paces behind Gita. They looked at Yasmin with irritation and wrath that she had hoped never to see again. Yasmin thought of the device in her pocket. Where was Ravi? He needed to get out.

Except he couldn't.

Not without her.

She wanted to take a step back and put more space between her and Gita, but Yasmin held her ground. "I did outsmart you."

The smile that spread over Gita's face was pure maliciousness. "Did you really think I would ever forget you, Yasmin?"

Yasmin barely had time to register her words before Gita tossed a powder into the air. A cloud of lake root enveloped Yasmin. She sucked in the toxic herb before she could stop herself. She gasped as her throat closed up, and breathing became a struggle. She clawed at her neck, choking and wheezing, but it was no use. The dose was one meant to kill.

32

Ravi slowed when he heard voices. He kept out of the light as he crept forward. He was gathering what little magic he had to use against the elves when the powder enveloped Yaz. He lurched forward to grab her as shadows abruptly shrouded him. His arms stretched outward as he saw her crumple to the ground. Then the corridor—and Yaz—faded from sight.

In a blink, the shadows receded. Ravi found himself in a room. He staggered from the shadows and spun to find a female. The Dark was clothed in a black and silver *lehenga*. Her long, white hair was gathered in a loose braid, while a silver band rested along the part of her white hair, a large oval onyx resting against her forehead. She took her time looking him over with her gray eyes.

He narrowed his. Was she Dain's informant? Or was the Dark working with Shaldorn? Ravi noted the door behind him and the clear passage to it. "Who are you?"

"Calm yourself, Ravi. I'm Arya. I'm here to help."

Dain had never given Ravi his agent's name. He hadn't even said whether the undercover operative was male or female. Ravi wouldn't assume anything. "You still haven't told me who you are."

"You know who I am. I've been watching you and your companion since you arrived."

"If I knew who you were, I wouldn't be asking."

Arya released a loud sigh of frustration. "Did that arsehole tell you nothing?"

"By arsehole, you mean...?"

"Dain, of course." Arya dropped her arms and rolled her eyes. "Life would be a lot less complicated if he would learn to use his words."

Ravi might have confirmation about who she was, but that didn't calm him. "Why did you keep me from Yaz? She was in trouble. We could've helped."

"Gita and the Trinity hadn't seen you. If you had made yourself known, you'd be going to the same place Yasmin is."

"You mean they would kill me."

The Dark shook her head and looked away. "Gita won't kill her. At least, not at first. She'll make Yasmin suffer. The human was a fool to return."

"They shouldn't have recognized her."

The Dark crossed her arms over her chest. "You thought some serum that altered her appearance would keep her from being noticed?"

Ravi turned his back to Arya and closed his eyes. After a moment, he ran a hand down his face as he tried to think of what to do next. He didn't have the device. Or Yaz. He opened his eyes and looked around the sparse room. "Where are we?"

"In a room on the staff level."

He faced her. "Get to Dain. He needs to tell Durga that we need more agents immediately."

"That isn't going to happen, Sunny. Shaldorn is on lockdown. No one can leave. Not even me."

"Yaz had a way out for us."

Arya quirked a brow. "Did she share it with you?"

"Nay."

"Then we're stuck."

"I can't be stuck." He fought rising helplessness and fury. "I have to get out there."

Arya tilted her head to the side, causing the thick braid to dangle over her shoulder. "To do what, exactly? Will you go after the device or Yasmin?"

"I..." He knew what he was supposed to do, what he *should* do. What his training told him to do.

Arya walked to a corner where a large bag hid in some shadows. "There are eyes everywhere at Shaldorn. Gita will know what you were wearing. We need to change."

"My clothes are... Shite. I don't know where they are." Yaz had warned him it was all a maze.

"Good thing I came prepared. Let's hope these fit," she said before tossing him some clothes.

Ravi caught them as they hit his chest. He glanced up to see her back to him as she removed her jewelry. He looked at the door, worry for Yaz clouding his mind. She had inhaled lake root. He'd heard her choking and gasping for air. He wanted to believe Arya that Yaz was alive, but he couldn't until he saw her for himself.

He never should've brought Yaz within the walls. She had warned him about the many dangers, but he'd had a mission. And he'd believed he could keep her safe. He'd promised her that he would. Now, she was once more held in Shaldorn. If she was alive, he couldn't imagine what they would do to her. He had vowed to free her if anything happened.

Don't make a promise you can't keep.

Ravi heard her words in his mind and wanted to hit something. He could tell himself she had known the dangers, but it didn't absolve him of his sins. He had to find Yaz. He couldn't leave her. Not after all she had done for him.

He dropped the clothes onto the floor and changed quickly. When he straightened after tossing his sodden garments aside, Arya was watching him. "Where will they take Yaz?"

"There are a couple of places we can look. The storm was a nice touch, by the way."

"It was a last-minute decision." Ravi shoved his wet hair away from his face. "I need to get to Yaz."

"No one has ever escaped Shaldorn before. No one."

"Meaning they'll make an example of her?"

The Dark unbraided her hair before gathering it behind her head and securing it. "I don't believe Gita will bring her in front of the guests or even the staff—not after everything that's happened tonight. The Moon Elf will take her revenge in private. She doesn't want to remind anyone that someone got out of her clutches. The guests let down their guards because nothing will ever get out."

"Who is Gita?"

"She is the mastermind behind Shaldorn. The elves behind her were the Trinity: One, Two, and Three. They answer solely to her and run Shaldorn with an iron fist."

Yaz had said a Moon Elf had brought her to the fortress. Had that elf been Gita? "I should've run faster. Had I gotten to our meeting point sooner, Yaz and I could've gotten away before Gita arrived."

"Then you would be in Gita's clutches along with Yasmin."

Ravi nodded and turned his mind back to his mission. "If this place is on lockdown, then that means the device is still here. I need to find it."

"There are four levels to comb through. Even with a hundred agents, we couldn't do it in time to find either Yasmin or the device."

Ravi squeezed the bridge of his nose with his thumb and forefinger. "I can't stand around. I have to be out there searching."

"For one, you don't know what the device looks like. Two, the storm ripped through everything upstairs. It was a monsoon. Indoors. It could still be raging for all I know."

"It would give us cover."

"I repeat. A *monsoon*," she said slowly as if he were addled.

And Ravi supposed he was. Everything was unraveling around him. All he wanted was to find Yaz and get her out of Shaldorn.

"My advice is to remain here for a bit. But by that stubborn look on your face, you're going to ignore it."

He turned his head to her. "I'm not good with being idle. Especially with my partner in trouble."

Partner. Yaz was that and more. But he couldn't say what he really wanted. He could only think it, *feel* it.

Arya eyed him. "You're one of the best in the DIA. You didn't get that way by being reckless or idiotic. Leave that to Dain."

"I need to know what's going on upstairs. Please," he added.

"Will you be here when I get back?"

"I give you my word."

She flashed him a flat stare. "You're on your own if you leave."

"Understood."

The shadows gathered around Arya within seconds. Then, she was gone. Ravi walked to a wall and put his back against it. He slid down it until he rested on his haunches. Then he dropped his head into his hands. "Hold on, Yaz. I'm coming."

Yasmin floated in the place between waking and sleep. Sometimes, sleep would tug her down, clutching her so tightly she was incapable of escape. Other times, she heard snatches of the world around her, teasing her to push through the veil and be a part of the living once more.

But sleep felt so good. She was comforted there.

Safe.

She didn't know what she should want to be sheltered from. Each time she attempted to figure out what it could be, it flitted from her mind like a shooting star across the night sky.

Yasmin drifted. She became cognizant of a little more each time she surfaced from sleep. Until she finally became aware of sunlight on her face. The warmth of it was heavenly. And the glow reminded her of something. Nay. Some*one*. If only she could recall who it was.

Her eyes were so heavy it took great effort to pry them open. They fell shut again almost immediately. She partially rolled onto her back and stretched, but sleep beckoned her again. She began to follow it when she recalled that she had something important to do. She couldn't remember exactly what it was but knew she had to get moving.

This time, when Yasmin opened her eyes, it was easier. She found herself staring at a familiar stone ceiling. Her lids grew heavy, but she kept her eyes open. She yawned and stretched again. Her body was so lethargic that she had to roll onto her side and use her arm to push up into a sitting position. Her brain was fuzzy, making thoughts difficult.

She tugged her feet from the covers, only to have one get caught. It felt like an eternity before she freed it. Her bare feet met a small rug. She squished her toes into the fibers before standing on wobbly legs. She saw the washstand and headed for it. It was only a few steps away but seemed more like a hundred.

Yasmin gritted her teeth when her feet met the bare floor. She heard a song in the distance she recognized but couldn't quite place it. She hummed along with it as she grasped the basin and turned on the spigot. The water was freezing as she cupped it in her hands before splashing her face.

She gasped as the chilly liquid met her skin, but it helped to shake off the last vestiges of sleep. She blinked the water from her eyes as she turned off the spout. Yasmin focused on her reflection in the mirror. She'd had the strangest dream. One where she had escaped Shaldorn only to return with a handsome Sun Elf on a mission for...she couldn't remember.

It had been so vivid that thinking of the elf brought a smile to her face. She rarely dreamed and almost never remembered more than bits and pieces. But this one had details. So many particulars she could still recall. She closed her eyes and immediately pictured the tent and the Sun Elf. His hard, naked body alongside hers.

His arms as they held her.

His beautiful, copper eyes.

The squeak of a door opening yanked Yasmin from her

thoughts. She dried her face and turned to the Moon Elf who had brought her to Shaldorn. Yasmin faced her as the elf came into the room. The strands of her blue hair were parted down the middle and gathered in multiple braids. She wore a navy *lehenga* with white embroidery. She looked more composed than last time.

The thought had come unbidden, but with it came the truth. Blood roared in Yasmin's ears as she realized she hadn't been dreaming. She had lived that life. She had been free to choose who touched her and when.

The room spun, making her grab the sink behind her to stay on her feet. She remembered the lake root Gita had thrown at her and the comprehension that she would die. For some reason, Gita had healed her. She was woozy because of elven magic.

Yasmin reached down for her pocket and the device, but she no longer wore the purple *lehenga*. She didn't need to ask to know that Gita had the device. But did they have Ravi?

"I see it's all coming back to you," Gita stated as she gathered her hands before her and grinned triumphantly.

Tears burned Yasmin's eyes, but she refused to let them fall. She wouldn't show weakness.

She couldn't.

Ravi's head jerked up when Arya returned. He stood and met her gaze. "Well?"

"They have the storm contained," she stated.

He waited for more. When it didn't come, he gave her a pointed look. "And?"

"And what? The elves have done their part, and the staff is already cleaning up. Guests are restricted to certain areas and are being questioned. The guards are also searching for you."

"Then we shouldn't tarry."

"Walking those halls right now is tantamount to suicide. You certainly won't get the device or locate Yasmin if that happens," she retorted.

Ravi raked his hand through his hair again. "I can't sit and do nothing!"

"Here." Arya held out a hand with a strip of leather in it. "Get your hair out of your face. Then we'll come up with a plan. I think I know where we can look for Yasmin."

"What about the device?"

"There won't be time for both. You have to choose. The device or your woman."

"She's not mine."

Arya shot him a skeptical look. "Whatever. We won't have long, whichever you decide."

33

Yasmin had known fear many times in her life. From the elf who called herself Mother as she slowly poisoned Yasmin. Fear of starving. Of sweating, pawing hands endlessly groping her.

But there was one above all the others.

The one where she died within the stronghold.

And she was about to meet that one head-on.

Yasmin curled her toes on the chilly stones. She looked down at the plain white gown. They were clothes she had sworn would never grace her body again. The gown locked her into her position more firmly than chains ever could. She hated the color white and what it had represented in her life.

She wanted her clothes. They were her armor. In them, she had found her freedom. The human who had fled the inescapable stronghold.

The woman who had survived.

Gita's nameless face had haunted her for years. It was time for Yasmin to take back her past and sever any links she had to Shaldorn. The stones hummed as they felt her anger and determination. She was a human standing against elves. Yasmin likely wouldn't win this battle, but she wasn't going down without a fight.

Gita took a step closer and raked her gaze over Yasmin. "You made us believe we had excised your willfulness. You had us all fooled. Yet you returned. I took you for a smarter woman than that. You had to know you wouldn't leave my fortress again."

Indeed, Yasmin had known. And still, she'd agreed to lead Ravi inside. For a moment, she had believed they would succeed. Her fingers curled into a fist. She wanted to ask about Ravi but knew the game they were playing. She had stood in this exact spot several times before.

Gita quirked a brow. "No biting remarks or witty retorts? Surely, there are things you wish to say."

"I'd rather you shut up and get on with whatever you plan to do." Yasmin fought to stay upright. She wanted to shake her head to clear the fuzz from her brain, but that wouldn't happen for hours yet.

"Oh, don't worry. I have much in store for you," Gita replied with a smirk. She walked to the other side of the small room. "The storm you and your accomplice released has been tamed. You've made quite a mess in my home, but there are plenty of staff to see it set to rights. Meanwhile, every nook and cranny of Shaldorn is being searched for the Sun Elf. Who is he?"

Yasmin bit the inside of her cheek to keep from smiling at the knowledge they didn't have Ravi. If he was still free, then there was a chance he could find the device and get out. She held that hope in her heart. "I don't know who you mean."

Gita tsked as she continued her slow walk. "Don't play dumb. It's never suited you. His name doesn't matter. Shaldorn is locked down, and it will remain that way until we locate him." She smiled like someone who had a secret. "I know just the way to draw him out, too."

"You're wasting your time. I came alone."

"I'm going to use you. I suspect that will bring him out quickly."

Yasmin knew Ravi's main focus was the device. He might have promised to find her if she got into trouble, but she knew he wouldn't fall for Gita's tricks. At least, she *hoped* he wouldn't.

Gita stopped before Yasmin. "As for the explosive you attempted to steal, it is once more in my control."

"You won't win."

"I already have."

Yasmin wanted to deny it, but she couldn't. She had failed. Now, it was possible tens of thousands could die.

Gita touched Yasmin's hair. "I thought you were something special. I gave you opportunities others never had. But you're just another boring human who tried to reach beyond herself."

But Yasmin wasn't just human. She had magic. She sought the stones beneath her feet and heard them answer with a loud rise of music. They had tried to warn her earlier, but the elf magic had muddled her brain and made it difficult for them to reach her.

Their song turned frantic as they sounded a warning. Her gaze moved to the door as it swung open, and two guards strode in. One was the Dark Elf she had tricked hours earlier. His sinister smile filled her with dread.

The lives of thousands versus one. The answer should be a simple one, yet it wasn't. Ravi's priority was obtaining the device, or at least preventing it from leaving Shaldorn. But he couldn't stop thinking about Yaz and what they might be doing to her at that very moment.

"Ravi? What's your decision?"

He shook his head, unable to look at Arya. "I don't know."

"You do. You just don't want to say it."

"I have an objective," he stated. "I always complete my missions."

She came to stand before him, her dark gray eyes holding his. "Things went to shite. No one will blame you."

"I will." He sighed. "I'll carry the weight of everyone who dies because I didn't get the device."

She shrugged indifferently. "You still can."

He could. All he had to do was set his mind to that and forget Yaz. Once he had the device, he could look for her. If she was still alive. It's what he would've done a week earlier. But his feelings interfered.

"If you wait long enough, you may not have to make a decision," Arya announced irritably as she stalked away.

He glared at her. "What's that supposed to mean?"

She paused and turned to him. "Your inability to make a choice will end up leaving Gita time to get the device away *and* kill Yasmin."

He'd told himself the very same thing, but hearing it aloud was like being punched in the gut. "Yaz never wanted to return."

"But she brought you here as promised. She's honorable."

She was that and so much more. That's when he knew. His decision had already been made. He just had to come to terms with it. "We find Yaz."

"It won't be easy," Arya warned.

"When is anything?"

Her lips flattened. "They know you two were together, and they'll use her to draw you out."

"Before or after they hurt her?"

"Knowing Gita? After."

That's what he feared. "Is there any way to find her before then?"

"Maybe."

"I leave here with Yaz or not at all," he stated.

Arya's brow furrowed. "What about the device?"

"That will be up to you and Dain."

She eyed him ruefully. "The instant they locate you, Gita will send the device out."

"You said she wouldn't bring Yaz out in front of others, but she'll have to if she intends to draw me out."

"Not necessarily."

Ravi was sure he didn't want to hear the answer, and yet he asked, "Meaning?"

"Information is passed around Shaldorn in many ways. Gita will ensure she uses all of them to find you."

"That doesn't matter. We're going to Yaz. Where do you think she's being held?"

Arya blew out a breath. "Someplace neither of you will probably get out of."

"I don't plan on dying here."

"I'm sure many have said that," she replied.

Ravi nodded as he looked around the room. "I thought Shaldorn was like any other place. Even when we were inside, I was sure we'd get out." He slid his gaze back to the Dark Elf. "I promised her I would free her if she got caught. Get me to her. I'll do the rest while you find the device."

"Gods," she said with a sigh. "You sound like Dain. I'm not leaving you, so don't push that agenda again. Got it?"

"Got it."

She rubbed her hands together, a small frown puckering her brow. "Traveling with someone takes a lot out of me. And we need to be careful. Don't move out of the shadows until I nudge you. How charged is your magic?"

"I haven't seen the sun in hours," he admitted.

Arya turned on her heel to walk to the bag. She dug around until she pulled out an amulet and handed it to him. "This should help."

Ravi accepted the necklace and studied the small, glowing yellow stone. He bowed his head to her. "Thank you."

"You can thank Dain. He thought you might need an extra."

Ravi placed the necklace over his head and dropped the sunstone against his skin. His magic immediately reached out to it, absorbing the rays captured within. He took only a little so there would be more if he needed it later.

"Expect anything," Arya warned.

"I always do."

She lifted her arms, and shadows began gathering and building. Ravi walked to her and turned so his back was to her front just as the shadows closed around them.

No matter how Yasmin tried, she couldn't distance herself from the pain that radiated from every part of her body. She had lost count of the number of ways the guards had struck her before Two and Gita had their fun.

The only reason she was still upright was because of the restraints holding her in place. Her left eye was swollen shut. Blood ran from her nose and the corner of her lip. She was sure her jaw was broken. Every finger had been broken, and her toes crushed. Both knees were shattered. One of her smashed ribs may have punctured a lung if the agony in her chest was any indication.

Her ribs made her think of Ravi and how he had brought her back from drowning. She tried to stay in that memory and drift away, but Gita wouldn't allow it. Each time Yasmin began to pass out, Gita would use a pinch of magical herbs to wake her.

"You always did have a high pain tolerance," Gita said as she slowly ambled around Yasmin. "We've gotten nothing from you other than a few moans when others would've been screaming long ago."

Yasmin knew that screams never helped. Besides, that would give Gita the satisfaction of knowing she'd hurt her. Yasmin might not be able to fight against them physically, but she could mentally. She tracked Gita with her one good eye.

"Imagine what you could've done if you had been born an elf." Gita chuckled. "But fate decided you weren't worthy."

Yasmin smiled inwardly. Fate had given her something even better.

Gita stopped beside her. "I applaud you for escaping. Not many dare to even think about it, much less act on it. But you did. Then you ran without a thought to anyone else. It didn't take us long to realize that Neela had aided you. You two were inseparable, after all. You should know that she screamed for you in the end."

Yasmin had never known the depth of hate she felt in that moment. Loathing for Gita for what she had done to Neela. And disgust at herself for not taking her friend with her.

Gita grinned in amusement. "Oh, if looks could kill, I'd be singed on the spot."

When she moved away, Yasmin spotted the clear box behind Gita. Fear snaked down her spine to settle in her stomach.

"Your special place. Made especially for you. I know how much you enjoyed the time you spent in it before. Did you miss it?" Gita shrugged. "It's fitting that your life should end in it."

Yasmin tried to fight as the guards unbound her, but her broken body wouldn't respond. The minute they wrapped their hands around her, she had to focus on holding back her cries of pain. Every step jarred her wrecked body. She desperately wished to pass out, but the gods weren't that kind.

They callously shoved her into the box. Yasmin was too consumed with agony to do anything as they shut the door. Then she heard the lid slide into place above her, blocking her air holes. The box was why she despised enclosed places. She had always feared suffocating. The only good thing she could think of was that they had done so much damage to her that she might not live long enough to asphyxiate.

Somehow, above the pain, she heard the stones. Their song rose up loudly to float around her. She let the calming melody fill her. It helped to distract her from the agony of her injuries. But it wasn't enough. She needed to take her mind somewhere else, somewhere she had been happy.

She found it with memories of Ravi.

34

Ravi held his patience as Arya took him to two places, then a third and a fourth before the shadows dissipated. He found himself back in the same room where they had begun. He spun around, his hands clenched into fists as rage coursed through him.

"You'd better have a good explanation for returning here," he said.

Arya's breathing was labored as she put a hand on the wall. Her gray skin had a sickly pallor to it. She shot him a heated glance. "In case you needed reminding, traveling with someone is exhausting."

"That doesn't explain why you didn't take me to Yaz." He was ready to fight, he *needed* a battle to release the tension building inside him. He had witnessed too much brutality within Shaldorn against those who couldn't protect themselves.

And he knew more was being doled out to Yaz.

Because the DIA had forced her to return.

Arya rested her back against the wall. "I went to the places I thought Yasmin would be, but she wasn't there."

"She's somewhere. You rest. I'm going to find her."

"Ravi, wait," Arya called when he turned and walked away.

He paused and looked at her over her shoulder. "What? I'm aware they're looking for me. I'll be careful."

"I came back here to rest because…"

Ravi pushed when she didn't continue. "Because?"

"I know where Gita took Yaz. I had hoped we wouldn't have to go there. It's why I looked everywhere else first."

He took a step to her. "Why don't you want to go there?"

"Some view Shaldorn as a hedonist paradise where any form of pleasure can be found. The truth is much more complicated. There is as much pain committed as pleasure. There are those who come here to hurt others. And sometimes even kill."

"Yaz told me as much."

Arya slowly shook her head. "The depravity I've witnessed left a lasting mark. Indulgence and agony ensue in every room at Shaldorn. But there is one where you can feel the pain, the utter misery, seeping from the very chamber before you reach it. It's a place used for those who have truly enraged Gita."

"Take me there. Now."

"You should prepare yourself."

Ravi sliced his hand through the air to halt her words. "Yaz doesn't have time for an argument."

She pushed from the wall and held out her arms as shadows gathered once more. Ravi walked to her as the darkness closed in around them.

Yasmin was jarred from her memories. Pain ratcheted up in her body as someone kicked the box. Her jaw was locked from the anguish. Otherwise, she would've screamed. She opened her eyes to see the Dark Elf flashing a menacing smile at her. He would be standing watch until she expired. No doubt he would be the one to toss her body outside for the animals to finish off.

Her nose brushed the box's door as her breath fogged it. Strands of hair lay over her face, unable to be moved. One of them poked her in the eye. She blinked to dislodge it but knew from experience that it wouldn't go anywhere. It didn't matter that her arms were broken. She wouldn't have been able to move them anyway. The box was barely big enough to hold her.

The guard kicked the box again, jolting her battered body so badly she nearly passed out. She could probably get him to do it again. If she was lucky, she'd die while passed out and not have to endure any more torture.

Yasmin glared at him through her good eye and then forced her cut lip to curve into a smile. The Dark's nostrils flared, and he pulled back his leg to kick again when his gaze whipped to the side. Yasmin turned her head as far as it would go to the left but couldn't see anything on that side because of her swollen eye.

She shut out the stones, trying to hear the muffled voices. Yasmin was able to hear Gita's, but she couldn't make out any words. The Moon Elf moved into her line of vision, the device in her hand. Yasmin could only stare at it while hoping Ravi was nearby, ready to snatch it away. Gita handed the device off before facing Yasmin.

That's when she realized that Gita had made sure Yasmin saw all of it. She tried to see who had taken it, but they were already gone. She couldn't do anything about it. The stones knew, though. They had been trying to talk to Ravi for some time, but he couldn't hear them. Every mountain around them could shout at him, but he was deaf to their words.

The Dark kicked the box again. Yasmin closed her eyes and sought her memories once more. She could feel her body failing. It wouldn't be long now. She wished she could say goodbye to the kids. And Ravi.

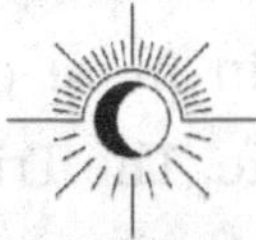

Ravi heard a male laugh through the shadows. He met Arya's troubled gaze.

She put her finger to her lips before mouthing, "*Wait.*"

He nodded, then faced forward and waited for the shadows to withdraw. Ravi focused on the voices in hopes of hearing Yaz. He picked up at least three different males and one woman. That must be Gita. His hands clenched into fists.

"The Sun Elf will come for her," Gita said. "I want only a few guards in the corridor. I want him to think he got to her before we capture him."

Ravi leaned forward, prepared to push through the shadows, but Arya's hands latched onto him, holding him in place. Her grip was tighter than expected, and she didn't allow him to budge an inch. He looked at her over his shoulder. However, her attention was directed outward. Ravi realized when he followed her gaze that she had opened the shadows enough for them to see into the room.

He took in the various torture apparatuses, and his heart sank. Murals of victims were on the walls. He spotted a female with her back to him, giving orders to her three henchmen. As ploys went, her plan to trap him was a good one. Not that he would've fallen for it. He narrowed his gaze on Gita. Her ruse was obvious. She must have something else up her sleeve. A second trap waiting, no doubt.

It's what he would do.

None of that mattered because he was already in the room. He leaned to the side to take in more of the chamber. Only more torture machines met his gaze. The Trinity left, but Gita continued to speak. Arya widened the shadows a bit more. Ravi tracked Gita to a hulking Dark Elf in a guard's uniform.

Arya nudged Ravi's side. He glanced at her to see her raise her brows in question. He nodded. He was more than ready to attack.

"Good luck," she whispered.

The shadows fell away. Ravi's gaze quickly scanned the entirety of the room. There were two other guards besides the one Gita spoke with. Then Ravi spotted the clear box and Yaz inside it with her eyes closed.

Arya moved to the two guards at the door, shadows billowing angrily around her. Ravi released magic, aimed like an arrow at the Dark's neck. Ravi gathered more as Gita turned to him.

"There you are," she said as she faced him. Her gaze skittered to the side, where Arya effortlessly killed the other guards. "I see you have help. Not that it will do you any good."

Ravi didn't want to hear anything she had to say. He brought his hands together and then spread them apart, yellow magic filling the space between them. "You're finished."

"You think I got this far alone? Think again."

He widened his arms as his magic grew stronger, drawing from the amulet against his chest. He felt the power swirling around his hands. He stepped forward, ready to unleash it to strike Gita. The Moon Elf didn't bother trying to protect herself as he released his magic. But she vanished before it reached her.

Ravi spun in a circle, his eyes darting about the room, waiting for the next attack. But there was none. Gita was gone.

"Where is she?" Arya asked, the shadows drifting behind her as if they couldn't stand not being near her.

Ravi glanced at the dead guard at the door. "Gone."

He raced to Yaz. His stomach churned at the sight of the blood covering her and the white gown. He swung opened the door. Gently, he moved aside her hair and saw her swollen, battered face. His hands shook as he brought it beneath her nose.

"She's alive," he said when he felt her breath. "Barely."

"We need to get her out before they return."

Ravi looked down and saw Yaz's fingers were in all directions, clearly broken. His heart cracked in two at what had been done to her. "Yaz?" he called. "Can you hear me? I'm getting you out."

He had to shift her to get his hands beneath her to lift her. The ragged moan that fell from her lips nearly brought him to his knees. It took both him and Arya to carefully lift her out. Even then, her pain was evident by her pinched lips. His stomach turned when he saw what had been done to her feet and lower legs, not to mention her arms and hands. He was going to kill every last person who had dared to hurt Yaz. The first to feel his wrath would be Gita.

The door to the room flew open, and four guards entered. Ravi and Arya exchanged a glance. They laid Yaz down as quickly and gently as possible before facing off against the newcomers, each taking two.

Ravi took his pair down quickly. He was turning to help Arya when he heard something behind him and spotted more guards pouring in from a door in the back that he hadn't noticed. He and Arya moved back to back as the guards surrounded them.

Magic came from every direction and had both of them dodging and using their own to shield. When an opponent got close enough, Ravi struck with his hands. He also snagged any weapons he could. He took two down with daggers before the guards got smart enough to back up.

Arya's gray magic swirled around them, striking quickly and ruthlessly. Ravi used his sparingly since he didn't know how much he could draw from the amulet. He spotted a discarded sword and lunged to the side to grasp it. The moment it was in his hand, he swung the blade, slicing bodies.

With every guard they killed, another came. He had no idea how long they fought. His magic was getting harder to use, and they still had to get Yaz to safety. He beheaded his last guard and turned to see Arya finishing hers off. Ravi's attention went to the door as Two walked into the room.

"Take Yaz," Ravi told Arya.

"Come with us."

He never took his eyes off Two as he stalked toward him. "Go. Now."

35

Yasmin couldn't take her good eye off Ravi. He was there. She couldn't believe it. He was covered in his enemies' blood, and given the cuts in his clothing, some of his, as well. She caught glimpses of a female Dark fighting with him, but Yaz couldn't stop watching him.

Even when he was outnumbered, Ravi didn't panic. He moved with a proficiency that spoke of years of training. He struck as quickly as a viper and with the fierceness of a bird of prey. She thought he might get beaten a few times, but he managed to get out of it. She wished she could join the fight, but it was enough that she got to see him one last time.

Yasmin spotted Two before Ravi did. She tried to shout a warning, but she couldn't manage more than a whisper. Then Ravi spotted him. She listened to the exchange between him and the Dark. Then, the female was beside her.

"Help him," Yasmin urged, her words a hoarse croak.

The female glanced over her shoulder before straightening and going to stand beside Ravi. Yasmin's vision wavered. She fought to cling to consciousness, but it became harder with every breath.

A crash yanked her back from the brink of oblivion. Beside her were chunks of wood from one of Gita's machines. Yasmin swung her gaze to Ravi, but he was gone. The sounds of battle raged around her, but she couldn't see where anyone was. Something smashed behind her. The Dark female flew over her and landed on her back before rolling to her feet, gray magic forming like interlocking bracelets around her hands.

Yasmin heard Ravi bellow. There was a moment of silence before something slammed into the floor. Then Ravi and the Dark were on either side of her.

"Hi," he said as he smiled down at her.

A lock of his golden hair had fallen into his face. Yasmin wished she could smooth it back. She tried to smile.

"Don't talk," he said as he glanced at the door. "Arya is going to get us out."

Yasmin swallowed. She had to tell him about the device. "Gi..."

"Gita?" Arya offered.

Yasmin tried to nod. "Gave...de-device..."

"Gita gave the device to someone?" Ravi asked.

Yasmin looked into his copper eyes and nodded again.

"Do you know where? Did the stones tell you?"

"Back," she croaked.

He frowned. "Back entrance? Is it on the main level?"

"Aye." She slid her gaze to the door. "Go."

He rushed to the doorway and looked out as Yasmin met Arya's gaze.

The Dark's brow furrowed deeply. "You're dying. We need to go now."

"His...mission."

"He chose you," she argued.

Yasmin pleaded with her expression since words were too hard.

"He has to know," Arya whispered.

Yasmin managed to shake her head.

"There's a chance I can track them," Ravi said.

Arya's shoulders dropped as she held Yasmin's gaze. "Go. I'll get Yasmin away and come back for you."

"*Thank you*," Yasmin mouthed. She closed her eyes and succumbed to the darkness.

Knowing Yaz would make it out of Shaldorn to the healers kept Ravi going. He was tired and hurt, but there would be time enough to rest later.

He didn't get far down the hallway before guards confronted him. He plowed into them with his sword swinging, his purpose renewed.

Dain stalked the passages of the city within the mountain. Navara was far older than Rannora or Belanore. The Mountain Elves were stingy with who they allowed into the hallowed halls. He was shocked that he was one of them. He doubted he would have been, had the current objective not been so important.

He was troubled that Arya hadn't returned with Ravi or Yasmin. Dain knew the pair had gotten to Shaldorn, but there were any number of reasons why the trio hadn't made it out yet. He was tempted to enter the fortress himself to find them. If anything happened to them, he might have to share with his superiors that he had been working with the DIA. And he knew how that would turn out.

They didn't believe the goings-on at Shaldorn were important enough to risk an agent. So, he had done the very thing he wasn't supposed to do. He had gone to the elves on the surface. Durga had been interested in his intel as well as his plan. She had brought her best agents onto the team to ensure things went smoothly. Dain would've gone himself, but his superiors were watching him too closely. Instead, Ravi had taken the position.

Dain turned a corner in hopes of locating Manu. The Mountain Elf governed Navara, keeping its occupants safe from the growing threat of Shaldorn. But Manu had yet to return. Manu waited outside the fortress, watching the comings and goings in case Ravi couldn't get the device.

Dain entered the grand house, nodding to workers. Manu had given Dain a place to stay in his home while he waited. He hated not knowing what was happening. What if the lengths they were going to weren't enough? What if the device made it across the border and into Idrias? He had notified Savita as soon as he got the information about the device. She had promised to contact her sister and Kendrick about it.

Savita had missed their last meeting. She was busy investigating the Conclave to see which of them had tried to kill Kendrick and Esha, which was as dangerous as what Ravi and Yasmin were undertaking. Dain did his best to help Savita, but it hadn't been easy. When information about the device had reached him, he had to shift his entire focus to it.

"Dain!"

He spun around in the hallway. He spotted Arya leaning against a wall, heaving, and raced to her. With one look, he knew she had been in the thick of battle. "Where are Ravi and Yasmin?"

"I had to get her out. Ravi stayed behind to track the device," Arya explained.

"What happened to Yasmin?"

Arya hesitated. "She's dying. She's with the healer, but..."

Dain nodded, not needing to hear more. "I'm going in after Ravi."

"Not without me."

He eyed her. She was fatigued and bruised, but he knew she wouldn't be left behind. Besides, he could use the help. "Let's go."

Staff scurried away at the sight of Ravi. He leaned against the wall and wished the stones would tell him the quickest way to the back exit. But he couldn't hear them, and he didn't have Yaz to translate. Which meant he was on his own. How had he ever thought that was what he preferred?

He heard more guards approaching. His magic was all but depleted, and he had no idea when he might see the sun again. He needed help. But he knew just the place. Ravi straightened from the wall and ran to the stairs, stepping over the dead. He reached the staircase and slid down the banister to the second floor.

His landing wasn't perfect, but he stayed on his feet. He rushed into the market area to see only two guards watching over the staff. Ravi caught sight of the children. They were drenched and shaking as they held on to each other. The bastards had left them to face the storm while everyone else went for safety.

Ravi locked his gaze on the guards and started toward them. They peeled back their lips in excitement at the sight of him. One rushed him, his arm up and his blade poised. Ravi saw the move coming and easily ducked the downward swing. As he passed the guard, Ravi used his sword to slice the guard's stomach. Ravi straightened and faced the second one as the first hit the floor with a thud.

The guard slowly withdrew his sword. Ravi saw that it was one the Asavori Rangers carried. The elf twisted his wrist to send the blade twirling around him. Ravi brought his weapon up, their blades clanging together. They each used their other hand to get leverage, but neither was able to gain the advantage.

Ravi stepped back and swung his blade down, using the guard's momentum. He shoved the elf to the side before he spun and sank the blade into the guard's back. A strangled cry gurgled from his opponent before he collapsed.

Ravi abandoned his weapon and turned to find the staff staring at him with a mixture of wariness and fear. Then his gaze slid to the children. He wiped the blood from his hands on his pants as he made his way to them. They squished tighter together as he approached.

He slowed his steps and lifted his hands as he smiled. When he reached them, he went down on one knee. "I'm not going to hurt you."

The way they clutched each other broke his heart. No child should have to endure such a life. It didn't matter if they were human or elf. He kept his expression easy as he found the lock on the chain that bound them.

"It's been a strange night, aye?" he said pleasantly as he called to his magic to unlock the latch. It took a moment for it to respond and break the padlock. "I bet you'd like to get dry. Maybe find some food," he said as he tossed aside the lock and began removing the chains.

The children didn't respond. Their wide, terrified eyes confirmed that their trauma went deep. Even when the bonds were removed, they didn't budge. He glanced at the staff. He wasn't sure he could trust them, but he also couldn't send the children out into the mountains on their own. But they couldn't remain either. Arya would've come in handy at that moment.

As if his thoughts had conjured her, she stepped out of a darkened corner. Another shadow appeared to the left and parted to reveal Dain. Ravi couldn't remember ever being so happy to see him.

"About time," Ravi said as he straightened.

Dain's yellow gaze flicked to the kids. "You've made a mess here."

Ravi ignored him and looked at Arya. "Can you get the children to safety?"

"Of course," she replied and walked to them with a smile. "Come, my darlings. We're going to be free of this terrible place."

To Ravi's surprise, Arya was able to coax the children to her. Her shadows enveloped her and the first two as she got them to safety. Ravi strode to the weapons booth and grabbed a Ranger blade from the display on the wall. He also took two daggers. He shoved one into the side of his boot, and the other went into the waist of his pants. Then he went from table to table, grabbing anything and everything he could find as Arya returned and removed more of the kids.

Dain glared at the market, his lip curled in disgust. But he also grabbed items.

"The device is headed toward the back exit," Ravi said as he passed the Dark.

Dain fell into step with him. "What are we waiting for then?"

They raced out of the hall to the stairs, where they found five guards waiting. Ravi and Dain exchanged a look, but neither slowed. A vine of magic shot toward Ravi's head. He slid to the ground, the momentum propelling him across the smooth tile. He lopped off the elf's hand as he passed, then popped back onto his feet behind the guard. The elf's screams of pain were silenced when Ravi shoved his blade into the guard.

Magic sizzled along the back of Ravi's leg as he turned. His muscles went lax, and his knee gave out as pain flooded him. Ravi spotted a Sun Elf striding toward him as he fell. With his leg seizing and stabs of pain running up and down his limb, Ravi released the last bit of his magic against the elf bearing down on him. Yellow coiled outward from Ravi's palm and wrapped around the guard's head, ripping it from his body.

"Impressive," Dain said as he helped Ravi to his feet. "You good?"

The pain was diminishing, but it would be some time before his leg was right again. Ravi glanced at the three guards the Dark had taken down. He nodded, and they were off again. Ravi didn't move as fast as before and had a limp, but he still managed to keep up with Dain.

The guards dogged their every step, making him and Dain stop repeatedly to fight their way through. Dain was lethal. Ravi might not like him, but he was glad the Dark was on his side. Even Ravi could admit that they made a great team.

Ravi blew out a breath when they finally reached the main floor. He scanned the area that had once been filled with guests. Shaldorn was as silent as a tomb. Did that mean the guests were gone? Or dead?

"How much magic do you have left?" Dain asked as they jogged down a long corridor.

Ravi shook his head. "Very little, if any."

They turned a corner and were met by seven guards, along with One and Three. He and Dain came to a halt.

"Who are the two in front?" Dain asked.

Ravi eyed the Star Elf on his left and the Wood Elf on his right. "The rest of the Trinity who runs Shaldorn. They go by One and Three, though I don't know which is which. I killed Two earlier."

Dain looked at him. "Then let's take care of these. You good?"

"I'm still on my feet."

The Dark grinned before facing the group. He raised his voice and said, "You have one chance to step aside, or we kill you where you stand."

The Star Elf laughed. "Not going to happen."

The Wood Elf motioned with his hand, and the guards attacked.

Ravi's sword was in his right hand, a dagger in his left. He held his position, saving his energy as the guards rushed them. Gray magic lashed out like lightning from Dain to zap into four of the guards' hearts, ending their lives instantly.

The other three didn't slow. Ravi dodged one shot of magic, but he wasn't quick enough for a second as it pelted his shoulder and spun him. The dagger fell from his hand and skittered across the floor when he landed on his side. Ravi quickly got to one knee, grabbing the second dagger from his boot as he did. He brought up the blade in time to block a blow from a guard's weapon.

Ravi surged to his feet and used his sword to slice the guard's stomach open. He glanced over to find Dain pulling his sword from an opponent's mouth. All seven guards lay dead around them.

Then, One and Three attacked.

Ravi flew backward from the force of the Star Elf's magic and landed with a bone-jarring thud on the floor. He rolled to his stomach and got to his feet. His fingers tightened on the pommel of his sword as he glared at his enemy. The Star Elf's purple gaze remained locked on Ravi as he strode forward.

"Gita wants your head on a spike," the elf stated.

Ravi shrugged a shoulder as they circled each other. "I'd like hers on one myself."

"You have no idea what you've done, do you?"

"I know I'm stopping evil. So, which one are you? Three?"

"One."

The Star Elf was dressed in finery with his long, silver hair in a queue at the base of his neck. One might appear noble, but Ravi saw the truth behind the façade. He was a fighter, an elf who lived and breathed conflict.

Ravi blinked the sweat and blood out of his eyes and sought his magic. It flared briefly but fizzled quickly. He needed the sun. It had been too long since he had felt it upon his skin, and he'd sucked the amulet dry. If he was going to get out of this alive, Ravi would have to use his other skills.

"What's the matter?" One asked with a smirk. "Having a hard time with your magic? You Sun Elves always think you're better than the rest."

"I don't think I'm better than others. I just think I'm better than you."

"By the time I'm done with you, you will beg for death."

"You've spent too much time tormenting humans who don't stand up to you. It's time you're reminded where you belong."

One smiled. "On top."

The words were barely out of his mouth before One raised his hand, and a coil of purple magic shot forward. Ravi moved his foot to the side and leaned away, rotating to watch as the magic slid mere breaths from his chest to hit something behind him. Ravi straightened and lunged as he thrust his blade at One. The Star Elf spun away and brought his hands up, his magic making a shield around him just as Ravi leaped into the air, his sword over his head.

He landed, and the tip of the blade pierced the barrier. Ravi grinned. "It's an Asavori sword."

Rage simmered in One's purple eyes. The elf brought the backs of his hands toward his chest and then shoved out with a bellow. Ravi didn't have time to move or get his sword free. He was flung, his body twisting in the air. His head slammed against the stone, and he slid a short distance.

Fingers wrapped around his throat a heartbeat before magic followed. Ravi opened his eyes to find One above him. Ravi curled his fingers, looking for the sword, but his weapon was gone. One's hand tightened painfully. The magic circling him constricted, choking him.

One leaned down, his lip curled in a sneer. "Take the back road and cut across the Cauthon Pass. It's the only way you'll get to the device in time."

Ravi blinked in surprise. Then, One was gone. Ravi coughed as his hand went to his throat. He sat up to find Dain using a wall to get to his feet. Three lay dead behind him.

"Where did he go?" Dain asked as he moved his gaze about them.

Ravi's body protested as he once more climbed to his feet. "Is One working with you?"

"I would've told you if he was."

"Nay, you wouldn't have."

Dain shrugged. "Probably not. But nay. He isn't. Where is he?"

Shaldorn might appear empty, but that didn't mean others weren't listening. Ravi walked to Dain and whispered, "He told me where to find the device."

"You believe him?" Dain asked.

Ravi shrugged. "Why tell me?"

"Because we were winning."

"I wasn't."

Dain shrugged. "Maybe to throw us off where the device really is?"

"Maybe. We won't know until we look." Ravi wiped blood from his eye.

Dain ran the back of his arm across his mouth to swipe away the blood there. "Where did he say it was?"

"He said to take the back road and cut across Cauthon Pass. Can you get us there?"

"I know less about these mountains than you. But I know someone who does. I'll be back."

Ravi was once more left on his own. He found his sword and a dagger before limping his way down the corridor. There was no exit in sight. This was where Yaz had said to get out, and she wouldn't steer him wrong.

He was glad she was safe now. It was the only reason he could keep his mind on his mission. Ravi paused and leaned a shoulder against the wall as he rubbed his injured leg, suddenly so weary it took every ounce of his strength to stay on his feet.

The only things left for him to do were to find the device and Gita. He'd added her to his mission because she had to be stopped. She couldn't be allowed to continue this operation.

He closed his eyes for a moment, and flashes of Yaz's bruised and bloodied body filled his mind. Ravi jerked open his eyes and tried to shake the images from his head. One had taken part in hurting Yaz. It didn't matter if he had told Ravi where the device was. Ravi was going to hunt him down for his role in Shaldorn.

He inhaled deeply before pushing away from the wall. He only made it a few steps before Dain appeared with another elf covered in furs. Ravi took in the dark brown hair, black eyes, and pale skin of the new arrival.

"No one knows these mountains like Manu," Dain said.

Manu looked Ravi up and down. "I know how to get to the pass. We're going to need to move fast." He tossed something at Ravi. "Put that on."

Ravi's hands closed around the soft white and gray fur. He was staring at an actual Mountain Elf. He could hardly believe it. Ravi had so many questions, but he saved them as he slid the coat on and fastened the closures.

"I hope you two can keep up," Manu said before he turned and ran.

Ravi and Dain exchanged a look and raced after him. Manu moved through the hallways as if he knew Shaldorn. There were no more guards to come for them, and Ravi only glimpsed a few staff before Manu led them to the back exit. They left the warmth of the fortress and ran into the ice and snow.

Ravi expected to feel the cold as before, but the fur kept him warm. He glanced into the gray sky, hoping the clouds would part so he could see the sun. At least, it was daytime, which gave him a slim chance of the sunlight peeking through. Ravi groaned in annoyance when he realized he had fallen behind. He pushed himself harder, forcing his legs to move faster to catch up to Dain. Manu was up ahead and getting even farther away.

"How bad are you injured?" Dain asked.

Ravi shook his head. "I'm fine."

Before Ravi knew it, Dain's shadows engulfed them as he ran. When they parted, he would've fallen on his face had Dain not grabbed him. They were now ahead of Manu, but the elf was catching up quickly.

"Rest while you can," Dain said.

Ravi looked at the Dark. "You should go on without me. I won't be able to keep up."

"I fucking hate the cold."

Ravi looked back at Shaldorn. "There are other staff who could be rescued."

"Shut up and move," Manu said as he neared.

Dain grabbed Ravi and shoved him as they began running

again. It wasn't long before Manu passed them. Ravi couldn't believe how quickly the Mountain Elf moved. There wasn't a path to follow. Just raw land and unforgiving mountains. Neither he nor Dain could keep up with Manu, but Dain didn't leave Ravi's side. When they fell behind too much, Dain used his shadows to get them ahead so they could rest for a moment, only to do it all again.

When they reached a mountainside, and Manu scaled it as if it were nothing more than a hill, Dain looked up and snorted. Ravi understood. There was no way he could follow. The Dark was tiring, and Ravi wouldn't ask Dain to haul him to the top. Yet Dain did it anyway.

There wasn't much time to rest with how swiftly Manu climbed. Ravi wondered if all Mountain Elves were like that.

"Get to the bottom," Manu told them as he launched himself over the top of the mountain and began jumping down vast sections onto narrow rocks that shouldn't hold him.

Dain said something under his breath that Ravi didn't catch. Ravi was mesmerized by Manu but didn't get to watch for long as Dain's shadows cut off his view. Once in the valley, Ravi turned to look for Manu.

"How long have you known him?" Ravi asked.

Dain grunted as Manu overbalanced but caught himself in time. "A few years. He doesn't talk much."

"So you two must get along great."

Dain chuckled. "He tolerates me."

"I know the feeling," Ravi replied.

Manu reached them, his breathing only slightly elevated. He nodded at the mountain in front of them. "I'll see you on the other side."

"Hold on," Dain said.

But Manu kept going.

Each time a Dark traveled by shadows, it drained them. The longer distances and having a passenger greatly increased that. But even if he hadn't sustained injuries, Ravi wouldn't have been able to keep up with Manu. If Dain wasn't here, Manu would be forced to slow his progress to wait for Ravi.

Or leave him.

Ravi knew the Mountain Elf would've left him. He didn't take it personally. Not when their mission was so critical.

Dain paused momentarily at the top of the next mountain before moving them to the snow-topped forest. There was a river nearby. Ravi hurried to it, lying flat on his stomach near the edge and cupping his hand into the freezing water to drink. He didn't rise until Dain called his name. Ravi was next to the Dark by the time Manu reached them.

Manu didn't stop jogging. "The pass is this way," he said as he moved to the right.

"Are we ahead of whoever has the device?" Ravi asked as he and Dain fell into step behind the Mountain Elf.

Manu shrugged. "Won't know that until we get through the pass."

"We don't know where the carrier will go after that," Dain said. "We need to beat them to it."

"I know where they'll go," Manu replied.

Ravi waited for him to elaborate, but the discussion ended. Which was for the best since Manu began running again.

It didn't take long for every breath that filled Ravi's lungs to feel like ice crystals stabbing him. Dain continued to get them ahead of Manu, but it was tiring the Dark Elf. Manu wasn't fazed at all. He kept a constant pace the entire time.

Cauthon Pass seemed to go on forever. Peaks towered on either side of them. In the distance, an animal released a loud roar. Ravi looked around for it, but Manu didn't seem to hear it. There was a brief respite for Ravi when the clouds broke for a moment, allowing the sun's rays to reach him.

Ravi wished he could stop and soak it all in, but it was enough that he felt his magic responding to the sunlight. Unfortunately, clouds soon blocked the sun again. They grew thicker as they traveled, denying the light.

Finally, Manu halted.

Ravi and Dain came up on either side of him, both of them breathing hard.

The Mountain Elf pointed ahead of them. "There's the road."

"I see only snow," Dain said as he squinted into the distance.

Manu grunted. "It's there. For now, we wait."

"Thank the gods," Dain murmured.

The three stood in silence, waiting. Ravi was about to say they needed to move on when he heard the jingle of a harness. They ducked as the sleigh came into view around the mountain bend.

37

"How do you want to do this?" Dain asked.

Ravi was surprised the Dark was conceding anything to him. He knew it was Dain's mission. He met the Dark's gaze. "Your call."

Dain bowed his head. "Ravi, stand in the road. I'll come in from behind the sleigh. Manu, be ready in case something goes awry."

Manu crawled backward and raced away, keeping out of sight.

"Ready?" Dain asked.

Ravi had his eyes on the sleigh. "Absolutely."

Ravi rose and made his way down the short embankment to the road. He stood in the center and faced the sleigh. When she spotted him, the driver flicked the reins to move the horses faster. A mass of darkness rose behind the sleigh. The driver was intent on Ravi and didn't look behind her. Ravi grinned as the shadows moved quickly to catch up to the vehicle, soon converging around it.

Yet the sleigh didn't stop.

Ravi held up his hands in an effort to stop the horse, but it wasn't working. His grin slipped when he had to step to the side or get run over. When the vehicle reached him, Ravi jumped and grabbed hold of a harness before dragging himself up atop one of the horses. He could hear the sounds of combat within the shadows as he tugged on the reins.

The horses drew to a halt. Ravi jumped down, wincing at the pain that lingered in his leg. Dain must have seen him approaching because the shadows fell away. He found Dain and a Sun Elf locked in combat. A dagger stuck out of Dain's chest on the right side near his shoulder. He had one of the elf's arms twisted at an odd angle while the female stabbed a second blade into Dain's right thigh with her free hand.

Ravi jumped into the sleigh just as Dain shouted his name. Ravi managed to lean to the side as a blade came near his face, followed quickly by a shot of yellow magic. He grabbed the elf's arm and pinned it to the seat before she could attack again. She bared her teeth and tried to bite him. Ravi rammed his fist into her jaw, knocking her out.

"Fuck," Dain muttered as he released the unconscious elf and dropped his head back.

Ravi rummaged through the female's pockets and the sleigh until he located the black orb. He held it up as he and Dain exchanged smiles.

"You did it," Dain said.

"*We* did it," Ravi corrected.

Dain bowed his head. "We did it."

Ravi shoved the unconscious elf to the floor of the sleigh and sat heavily. Then he jerked his chin to the weapons sticking out of Dain. "Want me to remove them?"

"I'm afraid you'll enjoy it too much."

Ravi shrugged. "Probably."

Without another word, he reached over and carefully removed the blade from Dain's leg first. Ravi tore off a portion of the Sun Elf's shirt to use as a bandage to help stop the blood flow.

Dain's face was pale, his breathing ragged. Ravi opened his coat and cut off the bottom part of his shirt. Dain nodded when Ravi wrapped his fingers around the pommel of the dagger. He pulled it free and quickly bandaged the wound. When he finished, Dain sat with his eyes closed, and his lips pinched.

"Fuck," Dain said after a moment.

"We need to get you to a healer soon."

Dain looked at him. "I'll be fine."

"Where's Manu?"

"He probably left. He'd show himself if he was still around."

Ravi took a moment to tie the Sun Elf's hands behind her back. Then, he gathered the reins and turned the horses around. The ride to Shaldorn would have been scenic if he had been paying attention. He ran the horses as fast as he dared, slowing them when needed. But he was in a hurry to find Yaz and let her know the mission was complete. He wanted to share that with her. She had earned it, after all. Maybe after that, he would see a healer and sleep for at least a day.

The last hour of the trip, snow flurries drifted in the air. He and Dain didn't speak much. They were too exhausted. It took everything Ravi had to keep going.

Elation pumped through him when he caught sight of Shaldorn. Even Dain sat up straighter in the seat. Their prisoner stirred. Dain set his feet on top of her, which made Ravi smile. He drove them to the back of the fortress and spotted Manu and Arya waiting for them.

Ravi pulled the sleigh to a stop and smiled at the pair. "We have a prisoner. Who wants her?"

"Leave her to me," Dain said.

Ravi dropped the reins and climbed out of the sleigh, walking around to help Dain. "Has the staff gotten out?"

Arya's lips twisted. "I got many of them away, but some chose to head into the mountains."

"My people will make sure they get where they want to go," Manu said.

Arya glanced at the doorway behind her. "Others are too frightened to leave."

"We can't make them," Dain said. He leaned heavily on Ravi until he could stand on his own.

Ravi passed the device to Dain. "Get this to Durga. I'll rest easy once I know it's in the DIA's hands." Ravi slid his gaze to Arya. "Can you take me to Yaz? I want to let her know we succeeded."

Arya's gray eyes jerked to Dain. Ravi frowned at her odd behavior. Then, he noted that Dain and Manu were watching him closely. His gut clenched in dread.

"Whatever it is, tell me now," Ravi demanded.

Had Yaz left? He could imagine her doing exactly that. Even though she technically wouldn't complete the mission until they were back in Rannora. He wouldn't hold that against her, though. Durga didn't need to know those details. Yaz had earned her freedom—from Shaldorn and the DIA.

Dain limped forward a step. "Arya, give us an update."

"She's not good," the female Dark said softly.

Ravi shook his head, not believing the words. He couldn't have heard right. "You got Yaz to a healer, right? She should be fine."

Arya swallowed. "Her injuries were extensive."

Ravi shook his head again. Yaz was a fighter. She wouldn't give up. Not after everything she had endured.

"There's a second healer with her," Arya continued.

Ravi held up a hand to silence her. He'd heard enough. "Take me to her. Please."

Thankfully, Arya's shadows wrapped around him without further argument. When they separated, he stood in a hallway outside a doorway with a pointed arch. He looked into the room and saw a large bed close to the floor. Lying in the middle of the mattress was Yaz. Someone had bathed the blood from her and brushed her hair. It lay in a single braid over one shoulder. Fur blankets were piled on top of her, stopping just beneath her chin. On either side of her was a Star Elf, their eyes closed and hands upon her as they worked their magic.

He started forward when Arya grabbed his arm.

"You need food and a healer yourself," she said.

Ravi shook his head. "I'd rather they save their magic for her."

"Then come. There is food and a hot bath waiting."

"I can't." Now that he had seen Yaz, he couldn't let her out of his sight again.

Arya moved in front of him and waited until he looked at her. "She's in good hands. You won't do anyone any good in your present state."

Ravi wanted to argue, but he was suddenly too weary. He let Arya lead him away, his gaze lingering on Yaz until he could no longer see her. Arya didn't take him far. She brought him to another room down the hall. There was a bed, a roaring fire in the hearth, and an oval tub that looked big enough he could stretch out in it and be covered by the water. The smell of food made him dizzy. Ravi was barely cognizant of Arya removing the coat Manu had lent him. Then he was seated at a table.

"Eat," Arya ordered.

He had no idea what was on the plate, but it didn't matter. He couldn't remember the last time he had been this hungry. Ravi ate until he couldn't stand to look at the food anymore. He sat back in the chair and scanned the room for Arya, but she wasn't there. She must have slipped out while he was eating. He didn't mind. It was nice to have a few moments alone.

The steam rising from the tub called to him. Ravi glanced down at his clothes and saw what was left of them. Suddenly, he wanted out of them. He kicked off his boots and got out of the ripped and bloodied clothing.

He climbed into the tub and let the water cover him, sighing in contentment. The heat felt good. Not even the sting of his injuries could get him to leave the bath. His eyes became too heavy to remain open. He found himself drifting off. Then, he remembered Yaz.

Ravi sat up and scrubbed the battle from his body. As he dried off, he saw clean clothes laid out on the bed. He dressed quickly, pausing long enough to rake his fingers through his wet hair before making his way back to Yaz.

The healers were still there. He stood in the doorway and stared as if he could somehow will Yaz to heal and wake up. He wanted to look into her dark blue eyes again.

"Any change?" Dain asked in a soft voice as he came up beside him.

Ravi glanced at the Dark to see that he, too, had washed and redressed. "None that I know of. I knew she was hurt, but I didn't know it was this bad."

"She asked Arya not to tell you. Yaz knew your mission was important."

Ravi closed his eyes and put his back to the doorway. "What did they do to her?"

"I just found out. Honestly, it might be better if you didn't know."

Ravi's eyes snapped open, and he pinned the Dark with a look. "Dain."

"They broke her. They snapped and shattered dozens of her bones. All of her fingers and toes. Her hands and feet. Her knees. Her hip. Her arms. Part of her spine."

Ravi looked away, his stomach churning. He couldn't stand to hear anymore, but it was nothing compared to what Yaz had endured. She deserved a life to live as she wanted. Without worry about anyone or anything trying to harm her. Free to communicate with the stones.

He spun to face Dain. "She shared a secret with me. One she has kept to herself her entire life."

"Then you need to keep it."

"But what if that hinders her healing?"

Dain's white brows drew together in a frown. "How could it?"

Ravi glanced at Yaz. "I don't know. It might." Still, he hesitated. "I want your word that whatever I share stays between us. You can't tell anyone."

"I can't give you that. If it will help or hurt her recovery, I need to tell the healers."

"Do you trust them?"

"I don't trust anyone."

Ravi slid his gaze to Yaz. "Our magic doesn't hinder our healing, does it?"

"How could it? It's magic that heals."

"What about a different kind of magic?"

Dain drew closer, his voice a whisper as he asked, "Are you telling me she has magic?"

"Of a sort." Ravi turned his head to him. "She can communicate with stones. That's how we reached Shaldorn. That's how we were able to get inside and move about as we did."

Dain blew out a breath and lowered his gaze to the floor. After a moment, he said, "Let me speak to the healers. I'll only tell them what I must."

Ravi watched Dain walk to the bed. The healers paused to look at him as he began speaking. Ravi couldn't hear what he said. He had never trusted Darks. He couldn't say he trusted Dain, but he put more faith in him and Arya than other Dark Elves. Ravi really hoped he wasn't wrong about them.

Dain returned a short time later. He paused with his back to the room. "They felt something different about her, but they don't believe it will hinder the healing process."

"Are they healing her?"

"It's slow. There's a lot of damage. They don't know if they can repair everything in time. One is keeping her body going as the other tackles the injuries."

"Then bring another healer," Ravi urged. "I'll go get one. Whatever it takes."

Dain placed a hand on his shoulder. "I brought another, just in case. He saw to my wounds and is healing others from Shaldorn. You should let him see to you."

"Bring him to Yaz. She needs him more than I do."

Dain dropped his arm to his side. "There is a chair inside. Take it before you fall over."

Ravi watched him walk away before he silently entered the room. The chair was near the bed, against a wall. He lowered himself into it and stretched out his legs. It wasn't long before his eyes became heavy. He propped his elbow on the arm of the chair and rested his cheek on his hand.

Whispers woke him. Ravi jerked awake and looked at Yaz, but she still lay unmoving. His attention moved to the source of the voices. Dain was with the two healers from before, both of which looked ready to pass out. Dain noticed Ravi's gaze on him and nodded to the healers, who walked out of the room.

"They need rest," Dain said.

Ravi sat up. "How far did they get in her healing?"

"Not far enough."

And the longer Yaz lay there without them, the quicker she would die. "I know of other healers. If you'll help me, I can get them here."

"The healer I spoke of earlier is on his way now. He'll take over while the other two rest. But, Ravi, you need to prepare yourself in case she doesn't ma—"

"I know," he said before Dain could finish.

The sound of footsteps grew louder until they turned into the room. Ravi looked up to see a Star Elf with bright violet eyes and dark purple hair walking to the bed. His attention was solely on Yaz. The healer held a hand over her and moved it from her head to her feet. Then he sat in one of the vacated chairs and placed his hands on her body.

This time, Dain remained. Ravi was grateful to have someone with him.

38

The hours bled into each other as the healers rotated in and out of Yaz's room. Ravi alternated between pacing and sitting as he watched the trio of elves continue to repair the damage Yaz had sustained.

And somehow, through it all, she clung to life.

Ravi ate when food was put in front of him and drank when a cup was placed in his hand, but he didn't leave Yaz's side.

He didn't know what day it was. He didn't even know what time of day it was. Worse, he had no idea where he was.

And he didn't care.

There were occasions when Ravi heard voices outside Yaz's room. He caught Dain's voice a time or two. A week ago, he would've been right beside Dain, wrapping up the mission or returning to Rannora for another. He had changed somewhere in the ice and snow of the Dangerous Peaks. Fundamentally.

He ran a hand down his face and shifted forward in his chair to prop his elbows on his thighs. Yaz had taken care of him when he was ill. Where had he been when she needed him? Fulfilling his assignment. He should've looked closer at her. He could've urged Arya to get the device. It didn't always have to be him saving the day.

Not at the cost of someone like Yaz.

There had been nothing outside of work for him in a very long time. No friends, no hobbies. Not even downtime. He was his job, and his job was him. Not that he hadn't had his share of affairs. He had. But they had been meaningless. He always held a portion of himself back, never giving anyone everything. Because he had known he couldn't have a life with them. The reality was that he hadn't *wanted* a future with any of them.

He had liked his perfectly ordered life where his emotions were always in check. Yaz had ripped apart the walls around him, though she hadn't come inside. Instead, she had made him see and feel things he hadn't dared to experience before.

Now that he had, there was no turning it off.

And he didn't wish to.

"You look like shite."

Ravi glanced up to find Dain beside him. There was no malice in the Dark's voice. Just truth. Dain sighed as he brought a second chair next to him and sat. Ravi was known for his attention to detail, but he had been so focused on Yaz that everything else around him had become fuzzy and distorted. Almost as if none of it were real.

"Arya and I have been scouring Shaldorn," Dain said.

In the past, this would've had Ravi on his feet and raring to go. He should make an effort. But he couldn't leave Yaz. "What have you found?"

"There's been no sign of Gita or One. I doubt they'll return anytime soon. We did locate more staff. We've spent a lot of time coaxing them to leave. Nearly all are out. Only a few remained. Arya is working to convince them they'll be safe."

"Will they?"

Dain shrugged. "You know the answer to that."

Ravi nodded before he dropped his head to pinch the bridge of his nose with his thumb and forefinger.

"My agency dismantled the device." Dain paused, letting it draw out. "Durga is waiting to talk to you."

"I know."

"We're not giving up on Yasmin."

Ravi looked up at Dain and nodded. "I'm not either."

Dain rose and left without another word.

The hours dragged after that. Each one without Yaz waking sounded like a death knell in Ravi's head. He let his thoughts drift, jumping from memory to memory. Inevitably, a picture of Yaz filled his head. He remembered how she had kept her head high as Durga's men hauled her into that small room behind the restaurant. The only time he'd glimpsed fear was when Durga had threatened prison.

Now that Ravi had seen the box used at Shaldorn, he understood Yaz's terror. He couldn't imagine how scared she had been sitting in that room with them. Yaz hadn't cried or begged to be released. She had waited to learn what Durga wanted. Even when Yaz grasped that she was in an impossible position, she hadn't taken it out on anyone else. She had focused on what she had to do to get it done so she could return to the kids.

A hand on his shoulder jarred him. Ravi's eyes snapped open, and he sat up at the sight of the male healer.

"I've healed your injuries."

"I told you, I'm fine. Save it and the herbs for Yaz and the others," Ravi snapped.

The Star Elf dropped his arm to his side. "We've done all we can for her."

Ravi glanced at the bed to find Yaz still as death. "Is she...?"

"She's sleeping." The Star Elf sat, his violet gaze intense as he regarded Ravi. "I can't promise she will wake. There was substantial damage. I'm amazed she's lived as long as she has."

"She's a fighter."

The healer nodded. "Aye, she is. There was a lot of scar tissue. This wasn't her first time being hurt in such a manner."

Ravi looked at Yaz. "What are her chances?"

"Hard to say. Her body has been mended. However, there could be psychological damage."

Ravi's head swung to him. "Meaning?"

"Her mind might not allow her to wake. I took the liberty of having a look for myself."

"And? Did you find anything?"

"The brain is a unique and powerful organ. Most healers don't delve into such things for fear of taking things too far."

Ravi swallowed past the lump in his throat. "You don't feel the same?"

"I've done more research than most, but I'm not an expert by any means. I couldn't detect anything in Yasmin's mind that caused me concern. That isn't to say there's nothing there," he cautioned.

Ravi digested that bit of news. "Thank you..." He frowned. "I don't even know your name."

The Star Elf chuckled. "I give it to very few, and Dain knows this. I'm Vijay."

"I'm honored to know your name. Thank you for all you've done for us."

Vijay bowed his head. "The honor is mine."

Ravi stood with him as the healer left the room. Ravi would find the other two soon and thank them. Words would never truly convey the depth of his gratitude.

Now that he was alone with Yaz, he brought the chair closer to the bed and lowered himself into it. He hesitated when he started to touch her, and instead fingered the end of her braid.

"It's time to wake, Yaz," he told her. "There are things to do. You need to get back to the children. They need you. I...need you. I need you, Yaz. Please, wake up."

Ravi hadn't expected her to open her eyes, but as the day wore on and she didn't stir, his worry grew. Hour after hour, she lay without moving or responding to him. Dain spoke to her. Vijay returned and talked to her, but she seemed too far away for anyone to reach. The sadness in the healer's eyes told Ravi exactly what he thought.

"Don't," Ravi told Vijay before he could say the words. "She'll wake."

The world faded away again. The only one who was clear and steady was Yaz. Ravi folded his arms on the bed and rested his head upon them. He allowed himself to nap, and each time he woke, he feared he would find her gone to a place he couldn't follow. He ate because he had to, but he didn't taste anything. It could've been dust for all the attention he paid to it—or cared.

He prayed to each of the gods, sending up prayers he hadn't said since he was a small boy in hopes one of them was listening. They had kept Yaz alive many times before. He only asked for one more. Yet each of those prayers went unanswered.

Rage set in. He paced the room like a caged animal, his hands fisted at his sides as he imagined what he would do to Gita and One when he found them. Ravi had never cared for torture, but he would take great pleasure in meting it out to those two. Then he would haul them to Durga and let them rot in jail, never to see the outside world again.

Never to hurt anyone again.

He meticulously planned the torture for each of them, imagining how they would scream and beg for him to stop. He would carry out his punishment at Shaldorn, in the very contraptions they had used on Yaz. It wouldn't bring her back, but it would be a smidge of the payback they deserved for Yaz and the countless others before her.

Ravi pivoted, only to come up short when Dain stood in his way. Ravi's stomach clenched, and he hastily looked at the bed. He watched Yaz's chest, waiting to see it rise and fall. When he did, he breathed a sigh of relief and noticed Arya fiddling with the covers.

"What?" Ravi demanded as he looked at Dain.

"I know what you're doing."

"I doubt it."

Dain's yellow eyes hardened. "You held on to hope for as long as you could. When that began to run out, you prayed to every one of the gods. The simmering anger boiled over when you didn't get a response. That's when you began to envision the vengeance you will unleash on those who hurt Yaz. Am I close?"

Ravi glared at the Dark but didn't answer.

"The gods don't ever answer," Dain continued. "I learned that a long time ago. Don't waste your time on prayers when you have me and Arya, who will join in your hunt for Gita and One."

Ravi slid his gaze to the bed and found Arya staring at him. She bowed her head in agreement. Ravi looked back at Dain. "Why?"

"Does it matter?"

"Nay," Ravi replied.

"Manu and his people have been keeping an eye out for them since we brought Yasmin here."

Ravi frowned. "Why would he care?"

"I wondered if Yasmin had shared that story," Dain said as his face softened. "Manu found her after she escaped Shaldorn. She was nearly frozen to death. He nursed her back to health and showed her the way out of the mountains."

Ravi ran a hand over his jaw, thick with a beard once more.

"I notified him that Yasmin was leading you to Shaldorn. He followed to make sure no trouble came upon either of you."

"I knew I saw someone trailing us."

Dain held his gaze. "The point is, you aren't the only one who wants revenge. We'll find them."

"Thanks."

The Dark turned on his heel, the loose edges of his coat billowing around him. "Take a bath. You stink," he said before leaving the room.

"You do," Arya added.

Ravi looked down at himself. He lifted an arm and sniffed, grimacing. He did need to wash and change. "Will you stay with Yaz until I return? I don't want her to be alone."

"Of course."

Ravi found his way back to the room he had been given. He hadn't seen it since he'd first arrived. He paused at the bed to find another set of clothes. Later, he would find out who was seeing to him and pay his respects.

He filled the tub as he undressed and wondered if magic heated the water or if there were thermal vents nearby. He had to admit that it felt good to stretch out in the tub and allow the heat to soften his tense muscles. His lower back ached from his time sitting. Not to mention his neck from falling asleep in such awkward positions.

Ravi reached for the soap, caught a whiff of sandalwood, and thought of Yaz. How long could she linger as she was? The healers could help keep her alive until she regained consciousness, but they couldn't do that forever. That was if she ever regained consciousness. There would come a time when someone would have to decide when enough was enough. He couldn't be that person.

He had failed to see how badly she was injured. All because he knew the device was nearby. His attention should've been on his partner. Because that's what Yaz was. And he had to admit, they worked well together—well, after they got past the hating-each-other part. He wanted a chance to tell her all of that.

He *needed* to say it.

Ravi could say it to her now, but he had been waiting until she woke. Perhaps he should prepare himself for the fact that he might never get to tell her when she was conscious. Maybe she would still hear it. There were elves who believed those caught between life and death could hear and see others. Ravi had never thought much about it until now. Could she see him? Could she hear him?

Would she know how sorry he was for leaving her?

Would she know the lengths he'd gone to for her?

Would she know how much he cared?

He thought about the way she had looked at him when they walked through Shaldorn. He was the one she had grabbed when the past rose up. He was the one who steadied her. But he was also the reason she had been in that godsforsaken place to begin with.

Ravi finished his bath and got out. He walked to the sink and stared at his reflection in the mirror. He ran a hand over his beard which had begun to grow in again. Yaz had liked his face devoid of hair. So, he found a razor and shaved. Then he put on clean clothes and left his room.

Halfway to Yaz's, he heard voices. As he approached, he saw a group standing outside her door. Their smiles and laughter had hope surging inside him. He shouldered his way through the crowd, halting at the doorway. Inside, he spotted Arya, Dain, and Vijay standing around the bed. And sitting up against the headboard was Yaz.

Ravi looked over to find Dain watching him. The Dark motioned him forward. All the things Ravi wanted to say to Yaz filled him. Then he remembered the sight of her bloody body in the box.

He backed up and walked away.

39

Yasmin had her eyes closed as Arya combed her wet hair. She had taken the longest bath of her life. Her skin was still puckered from the water. They'd fed and clothed her, and now she was being fussed over. She drew in a deep breath and listened to the soft melody of the stones. Their song had risen joyfully when she woke. Now, it sat in the background, playing softly without her having to touch anything. She didn't know what had changed, but something had.

"You have the most beautiful hair," Arya said.

Yasmin smiled. "Thank you, but yours is prettier."

"I'd much rather have yours." Arya set aside the brush. "Shall I braid it?"

"If you'd like."

If Yasmin thought it would be the simple plait she normally did, she soon discovered how wrong she was. Her eyes locked on the bed. She had spoken to Manu, Arya, Dain, and Vijay, but Ravi had yet to visit. No one had said much about him.

"It's good to see you up and about. You have no idea how worried we were," Arya said.

Her injuries were healed, but Yasmin would be weak for a little while yet. "How long did it take Vijay to heal me?"

"He and two others worked on you for two straight days."

"Two?" she asked in shock.

"Every hour. They were all shocked you were still alive when I brought you here. We weren't sure you would make it."

"What of the device? Did Ravi find it?"

"He, Manu, and Dain tracked the elf who had it. The threat is over."

"That's good." She wanted to ask if that meant Ravi had returned to Rannora, but she couldn't get the words out. "What of the rest?"

Arya's touch was light and gentle as she gathered small portions of hair. "Gita and One got away, unfortunately. We rescued everyone we could. Some of the staff didn't trust us to help."

"They were under Shaldorn's control for too long. I'm glad some were freed."

"Gita abandoned Shaldorn. At least, that's what we believe. Dain and I have been combing the fortress while Manu and his people look in the mountains for Gita and One. We found evidence that someone returned to Shaldorn, but they didn't remain long. I don't know what will happen to the stronghold. It's in Manu's territory, so Dain left it up to him."

Yasmin tried not to think of the horrors that had happened there, but she wasn't sure the memories would ever leave her. "I hope Manu tears it down."

"I'll be leaving soon."

Yasmin tried to turn her head to see the Dark Elf, but Arya tsked and continued braiding. "Must you?"

"You were healed for two days and slept for three."

She had lain in bed for five days. No wonder she was so weak.

"My superiors expected me back yesterday. I can't linger any longer," Arya said.

Yasmin reached back and covered the Dark's hand with hers. "I'm glad I got to see you before you left. Thank you. For everything."

"This operation succeeded because of you. We owe you thanks."

Once again, Yasmin almost asked about Ravi, but she feared what she might hear. "I did what I had to do."

"What will you do now?" Arya asked.

Yasmin shrugged. "The assignment isn't complete until we return to Rannora. At least that's what I was told."

"There. All done." Arya came to stand before her. "As soon as he learned about your injuries, he came straight here and didn't leave your side. For five days, he remained and watched over you."

Yasmin's heart squeezed at the words. "Who?"

Arya gave her a sad smile. "You know who. The only reason he wasn't here when you woke is because Dain made him bathe. He asked me to stay with you in his stead."

Yasmin wondered what it might have been like to open her eyes and find Ravi there. What would she have said? What would he have said? Neither had said anything about their kiss. Obviously, he cared if he stayed with her. But... "Why hasn't he come to see me since?"

"Males," Arya said with a roll of her eyes. "Who knows what goes through their thick minds? I can tell you he was willing to do anything to ensure there were enough Star Elves to heal you. He refused to let you die."

Yasmin couldn't work out how someone could be that committed to helping another but then ignore them. She'd thought they had become...friends.

"I don't know Ravi well. From what little I've learned, he's stubborn and immovable at the best of times. He was worried about you. I've never seen someone so visibly distraught like he was before. Ask him why he hasn't come. I know I would. He might not tell you, but you won't get an answer unless you put the question to him."

It was good advice. She forced a smile as she looked into Arya's dark gray eyes. "I say this with all honesty. I hope to see you again."

"I'll make sure it happens." Arya winked. "Good luck."

Yasmin watched the Dark close the door behind her as she walked out. She reached up and felt along her hair, her fingertips skimming many smaller braids that had been plaited together into a fishtail. If this expedition had taught her anything, it was that her hatred and anger shouldn't be directed at all elves. Only those who deserved it.

Elves had hurt her, but elves had also saved her.

She stood on legs that still wobbled some, but she was alive. Her bones were mended, her flesh repaired. No one looking at her would know that she had been so close to death. But it hadn't been her first brush with it. Her scars were on the inside, hidden from everyone but herself.

Yasmin had another chance at a future. One where she could continue to ignore the past and the role it played in her decisions or confront it. Face it. And heal. If the past four years were any indication, ignoring things didn't work. She didn't want to carry the anger and pain around anymore. It was time for a change.

She looked at the chair near her bed. Was that the one Ravi had used? She had soldiered on for others all her life, putting aside the things she wanted or needed. Ravi had kissed her. He hadn't been acting.

And neither had she.

Yasmin walked to the door and stepped out into the hall. Manu's home was large, but she would search every floor until she found Ravi.

Locating the Sun Elf proved more difficult than Yasmin had initially believed. She was about to give up when she turned a corner and saw him. She halted, her heart hammering in her chest with excitement and nervousness. His back was to her as he looked out across the city through an arched window with thick pillars on either side. For a moment, she simply stared.

There had been moments when she had been sure she would never see him again. Now, here he was. Everything she had thought about saying formed a lump and locked in her throat. But she couldn't walk away. Not now. For better or worse, she needed to know the truth.

Yasmin gradually made her way to him. From the first moment she'd seen Ravi, he had been confident and assured, an elf who saw the path he was supposed to walk and strode upon it boldly. He didn't appear quite so assured now. Like his world had been shaken vigorously and hadn't settled back the way it had been before. She knew a little about that herself.

His broad shoulders lifted as he drew in a deep breath. He raked a hand through his unbound golden hair, then turned to leave. She parted her lips to call out to him, but her voice didn't work. He did a double take in her direction and halted in his tracks.

A dozen things popped into her mind as they stared at each other, but none of them seemed right. Not until she opened her heart. "When Manu found me shivering on the mountain, I didn't have the strength to push him away when he lifted me in his arms and carried me to a nearby cave. I tried to tell him to bring me back and let me die, but he ignored me. He built a fire, hunted food he soon had roasting over the flames, and covered me with his coat.

"He said very little at first, which was fine because I didn't want to talk. I had wanted death and was angry that he had prevented that. Yet I didn't throw off the blanket and walk back out into the storm. Not even when he left to find food. I didn't refuse to eat either. That's when he started talking."

Ravi's copper eyes studied her. He said nothing, but he didn't walk away.

Yasmin took that as a sign to continue. She closed the few paces separating them to stand before him. "He talked about this city. Navara, he called it. He told me about his home and his favorite place." She nodded at the arches. "Here. He said that it gave the finest view of the city. He talked for what seemed like hours before I ventured to speak. I told him that a city couldn't be within a mountain. That it wouldn't be big enough. He just smiled. I never thought I'd get to see Navara myself."

She faced the arches and gazed at the city. Navara wasn't as large or grand as Rannora or Belanore, but it was still a sight to behold: the light pouring in from the opened tip of the mountain, the streets where the residents walked, and the beautiful buildings shaped from the mountain itself.

"Did you know the Mountain Elves used to be united? Now, they're split into different factions all around the peaks," she continued. "Manu is lord of Navara. His ancestors were kings of the Mountain Elves. By chance alone, he was born into that line of royalty."

"Yaz."

Her stomach fluttered at the sound of her name on his lips. She turned her head to meet his gaze. Her fingers itched to touch his face, to skim along his jaw and delve into his hair. "I hear you succeeded in obtaining the device."

"With your help."

"I did little. You did the most."

He glanced at the floor as he clasped his hands behind his back. "How are you feeling?"

"Good, considering I was apparently teetering between this life and the afterlife."

"It's good to see you awake."

She searched his eyes, looking for...what, exactly? Desire? Love? It was ridiculous to hope for such a thing. She had hunted for him because she needed an answer. The memory of his kiss still lingered. As did the pain of his absence.

"Why haven't you come to see me?" She hated how her voice wobbled.

"I was going to."

An excuse wasn't an answer. Then again, perhaps it was. He

didn't want to tell her the truth. Instead of pushing, she decided to accept his words and move on. To do otherwise would be senseless.

She nodded and turned to walk away.

"Yaz."

Her mind told her to keep going, but her heart urged her to stop. She halted, but she didn't turn around.

Ravi's bootheels sounded on the stones as he approached. He didn't stop until he stood before her. His throat bobbed as he swallowed. "I'm overjoyed to see you awake. I was about to get something to eat. Will you join me?"

40

Seeing Yaz had been as wonderful and excruciating as Ravi had known it would be. He could've told her that he had walked to her door a dozen times but had been unable to knock. He could've told her that he'd asked everyone for updates about her.

But he didn't, and he wasn't sure why.

As soon as they entered the kitchen, the Mountain Elves there were quick to give Yaz anything she wanted. They had finally warmed up to him, but he wasn't as welcome as Yaz. And he couldn't blame the elves for that. She had an openness about her that he never could. It worked well for him as an agent but not so much around others.

Ravi was content to sit and watch Yaz as the elves fussed over her. It did his heart good to see her soft smile and hear her smooth voice—both of which he had thought lost to him forever. Once the table was laden with food, the elves returned to their duties, leaving him and Yaz and the awkwardness he couldn't eradicate. It was worse than their first meal together, and he knew it was his doing. *He* was making things uncomfortable.

Yaz, who had never been bothered by silence, began filling it with inane conversation. He could stop it all if he just told her that he had feelings for her. He didn't know what kind exactly, but they were there. It had begun before they even reached Shaldorn.

But he didn't have relationships. They got in the way of his work. His emotions had clouded his judgment at Shaldorn, and they would continue to do so if he didn't cut them off immediately. He'd been attempting to do just that.

Except, he didn't want to. He wanted to finish what he and Yaz had started at the compound. He wanted another kiss.

"I'm sorry," he said over her.

She looked up from her plate, startled. Her dark blue eyes searched his. "For?"

Why were the words so hard to say? Why couldn't he just tell her? "I've a lot on my mind."

"Understandable."

Another silence was growing. He needed to fill it. And quickly. "The children from Shaldorn have been returned to the cities and villages they were taken from."

"I'm glad. You did a good thing."

"It was Arya who got them out."

"It was a team effort."

Ravi grunted as he sat back in his chair, pushing his half-eaten food away. He hadn't been hungry but wanted more time with Yaz. "Funny. I never would've imagined working with Dain or any Dark before, but they came through when I needed them."

"Like I said. A team effort."

"I wouldn't exactly call Dain a friend."

"Wouldn't you?" she asked with a grin.

Ravi shrugged. "I wouldn't have before, but I might now. Just don't tell him I said that."

Yaz laughed softly. Seeing her eyes light up brought a grin to his lips. It was the first time he had heard her laugh. She barely smiled, but he had made her laugh.

"My lips are sealed," she promised.

His lips parted, ready to tell her how beautiful she was. He was interrupted by the kitchen servants appearing to take away their plates. The next thing Ravi knew, he and Yaz were walking unhurriedly down the corridors.

"Are you helping Manu search for Gita and One?" she asked.

Ravi snorted. "I couldn't keep up with him. The only reason I was able to before was because Dain used his shadows."

"I realize I must bring you back to Rannora to fulfill my contract. I'm sorry if I've held you up. I'm sure there is another assignment waiting for you."

"There's nothing to apologize for." He didn't plan on going anywhere until she was ready. No matter how long that took. But she had brought up the future, and he couldn't stop his thoughts. "What will you do once we return to the city?"

"I can't continue to allow the children to starve and live in the same atrocious ways we have. They deserve better."

"You aren't leaving them, are you? I thought you cared about them." The last came out harsher than intended.

Yaz shot him a sad smile. "I've not been doing a very good job, though. I don't want them going back to their previous families, but I don't know if they should remain with me."

"No one could love them as you do."

"I love them with all my heart, and I want them to be happy.

But that won't be the case if things continue as they are. There is nothing for us in Rannora."

Ravi had been afraid she would say that. He almost said *he* was there, but what could he offer her and the children? He was always gone. "Leaving has always been what you've wanted."

"I want to make sure Durga wipes my slate clean."

"She will." Ravi would make sure of it.

They faced each other when they reached his room. He was close enough to see the dark blue around her irises. He yearned for her. Ached in a way he didn't think possible. It was agony not to reach for her and pull her close. To claim her lips.

But he wouldn't stop there. He would take it all, claiming Yaz as his. Then, he would find a way to bind her to Rannora so she would never leave. Yet he had nothing to offer in exchange. He couldn't give her something he didn't have.

It took every ounce of willpower he had to remain where he was.

"You should rest," he said and turned to walk away.

Yasmin stared at Ravi's retreating back. She opened her mouth to call out to him but didn't know what to say. Maybe it was better that things ended like this—if there had been anything to begin with.

She reluctantly walked to her room. Her mind was filled with thoughts of Ravi and their conversation. He had been withdrawn and quiet through the entire meal. He hadn't been much better on the walk back, but at least he had spoken.

He was different now. Or perhaps the Ravi she had come to know on the mountain was the different one. Maybe she was now seeing who he truly was.

Memories of their time together flashed in her head. The way he had held her as they slept. The way he had stroked her face to calm her. How he had protected her as they walked through Shaldorn.

And the kiss.

It all came back to that kiss.

Ravi pushed away from the door and forced his feet to take him farther into the room. He had nearly thrown open the door and called Yaz back. He halted in the middle of the space, gazing at the bed. His mind conjured images of him and Yaz tangled together. He closed his eyes and tried to ignore his desire. But he couldn't.

Because he couldn't stop thinking about Yaz.

He wanted to bellow and shout and hit something. Hard. There had never been a time in his life that he had felt so bereft. He didn't want to feel whatever it was banging against his chest. Yet it was there, and it didn't seem like it would go away anytime soon.

What was he supposed to do? Being around Yaz was too painful. He'd barely made it through their meal. He couldn't wait for her to get stronger on the chance they would run into each other again. Ravi groaned as he thought about making the return trek to Rannora with her. He wouldn't last an hour alone with Yaz.

Ravi briefly thought about looking for Dain. Maybe the Dark was still in Navara and would be up for sparring. It might help to ease some of his tension. There was a chance he would run into Yaz again. Or worse, go to her room.

He yanked off his shirt and wadded it in his hands. After a moment, he snapped the shirt open and carefully folded it before laying it over the back of the chair. Ravi took a step toward the tub when he heard the door open. He looked over his shoulder and spotted Yaz. Shock ran through him at the sight of her. He was afraid to move, scared that she would vanish.

She softly closed the door and took a few steps forward. "If you want me to leave, tell me."

Leave? Ravi wanted to bar the door to keep them inside and everyone else out. He turned to face her, his heart pounding like a drum against his ribs. He managed a few steps before he paused. If he got any closer, he wouldn't be able to keep his hands from her. He needed to know why she'd come before he gave in to his burning desire.

Yaz closed the distance between them. She was so close he could feel her heat. Unable to stop himself, Ravi gently touched her face, afraid it was an illusion, and she would fade.

His fingers brushed her soft skin. And in that instant, he was lost.

To her.

To the longing.

To the feelings he couldn't stop.

He brought a hand to her back and drew her against him as he lowered his head. Her eyes closed just before their lips met and briefly lingered. He cupped the back of her head with his other hand as he slid his tongue between her lips. She melted against him with a low moan. His balls tightened at the sound. Ravi deepened the kiss, needing more. Needing all of her.

And she held nothing back.

The kiss was everything he knew it would be. And everything he feared. With one taste, he was hers, body and soul. Utterly. Completely.

By the time Yaz ended the kiss, they were both breathing heavily. He tried to pull her back for another, but she took his hand and led him to the bed. Once there, she held his gaze as she removed her shoes. His blood heated, scorching him from the inside out. He couldn't take his eyes off her as she removed her pants and then her shirt.

He sucked in a breath as she stood for a moment in her undergarments. She held up a finger to stop him when he reached for her. Ravi gritted his teeth and held himself in place as she took off the last items.

Ever since he had woken with her naked body against him, he had imagined her curves. Now, he finally got to see her amazing body.

His gaze locked on her full breasts. Ravi groaned as her dark nipples pebbled beneath his stare. His gaze dropped to the triangle of dark curls nestled between her legs. He couldn't wait to spread those shapely limbs and wring cries of pleasure from her.

Ravi pulled her to him and claimed her lips in another heated kiss. He was well acquainted with lust and a quick fuck. That wasn't what he wanted this time. Not with Yaz. This was something different, something *more*. He tempted fate by exploring whatever it was, but there was no turning back for him.

Yaz tore her lips from his. She was breathless as she said, "I need to see you. To feel you. All of you."

He hastily shucked his boots and wrenched off his pants and undergarment to have them skin to skin again. His touch was gentle when he brought her against him. A moan escaped when she rested her palms on his chest before smoothing them up and over his shoulders. Her touch was light and sensual. He watched her face as her eyes followed her hands down his arms to his wrists. His fingers curled into her hip when she leaned back to trace her fingers along his stomach.

Then lower.

"Yaz," he said in a strangled whisper as her fingers inched closer to his aching cock.

Her gaze clashed with his as she closed her fingers around his arousal. He moaned as she moved her hand up and down his length. A small smile curved her lips when he rocked his hips forward.

If she could play, then so could he. Ravi locked an arm around her while his other slid between her legs. He groaned at the wetness that met his fingers. He found her mouth and kissed her deeply. His tongue tangled with hers just as he parted the folds of her sex and found her clit. A tremor went through her. Yaz's breath hitched as he circled the nub with a light, slow touch. It wasn't enough, though. He wanted her laid out so he could touch and explore at will.

Ravi gently pulled her hand away before he lifted her. Her legs wound around his waist as she gazed at him. The desire he saw reflected in her eyes sent a thrill rushing through him. Her hands returned to his face as she gently touched his cheeks and jaw. The pads of her fingers lingered on his lips. Then her hands were in his hair.

Her fingers ran over the points of his ears. At one time, their differences would've mattered to him. And to her.

His thoughts halted when her lips met his. Her hungry kiss

made him wild with need. Ravi turned and backed up until his legs hit the bed. He sat on the mattress and caressed a hand over her shapely bottom to the curve of her back. The tip of her braid brushed his hand.

Ravi leaned back to look at her. "I want your hair around me. I've dreamed of running my fingers through it."

She grinned and pulled the plait over her shoulder before tugging off the strip of leather binding. Her eyes never left his as he deftly freed her long tresses from the braids. Once her hair was free, Ravi sank his fingers into it. The locks were soft and cool to the touch, the weight heavier than expected.

Yaz closed her eyes and dropped her head back, exposing her throat. He placed kisses along the slender column and down to where her pulse beat erratically. Her answering moan had his cock jumping in expectation.

Ravi held her firmly against him as he turned to lay her on the bed. He looked down and saw her passion, raw desire reflected at him. Emotion threatened to overwhelm him. As if she knew, she drew him down for another scorching kiss. He would never tire of her taste. She was decadence and bliss. Splendor and sincerity.

And he knew there was no other like her.

41

Yasmin moaned in satisfaction when Ravi settled his weight over her. His thick arousal lay between them, and she couldn't wait to have him inside her. The brief touch she had gotten had made her hungry for more. *All* of him. From his touch to his kisses to the heated yearning in his copper eyes.

His lips left a hot, wet trail along her jaw and throat. And then lower. He braced himself on his forearms on either side of her before lifting his head to look at her breasts. She felt her nipples harden as he stared. His pleased grin said it all.

Her breath caught in her throat when his lips locked around a turgid peak, and he suckled. The pleasure shot straight to her center. She moaned and arched her back to press her breasts against him. His tongue swirled around the nub, causing her to grind against him. She was so consumed by the need growing within her that she didn't realize he had moved until he kissed down the center of her abdomen.

She watched him, torn between dragging him back to her breasts or pushing him down to her center. His eyes met hers as his fingers wrapped around the back of her legs and gently spread them. He slowly and leisurely skimmed his fingers along the insides of her thighs, stopping short of her sex.

Yasmin groaned in frustration. She couldn't help it. She *needed* his touch.

He slid one finger from the top of her sex all the way down. She dropped her head back, her eyes falling shut at the pleasure the simple touch brought her.

"So wet," he murmured.

His finger circled her entrance, but he didn't penetrate her. She lifted her hips, a silent plea for him to give her what she wanted. But she should've known he wouldn't give in so easily. His tongue replaced his fingers, lapping at the folds of her sex before licking upward to her swollen clit.

The first flick of his tongue nearly sent her off the bed. She cried out at the exquisite torture. But that first touch was just the beginning of the amazing buildup of pressure low in her belly. He put all his focus on her clit. It didn't take long for him to tease until she was mindless and begging for release. The orgasm crashed into her, taking her breath as pleasure rolled through her.

Then he slid a finger inside her and began moving it in and out.

Yasmin shouted as a second climax came amid the first. She was powerless to do anything but lay there shuddering with euphoria unlike anything she had experienced before. She drifted slowly to the present, her body still pulsating with aftershocks. Only then did she feel his finger still moving.

He added a second, and she felt another orgasm building already.

Ravi had nearly spilled at the sight of Yaz coming, combined with the tight walls of her body clamping around him. He slowly moved his fingers in and out of her, twisting them as he did. She moaned and rocked her hips for more. That was all it took to push him to the brink.

He withdrew his fingers and rose over her. He guided his rod to her sex and ran it along her labia before finding her entrance. She reached for him as she opened her eyes. Their gazes locked as he pushed inside her. He thrust and withdrew, thrust and withdrew, stretching her until he slid to the hilt.

She raised her knees, shifting him deeper. He braced his hands on either side of her. The feel of her wet heat was almost too much. He pulled out until only the tip of him remained before thrusting deep. Her moan mingled with his.

He kept his pace steady, only increasing when she began to lift her hips to meet his. As his tempo surged, so did his desire. He drove into her hard and deep. The sound of their bodies slapping together mingled with her cries of pleasure. Nothing mattered but the two of them and the passion they had found.

Yaz stiffened, her nails digging into his back an instant before her muscles contracted around his cock. He felt and saw her pleasure. His orgasm rushed up, crashing into him. He shouted his release, continuing to pump his hips as she wrung every last drop from him.

Ravi was dazed when he came to. He dropped to his forearms and pressed his forehead against hers, her body still clenching around him. Their labored breathing was the only sound in the room. When he could string two thoughts together again, Ravi lifted his head and opened his eyes. There was a smile on Yaz's face that brought one of his own.

"That was indescribable," she said.

"Aye."

She shivered, and he realized there was a chill in the room. Ravi gave her a soft kiss before pulling out of her. He tugged back the blankets, situated her head onto one of the pillows, and then crawled in beside her. She curled into his side, just as she had done in the tent. Her hand rested over his heart, and he covered it with one of his as his other arm held her against him. Nothing had ever felt so right.

Ravi had no idea how long they slept. He woke, needing her again. He reached for her only to have Yaz shove the blankets away and roll him onto his back. Then she straddled him. His balls tightened when she brought his arousal to her entrance.

His hands rested on her thighs, their eyes locked as she slowly took him into her body. She was unbelievably sensual. He thumbed her nipples until they were hard peaks as he began rocking her hips back and forth. He massaged her breasts, letting them fill his hands. His excitement and desire grew as he watched her. She was sexy, carnal.

And his.

At least for the moment.

He didn't want to think about the future. Not when he had such a perfect and beautiful creature in his arms.

She began to ride him faster. He dug his fingers into her hips, urging her on. Her palms flattened on his chest as she leaned forward, the curtain of her hair draped to one side. He raised his head and latched his lips onto a nipple, sucking it deep. Her responding moan drove him mad with need.

He moved to her other breast and teased that nipple until she was moaning loudly. Yaz planted her hands on either side of his head and rocked up and down on his aching cock. He tried to flip her onto her back, but she refused to budge. She wanted to be in control this time.

She sat up and resumed riding him, rotating her hips in a way that had him groaning. She dropped her head back and ran her hands over her breasts as she moaned. He gripped her and lifted his hips to drive into her. She sucked in a breath.

"Again," she demanded.

He repeated the move and pulled her down hard on his cock. Her thighs tightened against him. She cried out and gripped his wrists, lifting her head to look at him. Again and again, he plunged into her as she rocked her hips faster.

His orgasm was approaching swiftly, but he didn't want to reach it without her. He licked his thumb and brought it to her clit to circle the nub. She came apart immediately, her cries filling the room. Ravi shouted her name as he came with her.

Yasmin closed her eyes as the water lapped around her. Ravi's chest rose and fell against her back. His arms rested around her middle as if he needed to hold her there. They caught snatches of sleep between their bouts of lovemaking. Her body still tingled from him taking her from behind as the tub filled.

She couldn't remember a time she had ever felt so sated. It had been a gamble entering his room, but one she was glad she took. He could've refused her. There had been a moment when she stood there staring at his magnificent chest when she thought he might.

They had done little talking, but she wasn't upset about that. Each time she didn't think she could climax again, he proved her wrong.

"Did you fall asleep again?"

She chuckled. "You're the one who sounds near sleep."

"I nearly am. How about I get us some food? You need your energy. I'm not finished with you yet."

Yasmin shifted her head to look at him. He kissed her, causing her to grin. She loved that they couldn't keep their hands off each other. "I am quite peckish."

"Food it is," he said as he sat them up.

She remained in the tub and watched him climb out to dry off. He had a magnificent body that she had touched and kissed every part of.

He looked up to find her staring and winked. "When I get back, I expect you laid out in the middle of the bed."

"Maybe I want you laid out on the bed."

He finished putting on his boot and walked to the tub. Placing his hand on the edge, he bent down to press their lips together. "I do like the way you think."

Once he left, Yaz got out of the tub and drained the water. She grabbed another drying cloth to wipe off her body. She liked living among the Mountain Elves. They were shy but kind once they got to know someone. That was probably because they didn't see many strangers. She couldn't say that always happened in Rannora.

Her thoughts halted when the door opened. Ravi entered with a tray piled with food. He flashed a bright grin as he bolted the door behind him.

"Your food, madam," he said with a bow.

"Oh, I approve. Well done."

He took her hand and brought her to the bed. She dropped the drying cloth and climbed atop the mattress. Ravi set the tray down and promptly removed his clothes. She was too hungry to wait on him and dug into the feast. It wasn't long before she was cold and attempted to crawl beneath the covers. Ravi reached down to the floor and grabbed his shirt to hand to her. Yasmin slipped it over her head, smelling him.

"It looks better on you," he said between bites.

"Perhaps I'll keep it."

He grinned. "Consider it yours."

They ate in comfortable silence. Finally, she asked, "Do you know what time it is? Not being able to see the sky is an adjustment."

"It's nearly dinnertime, which is why I was able to get so much food. As soon as I told them it was for you, they gave me anything I wanted."

Yasmin chuckled. "They're very generous."

Ravi removed the nearly empty tray from the bed and pulled

her against him before yanking the covers over them. She wiggled out of his shirt before lying on his chest once more.

"What will you do when you get back to Rannora?" she asked. Speaking of the future was probably a bad idea, but she was curious about his plans.

He blew out a breath. "Durga will want a full report. I'll have to complete that before anything else."

"Will she send you on another mission?"

"That's usually how it goes." He paused. "What about you? You've spoken about leaving Shecrish."

She shrugged. "I don't want to be hungry anymore. I don't want the children to know that any longer either."

"There is still the option of working for the DIA," he said hesitantly.

Yasmin swallowed. "It would mean a lot of time away from the children. Who would watch them while I'm gone? If I'm going to care for them, I need to be there. They deserve that."

"I understand."

She wished she hadn't brought up the future now. She didn't want to think about their time ending at Navara or what she would do. Ravi's choice was obvious. But she didn't want to lean on him for employment or anything else. She needed to do that on her own.

At least they had the return trip to discuss different options. After that, she didn't know what would happen. But they had time to talk about it.

42

Ravi sat in the chair, his forearms on his knees as he watched Yaz sleep. He glanced at the wall he had pressed her against a short time ago, her legs around him as he plunged inside her. He could still hear her cries of release.

He hadn't been able to sleep since their discussion. She wanted to leave Shecrish, and he couldn't blame her. He almost begged her to remain. He had nearly offered his home to her and the children, but he knew she wouldn't accept it.

His feelings for Yaz were complicated. He'd tried to keep them simple, but there was no getting around the fact that he had real, deep feelings for her. It was possible they could have a good life together. She knew him as few did. He had the means to ensure she was given a job and found a proper home.

But it wasn't what she wanted.

He wasn't what she wanted.

She longed to find her people. Few could understand how she

felt. He certainly couldn't. But he sympathized and empathized with her situation. Elves had made her life a living nightmare. And not just her. The children under her care had received harsh treatment, as well. Ravi had always known they had a flawed governing system, but he hadn't realized to what degree until now. Until Yaz showed him.

If he stayed in her life, if they returned to Rannora together, she might not leave Shecrish. He wanted nothing more than for her to stay, but if she did, would she regret it later? Would she blame him? He wouldn't survive it if she did. He knew in his heart they could be happy, but was a few years of happiness worth her hatred after?

He couldn't do that to her or himself. Or the children.

Ravi got to his feet. He fisted the hand that wanted to stroke Yaz's face. He silently walked to the door before he changed his mind. With one last look at her, he slipped quietly out of the room.

It didn't take him long to find his target. Dain was in the kitchen talking to one of the Mountain Elves when he spotted Ravi. The Dark excused himself and walked to him. Ravi motioned for him to follow, and the two fell into step together.

"That's a serious look on your face," Dain said after a few moments.

Ravi made sure no one was about and stopped to face the elf. "I need a favor."

He expected a sarcastic comment. Instead, Dain said, "Name it."

"Actually, it's several favors."

"What's going on?" Dain demanded as he linked his hands behind his back.

"I need you to take me to Rannora. Immediately."

"What about Yasmin?"

Ravi paused. He had thought this through. It was a good decision. The right one. At least for Yaz. "When she wakes, take her anywhere she wants to go. Her and the children. They want out of Shecrish."

"You take them."

"It'll be faster if you or another Dark does it. I know it'll be a strain traveling with that many. I'll do whatever you want, pay whatever price. You name it, and it's yours."

Dain slashed his hand through the air. "I don't care about that. I want to know what the fuck is going on."

"She nearly died in the very place she escaped from," Ravi bit out, his anger rising. "She ran away from a horrific home and wound up at Shaldorn. For the first time, I want her to have what she wants."

"That's why the two of you have been locked in your room for the past day?"

Ravi ran a hand down his face. "Please, Dain. I'm trying to do the right thing."

"You're running because you're scared. You have feelings for her. Shite. You might even love her."

Ravi looked away. Was he so easy to read?

"Fuck me. You do." Dain shook his head. "Have you told her?"

Ravi shot him a dark look.

"Idiot. Talk to her. Let her decide," the Dark said.

"She'll choose to leave."

"You don't know that."

"Maybe she won't, but she hates living with elves. She'll come to regret her decision later. And...I can't handle that. I'd rather do this now before it hurts worse."

Dain sighed loudly. "No one can predict the future."

"Maybe not, but we can get pretty close. I want her to be happy."

"And what if that means being with you?"

Ravi threw up his hands. "What can I offer? I've never had a serious relationship for a reason. I'm always on assignment somewhere. I can't give her what she needs."

"Could be what you think she needs and what she actually needs are two different things."

"It has to be this way. Now, will you help me?"

Dain ran a hand over his jaw. "I don't agree with what you're doing, but aye. I'll help."

Yasmin stretched as she came awake. She rolled over, expecting to find Ravi. Instead, she found an empty spot cool to the touch. She sat up with a frown.

"Ravi?"

She knew with a glance that he wasn't in the room. She rose and dressed, thinking he might have gone to get them more food. Except he wasn't in the kitchen either. She asked anyone she met in the corridors if they had seen him, but they all had the same answer.

Yasmin returned to his room to wait for him. As soon as she opened the door, she found Dain standing there with his hands behind his back. She knew immediately that something was wrong.

The Dark smiled, but it didn't quite reach his eyes. "Good morning."

"What happened?" She didn't care what time of day it was. "It's Ravi, isn't it? I can't find him."

"He's on another mission."

She couldn't possibly have heard that correctly. "Mission?"

"It's what we do."

"I'm aware," she retorted. Yasmin closed her eyes for a moment and took a breath. She looked at Dain. "I apologize. I shouldn't have snapped. Why didn't he tell me goodbye? I thought I was supposed to return with him to Rannora to finish the mission. Durga was very clear about that."

Dain dropped his arms and held out a black velvet drawstring bag. "I bring a message from Durga. Your record has been wiped clean as promised. I've also been ordered to give you this."

"What is it?"

He jingled the bag so coins clinked. "Sounds like payment."

"That wasn't the deal we made."

"Neither was what you experienced. Take it. You've earned it."

Yasmin couldn't deny that the coin would make the children's lives better. She accepted the bag and held it against her stomach. It was so heavy, it took both hands.

"My instructions are to take you anywhere you want to go," Dain said.

She frowned at his words. "What? Why?"

"As I've said. You earned it. Tell me where you wish to go."

"I can't go anywhere without the k—"

"Kids," Dain finished with a grin. "Aye. I know. They will be joining you."

Yasmin shook her head in confusion. "I don't understand."

"We get paid to risk our lives. You were forced. The mission was a success, and you are being compensated. It's that simple."

Was it? She had more coin than she had ever seen before. She could return to Rannora and get a proper house. There would be enough funds to feed and clothe the children and tide them over until she found employment. That would be the safe thing to do. She knew what to expect in Rannora. She could go to Belanore for a change of scenery, but it would be more of the same. If she remained in Shecrish, her options were better in the two cities versus the smaller villages.

Or...she could fulfill her dream of leaving.

The problem was that she didn't know what was out there. She might find humans like her, but what if she didn't? What if she had Dain take her to the northern border of Shecrish and she found something worse? Or nothing at all. How would she support herself and the children? Feed them?

Then there was Ravi. They hadn't discussed any of it. If Ravi was on another assignment, there was no telling when he would return. *If* he returned. He hadn't written her a note or anything. He'd just left in the night.

Had she been wrong about what was between them? She couldn't have. He had felt it, too. She was sure of it.

"Yasmin?"

She jerked her gaze to Dain. He couldn't wait on her decision forever. But how could she make a choice without knowing where things stood with Ravi? "What do you do when the dream that always seemed just out of reach is suddenly right there, easily within your grasp?"

"You take it. Dreams only come around once. If they come at all."

"Do you know if there are other humans out there?"

Dain shrugged. "I couldn't say either way. The realm is a big place, and we inhabit a small portion. Anything is possible."

"May I have some time to think on this?"

"By all means. It's an important decision."

Yasmin turned and walked from the room. The entire way back to hers, all she could think about was that Ravi was gone. She couldn't understand why he hadn't woken her. Even if it had been sudden, he could've taken the time while he dressed to tell her.

She turned a corner and ran into someone. Yasmin bounced off them, only to be steadied by strong hands. "Sorry," she replied and looked up into Manu's black eyes.

"I was looking for you," he said.

"What can I do for you?"

Manu motioned for her to continue walking as he joined her. "I wanted to see how you were."

"Confused."

He quirked a dark brow. "About?"

"Ravi is gone. Apparently, on another mission. I've been given this," she said and hefted the bag to show him. "And told that Dain will take me anywhere I want to go."

"Anywhere?"

She nodded. "Anywhere."

"That's what you've always wanted."

"It has been."

They reached her room. Manu opened the door and waited for her to enter before following and closing the door behind them. "Dain told me about the children you've been looking after. Would you bring them with you?"

"Of course."

He leaned back against the door and crossed his arms over his chest. "Then what are you confused about?"

"I..." she started, then paused. Manu never said much, but he required honesty above all things. "I have feelings for Ravi. I believed he felt the same."

"Then he left."

She nodded. "Without telling me. That...hurt me."

"Did he make any promises?"

"None."

Manu looked at the floor for a heartbeat. "At least he finally came to see you."

"I actually went to find him."

Manu grunted in response.

"Do you know why he didn't come?"

"I have my suspicions. They were confirmed when you said you believed he had feelings for you."

Yasmin frowned. "I don't understand why that would keep him away."

Instead of answering, Manu said, "You told me when you escaped Shaldorn that you planned to leave Shecrish."

"Things happened that prevented that."

"You could've turned the children away."

"Like everyone turned me away?" She shook her head angrily. "I'm not like that."

Manu shrugged. "You have the means and opportunity now to find your people. Something is holding you back."

"Not something. Some*one*."

"Same difference. You have to decide what you want more."

"Ravi offered me a job with the agency. I refused because I knew I wouldn't be there for the children. Even if I find other employment, I know his duties would keep him away from me."

Manu dropped his arms and pushed away from the door. "You are welcome in Navara anytime. Bring the children. Live here. You have options. Consider each of them."

Yasmin sat on the bed once she was alone. She placed the bag of coins beside her and stared at it. For four years after escaping Shaldorn, she had done few of the things she wanted. Everything had been focused on the children. She loved them as if they were her own and would do anything for them. But she had been a shell of herself.

Until she met Ravi. She had slowly begun to remember who she was. Standing up to Gita had nearly cost her life, but it had been something she needed to do to heal herself. So had returning to Shaldorn and helping save all those she had left behind. No longer would she look over her shoulder in fear.

For the first time, she could do what she wanted. She had done it when she ran away from home. She had done it when she claimed her freedom from Shaldorn.

But this time, she would do it not to escape some horror, but to find the future she longed for.

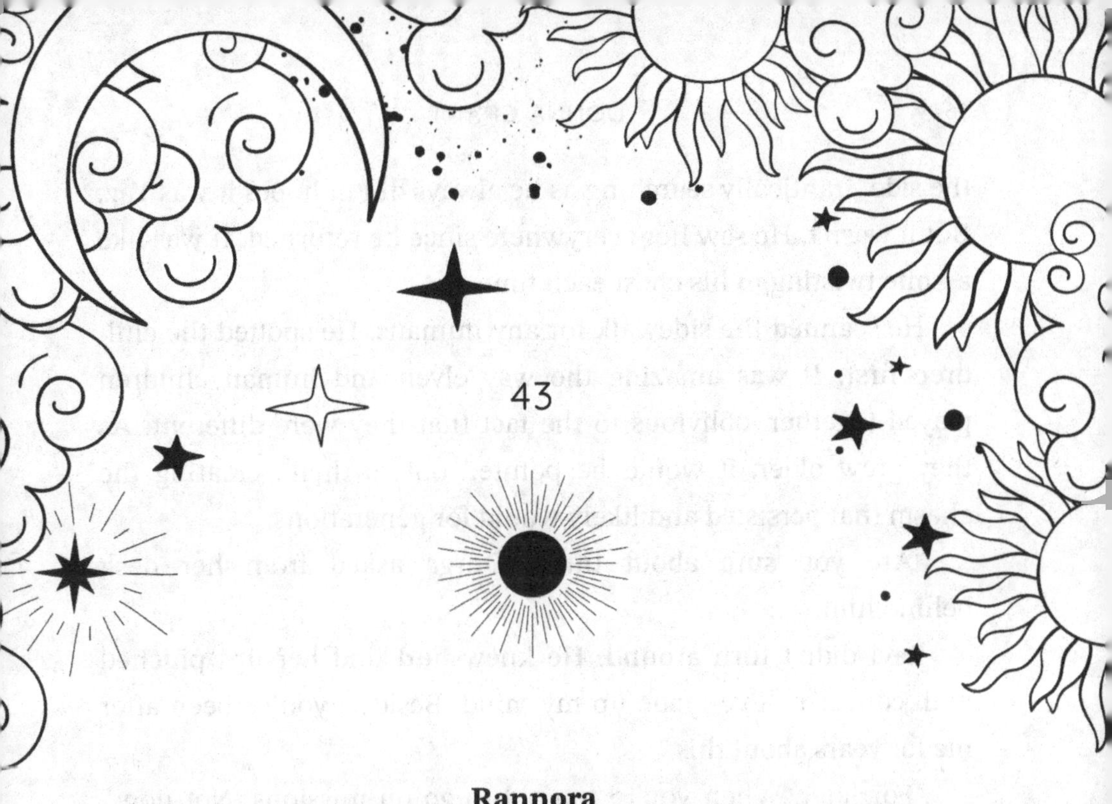

43

Rannora
Two weeks later

Ravi stood at the third-floor window of the nondescript building belonging to the DIA and looked down at the citizens below. He saw children playing around a group of adults. Two of them were scolded by a mother for getting too close to the street with the carriages. His parents hadn't known where he had gone or even cared.

They hadn't been bad people. They had just been preoccupied with their work. He had often wondered why they had wanted a child at all. Things might have been different if he'd loved academia as they had. They had clothed and fed him, but there could be an argument that they'd neglected him. He was fortunate that Durga had stumbled upon him instead of some criminal.

A flash of dark hair caught his attention. Ravi's gaze jerked to the side, frantically searching as he always did in hopes it was Yaz. But it wasn't. He saw her everywhere since he returned. It was like a knife twisting in his chest each time.

He scanned the sidewalk for any humans. He spotted the children first. It was amazing the way elven and human children played together, oblivious to the fact that they were different. As they grew older, it would be pointed out to them, creating the chasm that persisted and likely would for generations.

"Are you sure about this?" Durga asked from her desk behind him.

Ravi didn't turn around. He knew he'd find her lips pinched with concern. "I've made up my mind. Besides, you've been after me for years about this."

"For later. When you're too old to go on missions. Not now." She sighed loudly.

The chair squeaked as she pushed it back and rose. The thick rug dampened the sound of her approach. She stood beside him and sighed again. Two meant that she was trying to find a way to say something he wouldn't like.

"Why are you grinning?" she snapped.

He gave her the side-eye. "I know you."

"Oh?" she asked, the word both haughty and filled with doubt.

"You're trying to find a way to say something I'm not going to like. You're not particularly thrilled about saying it either. Hence, two sighs."

She snorted. "Know-it-all."

"That's your moniker, not mine."

They shared a smile before they went back to gazing out the window. After a long stretch of silence, Durga said, "You've changed."

"That's what we're supposed to do, is it not?"

"It is. I'm just trying to sort out the reason. Was it Shaldorn? The mountains? Y—"

"All of it," Ravi said before Durga could say Yaz's name. "What's the issue? You've always wanted me to train new recruits."

She rested her hands on the windowsill. "You're asking me to take my best agent out of commission."

"Not completely. I'll still be out there."

"Searching for Gita and One. You may never locate them."

An image of Yaz in the box flashed in his head. "I'll find them."

"At what cost to you?"

Ravi watched the children laughing as they ran around the adults playing tag. "Have you checked to make sure One doesn't work for us?"

"I've found nothing about him. It would be better if you had a name."

"In time," he promised.

Durga drummed her fingers on the sill. She swallowed and faced him. "While you were on your mission and I had the children watched, I found out their names."

Anger simmered in Ravi. Durga had promised to leave them alone. He turned to head to her. "Why?"

"I had to know the truth. The eldest, Sameer, is very protective of the others, but we managed to learn who they are. I reached out to a friend at the Ministry and discretely learned the names of the families they had been placed with."

Ravi faced her now. "And?"

"Yasmin didn't lie."

He wished he could say that he'd never thought she had, but it would be a lie.

"If the Ministry had done even a single check, they would've learned those families weren't the place for children. Abuse and neglect run rampant. I had them reported. Two of them had other children that have since been removed from the homes. Charges are being filed on all of them."

"What of Yaz? What of the children under her care?"

Durga's hazel eyes softened. "They know nothing of her, and they won't. I told them I was investigating the missing children."

Ravi lowered his gaze and nodded. Then he faced the window again. "Thank you."

"Did I ever tell you about my brother?"

He glanced sideways at her. "You never speak of your family."

"He was younger, and the sweetest person you would ever encounter. He loved everyone and everything. He had a way with finding hurt animals and nurturing them back to health. I never cared that he was human. My parents loved us both equally. He was a ray of sunshine on even the darkest days.

"As children, we had no idea of the differences between us. Our parents never said anything. We were around others who felt the same. It wasn't until he began his learning that things changed. He learned differently than others. My mum was a teacher, and she would spend her nights catching him up on what had been taught that day. He was very smart. He just required a different way, something the school wouldn't change for a single child. A human child."

Ravi looked at Durga, her pain evident in her words and stiff posture.

"The older he got, the more his differences set him apart from others. He was teased mercilessly. Eventually, that turned into beatings and pranks that bordered on cruelty. My brother stopped smiling. He turned into himself and shut out the world. One day, I found a wounded animal and brought it to him. He had always found comfort in animals before. Instead of helping it, he broke its neck in front of me. He said that it was better off dead instead of living in such a world."

Ravi watched a single tear roll down her face.

"He took his own life. It broke something in our family that day. My parents never fully recovered. It wasn't until I was cleaning out his room that I found the notes written to him. Every line was filled with such vitriol that it turned my stomach. There were piles and piles of them, in different handwriting. I was determined to find who had written those things to my beautiful, sweet brother. It took me nearly a year, but I found the three males responsible. I brought the evidence to the authorities, and they were arrested." She met Ravi's gaze. "That's how I found my calling."

"Why did you tell me that?"

She lifted one shoulder in a shrug. "Because some of us see everyone as equals. But there will always be those who see the differences in others and believe themselves better. I've seen you watching the humans since you returned. I see you scanning faces for her."

Ravi turned his head away. "I don't want to hear this."

"Too bad. You're the one always running toward something, not away from it."

"You and Dain are both wrong. I didn't run."

"Didn't you?"

He ran a hand down his face and sighed. "I tried to do the right thing."

"You should've talked to her. You still can."

Could he? He had purposefully not sought out Dain to learn where he had brought Yaz. Ravi hadn't even gone to her home, afraid to see it empty.

And terrified that it wasn't.

Had he run? If so, it wasn't far enough. He woke every morning clutching at air, aching for Yaz with a soul-deep longing that only became more unbearable with each passing day. He missed her.

He loved her.

Aye, he had finally admitted it to himself. The pain of her absence intensified by a thousand once he did. He found joy in nothing. The only thing that kept him going was tracking down Gita and One. He would get his vengeance on the two. It wouldn't bring him comfort—nothing but Yaz could do that—but it would make him feel better.

"I know where she is," Durga said.

Ravi spun and strode away before he whirled back around. "Leave it."

"We don't get happy endings, Ravi. There's always the next mission, until one day, our luck runs out. You found something special. You should hold on to it."

"What about what she wants?"

"How do you know what that is? You never asked her."

"I couldn't bear it if she didn't want me."

Durga gave him a sad smile. "You're not the running kind. You never have been. Stop doing it now."

Yasmin hid in the alley, staring down the street while searching for a familiar face. Her heart leaped when she spotted Ravi. She greedily took in the sight of his golden hair and full beard. A small frown furrowed his brow as he wove around others on the sidewalk. He was purposeful in his stride. An elf with a mission.

She could step from the shadows and call out to him, raise her hand and flag him down. It was the same thing she had told herself each time. Instead, she watched him march up the steps and unlock the door before disappearing inside. The brief glimpse wasn't nearly enough. Not when she longed to hear his voice, to have his incredible copper eyes on her once more.

There had been a hole in her chest since she'd woken to find him gone at Navara. Too many nights she had cried herself to sleep, wondering what she had done to drive him away. She wasn't brave enough to confront him. He had changed her life—and her heart.

Obviously, he hadn't felt the same.

It hurt. Probably always would. She had never thought to love anyone, not as she did Ravi. Yet love had found her when she least expected it. Or wanted it. The only reason she carried on was because the children depended on her. It was because of them that she stitched up her broken heart and faced the day.

Yasmin rested her cheek against the stone of the building. She no longer had to touch them to hear their song. The stones had led her to Ravi that fateful day. She stood across the street from him, waiting and hoping he might see her. But he hadn't. She told herself to let him go, and instead, she followed him home. She'd been returning to this spot every day since.

"See anything interesting?"

Yasmin jumped at the sound of Dain's voice behind her. She spun around and gave him an annoyed look. "You know I hate when you sneak up on me."

"But it's so fun," he replied with a crooked grin. It faded, and he glanced over her head to Ravi's home. The Dark's yellow gaze lowered to her. "Is everything set?"

"There are a few last-minute things to see to, but we'll be ready."

"Talk to him."

She firmly shook her head. "You know I don't discuss him."

"You two belong together."

"He made his choice. You should know, you were there."

Dain's lips flattened a moment. "Just talk to him."

"I appreciate everything you've done for me and the kids. It's more than I ever expected." She paused a heartbeat. "You know more than you're telling me about that day, but I've accepted that. I've accepted all of it."

"Yasmin," he began.

"I was the one who reached out to him at Navara. We had something spectacular. Then he left without a word. It made my decision easier."

Dain bowed his head. "You and the children have decided on a location then?"

"We have."

"I'll be by tonight."

She lifted her hand in a wave and began her last walk home.

Ravi came out of the kitchen when shadows billowed from the wall. He jerked in surprise, spilling his tea as Dain stalked out of them. The Dark glared. Ravi glowered back.

"Sure. Come in," Ravi said sarcastically. "Shall I make you some tea?"

"What the fuck is wrong with you?" Dain demanded.

"Oh, where to begin?" Ravi rolled his eyes as he turned and made his way to the kitchen to grab a towel. He set his cup on the counter as Dain's boots thumped angrily in his haste to follow.

"I'm not joking," Dain replied.

Would this day ever end? First Durga and now Dain? Ravi turned to face the Dark. "Perhaps if you told me, this would go quicker."

"Enough!" the Dark bellowed. Then, in a quieter voice, he said, "You know exactly what this is about."

Ravi held up his hand, a warning in his tone. "Don't. I told you *never* to say her name. I promised not to ask about her, and you vowed not to tell me anything. That's the way it has to be."

"Aye, I made that idiotic promise before I saw how you broke her heart. I did everything we agreed. I gave her your money and lied about where it came from."

"That's shite, and you know it. You crafted your replies so it *wouldn't* be an outright lie."

"We both know what the lies were," Dain said as he pointed a finger at him. "They all rest on you."

Ravi turned away and braced his hands on the counter. He was hungry for any news about Yaz. Durga had tempted him, and the fact that Dain was here said the Dark knew something. "What do you want me to say? That you were right? That I should've talked to her?"

"Aye."

Ravi pushed away from the counter and faced Dain. "It's too late."

"She's in Rannora."

"What?" The word was yanked from him.

Dain's eyes glittered as he smirked. "As a matter of fact, she was just outside watching you. She's done it for the past two weeks."

Ravi shook his head, refusing to believe it.

"I have no reason to lie," Dain replied. "She knows something isn't right about the way you left. You need to tell her. Everything."

"She's been watching me?"

The sneer faded from Dain's face. "I'm taking her and the kids away tonight. They decided as a family."

Yaz hadn't left. Yet. But she was about to.

Dain snorted loudly. The shadows rose and swallowed him. Then, he was gone. Ravi stared at the spot as more questions rose in his mind, questions Dain could've answered but likely wouldn't.

Ravi dropped the towel onto the counter and turned around to find Durga standing inside his back door. "How long have you been there?"

She lifted one shoulder. "What are you going to do?"

"I don't know. She didn't come see me."

Durga rolled her eyes. "You left her, Ravi. Of course, she isn't going to seek you out. Stop being stupid and go to her."

"And say what?" he demanded.

"You know what to say. It's what you should've said before you left her, but you were too afraid. She may come to resent you, but wouldn't you rather try and fail than never know?"

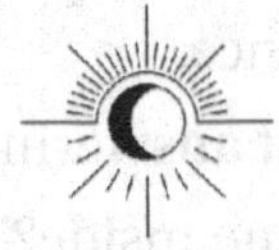

After Dain's and Durga's visits, Ravi needed time to think. He walked the streets to clear his head and looked up to find himself in the East Haffeb district. He made his way to Yaz's home. Ravi remained hidden as he watched the area.

One of the children ran past a window, followed by another carrying a bag. Sameer strolled behind them, laughing as he lifted one of the younger kids onto his shoulders. For weeks, Ravi had believed Yaz out of reach, and it had been a gut-wrenching experience.

He heard her laugh, and he closed his eyes to savor the sound. He knew what he had to do. Ravi squared his shoulders and focused on the door. Then he crossed the street to the building and stepped onto the porch. He rapped on the door he realized now hung correctly on its hinges.

"Is it Dain?" he heard the high-pitched voice of a child ask.

"It's Dain!" several of the kids said in unison.

On the other side of the door, he heard Yaz say, "It isn't time yet."

Ravi clasped his hands behind his back so he wouldn't yank her against him when he saw her. Then, the door opened. Deep blue eyes collided with his. Her smile faltered as she stared. His heart beat so fast he thought it might fly from his chest. Gods, she was beautiful. The two weeks had felt like two lifetimes.

Her hair was in a thick braid hanging over one shoulder. Some strands had come loose around her face. She pushed them behind an ear, only to have them slip back against her cheek.

"Hi," he said into the silence.

She stared at him without answering.

"I'd like to talk. May I come inside?"

Sameer moved to stand behind Yaz with his arms crossed over his chest. He looked taller, older. Or maybe it was the new clothes. "Nay."

"Sameer," Yaz reprimanded softly as she glanced at the lad. Then she refocused on Ravi. "Say whatever you need to say but do it quickly. We're on a tight schedule."

She spun on her heel and walked away.

Ravi swallowed nervously as he stepped over the threshold and shut the door behind him. When he turned, the children stood on either side of her, watching the entire scene. He noted they were all in new clothes and shoes. The scared, hollow look they had once worn was gone.

He cleared his throat. "I, um, I was hoping to have a private conversation."

"This is my family. Say it in front of them or not at all."

Ravi nodded and took a small step forward. "I'm sorry. I shouldn't have left the way I did. I...I could give you a bunch of excuses that, at the time, I believed legitimate. It has recently come to my attention that I'm an idiot."

Sameer snorted.

Yaz cut him a dark look.

Ravi swallowed past the lump of dread in his throat and moved another step closer. "The truth is, I was scared. Of how I felt about you and what you made me feel. I never let anyone close. How could I with my job? It's easier to keep everyone at a distance. That didn't happen with you."

Now that the words were coming, he couldn't stop them. "I think about you constantly. You're in my thoughts during the day, and you consume my dreams at night. I wake each morning thinking I'm holding you, only to discover I'm alone." He took another step. "I used to tell myself that I didn't need anyone, but it was a lie. I was too afraid of loving someone. Of letting anyone in. Until I fell in love with you." He paused, the pit in his stomach growing. "I should've stayed and talked to you that day. I should've told you how I felt. I should've done so many things differently. Please, forgive me."

He felt the eyes of six children studying him as he stared at Yaz. Her face gave nothing away. Had he missed his chance? He'd been too afraid to ask her if she wanted a life with him, and now he could lose her because of his fear.

"Why are you here?" Yaz asked.

"I just told you."

She shook her head. "Why are you here? Now?"

His hands itched to hold her. He needed her against him, her arms around him. He hadn't realized how much until that moment. "I love you. I know I messed things up, but I'm begging you for a second chance. I want to be with you. Always."

"You would leave Shecrish and the elves?"

"I would," he said without hesitation. "I'll go anywhere you are."

She wrinkled her nose. "You would hate it."

"I would be with you. And the kids," he said, looking at each of their young faces. He returned his attention to her. "Tell me you don't love me and I'll walk away and never bother you again."

"I can't," she whispered, her voice breaking.

Hope bloomed in his chest. Ravi took another step closer. "Yaz, be with me. Let's be a family. All of us. I'm not promising to be perfect. I'm going to make mistakes."

"We'll call you on them," Sameer stated.

Ravi grinned as he looked at the lad. "I'm counting on it." He slid his gaze back to Yaz. "I want to fight with you so we can make up. I want to make decisions with you. I want to have adventures as well as quiet nights at home. I want dinners to be loud and rambunctious. I want it all. With you."

"What about when you're off on missions?" she asked hesitantly.

He closed the distance between them but didn't reach for her. "As of earlier today, I've retired as an active agent. In between training new recruits, I'll continue searching for Gita and One to bring them to justice. Which means, I'll be right here."

Her brow furrowed. "But you love your job."

"I used to love it. Then I nearly lost you, and things changed. I haven't been in the right frame of mind to go out on assignment since Shaldorn. I made this change before I knew you were still in the city. But I would still make it if it meant I could be with you."

Yaz glanced at the kids. "You hurt me."

"I'm sorry. I hate that it happened. I'll make it up to you for the rest of our lives if you'll let me. Yaz, my heart is yours. It was yours before I realized it. Whatever you want, whatever you need, I'll give it to you. Just give me a chance to prove I'm the one for you. Let me love you like you deserve."

A tear dropped onto her cheek. "I've been waiting for you to find me."

"I know," he said as he pulled her into his arms. His eyes

burned with unshed tears when she melted against him. "I'll always find you."

She sniffed and leaned back to look at him. "I love you."

Ravi seized her lips in a slow, sensual kiss. The world fell away as desire flared. Gradually, the shouts of joy intruded upon their embrace, but he wasn't upset. He and Yaz shared a smile as they faced the kids.

All of them were clapping and shouting. Even Sameer was grinning. It would take some time to win over the lad and prove to him that he loved Yaz, but Ravi would do it. They were a family now.

"About damn time," came a voice from behind him.

Ravi and Yaz turned to find Dain. All but Sameer rushed the Dark. Dain stood there as the children dug into his coat for small toys and sweet treats.

"They adore Dain," Yaz said after Ravi looked at her in surprise. "He always has something for each of them, but they have to find it first."

Ravi viewed Dain with new eyes. He looked at the entire world differently now thanks to love. He squeezed Yaz to his side and kissed her temple.

"What remote section of Zora are we off to explore?" Ravi asked.

Everyone grew quiet as they stared at him with varying degrees of surprise.

Finally, Yaz said, "Dain was taking us to a house I've rented in the city."

"Rannora?" he asked.

Dain chuckled. "He's a little slow."

The children giggled. Sameer snickered.

"Aye," Yaz replied. "I'm also guessing Durga didn't tell you that she hired me to be her ears in the city."

Ravi laughed as he lifted Yaz and spun her around before claiming her lips once more. "To the future," he whispered.

"To *our* future."

"Aye, love. Our future."

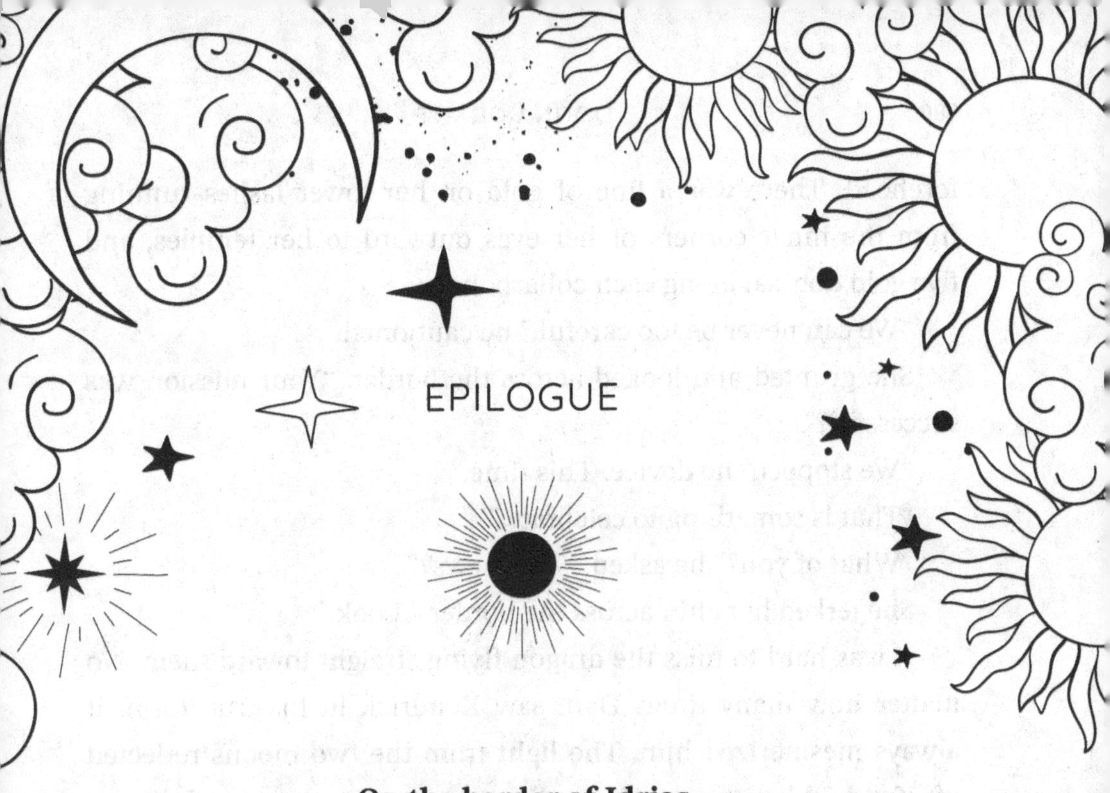

EPILOGUE

On the border of Idrias

The hour grew late as Dain waited for Savita to show. Both of them were walking a fine line navigating politics to determine who on the Conclave had set out to kill Kendrick. Dain lived his life in darkness and shadows. He knew how to read people and see through their lies and deceit. Savita wasn't trained as he was, but she was a Reader, and her runes would help lead her.

That didn't mean she wasn't in trouble.

"Is that frown for me?"

He sighed at the sound of Savita's voice and turned to see her walking in the moonlight through the tall grass, her white gown covered with a dark cloak. "I was getting worried."

"Rest assured, I'm careful."

Dain waited until she reached him. Even beneath the hood of the cloak he saw the large golden sun painted in the middle of her forehead. There was a line of gold on her lower lashes running from the inner corners of her eyes outward to her temples, and five gold dots sat along each collarbone.

"We can never be too careful," he cautioned.

She grunted and looked across the border. "Your mission was successful?"

"We stopped the device. This time."

"That is something to celebrate."

"What of you?" he asked. "Any news?"

She jerked her chin across the border. "Look."

It was hard to miss the dragon flying straight toward them. No matter how many times Dain saw Kendrick in his true form, it always mesmerized him. The light from the two moons reflected off Kendrick's sienna scales as his massive wings rose and dipped methodically. Atop his back sat his mate, Esha. Dain searched the skies for more dragons, but he found none. He prayed there wouldn't come a time when he stood there and saw an army of dragons about to invade.

Kendrick landed, and Esha slid off his back. By the time her feet hit the ground, Kendrick had shifted into his human form. Together, the pair walked close to the border. Esha had been banished after leaving with Kendrick, and after the attack, everyone knew it was safer if neither returned.

"Dain," Kendrick said in greeting.

Dain bowed his head in welcome. "It's good to see you two again. I'm happy to report the device has been apprehended."

Esha's tawny waves lifted in the breeze. "That's a relief."

"An attempt was made on our lives, and then a war nearly broke out when Esha returned with me," Kendrick said. "You've stopped this device, but I've a feeling there will be others."

Savita nodded. "Until we find who is behind all of this, there likely will."

"You think it's one person?" Esha asked her sister.

Savita shrugged. "I don't know."

"We're working on it," Dain told them. "It's slow with just the two of us investigating while continuing on with our normal lives."

Kendrick rubbed his hand on the back of his neck. "I wish I could help."

"We wish you could, too." Savita glanced at the moon. "I have to get back before I'm missed. Please assure the Kings we're doing the best we can."

Esha glanced at Kendrick. "We've got our hands full on our western border. It would be nice to know that the eastern border with Shecrish is peaceful."

"It is for now," Dain confirmed.

Kendrick hesitated. "Savita, wait. Before you go, have either of you heard of the Star People?"

"I hadn't, but we thought maybe one of you had," Esha said.

Savita frowned. "We have Star Elves."

"Not the same thing," Kendrick replied.

Dain crossed his arms over his chest. "Who are the Star People?"

"Beings more powerful than us. They come from the stars," Kendrick explained. "They move easily from realm to realm."

Savita asked, "Why are they here?"

"They have a grudge against the dragons. At one time, they enslaved them," Esha said.

Dain was shocked at the news. "What do they look like?"

"Like me in this form," Kendrick said.

"Human, then."

Kendrick nodded. "Aye."

"There are more like you,"—Dain motioned to him—"in this form?"

Kendrick frowned. "Many, many more. Nearly the entire population of my home world is human. Though some have magic. There are humans here, too."

"I know someone who would be interested in knowing that," Dain said.

Savita motioned to her sister. "Tell us everything about these Star People."

Gita sat in the opulent room and stared out the window in disgust. She had been driven out of her home. But she would return. No one would keep her from Shaldorn for long. There were secrets to the fortress that only she knew, ways into and out of it that only she could use.

She would let them think they had forced her out. While they had their fun searching, she was gathering the names of everyone who had dared to intervene. Even now, the staff who thought they had escaped were being rounded up and held in a secure facility until she could return to Shaldorn.

A single knock sounded on the door.

She uncrossed her legs and set her cup on the coffee table. "Enter."

The door opened and One strode in. The top portion of his silver hair was pulled away from his face, showing his striking features and purple eyes. He had once been a premier healer before she found him. Now, he was her right hand, the one she could count on for everything.

"Well?" she asked when he halted at the table.

He shook his head. "Yasmin still lives."

"How is that possible?" Gita surged to her feet and paced. She whirled around, her skirts billowing behind her. "Where is she?"

"Rannora."

"Then we go there."

"I wouldn't suggest it."

Gita halted and shot him a withering look that cowed most others. But not One. Never One. "Why not?"

"She now works for the DIA. It will be difficult to get to her without gaining their attention."

Gita slowly sank back onto the cushions. "I refuse to believe she's out of reach."

"I didn't say that," One replied with a slow smile.

Gita grinned as she sat back on the sofa. "Just what I wanted to hear."

Thank you for reading **RISING SUN**. I hope you enjoyed the story! I love the Elven Kingdoms world, and am looking forward to returning to it with the next book in the series, **DARK HEART** (available November 12, 2024).

BUY DARK HEART NOW
at www.DonnaGrant.com

***

To find out when new books release
SIGN UP FOR MY NEWSLETTER today at
https://www.tinyurl.com/DonnaGrantNews

***

Join my Facebook group, Donna Grant Groupies, for exclusive
giveaways and sneak peeks of future books.
https://bit.ly/DGGroupies

EXCERPT OF THE NEXT ELVEN KINGDOMS BOOK

DARK HEART, ELVEN KINGDOMS, BOOK 2

New York Times and *USA Today* **bestselling author Donna Grant returns returns for the next Elven Kingdoms story.**

Keep reading for an excerpt of DARK HEART…

DARK HEART
AN EXCERPT

The Crossing was that rare place on Shecrish that thumbed its nose at distinctions that everyone else seemed to be preoccupied with. It sat half in the Above and half in the Below, a place where Dark Elves ventured from the depths of the earth to mingle with the other elven races who dared to enter the tavern—but rarely any deeper. The Dark seemed to be the only ones who didn't fear the shadows.

The entrance of the pub didn't have a door. The dark rock had been chiseled smooth with a gentle, wide arch like a pair of open arms. Welcoming. Inviting. Everyone who entered The Crossing, be it from the narrow doorway from Below or the wide access from Above, all saw the same wall. If the entrance had been scored smooth, the wall was as smooth as silk. And on it was an enormous mandala. Half of the geometric symbol that represented the universe for elves sat in sunshine displaying vibrant colors while the other half with its white lines was bathed in shadow.

Arya's eyes were glued to the mandala. No matter where she

placed herself when she visited the tavern, her gaze always found the symbol. It meant something much more to her, something that she had tried to forget, to put out of her memory. She even succeeded a few times.

But that part of her past she couldn't seem to release completely.

Just like she couldn't forget Jai.

Time didn't lessen the pain. The wound occasionally scabbed over, but something would make her think of Jai and the future that had almost been theirs. The scab would be yanked off and the hurt would begin all over her. The scar was too deep, too jagged to ever fully heal. Even though she pretended otherwise. Her chest was empty, devoid of the heart that had once beat so steadily there. It had been ripped out of her chest and shredded to oblivion. There had been no pieces left to pick up and attempt to move on.

So, she didn't.

She was the walking wounded. A shell of who she had once been, a portrayal of what almost was. Of what should have been but never would be.

The hours she had spent at The Crossing waiting and hoping for Jai to show had been some of the longest, most agonizing of her life. But it was nothing compared to finally realizing that he wouldn't come. That he hadn't chosen her.

She pulled her gaze away from the mandala and down at the table where her ale sat untouched. It took her a moment to realize her superior had stopped talking. She swung her eyes to meet his. Yellow eyes that tipped toward gold stared intently at her. There was nothing soft about Dain Kelro. He moved with predatory grace. He saw everything in one sweep of a room and had skills no other Dark possessed.

His long, white hair was loose except for small, silver bands around locks of hair. He wore the scars of his battles like a warrior. The deepest ran from the inside corner of his left eye and cut diagonally down the left cheek to his jaw. Another dissected his mouth at an angle right to left. A third ran from his left temple through his left brow, across his nose and along the right cheek.

Even when he wasn't going into battle, Dain wore his favorite long black coat with the bottom cut into six thick strips and armor-plated shoulders. Beneath was a black shirt with chest and abdomen armor. Black trousers tucked into knee-high boots with more silver armor on the front.

And he had been mentoring her since she joined the Dark's elite Counter Corruption Division.

She would never dare to call Dain a friend aloud. Mostly because he didn't have friends. Or he hadn't before. Something had changed recently, and it all pointed back to Dain's recent encounter with a Dragon King.

"You're doing it again," Dain remarked.

Arya lifted the cup of ale to her mouth and drank. She held his gaze as she swallowed and slowly lowered her arm. There was no use denying it. Dain always saw through lies. Even hers. "Am I?"

"It's been four years."

She tried to school her features, but she wasn't sure she managed it by the way Dain's lips compressed.

"It was your first assignment. Those are always difficult."

Arya didn't want to talk about the assignment or Jai. She inhaled and released the breath as she looked away. Right to the mandala again.

"You attempted to warn him," Dain continued. "It didn't work. You know he wasn't captured in the search. He got away."

That should be enough. Why wasn't it? She had waited at The Crossing for Jai for two days, but he never showed. And that's what stung more than anything.

"I'm fine," she said.

Neither believed the lie.

She looked at Dain expectantly. "You didn't call me here to talk about the past."

"Actually, I did. Just not that far back." Dain scanned the room before he leaned his arms on the table.

Arya did the same. The Crossing was an entry point into the dominion of the Dark Elves who enjoyed an existence below ground. They could—and had—lived above with the other races of elves, but it wasn't normal. And while the Dark might occasionally mingle above, other races only ventured below when it was required. Same with humans.

No one could see into the shadowy depths of the Under like Dark Elves. The sunlight caused an issue with her people, making it difficult for them to see. Though it was a secret none *ever* shared. It would be considered a weakness, and that simply could never be known.

The pub was mainly occupied by Dark. There was a Sun Elf, two Moon Elves, and to her surprise, a Sea Elf. Like the Dark, Sea Elves had their preferred home and seldom left it. The Mountain Elves were even more reclusive. The Wood Elves seemed to be everywhere, but they had a particular abhorrence to the subterranean. The Star Elves were nomadic.

Arya glanced at Dain and saw his gaze was directed behind the bar now. She turned and spotted a human female pouring drink. It was the first time she had ever known the owner of The Crossing to hire a human.

"You need to be careful," Dain said in a low voice.

She swung her head back to him. "About?"

"There's been talk about recent exploits."

Shaldorn Stronghold. Arya inwardly grimaced at the thought of the mountain fortress. She had been undercover in the depraved, evil place where humans had been held as slaves and all races of elves had taken part in debauchery, corruption, and other sins. Her assignment had been a secret, one Dain had asked of her and kept from their supervisors. She hadn't understood why until she had been inside Shaldorn and saw firsthand those who fought for an invite to the exclusive citadel.

But she and Dain had merely been backup. It was Ravi, a Sun Elf working for the Defense Intelligence Agency, and Yasmin, the only human to escape Shaldorn, who had infiltrated the stronghold and halted the sale of a weapon intended to start a war with the dragons.

Ravi and Yasmin had accomplished their task and sent those running Shaldorn to ground, but it had nearly cost Yasmin her life. Each time Arya thought about the state she had found Yasmin, it made her stomach roil. And it was churning again, but for another reason.

"What about it?" Arya asked in a soft whisper. Despite their victory, they had yet to discover the tangled mess of just who was involved in Shaldorn. They knew it went up through the government, but how deep they had yet to uncover.

Dain held her gaze, his yellow eyes briefly showing his unease. "As you'll recall, a few got away."

Particularly the Moon Elf, Gita, who had been running Shaldorn Stronghold, and One, a Star Elf, the last of the Trio who answered to her.

"You're worried."

Dain shot her a flat look. "We'd be stupid not to be. It seems our friends are searching for us."

A shiver of apprehension snaked down Arya's spine. "How did you learn this? Can your source be trusted?"

"Unequivocally."

That made Arya's brows raise. Dain was distrustful of everyone. She couldn't name a single person he trusted unreservedly. Apparently, he did this source. "What did they say?"

"A bounty is out on us."

Six words. That's all it took for her stomach to drop to her feet. They had no idea how far Gita's reach was. The Moon Elf had mentioned that there were others working with her, and for all they knew, it could reach to the very top officials. It was something she and Dain had been looking into since their return. How else could the stronghold have stayed hidden for so long?

"They saw me," Dain said. "And the other two."

He wasn't saying Ravi and Yasmin's name for many reasons. Arya nodded. She had expected retaliation. They had halted a profitable location where criminals could buy, sell, and trade all manner of commodities, both legal and illegal. Mostly illegal. But it was more than that. The depraved had been able to release their true depravity by watching others being tortured, killed, and raped.

"Did anyone see you with us?"

Dain's voice pulled her from her thoughts. Arya shook her head. "I don't think so."

"It isn't a chance we can take. We all need to take precautions."

She shot him a glare. "You want to hide?" That wasn't something she ever expected Dain to say.

"Until we know who is pulling the strings, aye."

"We need to keep searching for Gita and One."

Dain slowly leaned back in his chair. "We will. Just more stealthily than we have been. Stay at your parents. They have enough security to keep anyone out."

She looked away briefly and drank another swallow of ale.

Dain's nostrils flared with his irritation. "You still haven't told your family you're working for us."

It wasn't a question. She couldn't hold his glare and looked away. Of course she hadn't told her family she was a spy. If they found out she was part of the Counter Corruption Division, they would force her to stop immediately.

And if she didn't, then her mother would put enough pressure on the CCD that they fired her.

"Fuck." A muscle jumped in Dain's jaw. "You promised."

"I lied."

His yellow eyes narrowed. "It won't be just your position they come after. It'll be mine for training you."

"I went to the CCD on my own," she argued. "No one recruited me."

"It won't matter to your family, and you know it."

Arya reluctantly nodded. "Fine. I'll tell my parents. I'm meeting them for dinner tonight," she stated when he gave her a glare.

"It might be too late for that confession."

There was an instant of elation of getting out of that lecture, but it quickly vanished. Dain didn't want her to tell her parents about the CCD, because she would then have to tell them about Shaldorn. If Dain's suspicions about how far up the corruption went was correct, then there was a good chance it might involve her mother who had been elected to the Dark council.

"Shite," she murmured.

Dain nodded after he tossed back the last of his ale. "Aye."

How had she not already thought of that connection? But she knew. It was because she didn't want to imagine that either of her parents could be involved with Shaldorn. But Dain had. She knew it without even asking him. She felt sick to her stomach.

Arya looked down at her hand that was still wrapped around the wooden cup. Her gray skin looked pale even to her. How was she going to act normal during the dinner? She had been trained by the best in the CCD. She could do it. It wouldn't be easy, but she didn't have a choice.

Her gaze snapped up to Dain to find his gaze on her. "How far have you investigated without me?"

"I kept you out because of the chance of conflict."

"That isn't what I asked," she said tightly.

He sighed, his gaze sliding away briefly. "Not far, but I won't ask you–"

"You don't have to. I'm part of this. We follow wherever things lead. To *whoever* they lead to."

"It's easy to say that now."

She lifted her chin. "If something is found..." She swallowed, not able to say the words. She could barely even think about her parents being involved with Shaldorn. "I have to see it with my own eyes, or I'll think it was falsified."

Dain stared at her a long moment before he nodded once. "Fair enough."

She pushed the ale away. If she drank anymore, she might vomit. She might have learned to repress her emotions so nothing showed, but she had yet to learn how to halt the effects of those emotions in her body.

"You can change your mind anytime," Dain told her.

"I won't."

"I know."

"I need to change before the dinner. Where do we start tomorrow?"

"Meet me here at midday."

Arya nodded as she pushed to her feet. "See you then."

"Be vigilant," Dain warned.

She paused beside him and smiled, hoping to make him believe she was fine. "You, too."

Arya scanned the establishment as she walked to the back were the lights and torches filling the tavern faded into darkness. There a door stood that was so cloaked in shadows only a Dark Elf could see it. She looked back to find Dain also studying the other occupants. She pushed through the door and skimmed the alleyway to see if anyone was about. There was a half dozen steps down that led to the tunnel that connected The Crossing to the Under.

She had a flat in the Deacos Corner neighborhood, much to her parent's horror. It was too near the surface for their liking. Then again, they wouldn't be happy unless she returned to their home. Preferably married. That's what this dinner was about. It's what *all* the dinners for the past year had been about.

To her parents, she should've already found her mate, settled down, and waited for the Domestic Ministry to give them a child. As if that's all there was to life. Her parents paraded men in front of her as if she were picking out a cut of meat. Her father would proudly list the contender's achievements and bodily endowments which never failed to mortify her. If it was that bad for her, she couldn't imagine what it was like for the males. Though, the ranking of her family meant that many put aside their egos and pride on the chance she might choose them. There was no way she would allow anyone to make her feel so degraded.

Not one of the men asked her anything about herself. They probably didn't care about her. It was her family name, its connections, and the money the males were interested in.

Actually, she was a slab of meat. She might not be flaunted about, but she was still on display.

And it was time that ended.

BUY DARK HEART NOW
at www.DonnaGrant.com

ABOUT THE AUTHOR

New York Times and *USA Today* bestselling author Donna Grant® has been praised for her "totally addictive" and "unique and sensual" stories.

She's written more than one hundred novels spanning multiple genres of romance including the bestselling Dragon Kings® series that features a thrilling combination of Druids, Fae, and immortal Highlanders who are dark, dangerous, and irresistible. She lives in Texas with her dog and a cat.

www.DonnaGrant.com

www.MotherofDragonsBooks.com

facebook.com/AuthorDonnaGrant

instagram.com/dgauthor

bookbub.com/authors/donna-grant

goodreads.com/donna_grant

pinterest.com/donnagrant1